Goddess of the Green Room

Due to illness, Jean Plaidy was unable to go to school regularly and so taught herself to read. Very early on she developed a passion for the 'past'. After doing a shorthand and typing course, she spent a couple of years doing various jobs, including sorting gems in Hatton Garden and translating for foreigners in a City café. She began writing in earnest following marriage and now has a large number of historical novels to her name. Inspiration for her books is drawn from odd sources – a picture gallery, a line from a book, Shakespeare's inconsistencies. She lives in London and loves music, secondhand book shops and ancient buildings.

Jean Plaidy also writes under the pseudonym of Victoria Holt.

D0887592

Also by Jean Plaidy in Pan Books

THE FERDINAND AND
ISABELLA TRILOGY
Castile for Isabella
Spain for the Sovereigns
Daughter of Spain

THE LUCREZIA BORGIA SERIES
Madonna of the Seven Hills
Light on Lucrezia

THE MEDICI TRILOGY
Madame Serpent
The Italian Woman
Queen Jezebel

THE TUDOR SERIES
Murder Most Royal
St Thomas's Eve
The Sixth Wife
The Spanish Bridegroom
The Thistle and the Rose
Gay Lord Robert

THE MARY QUEEN OF SCOTS SERIES
Royal Road to Fotheringay
The Captive Queen of Scots

THE STUART SAGA
Murder in the Tower
The Three Crowns
The Haunted Sisters
The Queen's Favourites

THE CHARLES II TRILOGY
The Wandering Prince
A Health Unto His Majesty
Here Lies Our Sovereign Lord

THE FRENCH REVOLUTION TRILOGY
Louis the Well-Beloved
The Road to Compiègne
Flaunting, Extravagant Queen

THE GEORGIAN SAGA
The Princess of Celle
Queen in Waiting
Caroline, the Queen
The Prince and the Quakeress
The Third George
Perdita's Prince
Sweet Lass of Richmond Hill
Indiscretions of the Queen
The Regent's Daughter

THE NORMAN TRILOGY
The Bastard King
The Lion of Justice
The Passionate Enemies

THE PLANTAGENET SAGA
The Plantagenet Prelude
The Revolt of the Eaglets
The Heart of the Lion

ALSO
Daughter of Satan
The Goldsmith's Wife
Evergreen Gallant
Beyond the Blue Mountains

Jean Plaidy

Goddess of
the Green Room

Pan Books London and Sydney

First published in Great Britain 1971 by Robert Hale & Company
This edition published 1979 by Pan Books Ltd,
Cavaye Place, London SW10 9PG
© Jean Plaidy 1971
ISBN 0 330 25626 2
Printed and bound in Great Britain by
Hazell Watson & Viney Ltd, Aylesbury, Bucks

This book is sold subject to the condition that it
shall not, by way of trade or otherwise, be lent, re-sold,
hired out or otherwise circulated without the publisher's prior
consent in any form of binding or cover other than that in which
it is published and without a similar condition including this
condition being imposed on the subsequent purchaser

Contents

Bibliography

Mrs Jordan and Her Family: being the Unpublished Correspondence of Mrs Jordan and the Duke of Clarence, later William IV edited by A. Aspinall

National and Domestic History of England William Hickman Smith Aubrey

The Life of Mrs Jordan including Original Private Correspondence James Boaden

In the Days of the Georges William B. Boulton

George III; His Court and Family Henry Colburn

Life and Times of George IV The Rev. George Croly

The Good Queen Charlotte Percy Fitzgerald

Life of George IV Percy Fitzgerald

Mrs Jordan, Portrait of an Actress Brian Fothergill

George IV Roger Fulford

Unsuccessful Ladies Jane-Eliza Hasted

The Life and Reign of William IV Robert Huish

The Story of Dorothy Jordan Clare Jerrold

George IV Shane Leslie

George III J. C. Long

The Sailor King William IV, His Court and His Subjects Fitzgerald Molloy

A History of the Late 18th Century Drama Allardyce Nicoll

The Four Georges Sir Charles Petrie

The House of Hanover Alvin Redman

George IV Joanna Richardson

Mrs Jordan Philip W. Sergeant

The Dictionary of National Biography edited by Sir Leslie Stephen and Sir Sidney Lee

Portrait of the Prince Regent Dorothy Margaret Stuart

The Four Georges W. M. Thackeray

The Patriot King, William IV Grace E. Thompson

British History John Wade

Memoirs and Portraits Horace Walpole

Memoirs of the Reign of George III Horace Walpole

George III Beckles Wilson

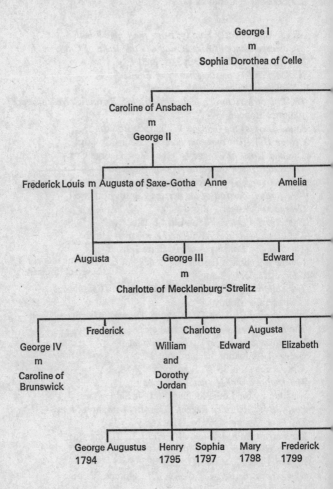

George I
m
Sophia Dorothea of Celle

Caroline of Ansbach
m
George II

Frederick Louis m Augusta of Saxe-Gotha   Anne   Amelia

Augusta   George III   Edward
m
Charlotte of Mecklenburg-Strelitz

Frederick   Charlotte   Augusta

George IV   William   Edward   Elizabeth
m   and
Caroline of   Dorothy
Brunswick   Jordan

George Augustus   Henry   Sophia   Mary   Frederick
1794   1795   1797   1798   1799

Sophia Dorothea

Caroline   George   William   Mary   Louisa
                      Duke of Cumberland

William   Henry   Frederick   Caroline Matilda
                                 Queen of Denmark

Ernest   Adolphus   Sophia   Alfred
      Augustus   Mary   Octavius   Amelia

Elizabeth   Adolphus   Augusta   Augustus   Amelia
1801   1802   1803   1805   1807

for William's and Dorothy's Great-Granddaughter,

Hebe Elsna

with admiration for her work,
gratitude for her friendship
and love for herself

Dorothy Jordan

Comedy in Crow Street

In a little room in South Great George Street in the city of Dublin two girls were discussing a matter of great importance to them. The elder, handsome and elegant in spite of the poverty of her clothes, was clearly in a state of tense anxiety; the other with the piquant face and the lively expression, was trying to calm her.

'You will do it, Hester,' she was saying. 'Why, it's in the blood. You inherited it all from Mamma.'

'I know,' said Hester, 'but you can't imagine what it's like, Doll, to face an audience for the first time.'

Dorothy was on her feet. 'Oh yes, I can,' she said. 'I've seen enough of it, Heaven knows. I remember when Mamma and Papa were playing their parts and we all had to listen to them. I can smell those tallow candles now. I always used to wonder what would happen if they toppled over and set the boards alight or perhaps caught the curtains.'

'I wish,' said Hester, 'that Papa had not died, and that we had more money.'

'People always wish for more money,' put in Dorothy quickly. 'And don't forget Papa deserted us before he died.'

'But he was kind. He always sent our allowance.'

'I'd rather have done without it, when I remind myself that he had to marry a rich woman to provide it. I'd rather earn my own money.'

'And that won't be much in your milliner's shop.'

'I dare say not to that famous actress, Miss Hester Bland.'

'Don't,' cried Hester. 'It's tempting the fates.'

'Nonsense,' retorted her sister. 'Of course you're going to be a success. Mr Ryder thinks so. Oh, he has great hopes of you. I heard him telling Mamma so. He thinks you are going to bring business to his Crow Street Theatre. Hester, it's a wonderful life, playing parts on a stage. And they have benefit nights which can bring in as much as thirty pounds. One day a manager from London may see you. How would you like to play at Drury Lane or Covent Garden?'

'Stop!' cried Hester. 'I can't bear it. I know I'm going to be a failure.'

'You are not, Hester Bland. The family fortunes are on the rise. No more skimping and screwing.'

'What expressions you use, Dolly!'

'Call me Dorothea, because that is what I am going to call myself when our fortunes are made. When I have a famous sister I shall boast to all the ladies who come into the shop. Try on this confection, Madam. The finest tulle I do assure you and the flowers are made of the best velvet as worn in royal circles. And you are being attended to, Madam, by the sister of the famous actress Miss Hester Bland. You will soon be obliged to travel to London to see her, for Dublin will not be good enough for Miss Hester Bland. Did you know that the King himself has sent for her to play before him in Covent Garden?'

'Oh, Doll, I'm so . . . *scared.*'

'Everyone is at first. Mamma says you should be if you are going to give a good performance. Do you know, Hester, I don't think I should be scared. I don't think I should *care.*' She laughed and, rising to her feet, she bowed before an imaginary audience:

'*Dead shepherd; now I find thy saw of might*
Who ever loved that loved not at first sight?'

'You'd make a tolerable Phoebe.'

'If I were to be a famous actress I'd like a singing part. Well . . .

"*Under the greenwood tree*
Who loves to lie with me
And tune his merry note
Until the sweet bird's throat . . ." '

'I'm in no mood for songs, Dolly, though I must admit you sing them sweetly enough. But your stockings are falling down and there's a rent in your gown.'

'I know. But as long as I am neat for the shop what matters it? Allow me to be as untidy as I please at home.'

'You'll be in the theatre tonight?'

'Of course. With the whole family. I expect even little George will be there. You can count on the family's support, Hester.'

'Oh, Dolly, suppose I forget my lines.'

'Let me hear them. Come on.' Dorothy was beginning to act the part Hester was to play that night when their mother came in. Grace Bland had clearly been a beauty in her youth, but that

14

beauty was much faded by years of struggle. There was a perpetual frown between her eyes which always moved Dorothy deeply; she wished that she could earn a great deal of money so that they need not be always wondering how to feed the family. But Hester was going to make their fortunes; and it did not matter which member of the family did it as long as it was done.

'I'm hearing Hester's lines, Mamma,' said Dorothy.

'That's right, dear. She must be word perfect. I remember my first part. Oh, that was years and years ago. But I recall going through agonies.'

'As I am now,' said Hester grimly.

'Never mind. It's all part of the life. When you've played through to the end and the audience applaud . . . then you forget all your qualms and you'll say to yourself: "This is the life for me." '

'Did you say that, Mamma?' asked Dorothy.

'I did. And I've never regretted it.'

Was it true? wondered Dorothy. Did she ever, during the difficult years, think of her father's parsonage where life must have been very different from this one for which she had forsaken it. Perhaps there would have been poverty in the parsonage though, for country parsons were often poor. Grace often talked of her girlhood and of life in a small Welsh village and the three girls – Grace and her sisters – deciding that it was no life for them and they were going to seek fame and fortune on the stage. 'Our father was horrified, as you can imagine,' Grace told her daughters. 'He called us "strolling players", but we didn't care. He said that if we went on the stage we could fend for ourselves . . . and we did.' They were courageous, Dorothy decided – three girls from the country coming to London to try their luck on the stage; and they had not done badly. Aunt Blanche, though, had tired of it and gone back to Wales where she had married and settled down in the village of Trelethyn; but the other two had stayed on. Aunt Mary now and then played in London, and their own Mamma had acted while she was raising a family; and now that they were deserted and there was no money coming in, they were looking to the stage again, and this time it was Hester who was to make their fortunes, for the little she and Dorothy had been bringing in from the milliner's shop would not keep them, and

15

something would have to be done. So now that Mr Ryder had offered Hester her chance – because she was Mamma's daughter of course – they must look to her.

Grace said: 'Dorothy, do go and tidy yourself. What if Mr Ryder should call. Now, Hester, I'll take you through your part.'

Grace studied her daughter. She has talent, she thought. This will be the beginning of better things, for she is young and there's no doubt that audiences like their players young . . . only great performers are allowed to grow old, and these are rare.

She could hear Dorothy, laughing with the boys. They were jumping on the stairs and Dorothy was shouting that she could jump more stairs than any of them. Grace smiled indulgently. Dorothy was a tomboy, not nearly as serious as Hester. It was amazing how lightly she seemed to take all their troubles. It was not as though she did not love them; she was ready to give up every penny she earned for them; it was simply that she could not accept the fact that all was not going well.

Perhaps it was for the best. It had been a hard life but a happy one until Francis had failed her. Until then everything had been worth while. Why had he done it? she wondered. But of course he had always been weak. In a way that had attracted her. She was thinking now of the day she had first seen him. He had sat in the theatre watching her and the next day he was there again and so it went on until she could not but be aware that the young army captain was interested in more than the play. And they had become lovers; Francis, fearing his father's anger, dared not marry her. He was after all under age, and he came of a family which did not approve of actresses. So they would have to wait until he was older. Like Francis, Grace had no wish to wait until then before they took lodgings together and very soon Hester was about to be born. Grace had not called herself Mrs Bland but Mrs Francis. Poor Francis, he was so much in awe of his father that he was afraid of offending him, which he would most certainly have done if he had given the family's name to an actress.

But it was impossible always to be known as Francis and sometimes she was called Bland and when Judge Bland, Francis's irate father, discovered that his son was living with an actress he let him know that any marriage would mean that Francis would be cut off without a penny.

Poor Francis, what could he do! And Dorothy was on the way by that time.

So they had lived happily enough though Francis had had to resign from the Army. He had little money of his own so it was Grace who provided their main source of income because by that time she was a considerable actress. The children came regularly and Dorothy was followed by Nathaniel and Francis and George.

And so they would have gone on. How many children would they have had by now? But there were troubles in Ireland and the theatre had closed. Grace was once more pregnant and Blanche in Wales invited the family to stay with her for a while until everything returned to normal in Dublin. Francis had not been well and his mother, who had kept in touch with him, wished him to take a trip to the South of France with her in the hope that this would restore him to health. Grace, who was also anxious for his health, advised him to take the opportunity offered; she and the children would be well taken care of in Wales. And to think, she mused now, that I was never to see Francis again! It was the biggest blow of her life. But she had known he was always weak. She should never have consented to his going. She could not believe it when she had received his letter, full of remorse, full of apologies; but that would not keep her and her children – and the new baby had now arrived to swell their numbers.

Francis was penitent, but with him and his mother had travelled a young heiress named Catherine Mahoney; and his mother, with the help of Catherine, had impressed upon him what an excellent match this young heiress would be. Grace knew that he had been disappointed of his inheritance and in view of this he had allowed himself to be persuaded.

Thus was Grace with six children to keep – and there would have been seven but little Lucy had died in Wales – deserted.

Francis was not a callous man – only weak. He had continued to send them an allowance; and what they would have done without it, Grace could not have imagined. They had stayed on in Wales until, with Francis's death, the allowance had stopped. Grace was informed of this by his wife Catherine who told her at the same time that she had no intention of continuing the allowance.

So they had returned to Dublin and Grace now being well into middle-age and not having won that fame, which would have made audiences regard her as ageless, was seeking to launch her eldest daughter on the stage.

It had been disastrous. Even Dorothy must realize this. They would never – any of them – forget that long-awaited moment when they had sat on the edge of their seats and waited in the old Crow Street Theatre for Hester to appear. Her name had been on the bills: Mr Ryder's great discovery – the young, beautiful, talented Hester Bland.

Hester came on to the stage; the audience waited, indulgent because she was young and not uncomely; but when she opened her mouth no words came.

'It can't be,' prayed Dorothy. 'Oh, God, let her speak.'

But Hester's fear had overcome her talents. She was suffering from acute stage fright and had completely forgotten the words she must say. Dorothy was repeating them under her breath, but how could she shout them to Hester in a crowded theatre. 'Please, please,' she prayed. 'Let her remember.'

There was a titter in the audience.

Mr Ryder came on to the stage. He waved Hester aside and she ran into the wings. Grace looked as though she would faint.

A little hitch, explained Mr Ryder. His new actress was unwell. He craved the audience's indulgence. Another actress would play her part.

Dorothy was sure she would never forget those moments: the hiss of conversation, the giggle here and there, the comments on young Miss who thought she could act; it wasn't often they had the chance (the pleasure, thought Dorothy angrily) of seeing such a stage tragedy. She was angry herself; she wanted to go up on that stage and play the part. She could remember most of the lines because she had heard Hester say them so often and she would make up what she did not know.

The family rose and went back stage to collect a numbed and tragic Hester.

She wept all night; she had disgraced them all; she was useless; why had she thought she could act?

Grace said: 'You *can* act. It was just stage fright. We all feel it but somehow we manage to overcome it in the nick of time. You didn't. You'll be better next time.'

'Next time,' cried Hester. 'I'd rather die.'

Then she wept afresh. She would never forget the disgrace; that moment would live with her for the rest of her life.

There was no way of comforting her. The whole family tried; and Grace was wondering whether Hester could get back the job she had had in the milliner's shop which she had left to go on the stage.

It was a morning of gloom. Mr Ryder, who was a kindly man and who knew the poverty of the family and knew also that what had happened to Hester did not mean that she was not an actress, called to see them.

He was immediately aware of the deep depression although he did not see Hester; Grace's eyes, however, were red-rimmed with tears and sleeplessness.

'Well,' he said, 'it was a bad business, Grace.'

'I can't think how it happened.'

'Easy enough. She's never faced an audience before. What are you going to do!'

'I don't know.'

'Now look here, Grace, there might be some parts for you. You must be a bit out of practice but you could get that back . . . say a small part to begin with. And what about that other girl of yours?'

'Dorothy?'

'I've noticed her. There's something about her.'

'She's a bit of a tomboy.'

'She'll grow up.'

'She's not as good-looking as Hester.'

'By God, are you telling me you're not going to let me try the girl in my theatre?'

'Try her in your theatre! Why, she has never shown any inclination for the stage.'

'Call her in.'

'Good gracious me, I doubt she's fit to be seen.'

'Fit for me to see. I'm not looking for a tidy Miss but an actress.'

'Dorothy an actress!'

'Please may I see her?'

'Dorothy,' called Grace, 'come here.'

She came. Ryder studied her. She had something. What was it? A gamin quality. She might have been an untidy schoolboy except for the fact that she was so dainty. Yes, there was some quality – latent perhaps, but he was sure it was there.

'Hello, Dorothy,' he said. 'Let's hear you play a part. Do you know any?'

Her imperturbability delighted him.

'Phoebe,' she said, 'from *As You Like It.*'

'Good,' he said. 'That'll do.'

To see her strut before him like that was amazing, thought Grace. She did not declaim as an actress would. She played it naturally as though Dorothy Bland was a shepherdess, and for a moment one felt that the shabby room was the forest of Arden. It wouldn't do. It wasn't acting. It was being natural.

Ryder felt differently. Her voice was most unusual. It was almost as though she sang the words. She seemed to give them a music of her own.

'Look here, Dorothy Bland,' he said, 'how would you like to take your sister's place? H'm? I'd pay you what I've been paying her. I don't think you'll suffer from stage fright.'

'I'll do it,' said Dorothy as though she were promising to wash the china or make a dish of tea.

'That's the spirit,' said Ryder. 'I can give you a part in *The Virgin Unmasked*. It's not much, but it'll be a good way of making your stage début. Be at the theatre tomorrow morning.'

He left them and Grace looked in astonishment at her daughter. Dorothy was smiling. Everything had turned out for the best. The only difference was that she, not Hester, had to make the family's fortune.

So Dorothy became an actress. She played in *The Virgin Unmasked* without causing a great stir in Dublin theatrical circles; and after that she was Phoebe in *As You Like It.*

Thomas Ryder was not displeased; he might not have a star performer, he told himself, but at least he had a tolerable actress.

Dorothy was delighted. It was more fun than making and selling hats; moreover, she had prevailed on Hester to accept a small part and once Hester had done this successfully, she was ready to undertake bigger parts and so overcome the terrible fear of appearing on the stage.

Life was easier; there was more money. Ryder often talked to

Dorothy in whom he felt a special interest because he had selected her to play in his theatre before she had realized she was an actress.

'We have to do better business,' he said, 'or we'll be running at a bigger loss than I can afford. Did you know the house was half empty last night?'

'I was aware of it,' Dorothy told him.

'And I have Smock Alley standing empty. There's not room for two theatres in Dublin. If it goes on like this I'll have to get rid of my lease of Smock Alley – and who's going to take it, eh? If Dublin can't support one theatre, how can anyone open up in Smock Alley?'

Dorothy shrugged her shoulders; she was thinking of her newest part.

'If you would let me sing a song,' she said, 'I'm sure that would bring them in.'

'There's no place for a song in the play.'

'We could make a place,' she wheedled.

'Rubbish,' said Thomas; and went on to brood on a new means of luring people into Crow Street.

Shortly afterwards he came up with an idea. 'I've got it,' he said. 'We'll have a play with men playing the women's parts and women the men's.'

It seemed a crazy notion. To what purpose? But when some of the women appeared in breeches the purpose was obvious, and this was particularly so in the case of Dorothy. Her figure was enchanting, her legs long, slim and beautifully shaped.

Yes, said Thomas Ryder, this could well give them the opportunity they were looking for.

The play, Ryder announced, would be *The Governess* – a pirated version of Sheridan's *The Duenna*. He had not intended such an inexperienced player as Dorothy to have a big part, but when he saw her in breeches he decided she should have that of Lopez.

Dorothy was delighted. She would make something of the part. How pleased she would be if she could sing!

'Sing!' cried Ryder in exasperation. 'Now why should Lopez sing?'

'Because,' replied Dorothy, 'Dorothy Bland would like to sing and the audience would like to hear her.'

'Nonsense,' retorted Ryder. 'You play your part, my girl. That's all the audience ask of you.'

'Don't forget the theatre has been half empty these last weeks.'

'*The Governess* will pull them in.'

Dorothy posed before the mirror in her breeches. Grace said: 'I don't know. It's not modest somehow.' Dorothy kissed her. 'Don't you worry, Mamma. I'll take care not only of myself but of the whole family.'

Poor Mamma, she was terrified that Hester or Dorothy – and more likely Dorothy – would get into some entanglement and, always having longed for the blessing of clergy on her union, was fearful that one of the girls should find herself in a similar position. She was constantly saying that if their father had married her they would not now be wondering where the next penny was coming from, for Judge Bland would surely have relented when he saw his grandchildren. But because she lacked marriage lines she lacked security. Security! It was an obsession. She wanted it for her girls.

So she was constantly warning. And she was right, said Dorothy to Hester. But she need have no fear.

At rehearsal Dorothy swaggering on the stage in her male costume designed to show off her figure so amused Thomas Ryder that in a weak moment he gave way to her pleading to let her sing.

The first night of *The Governess* arrived. The theatre was full, as it had not been for some nights, because people had come to see the women in male costumes and they were not disappointed. Particularly admired was the young actress who took the part of Lopez; her figure was trim and yet voluptuous; she was so completely feminine that her masquerading in male attire was an absurd delight. The audience was intrigued. They were beginning to notice Dorothy Bland.

When at the end of the play she came to the front of the stage and sang for them they were spellbound. There was an unusual quality in her voice; though it was untrained it was sweet and true, but so were many other voices. Dorothy's had a quality purely her own which touched them; it had a haunting charm, warm, full of feeling, tender and sincere.

The song she had chosen to sing was one they all knew about an Irish colleen who came to Milltown, a district of Dublin, to ply her

22

trade as an oyster seller. They had heard it many times before but never as sung that night.

They called for her to sing again, which she did; and it was clear from that night that Dorothy Bland was no ordinary actress.

Grace read the letter to her daughters. It was formal and from a lawyer who represented Francis's relations. The family resented the fact that Miss Grace Phillips allowed her actress daughter to use their name and to have it appearing on play-bills. As she had no right to this, they must ask her to stop doing so.

Dorothy could not restrain her feelings. She had a temper, as the family well knew; but it did not greatly worry them because although it would flare up suddenly it was quickly over.

'Impudence!' she cried. 'They have done nothing for us and now they are telling us what we should do.'

'Take no notice of them,' advised Hester more calmly. 'You've made something of a stir as Dorothy Bland, are you going to throw it away because Papa's family are ashamed of us?'

'I am not,' Dorothy assured her. 'And I may well make it known that I am connected with the high and mighty Blands of Dublin's fair city – yes, and that they will have nothing to do with us although it is their plain and bounden duty to keep us from starvation.'

'You're not on the boards now, Dolly,' Hester reminded her sister.

'Now, girls,' put in Grace, 'I've been thinking about this; and it's not wise to go against your Papa's family. It's always been my hope that one day they would do something for us. Now that your grandfather, the Judge, is dead, it may be that the rest of the family will feel differently.'

'It doesn't seem like it,' retorted Dorothy. 'And why do you imagine they should suddenly turn so virtuous?'

'You never know,' insisted Grace; 'and it's always wise to be on the safe side.'

Dorothy laughed suddenly. Dear Mamma, who had been so badly treated by life, who had really believed that Papa was going to marry her one day – how she always wanted to be on the Safe Side.

Dorothy kissed her suddenly. 'All right, Mamma. We'll be on

the safe side. We'll compromise. I'm not going to give up Papa's name altogether. But we'll meet the high and mighty Blands half way. I'll be Dorothy Francis. They couldn't object to that.'

They all thought this was a good idea; and from that day Dorothy became Miss Francis.

Miss Francis was a considerable actress. She could dance prettily; her singing voice was unusually appealing and when she sang on a stage the audience were always loth to let her go. If the play was not going well it was always advisable to bring in Dorothy Francis to sing or do some sort of a jig on the stage and the audience could usually be put into a good humour. In addition her speaking voice had a soothing effect and when she spoke a prologue the noisiest audience grew quiet. It was not so much that she was a good actress as that she was Dorothy Bland – or Francis as she had now become – with a carefree diffidence, a gaiety, an insouciance . . . who could say what it was? But whatever the description it was Dorothy – and the people liked it.

Is it those shapely legs? wondered Thomas Ryder, determined to get her into breeches parts as much as possible. Is it her singing voice? Her speaking voice? Her way of romping through a part as though she enjoyed it? Even a tragic role seemed less tragic in her hands. There was something about Dorothy which assured him that the day he had decided to let the young sister try where the elder one had failed had not been an unlucky one for him.

Dorothy – with Hester and the rest of the company – went to Waterford and Cork to play under Ryder's management while Grace stayed behind in Dublin with the young children because her two daughters were earning enough to make this possible.

By the time she was back in Crow Street Dorothy had come to regard herself as a professional actress. The smell of tallow candles, the draught that blew in from the wings, the excitement of facing an audience and the gratifying ring of applause were a part of her life; and she asked for no other.

She had her friends – and enemies – in the company. Ryder was one of the best of the former; the latter were made up of those actors and actresses who were jealous of her popularity with audiences, those who declared that the young upstart took more than her share of the applause.

There were many ways in which they could make life burdensome; they could try to distract the audience's attention from her; they could discuss her disparagingly in the Green Room; they could talk of her in the taverns as a girl who had achieved success through a fine pair of legs and hint at the reason for her favouritism with Ryder.

Dorothy could take these taunts better than Hester. In truth she enjoyed a fight, and the attitude of some of her fellow players increased her determination to succeed. She could retaliate by displaying her superior talents on the stage, by singing with more and more feeling, dancing with more and more verve. In those early days life was a battle – a gay and exciting one which seemed to offer certain success.

There was one man in the company who gave her a few twinges of fear. His name was Richard Daly and he was a swaggering braggart of a man – not a great actor but the opinion he had of himself made up for a lack of acting ability. There was a quality in him which made it impossible for anyone to be unaware of him. He was tall and well made; in fact he would have been extremely handsome but for the fact that he squinted. This squint added a diabolical touch which many declared to be entirely fascinating. He was constantly boasting of his successes with women and it was obvious that this was no idle boast. He was a real dandy – the most elegant man in the theatre and any casual observer would have thought he was the manager rather than Ryder. He was a great duellist, adept with sword and pistol; and he wore a diamond brooch in his coat with great pride because it had once saved his life. It seemed he had challenged a college acquaintance, Sir Jonah Barrington, to a duel – for what reason no one seemed sure – and Sir Jonah had fired first. The bullet would have gone through his heart but for the diamond brooch; in fact some of the gems had become embedded in his chest. He had had the brooch reset and wore it always that everyone might remember how ready he was to make a challenge and that he was Devil-May-Care Daly.

Daly was a gambler, and if his acting was not of the highest standard, having graduated from Trinity College, he was educated and could quickly memorize a part; moreover he had an excellent wardrobe of his own which was useful in business. Daly had no sooner joined the company than he began to dominate it.

He was a deeply sensual man and greater than his interest in gambling and duelling was his interest in women. There was not a woman in the company on whom he did not cast his speculative eye, and it was scarcely likely that Dorothy would escape.

He would waylay her on the way to her dressing room; he would bar her way almost playfully but she was aware of his brute strength and he wished her to be.

'Dear Miss Francis, why in such a hurry?'

'Dear Mr Daly, what concern is that of yours?'

'All Miss Francis's actions are a concern of mine.'

'Then it's more than Mr Daly's are of mine.'

'A kiss for a free passage.'

'These passages are already free,' she told him. 'Or so I believe. I must verify this with Mr Ryder.'

A threat of course. Ryder had it in his power to dismiss Daly.

'I am in no mood to take orders,' he told her.

'I know. You solve your problems with bullets. But don't spoil that nice diamond brooch again.'

She would dodge past him with a derisive laugh; and he would laugh with her, but his eyes, as far as the squint would allow her to see, were smouldering.

He was the sort of man whom her mother would wish her to avoid. And I am in complete agreement with her, thought Dorothy.

But for the existence of Mrs Lyster, the leading female player in Ryder's company, Dorothy might have been uneasy, for she sensed something evil in the man.

Mrs Lyster was a fine comic actress. Dorothy liked to stand in the wings and watch her perform for she had great talent and there was much to be learned from her. She had been a Miss Barsanti before her marriage to Mr Lyster who had recently died leaving her a comfortable income. Dorothy admired Mrs Lyster not only for her acting ability but for her poise and that comfortable and apparent sense of security which having an income apart from her theatrical earnings gave her.

There was someone else who admired Mrs Lyster and that was Richard Daly; and Mrs Lyster like so many women seemed to be completely fascinated by the man and not in the least revolted by his squint; on the contrary to find it an added attraction.

Daly's interest in the widow did impede to some extent his pursuit of Dorothy, but in spite of the fact that everyone knew his intentions towards Mrs Lyster were serious and honourable (Dorothy laughed at the word because it was clearly Mrs Lyster's income which made her so overwhelmingly attractive) he still turned that smouldering gaze on Dorothy.

She was repelled by it and yet excited. She had welcomed the opportunity to let him know that although most women found him irresistible, she did not. She was relieved however when Daly announced to the company his intention to marry Mrs Lyster.

The wedding was celebrated by a party back stage, which Dorothy attended with the rest of the company. Mrs Daly was very proud of her swaggering squinting husband and, thought Dorothy, welcome to him.

The bridegroom had a word or two with her.

'I'm disappointed in you,' he told her. 'I'd hoped to find you heart-broken.'

'Although I condole with the bride,' retorted Dorothy, 'I can hardly be expected to break my heart for her.'

'And what of the bridegroom?'

'He's a man who will know how to look after himself, I don't doubt.'

'True, Miss Francis. I know a wise woman like you would recognize in him a man who won't be denied what he wants.'

'I am sure Mrs Daly will be able to satisfy all his needs.'

With that Dorothy turned away. In spite of her mockery, he disturbed her.

Shortly after the wedding Ryder told her that he had had to relinquish the lease of the Smock Alley theatre.

'What will that mean?' asked Dorothy. 'If someone else takes it they'll set up in opposition to Crow Street.'

'It means exactly that. But I can't pay the rent just to stop someone else opening up.'

'But two theatres can't be filled. You know how hard it is to fill one.'

'That's what I'm afraid of. I'm in debt to the tune of thousands of pounds and the owners have offered to waive the debt if I give up the lease. There's nothing I can do but give it up. It may be that they'll use the building for something other than the theatre.

I can tell you this, it will be a great weight off my mind and off my pocket to be rid of the place.'

The deal went through and Ryder was more at ease than he had been for a long time. Richard Daly was strutting about the theatre as though he were premier actor, manager and owner of the place. He was clearly delighted with his marriage.

Dorothy heard the news through Ryder.

'Who do you think has taken over Smock Alley? Richard Daly! And he's going to open up in opposition.'

In the stalls every night sat a young soldier. There were many soldiers in Dublin who came regularly to the theatre but there was something persistent about this one and very soon the company was referring to him as Francis's admirer.

He was very young – scarcely good-looking, but extremely earnest; and there was no doubt that he was in love.

Flowers and gifts were arriving back-stage for Dorothy and at length she consented to see the young man. She could not help being touched by his naïvety. On the first meeting he proposed marriage.

Very soon Dorothy took him to the family's lodgings where Grace eagerly studied him. Dorothy was amused because her mother's dearest wish to see her married was becoming more of an obsession. 'You are doing well now,' she would say, 'but never forget that the life of an actress is a precarious one. The public can drop you as quickly as it takes you up. Look what a private income did for Mrs Lyster.'

'It bought Richard Daly,' mocked Dorothy.

'I don't mean that. He'll doubtless run through her fortune for her.'

'Not he. She's too good a business woman and he too good a business man for that to happen.'

'Dorothy, *you* must learn to be a business woman.'

'Very well. I'll start taking lessons.'

'But best of all is a rich husband to take care of you,' affirmed Grace. 'We must find out more about Charles Doyne.'

Dear Charles, he was so young and so much in love! She was sure she could be quite happy married to him. He would never interfere with her career, and it would be pleasant to have a constant admirer. She had to admit that she was not deeply in love with the young man though she liked him well enough, and the more she compared him with Richard Daly the more she liked him. Though why she could compare him with that man seemed irrelevant. What was important was that he would be a docile husband, and there would be children. She had discovered in herself a great desire to have children. It was not that she was so fond of other people's children; it was those of her own which she wanted. And one of her mother's most constant fears was that – as in her own case – there might be children without marriage.

Grace was making inquiries. A cornet in the Second Regiment of Horse. A cornet! What did Dorothy think they were paid? The young man was of good family though, his father being Dean of Leighlin, but Grace knew how such families viewed the marriages of their sons with actresses. She must consider with extreme caution.

It was Grace who discovered that Doyne's income was of the smallest and so was his pay; his family might be good but they were not wealthy and it was clear that the couple would get no support from them.

'I can continue acting,' pointed out Dorothy, 'and we shall be much in the same position as before.'

'There is the family to be supported and what if you started a family of your own? No, my dear, I see nothing but a life of drudgery. Consider this very carefully. Fortunately you are not in love with the young man.'

No, conceded Dorothy, that was true. And a rising actress did not accept marriage from an impecunious young man merely because she wanted legitimate children. Hester joined her voice to Grace's and since Charles Doyne was too meek to be a persistent suitor and Dorothy herself could view the relationship from the most practical of viewpoints, she quietly told him that she could not accept his proposal.

Young Charles was desolate and when the company went on tour he made the most of his leave to follow it to Waterford in the hope that Dorothy would change her mind. But she was firm in her resolve and this was strengthened by the fact that the opening of Smock Alley had taken so much business from Ryder that he was forced to cut salaries.

'Business,' he said mournfully, 'is bad. We're playing to empty houses. Most of it's going to Smock Alley.'

Ryder grudgingly accepted the fact that Daly was a good business man and with his wife's money behind him a formidable rival.

It was clearly no time for an insecure actress with family responsibilities to consider marrying a young man who had little beyond his pay as a cornet in a regiment of horse.

Dorothy was firm, and accepting defeat Charles Doyne began to look elsewhere for a wife.

Another cut in salary. Dorothy was getting worried. Grace said: 'I don't know how we'll manage. The public is deserting Crow Street for Smock Alley every night. I've seen this sort of thing happen before. People like something new. And they say that Daly has engaged John Kemble.'

'How will he be able to pay his salary?' pondered Hester.

'Daly was wise,' replied Grace. 'He married a woman who could not only help to fill his theatre by her own performances but could pay for those of others. He's a very clever gentleman. He'll go up and the more he rises the lower will Tom Ryder fall.'

'It's a gloomy prospect,' agreed Dorothy. She hated playing to half empty houses almost as much as receiving a small salary, but it was no use complaining to Tom Ryder, for what could he do?

While they were discussing the state of affairs a young boy arrived with a note for Miss Dorothy Francis.

Grace, recognizing whence the boy came, could scarcely suppress her excitement.

Dorothy opened it and read that Richard Daly requested the favour of a visit from Miss Dorothy Francis to his office at the Smock Alley Theatre that afternoon as he had a proposition to put before her.

Grace and Hester could not hide their delight which was mostly relief. Here was a way out of their troubles for there could be no doubt what that note meant. One of the remaining draws at Crow Street was Dorothy Francis and Daly wanted her at Smock Alley.

Dorothy hesitated while her mother and sister looked at her in astonishment.

'Don't you know what it means?' demanded Hester.

'Of course I know what it means.'

'Well, what are you waiting for?'

'Tom Ryder gave me my chance.'

'He would be the first to say Go. Besides we can't live on what he's paying you.'

'And then . . .'

'Then what for Heaven's sake?'

'With Mrs Daly in the company what parts should I get?'

'Nonsense. They're in business. They're going to give the parts to the actress the public wants to see in them. You've got to go and see him.'

'I'll see Tom first.'

Grace lifted her eyes to the ceiling. Sometimes she thought Dorothy's heart would rule her head; but Hester thought Dorothy would make the right decision because always she considered her duty to her family before anything else.

Tom Ryder regarded her sadly.

'You've got to go, Dorothy,' he said. 'Crow Street will be closing down if we go on like this. I said there wasn't room for the two of us, didn't I?'

'I shall never forget what you did for me.'

'All in a matter of business, my dear. And that's what you must consider. If you don't accept this offer now, there might not be another. The profession was never a bed of roses.'

So she saw that she must go. She had been hoping all the time that they would persuade her against this.

Daly! She could not get that sly lecherous face out of her mind. She had in a way enjoyed their encounters in Crow Street; it would be different in Smock Alley where he would be something more than a fellow performer.

In Smock Alley she would be to some extent in his power. On him she would depend for parts and salary.

It was a challenge, but a disturbing one.

Moreover, there was the family to consider.

Tragedy in Smock Alley

Daly received her with a mixture of effusiveness and mockery.

So she wanted to come to Smock Alley. He had thought she would. He would pay her three pounds a week as he was paying Kemble only five. What did she think of that?

'It is what I expect,' she told him.

'Then I am delighted to satisfy your expectations. I hope you will satisfy mine.'

'I have not quite decided whether I wish to come.'

'Not for a chance to play opposite Kemble for three pounds a week?'

'Ryder gave me my first chance.'

'Don't be an idiot, girl. This is the serious business of the theatre. There's no room for sentiment.'

'I happen not to agree.'

'That's what I like about you, Dorothy. You always make me convince you.'

'You have never yet succeeded in convincing me on anything.'

'That's to come,' he promised.

Mrs Daly appeared. He said: 'My dear, Miss Francis wants to come to Smock Alley.'

'Of course,' said Mrs Daly. 'Crow Street can't hold out much longer.'

Mrs Daly was a satisfying presence. Daly was not so much in awe of her as of her money and she was wise enough to keep a firm hold on the purse strings which was the only way of keeping a firm hold on Daly.

It will be all right, Dorothy assured herself. There's always Mrs Daly.

Grace was delighted. What a good move it had been over to Smock Alley! Dorothy was now getting her chance and her reputation had grown considerably.

True to his word Daly had given her some good parts.

Walpole's successful Gothic novel, *The Castle of Otranto*, had been dramatized under the title of *The Count of Narbonne* and it was played with Kemble in the main part and Dorothy as

Adelaide, Dublin flocked to see it and theatregoers were all talking of the brilliant young Miss Francis.

One evening when she came off stage flushed with triumph Daly sent for her to come to his office where she found him alone.

'Well,' he demanded. 'Ryder didn't know how to treat his actresses. It's not the same with Daly. Grateful?'

'Grateful indeed for a chance of a good part.'

He put a hand on her shoulder; it was a habit of his to lay his hands on female members of his company when he was near them. Dorothy tried to shrug him off without appearing to do so; but he smiled fully aware of her intentions.

'You don't show your gratitude,' he complained.

'I have thanked you. What more do you expect?'

'A great deal more.'

'What more can an actress give than to play a part well.'

'There are many parts to be played, Dorothy my dear; and if you wish to succeed you must play them all with skill.'

'I hope you have some good ones for me,' she said lightly.

'Excellent ones, my love. And because you are wise as well as devilishly attractive you will play them magnificently.'

'I shall do my best; and now I will say good night.'

She had turned, but he was between her and the door.

'I did not send for you to receive a mild "Thank you for giving me a good part, sir." '

'Then what?' she said.

He seized her by the shoulders. The strength of the man alarmed her.

'Kiss me to start with,' he said.

She turned her face away. 'The prospect does not enchant me.'

She was bent backwards so violently that she cried out in pain. He laughed and forcibly kissed her lips.

She struggled and tried to grip his hair but she was powerless against him.

She gasped: 'I hear footsteps. They sound like Mrs Daly's.'

He held her, listening. Indeed there were footsteps. She was not sure that they were Mrs Daly's; nor was he; and he could not afford to be unsure. She took her opportunity to throw him off and in a moment she had opened the door and was gone.

She was shaken. It was not unexpected. If it were not for the presence of Mrs Daly in the theatre she would be in real danger.

Her great chance to show her talents had come. Only in Smock Alley could she do so. If she left where could she go? There was nowhere else. To England? Could an actress – unknown in that country – hope to get a chance? She saw penury ahead; the entire family in acute poverty.

She was between that and the unwelcome attentions of Richard Daly. Never had her prospects as an actress been brighter; never had her reputation been in greater danger. In Smock Alley she could be seen by English managers, perhaps even London managers. She must stay in Smock Alley until she had enough fame to carry her elsewhere. And she could only do this if Daly permitted it. But what did keeping his good will entail?

She wanted to discuss this with Grace and Hester, but what was there to discuss? Grace would be terrified; it was the sort of situation which she had always feared, and what advice could she give? It was either leave and start again in the hope of getting employment – and where? – or remain and fight Daly.

There was no point in discussing it. It was a clear-cut case.

The brightest aspect of the affair was the presence of Mrs Daly. Dorothy staked her chances of victory on that lady.

In the office at the Smock Alley Theatre Mr and Mrs Daly were quarrelling.

'I'll not have you seducing every female member of the company,' she declared.

'Now, my dear, that is an exaggeration.'

'All right. I'll not have you seducing *one* member of the company.'

'It is nothing. I must keep on friendly terms with the actresses. You know how temperamental they are. One has to flatter them all the time.'

'You leave the flattering to me.'

'My dearest, you are the cleverest woman in the world, but you are wrong in this case. I never give a thought to any woman but you.'

'You'd do well to keep like that.'

He sighed. Without Mrs Daly he could really enjoy life. Business was tolerably good; Kemble was bringing them in and so was

Dorothy. He had some good female parts to dispose of and, good business woman that Mrs Daly was, she had not always objected to their going to Dorothy, providing she herself had a better one – or at least as good. She had not put money into this venture to remain out of sight. The Smock Alley Theatre was to make money for them both and fame for herself. It was not asking too much, for even her greatest enemy would agree that she was a good actress.

She had continually to watch Richard; he simply could not leave women alone. Only the other day she had heard the mother of a young Italian Jewess demanding that he stop pressing his attentions on her daughter. 'What do you want with my daughter?' she had asked. 'You have a fine wife of your own.'

It was humiliating and embarrassing; but in her opinion Richard was so attractive that most of the actresses must find him irresistible.

His power to dismiss them was certainly proving effective and it was whispered in the Green Room that there was scarcely a woman in the company who had not yielded to him. There was one, however, who constantly evaded his advances and this exasperated him beyond endurance. Did she think she was such a draw that she could afford to flout him? He was determined to show her that he would not be flouted; and as the days passed he could think of little but Dorothy and was determined to make her his mistress sooner or later.

He pretended to change his tactics, laughingly accepting her refusal to become his secret mistress. The relationship between them was to be manager and actress; and he hoped, he implied, one of friendship. He appreciated her talents, and whenever he could without alienating Mrs Daly he would give her the best parts.

Kemble was one of the greatest actors she had known and it was an education to play with him; it was not that she wanted spectacular parts as much as a chance to learn; Kemble was a good teacher. Delightedly she played Anne to his Richard III; she was given Maria in *The School for Scandal* – not as important a part as Lady Teazle but a good one nevertheless; she was Katharine in *The Taming of the Shrew* with Kemble a stimulating Petruchio. And she was happier than she had been for some time because she believed that Daly had at last accepted her persistent refusal to accept his advances. She was constantly hearing of the seduction of this and that small player and Mrs Daly's jealousy. Let them, she thought. It has nothing to do with me. I'm becoming a great actress and one day I shall play comedy all the time and shall succeed in convincing managers that what the public like from me is a song and a dance.

She was certain now that she had done the right thing in coming over to Smock Alley.

One day life changed dramatically. It was after the performance and she was about to return to her lodgings; as she came out into one of the corridors of that warren which was Smock Alley Theatre she heard her name called faintly. She paused. She did not recognize the voice but it sounded like one of the young girl players.

'Miss Francis . . . oh . . . come quickly . . . up in the attic . . .'

She hurried up the narrow stairs to the top of the building.

'Miss Francis . . .'

She opened the door of the attic; it was dark inside.

She called. 'Who is it? Where are you? Wait . . . I'll get a candle.'

She heard the sound of a key turning in a lock; and there was a chuckle from behind; she was seized in a powerful pair of arms.

She knew immediately. What a fool! she thought. Of course he could imitate one of the girls. He was enough of an actor for that.

'Dorothy, you idiot,' said Daly. 'How long did you think you could say No to me?'

'Let me go immediately.'

'All in good time.'

'Mrs Daly . . .'

'Is not in the theatre tonight.'

'You're a devil.'

'I don't deny it.'

He was laughing as she hit out at him. She shouted and screamed, but he laughed. 'No one can hear.'

'I . . . I'll kill you.'

'You can try. Most of them want to smother me with their caresses.'

36

'I will never, never do that.'

'In time you will. Go on. Kick . . . scream. I like it. It's a novelty . . . and it's all useless.'

She fought until she was exhausted, but he was the stronger. Crying with rage, frustration and shame she was forced to submit to rape.

She crept into her bedroom. Thank God she did not have to share with Hester or Grace for if she had, how could she have kept this hideous secret? Her clothes were torn, her body bruised and battered, and she herself was bitterly humiliated.

She should have known. All that care she had taken in the beginning and then to be lulled into security, and caught like that. She would never forget; she would go on remembering every nauseating second.

And he had laughed triumphantly, knowing all the time that he would win.

What could she do?

Her impulse was to pack and leave. But how could she explain the reason to her mother? She pictured Grace's terror. It was what she feared would happen to her daughters – only even she had not thought of rape.

I hate him, she thought. He's a devil.

She wished she could stop thinking of it. The darkness of the attic, the losing battle virtue and decency had fought against brutal and bestial strength.

What chance had she had?

She could not stop thinking of him, brooding on him, hating him and yet . . . she would not admit it. She was *not* fascinated by him. She was not one of those silly little girls who were ready to run when he beckoned.

'I hate him,' she said aloud.

But what could she do? She took off her clothes and wrapped herself in a dressing gown. She could go into her mother's room now and say, 'We are leaving in the morning. I shall never go into Daly's theatre again.' She thought of the parts he had given her, playing opposite Kemble, and giving all that up. For what? To start again in England? Where? And who would give her a chance?

Time was what she needed. Time to think about the right course of action.

I have not only myself to consider, she reminded herself.

She saw him the next day and scornfully turned her head away.

'Don't be despondent, my dear,' he said. 'I'll arrange another little rape for you very very soon.'

'You're loathsome,' she cried.

'I know.'

'I wish I'd never seen you.'

'My dear Dorothy hates me so vehemently that it's almost love.' he said.

She turned away, suppressing a great inclination to burst into tears.

She was careful never to be alone with him; but he was constantly in her thoughts. It must be so, she told herself, because she must be continually on the alert against him.

Once or twice when by some mischance he encountered her alone he would ask her to step up once more to their attic.

'Never,' she retorted, 'and I am in a mind to tell Mrs Daly what has happened.'

'She would believe you were very willing – in fact that you lured me there, for in common with every other woman in this theatre – including Miss Francis – she has a high opinion of my prowess in love.'

Dorothy turned away. There might be something in that, she had long decided. To have reported what had happened to Mrs Daly could well have meant her dismissal.

He was secretly amused because she had told no one of what had happened. That fact gave him confidence to proceed with his plans.

He ceased to pursue her. In fact he told her that he was sorry he had behaved as he had and he hoped the incident might not impair their friendship.

'That which never existed could naturally not be impaired,' she retorted.

And from that day she was no longer offered the best parts. She was not well known enough to insist; she was entirely in his hands; and naturally since she was not playing important parts she could not expect to continue with her salary of three guineas a week. It was promptly cut to two and, she was told ominously, even that was more than the parts warranted.

Grace was bewildered. What had happened? Dorothy had been doing so well. Why had it suddenly been decided that she should be given such silly little parts? Grace began to worry. Were the Dalys displeased? It was difficult to balance the household accounts. Worrying made her ill and it was necessary to incur doctors' bills. They were in debt.

'You're looking scarcely yourself, my dear,' said Daly one day when she saw him alone. 'I'm getting concerned about you. Mustn't lose your bloom, you know. The audiences won't like it.'

She tried to push past him but he detained her and said gently: 'I hear that your mother has been ill. Is it doctors' bills and invalid's fare?'

'My mother has been ill,' she admitted.

'In debt?'

'It's my affair.'

'That's where you're wrong, my dear. My actresses' good looks are *my* affair. And I feel guilty. You haven't been the same since our little adventure. You worry too much. I'm sorry. I was under the impression it was what you wanted. I didn't understand that you really meant what you said. Dorothy, will you accept a loan?'

She hesitated. She must find the money. And after all why shouldn't he help?

'I'd rather have my old parts back with my old salary.'

'Have the loan first, settle your affairs . . . and then you'll be able to concentrate on work.'

'You owe it to me in any case,' she said.

'That's the spirit. More like the old Dorothy. I'll lend you a hundred pounds. You can pay me back when you've got it. Come to my office tomorrow and I'll get it all signed and sealed.'

So she did and she paid the bills and she told Grace how kind Mr Daly had been. That cheered Grace considerably. 'He must think highly of you, Dolly,' she said. 'I expect that wife of his is jealous.'

'Jealous?' said Dorothy sharply. 'Why should she be jealous?'

'Of your success, of course.'

Dorothy sighed. Grace must never know about that frightful scene in the attic.

A few weeks passed. True to his word Daly offered her a better part; her spirits rose. It was going to take a long time to pay off her debt but that would come.

Wherever she went she seemed to see Daly's eyes upon her. She became alarmed because she knew that it was not true that he had lost his interest in her.

When the ultimatum came she was not unprepared for it. The kind Mr Daly disappeared and there was the rogue, whom she had learned so tragically how to distrust, with another proposition. He wanted her to come to him willingly this time; he had no intention of using physical force.

'An anti-climax,' he told her. 'The first time . . . that was exhilarating. But we don't want a repeat performance. I have rented a place for us; we will go there whenever I say and you will be pleased to come, my dear, I promise you.'

'And I promise you that you can keep your little places for others.'

'I've had a surfeit of others – by no means enough of Dorothy.'

'You are insufferable.'

'I know it. And you are fascinating. That is why I must go to such lengths to win you. For you are too cold, my dear. I could never abide frigid women. That's something we must change – and I think we shall. I have a notion that that experience we shared was not as repulsive to you as you would like to delude me and yourself into believing.'

She turned away, but he caught her arm. 'Don't forget you owe me money. I can have you sent to the debtors' prison.'

The debtors' prison! The shadow which overhung the poor of every class! The descent into despair from which so often it was impossible to escape. He laughed to see her turn pale.

'No need to be afraid, my dear. Be kind instead. It's all I ask.'

'You promised that you would allow me to pay you back by degrees.'

'I've changed my mind.'

'But . . .'

'I want the money now. Don't be a fool, Dorothy. You don't have to pay your debt in cash.'

'Oh . . . you are . . .'

'Insufferable! You've already said it. Don't repeat yourself, my dear. Shall we say after the theatre tonight? I'll give you the address. It's close by. Stop being Miss Prude. It doesn't become you because you're not, you know. You were meant to enjoy life and by God you shall. You be there tonight, kind and loving, and I promise you you'll have no fear of either debtors' prisons or small parts. You'll come well out of this, Dorothy, my dear. All you have to remember is that it does not pay to flout the manager.'

He gave her an affectionate little push. He was sure of success.

Dorothy walked away blankly.

What could she do? Run away with the family. Where to? Grace was not fully recovered. This would kill her.

Whereas if she gave way Grace would know nothing . . . She would get her big parts back . . .

What can I do? she asked herself.

From that day she became Daly's mistress.

There was a clever likely lass,
Just come to town from Glo'ster;
And she did get her livelihood
By crying Melton Oysters.

She bore her basket on her head
In the genteelest posture;
And every day and every night
She cried her Melton Oysters.

And now she is a lady gay,
For Billingsgate has lost her
She goes to masquerades and Play,
No more cries Melton Oysters.

So sang Dorothy on the stage at Smock Alley and the audience roared its applause. It was not the banal words of the song nor the simple melody; it was Dorothy Francis, small, dainty, provocative, looking for all the world as though she might have carried a basket of oysters on her head at one time and now was the lady who went to masquerades and plays.

Now that she was getting better parts her fame was growing and on the nights when she appeared the theatre was full; when she sang one of her songs the audience would not let her go immediately after but insisted on several repeats.

There was no doubt of Dorothy's popularity. Mrs Daly grumbled a little. 'Must that young woman have all the best parts, Richard?' 'No, my dear, only those that wouldn't become you. Dorothy's a comedy actress. She lacks your dignity. Let her have the light-weight parts. You have the real drama.' And Mrs Daly was not discontented with that. She had given up being jealous of Richard. It was well known that he was the lover of almost every personable young woman in the company, and she had grown tired of protesting about that. What she cared about was that the best parts should be reserved for her – and if that were so and the money came in, let Richard amuse himself.

The winter and spring had been a trying time for Dorothy. She despised herself and the position into which she had fallen; and her hatred of Daly, who had put her into it, was growing so intense that she felt she could not accept her position at Smock Alley for much longer.

As she lay in her bed in the room next to her mother's and Hester's she examined the possibility of departure. She had acquired some fame, but was it enough? Would they ever have heard of her across the Irish Channel?

Extreme poverty was something she could not face. Daly had refused to accept small payments for the loan and she knew that he intended to hold it over her. It was no generosity on his part; he liked to have women in his power particularly when they were good actresses as well as physically attractive to him.

So far she had managed to keep the affair secret from the others but could she hope to continue to do this? From a carefree tomboy she had become a woman of responsibilities. Had she had only herself to fend for everything would have been different. She thought longingly of the old days at Crow Street, and the more she thought the greater her hatred of Daly grew.

She had always been aware that something would have to be done. The question was what.

She knew that fate had decided for her when she made the alarming discovery that she was pregnant.

It could not remain hidden for much longer and Grace, ever watchful, made the discovery. She could not believe it – except that it was something she had always feared for her daughters.

Never had Dorothy's hatred of Daly been so intense as it was when she saw the anguish in her mother's face.

'Yes,' she said, 'I'm going to have a child. It's Daly's. He forced me in the first place and after that threatened me with the debtors' prison.'

Grace wept bitterly. 'You did it for us,' she said. 'For me and for the family.'

'I could see no other way out and after that first occasion . . .'

She shuddered and Grace cried out: 'Don't go on. I understand, my dearest child. But this must stop. I can't have you treated in this way.'

'But what can we do? Where can we go? Don't forget that now . . . there will be the child.'

Grace threw off her invalidism and became the courageous woman who had run away from a parsonage to seek her fortune on the stage. This was her daughter whose very devotion to the family had put her into this terrible position. Grace had always feared it but now that it had come she would face it boldly.

'We must leave here at once,' she said.

'But where could we go?'

'To Leeds,' replied Grace promptly. 'I was reading not long ago of Tate Wilkinson's company. I once played Desdemona to his Othello. He couldn't refuse help to an old friend.'

Dorothy was relieved. At last she was sharing her hideous secret; and her mother knew too much of theatrical life not to understand how it had happened.

She felt happier than she had for months.

Tate Wilkinson's company

There was enough money to buy passages to Liverpool for the family and during the next few days they secretly made their preparations to leave. When the time of departure arrived they quietly slipped out of their lodgings and took ship to Liverpool; and from thence made their way to Leeds.

It was easy to discover the whereabouts of Tate Wilkinson for most people knew the manager of the theatrical company who had not long ago inherited theatres in York, Newcastle and Hull when his partner had died. He lodged at an inn near the theatre and Grace said they must lose no time in seeing him, for they had scarcely any money left and had not been able to bring all their clothes with them for fear of someone's seeing them and reporting to Daly, who would legally have been able to stop them since Dorothy not only owed him money but was under contract to him.

When Tate Wilkinson heard that Mrs Grace Bland recently come from Dublin was asking to see him he remembered who she was at once. He would never forget that *Othello* in Dublin in the days when he had been a young and struggling actor.

He was kindly and as sentimental as most theatre folk so he received Grace warmly but was unprepared for the rest of the family.

He bade them be seated and when Grace told him that they had come from Dublin and that her daughter who had made a name in Ireland wanted to give her talents to the English, Wilkinson was dubious. He was like any other theatrical manager, always looking for talent; but if the young woman had been doing as well as her mother said why had they left Dublin? He was constantly being approached by impecunious actors and actresses for a chance, and he was after all a business man.

'My daughter Dorothy is a first rate comedienne,' declared Grace. 'You should have seen her filling houses in Ireland. It was the same wherever she went . . .'

Wilkinson looked at the dejected and weary young woman, who did not look exactly like a comedienne.

He wanted to say he could do nothing, but there was the past connection with Grace and something about Dorothy, in spite of her listlessness, appealed to him. Perhaps she would recite something for him, he said. She replied that she was too tired and would prefer an audition actually on the stage in a few days' time.

The mother was anxious; there was some mystery here, Wilkinson decided.

He sent for a bottle of Madeira wine and some food. The

family, he noticed, ate heartily and while they did so he talked of the old days at the Dublin theatre; and of Grace's sister, Miss Phillips, who was now playing with his York company.

He was studying Dorothy all the time and he mentioned that her aunt, Miss Phillips, had made an excellent job of the part of Callista in *The Fair Penitent*. Dorothy said she knew the part well and when, of her own accord, she started to recite some of the lines, Wilkinson was immediately aware of the quality of her melodious yet resonant voice and that she was undoubtedly an actress.

'What is your particular line?' he asked. 'Tragedy, comedy or opera?'

'All,' she answered, to his astonishment.

Before they left the inn Wilkinson had agreed to sign Dorothy up and that her first part should be Callista in *The Fair Penitent*.

It had been an excellent idea to come to Leeds. Grace congratulated herself and in fact felt better than she had for a long time. The family needed her. When Dorothy was in trouble she turned to her mother and it was Grace who had found the solution to their troubles.

Wilkinson could only offer Dorothy fifteen shillings a week to start. It was a fair salary for an unknown actress and she had her way to make in England, but it was very different from the three guineas she had received with Daly. But peace of mind goes with it, said Dorothy with her usual optimism.

Peace of mind, yes, thought Grace. Provided Daly did not discover where they were and sue for breach of contract, which Grace would be the first to admit he had a perfect right to do, the scoundrel.

Remembering that it was her singing which had brought her the warm appreciation of audiences in Dublin, Dorothy was eager to introduce a song at the end of the play.

Wilkinson was dubious. 'Callista is dead. How can she spring forth and sing?'

'It won't be Callista. It will be Dorothy Francis. You'll see. Please, I beg of you, give me a chance to do this. If it isn't a success immediately I'll stop it.'

'Sing for me now,' said Wilkinson, expecting a moderately

good voice, for had it not been so she would not have wished to use it.

But when she sang *Melton Oysters* she won his instant approval. This young woman had all the gifts an actress needed for success – an exciting personality which was entirely individual; a trim figure, neat yet voluptuous; a face that while not beautiful was piquant, jaunty and irresistible when she smiled; a voice that made her rendering of her lines a joy to listen to; and in addition she could sing with such feeling, charm and sweetness that she must enchant all who heard her. He was beginning to be glad her mother had brought her to the inn that day. But why had they left Dublin? Why hadn't some manager there determined to keep such a talented creature?

He had billed her as Dorothy Bland and she told him that that must be changed. She was Dorothy Francis. She was talking of this to Grace when she suddenly realized that if she made a success of a part it was not unlikely that Daly would hear of it; and he would then know where she was.

'I must change my name at once,' she declared. 'Dorothy Francis must not appear on a play-bill that could fall into Daly's hands.'

Grace agreed that this was so and Dorothy who had in this short time found that she could talk over her problems with Wilkinson went to see him.

'There is something I must tell you,' she said. 'I am to have a child.'

His face fell. Actresses constantly became pregnant and usually did not manage to lose much working time because of this event, but he had not considered this would happen to Dorothy and that it was already about to was a shock. On the other hand it might explain her flight from Dublin, and if it were an emotional entanglement that was not so disturbing to him as a theatrical upheaval.

'When?' he asked.

'In six months' time.'

'Six months . . . well, that gives us a little time.'

She was relieved. 'I shall work up to the last minute. But I wish to change my name.'

He nodded. 'That shouldn't be a great difficulty.'

'In the circumstances I prefer to be known as Mrs.'

'Naturally. You don't want Bland?'

'No, my father's people object to that.'

'And you can't be Phillips because of your aunt. We don't want two actresses of that name. It could be confusing. I might call you Jordan because you've just crossed the river.'

He had spoken jocularly, but she said: 'Mrs Jordan. Dorothy Jordan. That's as good as any other.'

So from then she was known as Mrs Dorothy Jordan.

She was a success. No sooner had she appeared in a simple muslin dress and a mobcap and had sung *The Greenwood Laddie* than she knew she had made an excellent start. What did it matter that the tragic Callista had died? She was resurrected in the enchanting form of Dorothy Jordan, and she sang for them so delightfully that they would not let her stop in a hurry.

She stood accepting their acclaim. One of these days, she thought, I'll play comedy; I'll sing and dance; and I'll refuse to play parts like Callista.

For the time, though, she would be glad of what she could get; and she could not believe that it was a short while ago that she had been planning her escape from the villainous Daly.

If that man did not exist, if she did not carry the fruit of his lechery within her, she could be completely happy. But she would be happy. Although the child had been forced on her she would love it when it came. As for her contract with Daly, she would do her best to forget it. Tate Wilkinson was pleased with her.

Life in the theatre had taught her not to expect too much, and while her success pleased the family and Mr Wilkinson it was not received so enthusiastically by some members of the company. Who is this Dorothy Jordan? some of the female members of the company wanted to know. Why should she appear from nowhere and suddenly take the best parts? How had she managed to win public approval? Wilkinson has done more for her than he ever did for us.

The old envies were beginning to rise.

'The devil take them!' cried Dorothy. 'They'll get as good as they give.'

'*Mrs* Jordan,' said Mrs Smith, one of the leading ladies who had not only a following with the public but a husband to substantiate *her* right to the title of Mrs. 'Where is *Mr* Jordan then – for I'll swear the woman's pregnant!'

Mrs Smith herself was in that condition and, as she said, proud of it. One did wonder about Mrs Jordan who had appeared suddenly in their midst with her faintly Irish accent which some people seemed to find so fascinating, and her forward ways. And if she were pregnant that might account for her sudden appearance. She was running away from the scene of her shame with some tale of having recently become a widow. Or at least if she had not deigned to tell such a tale, it was what she implied.

Mrs Smith would stand in the wings while Dorothy was on stage and criticize her acting audibly. Dorothy laughed. She could always do the same for Mrs Smith.

Mrs Smith imitated Dorothy and went round singing *Melton Oysters* and *Greenwood Laddie*; but her singing voice was not of the same calibre as Dorothy's and this attempt was a failure. She talked to her friends of the poverty of Dorothy's acting. Grace was furious and joined in the battle on behalf of her daughter. She would come to the theatre and groan whenever Mrs Smith appeared, demanding of all within earshot what the theatre was coming to when people like that were allowed to perform. Tate Wilkinson turned away from these battles, which were familiar enough in the theatre.

Meanwhile Dorothy had scored her greatest success to that time as Priscilla Tomboy in *The Romp*. There was no doubt that this was the kind of part in which she excelled. Small and dainty with great vitality and a rare ability to clown she had the house shrieking with laughter. She followed that with Arionelli in *The Son-in-Law*; and the fact that she wore breeches and took this male part enhanced her reputation. Audiences wanted to laugh and Dorothy Jordan could make them do so. They wanted to see a fine pair of legs and she could offer these as well. No member of Tate Wilkinson's company looked quite so well in male costume as Dorothy Jordan.

'In a few months it will be different,' said Mrs Smith gleefully. She was delighted because though Dorothy might be able to get ahead of her during her enforced absence Dorothy would have one of her own to follow, when she could be reduced to her proper place.

Wilkinson was not entirely displeased with this jealous bickering; he remarked to Cornelius Swan, the theatre critic, that he believed it kept the company on the alert. Mrs Smith was so eager to excel Mrs Jordan's performance that she gave of her best – and the same thing applied to Mrs Jordan.

'Mrs Jordan is a great little actress,' said Cornelius Swan. 'She wants a little coaching here and there; but I think if she had it she might make London.'

'I prefer to keep her up North.'

'Ah, but you can't stand in her way, my good fellow. Give me an introduction to the lady. I want to tell her how I enjoyed her performance.'

'And suggest a few improvements?'

'There is usually room for improvement in any performance – even Mrs Jordan's; and I think you may well agree that I am qualified to suggest where.'

So Wilkinson introduced Cornelius Swan to Dorothy and she found him entertaining. He told her that he had even criticized Garrick and advised him how he might improve his roles. Would she listen to him?

Dorothy replied that she would with pleasure for she felt she had much to learn; and although she might not always feel that she could take his advice she would always be pleased to listen to it.

This reply delighted the old man, who came constantly to the theatre and watched Dorothy's progress with great interest and his notices of her performance were eulogistic with just the right flavouring of criticism to dispel any accusation of favouritism.

The friendship meant a great deal to Dorothy during those months. Her pregnancy was becoming irksome; she blamed herself for not confessing to her mother earlier and leaving Dublin before this happened. If after that humiliating experience she had left she would have been able to pursue her career without this added encumbrance, but by remaining and submitting to his blackmail she had not only burdened herself with his child but had destroyed her own self respect.

But it was not in her nature to look back and she must not do so now. Her excuse was that she had been young and inexperienced; and she had paid dearly for that inexperience.

The company was to play in York and when they arrived in that town a message awaited Grace from her sister Mary.

'I trust, dear sister,' wrote Mary, 'that you will come in time. I long to see Dorothy. I have heard reports of her acting and she is going to be a credit to us.'

Grace and Dorothy and Hester went to Mary's lodgings and when they arrived there were horrified to find that she was on her death bed.

Grace embraced her sister and wept, thinking of that day long ago when they had run away from their father's parsonage, of all their ambitious dreams which had come to nothing . . . or very little.

Mary understood her thoughts. She grimaced. 'Well, Grace, this is the end of me,' she said. 'But it was a good life and I've no regrets.'

Her eyes were on Dorothy. She held out a trembling hand to her. 'See,' she said. 'It's the drink. Don't let it get the better of you, dear, I've heard of your performances. They're shaking up some of the dear ladies, I can tell you. Never mind, my dear. You go in and beat the lot of them. She's going to make it worth while, Grace. One day you'll say you were glad you ran away because if you hadn't there wouldn't have been a Dorothy Jordan.'

'You're tiring yourself,' said Grace.

'What does it matter? I haven't much longer in any case.'

Mary talked rapidly and excitedly of past triumphs, failures and her love of what she called the bottle which had been her downfall. 'We all have our weaknesses. Don't let yours interfere with your career, Dorothy. I ought to have worked harder. I might have done it then. But you'll do it, Dorothy, I know it.'

She was like a grim prophetess lying back on her pillows, her feverish eyes fixed on her niece.

She died a few days after; but it was said that she seemed contented after she had seen Grace and her daughter. She left all she possessed to her niece Dorothy Jordan. It was mostly clothes and many of these were in pawn; but she had some fine costumes.

*

They were getting better off now. Dorothy had her fixed salary which Wilkinson had raised to twenty-three shillings. This was not riches, of course, but Dorothy was careful; and with the little Aunt Mary had left her she felt that she would be ready to give the coming child a good start in the world.

Cornelius Swan had followed the company to York because he was eager to see all of Dorothy's performances. When Dorothy was feeling ill, which she was more and more frequently now, he would come to see her and sit by her bed going over some of her parts with her.

This passed the hours of enforced rest pleasantly enough; and they were a delight to the old man.

He said that she was like his adopted daughter and he had great plans for her future.

With her aunt's prophecies and Cornelius' interest Dorothy felt more and more ready to face the ordeal ahead. Mrs Smith's unpleasantness could be borne, even when she tried to wreck Dorothy's benefit.

All appeared to be going well but it seemed impossible to have too much good fortune; and it was her very success which was proving her downfall.

Daly's letter reached her in York.

He had heard of her recent successes and knew where she was playing. She had deserted his company and so broken her contract and for this he demanded the immediate payment of £250. There was also a matter of an outstanding debt. He offered her three courses of action: she must return to Dublin and complete her contract with him; she must pay up what she owed; or she would be arrested at once and committed to a debtors' prison.

Grace found her staring at the letter and taking it up read its contents with horror.

'This,' she said, 'is the end of everything. We cannot fight this. We are trapped.'

Cornelius called at the lodgings. He was excited.

'I have persuaded Wilkinson to revive *Zara* so that you can have the title role. You'll need some coaching but I am prepared ... But what's wrong?'

Dorothy held out Daly's letter. 'I don't think I shall be playing Zara or anything else,' she said. 'I've thought of running away. But where to? If I go on acting and make any sort of name he will find me. If I don't, how can I live?'

'Well, what are you planning to do?' he asked.

'I'm trying to make some plan.'

'And didn't it occur to you to consult me?'

Dorothy shook her head. 'There is nothing to be done. I see it all clearly. From the day I set eyes on that man there was no hope for me.'

Cornelius laughed. 'You forget, my dear, that I am not a poor man. You forget too my interest in you as my adopted daughter and one of our finest actresses. Daly shall have his money at once and that will be an end of the villain as far as you are concerned. I will send off the money without delay then we can continue with the serious business of rehearsing for *Zara*.'

It was like a great weight which had burdened her for a long time suddenly dropping from her. She was free. She need never wake in the night from a dream of a dark attic, and lecherous tentacles stretching out for her across the sea.

Her dear friend Cornelius Swan had severed the chains which bound her to that evil man.

She was free . . . almost, but not entirely.

She still had to bear his child.

One night when Dorothy was playing Priscilla Tomboy there was great excitement in the theatre because an actor from London had arrived in York to see the play.

It was stimulating to know he was there and Dorothy, free from menace for the first time for more than a year, gave a sparkling performance, after which Mr Smith – who was no relation to the envious actress of the same name – came backstage to congratulate the performers and in particular Dorothy.

'You have a genius for comedy, Mrs Jordan,' he said. 'By Gad, I never saw Tomboy better played.'

This was great praise indeed coming from an actor who played in Drury Lane and had won the approval of London audiences.

Mr Smith was known as 'The Gentleman' because of his exquisite manners – he followed the Prince of Wales in his dress, they said; and he certainly had an exquisite way of taking his snuff. He bowed with elegance and flattered most of the players, but Dorothy sensed that there was a certain sincerity in his praise for her. Why else should he be in the theatre every night she played? She was excited to know he was there, and was fully aware that when he was she played her best.

There were rumours throughout the theatre. Mr Sheridan had sent him up to look for talent. There was a chance that some of them would be invited to play in London. Covent Garden and Drury Lane were not an impossibility.

Wilkinson was a little dismayed. He did not want his big draws lured to London; he was particularly afraid of losing Mrs Jordan, for he had seen how interested The Gentleman was in her.

He raised Dorothy's salary and said she should have another Benefit. Dorothy was delighted, but when Gentleman Smith returned to London and no offers came, he was forgotten.

While Mrs Smith was obliged to leave the theatre temporarily to give birth to her child, her parts fell to Dorothy who played them with a special verve and won great applause. She could not repress a certain malicious delight in picturing the incapacitated actress grinding her teeth wondering how much progress the Jordan was making during her absence. 'Hers will come,' declared Mrs Smith delightedly.

And in due course Dorothy retired from the stage to give birth to her child. It was a healthy girl and she called her Frances.

Mrs Smith had been working hard during Dorothy's absence – both in the theatre and out. The company had gone to Hull where Dorothy would play her first part since her confinement. 'Return of Mrs Jordan after a six weeks' absence,' ran the play bills, but Mrs Smith was determined that her rival was to have a cool reception.

Through friends in Hull she made the acquaintance of some of the leading citizens, and in the seclusion of their houses to which the famous actress was asked as a welcome guest she spoke of 'that creature Jordan. A loose woman if ever there was one.' She did not think that gentlemen of Hull would wish their wives and daughters to see her perform if they knew the whole story. It was nauseating. The creature had been absent to give birth to a bastard – father unknown. Such was their Mrs Jordan!

The ladies were duly shocked and declared their intention of staying away from *The Fair Penitent* in which Mrs Jordan was playing the part she had made famous – that of Callista.

Some, however, were determined to make their disapproval known.

Dorothy, who during her enforced absence had been longing to return to the stage, was immediately aware of the attitude of her audience. They were hostile. She had never before played before such a house.

They seemed to have come to the theatre for anything but to see the play and when they should have been spellbound they chatted and laughed together. What has happened? wondered Dorothy. Can it be that I have lost the gift of holding an audience?

The play was a disaster. When she died they applauded derisively. She caught sight of Mrs Smith's delighted face in the wings and guessed she had helped to bring about this fiasco. Could she have carried her enmity to this degree? Yes, because people had crowded into the theatre to see Dorothy in those roles which Mrs Smith had reckoned to be entirely hers.

Mortified, she changed into her simple gown and mob cap. *Greenwood Laddie* had never failed to charm them, yet it did on that night, and her voice could not be heard above the hissing and boos.

The curtain came down. It was disaster. For the first time Dorothy Jordan had failed to please an audience.

There was a knock on the door. It was one of the male actors.

'Oh,' he stammered. 'I thought I'd look in.'

'Why?' demanded Dorothy.

'Tonight ... You shouldn't let it worry you. You know who's responsible, don't you? It's that confounded jealous woman. I could wring her neck.'

He was moderately good-looking and a moderately good actor. She had always liked George Inchbald. He had shown her little acts of kindness often but tonight she felt drawn towards him because after her recent humiliation she was in need of comfort.

'You don't want to take any notice of it, Dorothy. It was arranged ... deliberately.'

'Do you think so, George?'

'I know it. Why, she has been talking of nothing else for days. I've heard all the whispering in corners.'

'How can she be so malicious?'

'Because you're a better actress than she is and because she's jealous.'

She knew it, but it was comforting to hear George say it.

'Ignore it,' advised George. 'Go on playing as though you don't notice it.'

'Don't notice what happened tonight!'

'Well, go on playing then. She can't go on turning them against you. They come to see a play well played and nobody can play better than you.'

'Oh, George . . .' She held out her hand and he took it suddenly and kissed it.

She felt then that something good had come out of this unhappy night.

George Inchbald was right. That night had been an isolated incident. The citizens of Hull wanted to see Dorothy Jordan in her parts and when she wore male attire no one was going to boo her off the stage. They liked to hear her sing; and in fact preferred her performances to those of Mrs Smith.

Tate Wilkinson sighed over the tantrums of his company and deplored the fall in takings which had resulted from the absences from the stage of his two chief female players; but there was no doubt that Dorothy was a draw and all Mrs Smith's malice could not alter that.

As for Dorothy she was more light-hearted than she had been for a long time. Every morning when she awoke she remembered that Daly no longer had any power to harm her; that in itself was the greatest blessing she could think of. Young Frances was well and Grace enjoyed looking after her. Hester was playing small parts and growing into a tolerably good actress. There was an occasional part for Francis, the eldest of the boys. At last she was no longer worried about money; and she had given the clothes her baby had worn to a hospital for the use of some poor mother. In her desire to show her gratitude for her changed position she added several layettes to the one she had used and gave these too, for she would never forget her fears when she had believed herself to be in debt to Richard Daly. It was a sort of thanks offering for deliverance.

So she was lighthearted and George Inchbald was an attractive young man. They fell in love.

Grace was pleased; there was nothing she wanted so much as to see her daughter settled with a man to look after her and help shoulder responsibilities. She could have hoped that Dorothy might have made a brilliant match but as she said to Hester, it was not marriage rich men were after; and she thought Dorothy ought to be married. Little Frances wanted a father, and George Inchbald would do well enough.

George's stepmother, Mrs Elizabeth Inchbald, a novelist, playwright and herself an actress, believed that it would be a good match for she had a high opinion of Dorothy and thought her singing and speaking voices charming, though, she had pointed out, she had a faint Irish accent but that would disappear in time. So there would be no difficulty between the families.

Marriage, thought Dorothy. Yes, she did want it. Sometimes she asked herself, Was it George she wanted as much as marriage? She longed for her mother to be satisfied; she wanted no more anxiety, and she was still smarting under the rumours Mrs Smith had spread of the immoral life she led.

Dorothy wanted respectability and she saw it in George Inchbald.

Gentleman Smith came again to the theatre, bringing with him an air of elegance from London. He talked knowledgeably of what was going on there. Names like Sarah Siddons and Richard Sheridan crept into the conversation. He spoke knowingly of the affair between the Prince of Wales and Mrs Robinson which had ended in such a burst of scandal. The whole of the company could not hear enough of gay London society and there was not one member of the company who did not hope that Gentleman Smith would go back to London and report that he – or she – deserved to play in Drury Lane or Covent Garden.

But everyone knew that Gentleman Smith was more interested in Mrs Jordan than in anyone else.

'She has the quality,' he had been heard to say. 'It's indefinable . . . but it's there.'

The envy of the women players was as evident as ever, but as

Dorothy's position grew stronger it had less effect on her.

George Inchbald would call at the lodgings and talk for hours to the whole family of what would happen if Dorothy was invited to play in London. It would make all the difference, he said. To continue to play in the provinces was death to an actor or actress. There was no chance really; and they had to be noticed before they were too old.

'He is on the point of proposing,' said Grace after he had left. 'He thinks you're going to London, Dorothy, and he's afraid that he's going to lose you.'

'And he always speaks as though when you go he'll be with you,' pointed out Hester.

'He'd be a good husband,' put in Grace almost pleadingly. 'Quite serious . . . and reliable.'

Yes, thought Dorothy, serious and reliable; a good husband for her and a father for Frances.

Gentleman Smith went back to London. Almost daily Dorothy waited for a message, but none came.

If I were going to be asked, she thought, I should have been by now.

It was some time before she noticed that George's visits to the lodgings were less frequent. She saw him often in the theatre as a matter of course, but he did not seem to be waiting for her when she came off to give her the usual congratulations.

Grace invited him to supper and he accepted with pleasure; and during that evening Dorothy realized what his devotion had been worth, for he talked of the precarious existence of stage folk, who could never be sure of financial security. He hinted that he believed it would be folly for impecunious actors and actresses to marry. How could they be sure when their playing would not separate them? But chiefly how could they be sure that they would keep a roof over their heads? It did not seem to him wise to bring children into such an uneasy existence.

Dorothy understood.

He was telling her that while he had considered marrying an actress who had a chance of a London success, he did not want to unite himself with one who was a provincial player.

When he had gone she gave vent to her temper.

'That is an end of Mr George Inchbald!' she cried. 'Reliable . . . oh, very! Reliable in his desire for a wife who can bring home a good salary. Serious in his intentions! Oh, yes. In his intentions to marry a woman with money! Men!' she went on: 'They are all alike. I have not linked myself with one so far. That has been wise of me. I shall go on in that way.'

And she was not sorry, for she had never had more than an affection for him.

'I shall have to be besottedly in love,' she told Grace, 'before I consider sharing my life with a man.'

It was Grace who was heart-broken. The longing to see Dorothy respectably married was the dearest wish of her life.

The next three years passed quickly. Dorothy devoted herself absolutely to the theatre, Cornelius Swan coached her and she was never too sure of her own ability not to learn from others. Her spontaneous generosity brought her the friendship of beginners; her talents brought her the envy of her rivals; she was careless of their enmity and devoted herself to her family.

Then one day the letter arrived. Dorothy could scarcely believe that she was being offered a chance to go to London and appear at Drury Lane that autumn.

She called to her mother and Hester. 'Read this,' she cried. 'Read this. Tell me that I'm not dreaming.'

Grace snatched the letter from Hester; they read it, their cheeks flushed, their eyes round.

At last – the great chance. Gentleman Smith had not failed them.

The news spread rapidly through the theatre. Dorothy Jordan is going to Drury Lane. Those jealous actresses, Mrs Smith and Robinson, ground their teeth in fury, but there was nothing they could do about it. They were sure Mr Sheridan would be unmoved if they tried to pass on to him news of Dorothy's scandalous life. What scandals could a provincial actress hope to create to compare with those which circulated about him? Dorothy was going. In spite of them she was the one who had been given the great chance. She was to act in the same theatre as the great Sarah Siddons.

It was unfair; it was favouritism; it was intolerable; but there was nothing they could do about it.

Tate Wilkinson grumbled. 'No sooner do I train an actress and make her of some use to me than I lose her.'

Grace tried to put a sympathetic façade over her elation.

'She'll never forget what you did for her,' she soothed. She believed that Tate Wilkinson's reward would be posterity's gratitude to the man who had helped Dorothy Jordan when she most needed it.

Dorothy could think of nothing but her London début; she played indifferently; she even forgot her lines.

'My God,' cried Mrs Smith. 'Is this our London actress?'

George Inchbald came to offer his congratulations, his eyes alight with speculation. Dorothy received him coldly. 'When I'm in London, George,' she said, 'I shall think of you playing in Leeds and Hull and York.'

He flinched; but he told himself an offer to play in London did not necessarily mean an actress's fortune was made.

Dorothy dismissed him from her mind. She could not wait for the summer to be over.

She was in her dressing room preparing to play Patrick in *The Poor Soldier* when Tate Wilkinson came in.

'There's a distinguished visitor in the theatre tonight,' he told her.

'Oh?'

'The great Siddons herself.'

Dorothy felt as she had never felt in the theatre before: nervous. The great Sarah had surely come to see her because she would know that in a short time they would be playing together in Drury Lane. It couldn't be that Sarah would regard her as a rival – scarcely that – but all actresses were uneasy when someone younger and reputed to be very talented was about to share their audiences.

'You'll be all right,' said Wilkinson.

When he left her she studied her reflection in the glass. She looked really scared. She *would* be all right once she trod the boards. She was actress enough for that.

But she could not forget that everything depended on what happened at Drury Lane. And Sarah Siddons, at this moment, was seated regally in her balcony box over the stage, come to pass judgement.

Dorothy played for the statuesque woman in the box which was poised above the stage – a place of honour for Sarah – but it was not one of her best performances. It was not the way to play. One did not act to impress. One forgot an audience when on the stage; one became the part which was the only way to play it. But who could forget Sarah? Sarah herself had no intention that anyone should.

The eldest daughter of Robert Kemble had acting in her blood. She was the Queen of the Drama and she intended to keep the crown until she died.

She was some thirty years old and had appeared at Drury Lane when she was seventeen and David Garrick had been the actor-manager, so she was not going to be easily impressed by the performance of a provincial player. And she made it quite clear that she was not.

When the performance was over she was escorted back-stage with the ceremony of royalty – for the part she played off-stage was that of a queen – and asked for her opinion of Mrs Jordan's performance.

'Since it is asked,' said Mrs Siddons, pronouncing her words clearly as though to reach the back of the house, and striking the pose of a seer, 'I will give my considered opinion.' She never used one word when six would fit the same purpose. 'I have come to a conclusion while watching this performance and it is this: Mrs Jordan would be well advised to remain in the provinces rather than to venture on to the London stage at Drury Lane.'

It was what Dorothy's enemies had wanted to hear.

Dorothy herself laughed. Nothing Mrs Siddons could say could stop her. She was under contract now. It had been signed by Richard Brinsley Sheridan himself together with his business partners Thomas Linley and Dr James Ford. With such a contract in her pocket should she care for the attempts of any actress – even Sarah Siddons herself – to undermine her?

'The woman's jealous!' declared Grace.

And although it seemed incredible that the Queen of Drury Lane could be envious of a little provincial actress as yet untried,

Dorothy liked to believe this was so. After all she was some seven or eight years younger than the great tragedienne; and although Sarah was one of the most handsome women she had ever seen there was something forbidding about her.

In any case, what was the use of brooding?

She was going to Drury Lane to seek her fortune.

And that September she left the North for London, taking with her her mother, Hester, her daughter Frances and brother Francis. The rest of the children went to Aunt Blanche in Wales; but Dorothy would support the whole family on the wages she was to receive in her new position.

Début at Drury Lane

London delighted and fascinated. Dorothy knew as soon as she set eyes on it that it was here she wanted to stay. The bustling streets with their noisy people who shouted and laughed and seemed bent on enjoyment were full of life; and the carriages, the sedans with their exquisitely dressed occupants, powdered and patched, their faces made charming and sometimes grotesque with rouge and white lead were in great contrast to the beggars who whined in the alleys and the street traders calling their wares. Here was the lavender seller thrusting the sweet-smelling branches under the noses of passers-by; the piemen offering to toss for a pie; the shoe black; the ballad sellers singing their latest offerings often to thin reedy voices; the crossing sweepers ready for a penny to run under the horses to sweep a passage across the muddy roads. It was life as she had never seen it before.

Dorothy was determined that she had come to stay.

They took lodgings in Henrietta Street, which was not very grand, for Dorothy was going to have many calls on her purse; but the whole family was enchanted with London and to be in those streets, Grace declared, just did you good. You knew that this was the only place worth being in.

The theatre was different from anything Dorothy had played in before. Royalty came here quite often, she understood. The Prince of Wales was a frequent visitor and came with his friends, his brothers and his uncles. Sometimes the King and Queen came; then of course it had to be a most moral play. They accepted Shakespeare because everybody accepted Shakespeare, although the King did not think much of it and had been known to refer to it as 'sad stuff', but the people expected the King and Queen to see Shakespeare so they saw it.

It was different with the Princes – those gay young men – who were always satisfied by the appearance of pretty actresses, especially in breeches parts.

Then every actor and actress must be thrilled to meet Richard Brinsley Sheridan, for the author of *The School for Scandal*, *The Rivals* and *The Duenna*, the notorious wit and friend of the Prince of Wales was the biggest name in the theatre. And now that he was going into politics and had become Secretary to the Treasury in the Coalition Government and had allied himself with that great statesman Charles James Fox, one could not even compare him with managers like Daly and Wilkinson. Sheridan was as different from them as London was from the provinces.

No sooner had Dorothy arrived in London than she was completely convinced that this was the great opportunity and that she needed all her special gifts, everything she had learned since she had begun, to hold her place there.

She talked over her affairs with Grace and Hester. Her great anxiety was Sarah Siddons.

'I think I know,' she said, 'why they have brought me here. They want a rival for Sarah Siddons, and what worries me is that I can never be that.'

'Why not?' demanded Grace indignantly.

'Because we are not the same type. She has all that dignity; and you must agree, Mamma, that my dignity is more often off-stage than on. She wrings their hearts: I make them laugh. She's Lady Macbeth; I'm the Romp. There's room for us both, I'm sure, but I have to make them see this.'

'You are going to make *Mr Sheridan* see?'

'I have to, Mamma. I can never rival Sarah. How could I!

She's already there. They accept her. She's the Queen of tragedy and nobody is going to jostle her off her throne. As well try to take the King's crown from him. I'm not going to let them put me into tragedy. I'm going to insist that I choose the play for my début – and it's going to be comedy.'

Hester said: 'She's right, Mamma. Absolutely right.'

'Do you think they'll allow you to choose?' asked Grace fearfully.

'Surely it's the right of any actress to choose her first play.' Dorothy laughed. 'Don't be frightened, Mamma. Leave it to me. I'll make them understand. There's one thing I'm determined on. This is the great opportunity. It may come only once in a lifetime. I'm not going to miss it.'

It was easier to persuade Mr Sheridan than she had anticipated. With his manager, Tom King, he received her in his office and listened courteously to what she had to say. She was earnest and very appealing, he thought, and he was quick to recognize that quality in her which was rare and yet so essential to an actress. It was not beauty – in fact when she was not animated she was not even pretty – but when her face lit up and that inner vitality was visible she had a fascination which he guessed would be irresistible to an audience.

'You see, Mr Sheridan,' she said, 'it is no use my trying to rival Mrs Siddons. The public has made her its Tragedy Queen. They'd accept no other, however good. Miss Elizabeth Farren plays like a perfect lady and the public accept her for that. I have to be different. They love Mrs Siddons for her dignity, Miss Farren for her elegance; I have to win them through laughter. I *must* play comedy, Mr Sheridan. It's necessary if I am going to succeed.'

She was vehement. Sheridan looked at Tom King and knew what he was thinking. An actress must have the chance of choosing how she would make her début. And she was right when she said she could not take over Siddons' role. It was hardly likely that she could out-tragedy the Tragedy Queen and if she did there would be trouble.

'All right,' said Sheridan. 'Comedy. What do you say to *The Country Girl*?'

She smiled delightedly. 'I'd say yes please.'

'Good. *The Country Girl* it is.'

'Well, Tom,' said Sheridan when she had left them. 'What do you think of our actress?'

'I'll reserve my judgement till after the play.'

'Coward. I wasn't asking for the judgement of the audience. I was asking but yours.'

'I don't know. She's small.'

'You're thinking in terms of Siddons. We don't want another Juno striding across the boards.'

'Her voice is good but it doesn't boom . . .'

'Like Sarah's. I tell you this, Tom: One Siddons is enough in any company.'

'I thought you were looking for another Siddons.'

'Then you haven't been thinking enough. Consider all we suffer from our divine Sarah. Do you think I want to double trouble. Do you?'

'She's a draw.'

'Sarah's a draw. No one denies it. But she does condescend somewhat, eh, Tom? I feel I should bow from the waist every time I approach and walk out backwards after being received.'

'You would know how to behave in the presence of royalty better than I.'

'Sarah's more royal than any of their Royal Highnesses. As for Their Majesties there's little royalty in the Hall of Purity at Kew, I do assure you. I'd sooner ask a favour of His Royal Highness, the Prince of Wales, than of Our Majesty Queen Sarah. I pin my hopes on little Mrs Jordan. I want Sarah to have a rival . . . here in the theatre. I want the carriages to cram the streets on the way to the Lane to see Dorothy Jordan just as they do to see Sarah Siddons.'

'And you think you're going to bring about this miracle, Sherry?'

'My dear Tom, didn't you know I was a worker of miracles? We need a miracle or Harris over at the Garden will be taking our business away. You'll consider yourself lucky that I brought Jordan to the Lane before Harris got her for the Garden.'

'I sense that you feel some confidence in this young woman.'

'I do – and you know that – theatrically – I am invariably right.'

King looked dubious and Sheridan burst out laughing.

'I'll persuade the Prince to patronize the show.'

'He won't want to be caught by another pretty actress just yet.'

'He's always interested in pretty actresses and he's forgotten poor Perdita by now. We'll see what she's like on her first night and if she's good enough she shall play before His Highness.'

King continued to shake his head, but Sheridan only laughed. His unerring theatrical sense insisted to him that he had done right to bring Mrs Jordan to London.

She was nervous. How could she help it – her first night at Drury Lane! Grace and Hester were anxious as she was – more so. She could assure herself that she knew the part backwards, and she did know that as soon as she got on to the boards and started to act all her fears would disappear. But poor Hester would be recalling the fiasco of that night in Dublin. Grace would be trembling, too.

'Don't worry,' said Dorothy. 'I'll do it. I couldn't have better than *The Country Girl.*'

'It's somewhat bawdy,' said Grace timidly.

'That's what they like about it, Mamma.'

'At least Mr Garrick adapted it,' Hester reminded them. 'So if he thought it was good . . .'

'I believe you could have outdone that Siddons woman, Dolly.'

Dorothy began to play Lady Macbeth in an exaggerated manner reminiscent of Sarah Siddons.

'You'll be the death of me, Doll,' laughed Hester.

'Only hope they'll be as easily amused tonight,' prayed Dorothy. 'Peggy is just my part. As good as the Priscilla Tomboy in *The Romp* really. I think Peggy will go down better in Drury Lane than Priscilla would have done. Stop worrying, you two, or you'll make me nervous.'

She was rehearsing the part, remembering how she had watched Mrs Brown play it up in York, saying to herself: This is just the part for me. She would play it as no one had ever played it before. She would have that sophisticated London audience laughing or if she did not she would give up the boards altogether.

'Stop fretting,' she cried. 'I'm not worried . . . if you are.'

It was not a full house. Had she been foolish to hope for it? Why should the fashionable people of London come out to see a little provincial actress who had not yet proved what she could do?

She wondered what it was like over at Covent Garden. Was there a full house there tonight?

Although she was as yet of no importance the critics would be there in full force. She could almost hear their comments: 'Is this Sheridan's newest venture? Does he hope this little girl is going to pay his debts?'

I'm going to prove to him and to them that his trust in me is not misplaced, she told herself.

Gentleman Smith was in the audience. She must not disappoint him either for she owed her presence here to him. She had to play as never before. And she was going to.

The joy of being on the stage was to forget all anxieties; she *was* Peggy and those who had come to see her recognized an actress when they came face to face with one. She had the true comic quality and there was something indefinable but definitely there, a charm which Siddons lacked. Dorothy wanted to make them laugh; Siddons wanted them to do homage to the muse and to Siddons. There was a difference. Sheridan recognized this quality at once; he grinned at Gentleman Smith who lightly flicked a fly from the lace ruffles at his wrist and looked, as Sheridan pointed out to him, 'smug' – and with reason.

'You like the little Jordan, Sherry?' asked Smith.

'We might well keep her,' was the reply.

'I saw Harris of the Garden in the house.'

'Ha! Worried about my little Jordan, no doubt.'

'He has need to be.'

'We'll see.' The applause at the end of the play was moderate. Dorothy, who had been used to northern audiences who expressed their appreciation or scorn with more abandon was a little disturbed; but Mr Sheridan came to her dressing room and kissed her warmly.

'Well done, my dear,' he said.

Grace could not wait to read what the critics had to say. They were not enthusiastic, but at the same time not all unkind.

The *Morning Herald* was the best. It commented on her

delightful figure, pointing out that though small it was neat and elegant and shown to advantage when she appeared dressed as a boy in the third act. Her face might not be beautiful but was pretty and intelligent. Her voice if not peculiarly sweet was not harsh, if not strong was clear and equal to the demands of the theatre. She was active and brought out best in the comic aspects of the play and the conclusion was that she would be a valuable asset to the stage.

No one could have said more than that. Dorothy was a success.

This satisfactory debut was not in the least impaired when Harris of the Garden tried to denigrate her. She was a vulgar little piece, he said, and might do for Filch in *The Beggar's Opera*.

Some wit standing by, laughed at Harris' envy of Sheridan's find.

'Certainly she would,' was his reply, 'for she filches our hearts away.'

So the world of the theatre after one performance of *The Country Girl* was sure that Dorothy Jordan had come to stay.

It was disappointing after that initial success not to be able to play for a week, but Mrs Siddons who was expecting a child was anxious to appear as often as possible before her enforced retirement and Dorothy quickly learned that every other actress and actor was expected to stand aside for the Queen of the Theatre.

But in due course Dorothy's chance came and this time her fame had spread and it was a full house.

How right she had been to insist on comedy! She knew there was no one at Drury Lane to equal her in that sphere and she had always believed that although they might thrill to Sarah's drama, audiences liked above all things to laugh. She had that god-given gift – to amuse while she entertained. She was going to use it whenever she had an opportunity.

There came the wonderful occasion when she had her first glimpse of royalty. The rumour ran through the theatre: Tonight the Prince of Wales is coming with his uncle the Duke of Cumberland.

There was a great deal of chatter about the royal family. The Prince was at loggerheads with his father. It was an old Hanoverian custom for fathers to quarrel with their sons. The puritanical old King who had remained faithful to his ugly wife for years and whose joint efforts had been to give the nation fifteen royal children to provide for, was estranged from his brilliant, clever and wild son, the Prince of Wales, who had already shocked his family and delighted the scandalmongers by his affair with an actress, Mrs Robinson, who had produced his letters and threatened to publish them if she were not amply rewarded.

The Prince's friend, that wily politician Charles James Fox, had arranged the deal to the satisfaction of all parties and had himself become the lover of Mrs Robinson for a while which apparently seemed to the Prince a satisfactory conclusion, for his friendship with Fox was greater after the affair than before; and Fox and Sheridan were close friends, which meant that the manager of Drury Lane was on terms of intimacy not only with Mr Fox but with the Prince of Wales. Now there were rumours of his love affair with Mrs Fitzherbert and some went so far as to say he was married to her.

Harris was furious that royalty should patronize the Lane more than the Garden and there was little that delighted Sheridan more than Harris' jealous rage.

Mrs Siddons believed that she should perform on the occasion.

His Highness would surely wish to see the very best the Lane had to offer.

'Tonight, my divine Sarah,' Sheridan told her, 'the Prince does not wish to be greatly moved. And how could he look on one of your performances and not be? He wants a light evening's entertainment. He will come later to see real theatre.'

Sarah was mollified and graciously inclined her head. She thought it was wrong to put on the Jordan woman; it was said that she was unmarried, and whose child was that Frances in that case? And did it not let down the tone of the theatre to give prominence to people like Jordan?

'I fear the tone of the theatre is so low, Sarah my dear, that Jordan could not bring it lower. It is respectable married ladies like yourself who lift it – with your acting and your exemplary private life. You are an example to us all.'

'Well, you must do what you wish.'

Indeed that is one thing you can be sure of, thought Sheridan.

'But I think you are wrong to bring that creature to the notice of His Highness.'

'My virtuous Sarah is thinking that His Highness might wish to repeat the Robinson adventure?'

'I do not. Jordan is vulgar. Mrs Robinson tried always to be . . . refined.'

How hard she tried! he thought. Poor Perdita! 'You have taken a weight off my mind, Sarah my dear. Now I shall feel happier. Our little Jordan's shortcomings will save her from Perdita's fate. And you should rest. Moreover, His Highness's affections are firmly held elsewhere. William will be angry with you if you forget your condition and tire yourself.'

He smiled, thinking of poor Will Siddons who scarcely dared raise his voice in Sarah's presence.

Sheridan went on: 'It is because of your condition, Sarah, that I have to offer His Highness second rate fare tonight. I could not allow William to reproach me for putting you through an ordeal which at the time is too much for you.'

She was placated.

It was time, Sheridan told himself, that he had an actress with the ability to draw as full a house as Sarah. It was the only way of controlling her.

His hopes were fixed on Jordan.

So this was Royalty. This good-looking young man with the plump freshly coloured face, the pert nose which gave a friendly touch to his face, the alert blue eyes and the elegant person. The diamond star on his velvet coat was dazzling – but not more so than he. He was elegant in the extreme; and the manner in which he bowed to the audience was quite exquisite. His box on the stage was so close to her that she could see him clearly and his eyes followed her and were particularly appreciative when in the third act she appeared in male costume.

With him was a less attractive member of the royal family: his uncle, the Duke of Cumberland, glittering and royal, but debauched and completely lacking the Prince's fresh good looks.

Cumberland was in disgrace and not received at court because he had married without the consent of his brother, the King, a lady who had had many amatory adventures before she had captivated Cumberland and who, Horace Walpole had said, was possessed of the most marvellous eyelashes he had ever seen; they were 'about a yard long'. Because of this marriage the King had introduced the Royal Marriage Act which forbade any member of the royal family to marry before he reached the age of twenty-five without the consent of the King.

Cumberland might not be received by his brother but he had become the constant companion of his nephew, the Prince of Wales, and now the Prince was growing up – he must be about her own age, Dorothy thought – he had his own little court and it was becoming like a repetition of previous reigns when there had been a King's and a Prince's court in opposition to each other. The Prince's friends were Whigs; the King's Tories. The Prince's friends and mentors in politics were Mr Charles James Fox and Sheridan, and the King was relying more and more on young Mr William Pitt, who two years before, at the age of twenty-five, had become his Prime Minister.

In the new world into which she had come Dorothy learned of these matters. Royalty was closer. How could it be otherwise when it came to the theatre and sat in a box a few yards away. Here in London she could see the important members of the government in their carriages on their way to Parliament. One day she would catch a glimpse of the King and Queen, the Princes and the Princesses who made up that large family.

Here in London, in Drury Lane, was the centre of affairs.

And now she was playing before the Prince of Wales.

She heard his laughter. It stimulated her. He leaned over the box and applauded her. When at the end of the play she turned to his box and curtsied, he rose and bowed in such an elegant manner that she might have been royalty. The applause was thunderous.

A successful evening. The approval of royalty! What more could an actress eager to make her name desire?

'His Royal Highness is impressed with Mrs Jordan,' said Sheridan to Tom King. 'But for the disaster with Mrs Perdita Robinson and the fact that his love is dedicated to Mrs Fitzherbert we might have a royal romance on our hands.'

Dorothy followed Peggy in *The Country Girl* with Viola in *Twelfth Night* and then Miss Prue in *Love for Love*.

There were many appearances for Dorothy that autumn for Sheridan wished to get her known to audiences as quickly as possible.

He need not have been concerned. Audiences had taken her to their hearts. Her daintiness, her extreme femininity, which was accentuated by her breeches parts, delighted them. They had begun to associate Dorothy Jordan with laughter.

Mrs Siddons, as her confinement grew nearer and nearer, ground her teeth with annoyance. Much as she wanted the child and her children meant more to her than her ineffectual William, she deplored the ill timing of the child's arrival. 'A little later, William,' she declared, 'and I could most certainly have put the Jordan back where she belonged.'

William agreed but secretly thought with everyone else that the Jordan had come to stay and there was something likeable about her friendly attitude which was completely lacking in Sarah's. Loyally he supposed that actors and actresses should be grateful for the opportunity of working with Sarah and audiences of the chance to see her, but even apart from the usual theatrical jealousies, Dorothy Jordan did seem to be more liked than Sarah by both the company and management.

The carriages which stopped outside Drury Lane on the night when Dorothy was playing were as numerous as those which came for Sarah Siddons.

'Wait until I am ready to come back,' said Sarah.

In the meantime Dorothy enjoyed her success. She was fully aware of her value. Sheridan had offered her four pounds a week to start and that had been affluence when compared with the thirty shillings Wilkinson had paid her; but after that first performance he had of his own free will offered her eight because he was afraid that Harris would come over with a bigger offer; and greatly daring, for living was dearer in London and she had the whole family to think of, she asked for a further four pounds a week and to her astonishment Sheridan said that he would consider it.

This was success.

A delighted Grace declared that it was nothing more than she had anticipated and she only wished that Aunt Mary had lived to see this day. She wished, too, that Dorothy's father had seen it – and his family; perhaps they might have been eager then to link themselves with such a famous and respected figure as Dorothy Jordan.

'Oh that's all over and done with,' said Dorothy.

'I only want one thing to complete my happiness,' said Grace, 'and that is to see you nicely settled and respectably married.'

'Do you think I should have time for a husband with all the new parts that are coming along for me?' demanded Dorothy.

'A woman always has time for a husband. And I want a nice steady one for you.'

'Someone mild as milk like Will Siddons?'

'Ah, she has done very well. Fame *and* respectability. What more could an actress ask for?'

'Which reminds me,' said Dorothy with a laugh. 'I have to make the most of it while Sarah gets her respectable child respectably brought into the world. I'm to have the part of Matilda in that odd play *Richard Cœur de Lion*. I think I can make something of that.'

Dorothy lured the talk back to the theatre and her future parts which was so much more comfortable than the subject of marriage. She could never think of it without recalling that nightmare with Daly and the rather humiliating position in which George Inchbald had put her.

She would leave men alone. Parts pleased her more.

In December of that year, two months after Dorothy's first appearance at Drury Lane, the great comedy actress Kitty Clive died. It seemed significant; a star had set and a new one had arisen to take her place; that new one was Dorothy Jordan, for so had Dorothy's fame grown that people had already begun to compare her with Kitty Clive and Peg Woffington.

And by that time she had met Richard Ford.

Her meeting with this young man was momentous for in a very short time he had made her change her opinions about his sex. He was different from any man she had hitherto known – young, eager and passionate; he wanted above everything else, he declared, to please her, to make her happy; and that would from henceforth be his main purpose in life. Shortly after their first meeting he told her he had made up his mind to marry her.

She reminded him of her career. It was not easy for an actress to lead a married life. Why not? he wanted to know. So many of them did. Look at the great Siddons herself.

'And see how she had to leave the theatre to a rival while she retires to have her babies.'

'She'll come back as popular as ever.'

But she was not really arguing against marriage. She only wanted to be sure of Richard. Her experiences with Daly and George Inchbald had made her very wary. And as Richard broke down all her arguments against it she gave herself up to the luxury of contemplating it. She thought of him as a father to Frances – who could be a better? He was gentle and kind, all that Frances's own father was not. She thought of other children she would have, for she knew that once she had made her family financially secure she would love to add to it. Frances born in such bitter circumstances was very dear to her; how joyful she would be to have children of a happy union! There was her mother, who longed for one thing to complete her contentment: Dorothy's marriage.

Yet she wished to wait for a while. I must be absolutely sure, she told herself. Moreover, in spite of her recent success did she stand firmly enough in her new position? The people were flocking to see her, but she had formidable rivals and once Sarah came back the battle to hold her place would begin in earnest.

They would wait for a little while and in the meantime tell no one. There was too much gossip in the theatre already; she had many enemies who would seek to blacken her character; and if her mother knew of Richard's intentions she would undoubtedly attempt to hustle them into marriage.

Richard was the son of Dr James Ford, a co-shareholder in Drury Lane Theatre with Richard Sheridan, though he took no part in the running of the theatre; for him it was purely a business adventure. He was rich, a court physician and on friendly terms with the royal family, and he had invested a large sum of money in the theatre to help the ever-impecunious Sheridan. Because of his father's position Richard came and went as he pleased while he himself trained for the bar.

Whenever Dorothy played he was at the theatre and as when she was on stage he never took his eyes from her, it was soon common knowledge that he was mightily taken with her. Then so were many others. Even the Duke of Norfolk came to see her play and showed his appreciation.

But Dorothy refused to dally with any. She was an actress, she reminded them; she needed to devote herself to her work. Life was a constant round of rehearsals and learning new parts.

Not yet, was her continual excuse. 'First I must make sure that I've come to stay.'

She was to play Miss Hoyden in *A Trip to Scarborough*, a version of Vanburgh's *The Relapse* which Sheridan had arranged for his theatre. This part was the sort at which she could excel – the bouncing young woman just out of the nursery, without social graces, wayward, full of high spirits. It was a similar part to that of Priscilla Tomboy in *The Romp*.

She expected to enhance her reputation in this role and put everything else from her mind.

As soon as she stepped on the stage in her scanty costume, purposely not fitting and falling from her shoulders, and her hair in very charming disorder under a rakish cap, she was hailed with delight.

Sheridan watching from the back of the theatre was certain in that moment – although he assured King that he had never had a doubt before – that Dorothy was going to be one of the biggest draws they had ever had.

It was not the tradition of the London theatre to play comedy all the time. Tragedy had been more acceptable and the great Sarah herself was a confirmation of this. 'Ask anyone,' said Tom King to Sheridan, 'who is the greatest actress on the boards today and the answer is Sarah Siddons. People will always come to see Sarah throw herself about in her agony and declaim disaster in that magnificent voice of hers. It'll go on when they're sick to death of a young hoyden romping round the stage.'

King was not as enamoured as Sheridan with the newcomer. He thought her rise had been far too rapid. She was young and had an appeal, he knew; but an actress must act. She couldn't rely on her youth because it was a stuff that did not endure, as the bard told them; as for her beauty that was equally perishable. If the Jordan was going to prove her worth she would have to act tragedy as well as comedy.

Sheridan was persuaded and Dorothy was dismayed when she was told she must play Imogen in *Cymbeline*.

She could not say she would not. She was not in the position to do that. She could not declare her inability to play the part, for that was something an actress must never do.

She would do Imogen, but, she pleaded with Sheridan, could she not do Priscilla Tomboy in *The Romp* afterwards? The public would be in a serious mood and there was nothing it liked better than to go home in a merry one. When the curtain had fallen on *Cymbeline*, let it rise again on *The Romp*, which would give them good measure for money.

Sheridan knew his actress and applauded her energy. He had given way to King on this matter of *Cymbeline* and now he was going to give way to Dorothy. So *The Romp* followed *Cymbeline* – and what a stroke of luck that it did! Her performance as Imogen was indifferent. How could it be otherwise when her heart was not in it; she was not made for tragedy. She was a comedienne. She knew it. The audience must know it and accept her as such.

The audience, a little depressed to see their new idol scarcely at her best, were soon laughing at the antics of Miss Tomboy who threw herself into the part with even more verve than usual. Desperately she had to eradicate the impression of Imogen with Priscilla Tomboy; and she did. Next morning the papers were full of the performance of Mrs Jordan in *The Romp*.

'In the farce Mrs Jordan made amends for her deficiency in the play,' the *Morning Chronicle* announced. 'The audience were in a continued roar of laughter. The managers of Drury Lane have a most valuable acquisition in this actress.'

'Saved!' cried Dorothy when she read the papers in the company of Grace and Hester. 'I'll have to fight off these tragic parts with all my might. The fact is I could never compete with Siddons. I should burst out laughing if I beat my breast and cried out in agony as she does. The point is that no one ever behaved in real life as Sarah Siddons does on the stage.'

'And they call that acting!' cried the loyal Grace.

'Which, dearest Mamma, is exactly what it is.'

So all was well for the time being; but how could she think of marrying just now when there was so much to be done? She was in love. She was aware of that now. She believed that if she married Richard she would want to give all her thoughts to pleasing him, to building the foundations of a happy marriage. She would neglect her career; and how easy it would be to let slip all that she had so far grasped. The recent experience with Imogen had shown her that very clearly.

Mrs Siddons returned to the stage after the birth of her child – an avenging angel of the Tragic Muse ready to do battle against the enemy Comedy.

'What will happen to the theatre if this persists?' she demanded of King and Sheridan, striking one of the poses which had held an audience spellbound. 'It will sink to the level of a peep show.'

King was inclined to agree with her; Sheridan shrugged his shoulders.

'Now you've returned, Sarah my dear,' he said, 'you can lead them back to tragedy and show them how much they prefer you to little Jordan.'

'They will not need much leading.'

But they were not to be led. They showed clearly that it was laughter not tears they wanted.

'If they want laughter,' said Sarah, 'I will play some of my lighter roles. I'll give them Portia. They have always responded to her.'

But brilliant as Sarah was, beautiful as was her face – though her figure had suffered from childbearing and she had always been Junoesque – and magical her voice, she lacked the gamin quality of Dorothy Jordan and it was to Dorothy's performances that the people were flocking.

Even King must see the importance of bringing in the money and *The Romp* had become a recognized afterpiece. The Prince of Wales came to see it twice in a week. Mrs Fitzherbert accompanied him and they sat laughing and applauding in their box.

'The success of *The Romp* rests almost exclusively on the spirited performance of Mrs Jordan,' wrote a critic in the *Morning Post*, 'and it must be confessed that there has not been seen a more finished acting of its kind. It is not to be doubted therefore that this ludicrous little afterpiece will become a favourite notwithstanding the fastidious taste of certain critics who seem ashamed of being so vulgar as to indulge in a hearty laugh.'

No, her power was too great for anyone to break. She had what the people wanted and were ready to pay for and no carping critic, no jealous actress, could stop her.

'This will show Madam Sarah that she is not the only pebble on the beach nor the only actress in the world,' commented Grace triumphantly.

Dorothy smiled at her indulgently. How lucky she was to have a mother who cared so passionately for her welfare!

One morning when Dorothy was sleeping late after a late night at the theatre Grace came into her room, her eyes shining with excitement.

She sat on the bed and cried: 'What do you think? George Inchbald is in London. He arrived last night. You can be sure he'll be calling today.'

Dorothy yawned. 'Well, what of that?'

'What of it! He's come to see you. You can depend upon it.'

'Well, I'm not all that eager to see him.'

Grace laughed knowingly. 'He wouldn't have come all this way for nothing.' She was a little arch. 'It wouldn't surprise me if he has a proposition to make.'

'I can't see that he would have any proposition to make to me which I should want to act on. He's not a theatre manager and what could be better than Drury Lane unless it's Covent Garden. And talking of Covent Garden I heard that Harris is going to bring Mrs Brown down to play in *The Country Girl*.'

'That old hag!' cried Grace. 'London would never accept her. She's too old.'

'She's a fine actress. And you'll remember how I used to stand in the wings when she was on stage and watch how she played Peggy.'

'She'll be a fool if she comes. Harris is a fool to ask her. What chance would she have against you! But do get up and put on a pretty gown and Hester can do your hair, for I do believe that George will be calling soon.'

'I'll be ready for George when he comes,' said Dorothy.

Grace nodded. Good Heavens, thought Dorothy, she believes he has come to ask me to marry him and that I'm going to accept him! Does she think I have no pride. But I do believe dear Mamma thinks it is wise to sink everything for honourable marriage. Honourable indeed! He'd be marrying twelve pounds a week and an almost certain brilliant theatrical future whereas thirty shillings and uncertainty was not good enough for him.

Hester came in. 'Can I help you dress, Doll?'

'Thank you. I feel grand with my lady's maid.'

'So you should. What should we do without you! I'm happy to be your lady's maid, as you know.'

'Dear old Hester. I was just thinking how fortunate I am in my family. And being so why should I think of adding a fortune-hunter to it.'

'George was always cautious, you know.'

'And Mamma cares so much about my marrying that she would want me to accept him.'

'Oh, you know what she is. She worries. She's haunted by insecurity. Which dress will you have?'

'The blue. You can be just as insecure married as unmarried – more so, if there are children to feed.'

'You'll never get Mamma to see that. Besides, it's respectability she's after.'

'It's strange, Hester, but I hanker for it myself. I think that Daly business did something to me.'

'Don't think of it.'

'I don't often. But when Siddons sweeps into the theatre so assured, so certain of her genius, the greatest tragic actress on the boards, with a nice meek little husband, children and a reputation beyond reproach, I confess I find something rather enviable about that.'

'For Heaven's sake don't you start being envious. There's enough envy about this place already.'

'But you see I've got Frances . . . and she's illegitimate. It's a handicap for the child. Oh, yes, I might like a little respectability.'

'You're not telling me that you're going to accept George Inchbald.'

Dorothy laughed scornfully.

'I didn't think you would,' said Hester with significance.

I believe she knows about Richard, thought Dorothy. Well, they would all have to know soon because she was fast making up her mind that she was quite capable of managing her career and marrying.

George cried: 'Why, Dorothy, you've become even more beautiful!'

'Thank you. It's the London air.'

'Success!' murmured George. 'I always knew you would achieve it. There was a quality about you, Dorothy.'

'*Did* you always know it, George? I remember a time when you talked so earnestly about the insecurity of a stage career.'

'That's for most people, Dorothy. Not for you.'

'But I have always been ambitious.'

'It must be wonderful to know that London is talking of you, and to play before royalty. Oh, wonderful indeed. But don't forget there is another side to life. Love, marriage.'

'I don't forget it, George,' she said softly.

He would have taken her hand, but she eluded him.

'I knew you would be the same Dorothy who played with Wilkinson's.'

'You're wrong, George. I've changed. We all change. You've changed too, you know. I have a fancy that you don't feel quite the same about certain matters as you once did.'

'We grow wiser.'

'You were always wise, George. I trust I have learned to see those about me more clearly. It's a great help, you know.'

'Dorothy, I was most unhappy when you left. The only brightness was hearing about your triumphs. My stepmother says you'll be a great actress.'

'Earning twelve pounds a week,' put in Dorothy. 'That's a little better than thirty shillings, eh?'

'And it's not the end. You'll be rich as well as famous.'

'I have my family to care for.'

'And you would always care for those who depended on you, Dorothy.'

She smiled at him almost fondly. She wanted to lure him on so that he would suffer fully the extent of her scorn.

He told her how he had followed her career; how excited he had been; how he had feared for her – though not really for he knew she would succeed, but as one member of the profession to another they knew what it meant to face an audience on whom one's future could depend.

'Dorothy,' he said, 'when you had gone I knew what I missed. I should never have let you go.'

'Then I shouldn't have come to London and started out on the road to fortune.'

'You had to come. You're a great actress, but you need someone to look after you. How happy I should be if you would decide I was the one—'

'You have changed your mind in these last months.'

'I want you to marry me, Dorothy. Being away from you made me realize that.'

'Not so much my being away from you as my twelve pounds a week and prospects. That's what made you change your mind. George Inchbald, do you think I'm a fool! Do you think I don't see through your feeble efforts. I'll tell you one thing. You will never suceed on the stage if you can't play a part better than you're playing it now. Enter ambitious suitor who has learned the penniless actress of the past is now rich and famous. He pleads with her. George, you're a fool. I'd never marry a fool. I'd almost sooner marry a mercenary gutless schemer.'

'Dorothy!'

'Curtain,' she said. 'This little drama is over. Go back to York or Hull or Leeds, wherever you're playing. Your proposal has been most definitely refused.'

George would have protested, but she laughed at him; and since he did not leave she went out and left him.

She had made up her mind. The next time Richard asked her to marry him she would accept him. He was not long in doing so and she gave her promise.

He was the happiest man in London, he told her. He would love her for ever; his life would be subjected to hers for he knew that she would never be happy away from the theatre.

'I want my mother to be the first to hear,' she told him. 'I know she will be delighted.'

'And after that,' he said, 'I will tell my father. Until these two know, it must be a secret.'

So they went to Henrietta Street and when Grace heard the

news she was overcome with joy. No wonder Dorothy had sent George Inchbald about his business. And all the time she had been in love with Richard Ford and had kept it secret!

When was the wedding to be? Clearly it could not be too soon for Grace.

'I think after I come back from my northern tour,' said Dorothy. 'So long!'

'Oh, Mamma, that is not really very long.'

Richard said fondly that he agreed with Dorothy's Mamma and it was far too long.

Grace brought out wine and they drank to the future.

That was a happy evening.

Richard left Henrietta Street in an uneasy mood. He loved Dorothy; he sincerely wished to marry her; but he was not looking forward to telling his father that he had proposed and been accepted.

His father was a wealthy and ambitious man, and Richard knew that it had always been a desire of his that his son should make a good marriage. He had excellent prospects; all he had to do was qualify at the Bar and with his father's money and connections at court that could lead anywhere. And as he had so often impressed on his son the first step towards advancement had often been the right marriage. There were several wealthy and influential families into which Richard could marry.

Richard was not very courageous. He was devoted to Dorothy; he thought her the finest actress in the world; he was happy watching her perform all her parts; he was content to talk to her, be with her; and he longed to be her husband. If only his father were not so ambitious.

But now he had been accepted and he had to tell his father. He had definitely promised to marry Dorothy and nothing, he told himself boldly, would make him go back on his word. Dorothy was the only woman in the world he would have for his wife.

When he dined with his father that night it was obvious that Richard had something on his mind. His appetite was poor; he played nervously with his glass and every now and then opened his mouth to say something and changed his mind.

Dr Ford had a very good notion of what this might be for Sheridan had told him that young Richard had haunted the theatre for some months past and was almost always in one of the balcony boxes when Dorothy Jordan was playing. It was Sheridan's belief that young Richard harboured very tender feelings towards his little actress and Sheridan was not surprised; she was a dainty piece, a clever little piece, full of charm; and it amazed Sheridan that a Duke or an Earl or at very least a baronet had not installed her in some charming little love-nest by now.

In fact it was Sheridan's view that but for H.R.H.'s preoccupation with Mrs Fitz, there might have been a royal offer. But his little actress was by no means promiscuous; she was indeed a very virtuous lady. There had been one slip with young Miss Frances and 'never again', said Mrs Jordan. Sheridan fancied that she was holding out for marriage lines.

'Our divine Sarah sets a very moral tone at Drury Lane,' he added.

Dr Ford was remembering this as he noticed his son's uneasiness. If Richard had made a fool of himself that must be stopped without delay.

'As soon as you've qualified, Richard,' he said, 'I can put you into the way of making a fortune for yourself. Your future is rosy, my son. There's no doubt about it. Of course you'll have to work. Can't be hanging around the theatre every night. Who was it was talking to me the other day . . . Son got a fancy for some actress. Married her on the sly. *Married* her. That was the end of him. A nobody if you please. The fellow's prospects ruined. Imagine what it'll be like for them. Love's young dream at the moment, but how long will that last when the babies come and the money's short, for you can be sure the silly fellow will be cut off from his inheritance. I understand he'll get nothing. I'd be the same myself. Why, if you came along and told me that you'd made such an idiot of yourself, I'd do exactly the same. Well, no fear of that. More sense, eh?'

Richard grinned feebly.

How could he tell his father that he was engaged to marry Dorothy Jordan after that?

*

He tried to explain to Dorothy.

'You see it would break his heart. He'd never accept it. He was talking about a fellow who had married and been cut off by his father. He said he'd be the same.'

'It seems,' said Dorothy, 'that someone warned him about us.'

'I don't know who. We told no one. I can't tell him yet . . . and yet . . . how can we wait like this? You love me, Dorothy. You love me enough not to give me up because of this. As soon as I'm making money at the Bar we'll be married. As soon as I don't depend on him.'

He looked so young, so helpless that she was so sorry for him.

She was not the sort of woman to make bargains; and yet she longed for a respectable ceremony, for a father for Frances, for children who would be born without the slur of illegitimacy.

She told him all this; he wept and entreated her. He understood. They would take a house together; she should be Mrs Ford; it would be the same as though they were married. No difference at all, except that they wouldn't go through the ceremony. In time he would persuade his father, but as yet the old man would not listen. He considered his son too young. In a few months' time it would all be different. But he could not wait those months. He wanted Dorothy; he needed Dorothy . . . now.

Dorothy could not bargain when it was a matter of love; and she loved him. Only when she had seen George Inchbald again had she realized how much.

They would wait no longer. She had his solemn promise that as soon as it was possible he would marry her. In the meantime they could live comfortably enough on his private income and her salary.

It was not what they had planned but the next best thing.

So Dorothy and Richard Ford became lovers.

Grace was bitterly disappointed, for it seemed as though her greatest wish would never be realized.

'They are in love, though, Mamma,' pointed out Hester, 'and it is time Dorothy had a little happiness. I began to fear that her terrible experiences with Daly had made her turn from men for ever. I think she needs to love and be loved.'

'Well, she *is* earning well now and I daresay will always be in a position to keep herself.'

'And us all,' said Hester with a grimace.

'And, Richard is not a pauper.'

'I'm sure that when he can do so he will marry her,' added Hester, 'for he truly loves her and she loves him.'

So they had to be contented with that.

A royal command and a battle

That summer Dorothy went on tour visiting the old theatres at which she had played in the past; and she could not help but enjoy returning to the old haunts and remembering her early struggles; some of the actors and actresses who had played with her in the past were still there.

She played *The Country Girl* and *The Romp* to overflowing houses in Leeds; she saw the envious looks and heard the references to her 'luck' and she smiled on them all, pitying these poor provincial players and understanding their envies.

She went to Edinburgh where she was received with some reserve. The inhabitants of Edinburgh did not care for frivolity and their idea of acting was that portrayed so admirably by Mrs Siddons. It was different in Glasgow. Here she was an immediate success and before she left she was presented with a gold medal.

When she returned to London it was to receive a letter from her brother George who longed to go on to the stage; he was asking if he might now join the family and try his luck.

In the autumn George arrived in London and Dorothy and Richard took number five Gower Street where they set up house together and Dorothy was known as Mrs Ford. It was understood that in a few years they would be married and because of their devotion to each other and the domestic atmosphere which they created at Gower Street she was accepted as Richard's wife by their circle of acquaintances.

Grace referred to Richard as her dear son and refused to think of Dorothy's position as anything but the desired married state.

Her eldest son Francis had joined the army but here was George in his place; and the aim of the family now – greatly assisted by Dorothy – was to get him parts in the theatre.

They were comfortably off – Dorothy's salary seemed like near affluence; Hester's occasional appearances and Richard's private income added to the exchequer; and they were all content to wait for the day when Dorothy would become Mrs Ford in truth.

Dorothy was happier than she had ever been before. She had success in her profession and she loved and was loved.

What more could any woman ask? But there was always the echo to come back to her: Marriage.

The inevitable happened. Dorothy was pregnant.

Grace was inclined to be alarmed, remembering the lack of marriage lines, but Dorothy was serene.

'I shall play till the last month. It'll make little difference,' she assured them.

'There's the tour,' cried Grace aghast.

'Never mind the tour. I shall go.'

'But what if ...'

'Do stop fretting, Mamma,' said Dorothy. 'Babies are born in Leeds and Hull and York, you know.'

'I don't know. I wish ...'

But Dorothy would not let her voice her wish. She knew that what she wanted was Dorothy to be respectably married and received by Dr Ford and allowed to have her confinement in luxury.

Dorothy set off and was in Edinburgh when she gave birth to her child – a daughter. She named her Dorothy but she was soon known as Dodee which avoided confusion. Dorothy loved her child from the moment she held her in her arms and she realized that although she had believed she had loved Frances in the same way, it was a fact that she could not forget the child's father and the manner in which she had been conceived. How different was little Dodee's coming.

She wanted lots of children. She imagined herself far away from the theatre, the thrills and depressions, the spite, the envy and the malice, the smell of guttering candles, the callousness of audiences with their boos and catcalls and their wild applause. Peace, she thought, with her children growing up round her. Perhaps a house in the country with lovely gardens and the children playing and Richard beside her. It was a pleasant dream, but not for her. And did she really want it? Could a woman, born to strut the boards, ever really do without the clamour and glamour, the glittering tinsel existence?

She laughed at herself. Why, I'd be aching to be back in less than a month. Having a baby made one sentimental.

The press was far from sentimental. It chortled over the adventures of its darling comedienne.

An advertisement in the *Public Advertiser* ran:

'The Jordan from Edinburgh – a small sprightly vessel – went out from London harbour *laden* – dropped cargo in Edinburgh.'

The theatrical world was well aware that Dorothy Jordan had borne Richard Ford a child.

That spring rumour concerning the royal family was discussed in Drury Lane almost as much as theatrical events. There was always the relationship of the Prince of Wales and Mrs Fitzherbert, and the question: Was he married or was he not? was on everyone's lips. Mrs Fitzherbert behaved as Princess of Wales and when the Prince came to the theatre it was always in her company. Sheridan received her with the utmost homage which she accepted with as much dignity as visiting royalty; and the Prince was clearly delighted with her.

Then a more extraordinary rumour arose which put that of the Prince's marriage temporarily in the shade. It was the state of the King's health. Stories of his extraordinary conduct leaked out from the royal household. He had tried to strangle the Prince of Wales; he had talked gibberish to the Prime Minister; he had shaken the branch of a tree under the impression that it was the King of Prussia.

Was it true? Was the King going mad?

There would be a Regency, said some. There were quarrels

between the Queen and the Prince of Wales. The Whigs wanted the Prince to have the Regency; the Tories wanted the Queen. Mr Fox who had left England after his estrangement with the Prince – for the statesman had denied the Prince's marriage to Mrs Fitzherbert in the House of Commons and by so doing had incensed Mrs Fitzherbert to such a degree that she had left the Prince, who had great difficulty in winning her back – returned to England to be beside the Prince should he become Regent.

There was a tension everywhere; people talked of the King's illness in the theatre; they talked during the play itself if the players failed to hold their attention.

As for Sheridan, he seemed aloof from theatrical affairs. It was clear that he saw great things for himself through a Regency. The Prince was his friend and if the Prince became the King in all but name, that would be a good augury for those who had been his friends when he had scarcely any power against his antagonistic parents.

Sheridan had always preferred drinking and gambling to work; he squandered his genius in conversational quips instead of preserving them for posterity. He had written brilliant plays but that was years ago; he was too intent on carousing with the living to work for posterity.

Who knew what Sheridan might become? Who was there to stand in his way since Fox was out of favour and some said could never come back completely, for all his sly genius, while Mrs Fitzherbert reigned with the Prince, for Fox had offended her mortally when he had denied her marriage. 'Rolled her in a kennel as though she were a streetwalker,' she had said. She would never forgive him; and although it was really the Prince's lack of courage which was to blame and Mr Fox had acted in the only way to save the Prince's hope of the crown, Mr Fox must be the scapegoat. But Mr Fox was coming home. Great events were in the air. Life was stimulating, full of excitement; and no one knew what would happen from one day to the next.

A young woman whom Dorothy had known in Dublin came to play at Drury Lane. This was Maria Theresa Romanzini. She was an Italian Jewess, small, inclined to plumpness with magnificent black eyes and hair which offset her heavy features. She had a beautiful voice and this it was which had secured her engagement.

She was delighted to see Dorothy and together they recalled some of the old Dublin days.

Maria shivered. 'I was terrified of Richard Daly,' she said.

'You too?' said Dorothy.

'Were not all of us? I tremble to think of what would have happened to me if my mother had not been with me. He was always trying to seduce me and I told my mother. She knew we should very likely be turned out of the theatre but she said that she would rather that than that I should fall into his hands.'

Dorothy nodded. Mrs Romanzini had been more watchful of her daughter than Grace had been of hers. That was not fair. Maria had been younger – only a child; and she Dorothy had been seventeen, old enough, one would think, for an actress to take care of herself.

'Mamma shrieked at him once in Mrs Daly's hearing,' said Maria with a little laugh. 'I shall never forget it. Mamma was so angry. "You have a fine wife of your own," she said. "Leave my daughter alone." And he did. He dared do no other. And we were not turned out of the theatre and it made no difference to my career. But I am glad to be free of him.'

Dorothy took Maria under her care and praised her to King and Sheridan; but Maria was ambitious enough to look after herself and because of her very fine voice quickly became quite a favourite with the audience. Her personality did not match that of Dorothy, Sarah Siddons and Elizabeth Farren, who were clearly destined to remain the three queens of the stage, but young Maria was an asset to the theatre.

When George arrived he and Maria took an immediate liking to each other which meant that Maria was frequently invited to Henrietta Street as well as to the Ford household in Gower Street.

Dorothy was winning praise in many roles. People flocked to see her Sir Harry Wildair in *The Constant Couple* – one of those ever popular breeches parts.

In the summer when Drury Lane closed and the more famous actors and actresses went on tour she hoped to play in Edinburgh again but learned that Mrs Siddons had accepted an offer to play there which would mean that the Queen of Tragedy would be in direct rivalry; and it was hardly likely that good business would result from it. The dour people of Edinburgh did not care for the laughter-makers; tragedy was more to their taste; and in their view pert little tomboys – whose private life Mrs Siddons and her adherents would not hesitate to inform them was not all to be desired, unlike that of the great tragedienne herself which was without reproach – could not be accorded respect in a town like Edinburgh.

'They wouldn't be able to stand out long against you,' said Grace. 'You'd soon have them laughing their heads off.'

'Not in Edinburgh,' replied Dorothy glumly.

She had an increasingly large family to support. There was now little Dodee, and George was getting only the smallest walk-on parts; Hester was home most of the time taking care of the children and Richard's income was not large. She could not view a long rest from the theatre with any complacence – much as she would have liked to have more time for her family.

An unusual piece of good luck occurred then. The King, whose illness had given rise to so much gossip, recovered and the Queen decided that it would be an excellent idea for him to recuperate somewhere right away from London and his royal duties. Brighton would have been ideal, but the Prince of Wales had made that delightful town his own, and relations between the royal parents and their son were strained, so definitely it could not be Brighton.

Cheltenham was little known but it was recommended to the Queen as a very healthful spa where the waters were most beneficial, so she decided that she, the King, the Princesses and their suites should spend a few weeks there while they nursed the King back to health.

Cheltenham for the first time in its life was on the map. There happened to be a theatre in the town, and since there was to be a royal visit that meant that the place would be full not only of the royal entourage but of many visitors.

A full town needed good players in its theatre.

Mrs Siddons was going to Edinburgh; clearly Mrs Jordan must come to Cheltenham.

*

Cheltenham was pleasant although Dorothy always preferred London audiences to those of the provinces. At this time, though, the town had three times its usual population and it was said that if royalty made a habit of visiting it, it would soon resemble Brighton. She heard that sixty-seven hairdressers had followed the King and Queen to the town because where the Court was there was the *ton*; and constant hairdressing was essential to the fashionable world.

The theatre was a converted barn but a royal box had been erected, all sorts of comforts added and the inhabitants were all prepared to enjoy the amenities induced by elegant society.

They even had Mrs Jordan.

She was greeted wherever she went with great enthusiasm. People stopped her in the streets and told her how much they were looking forward to seeing her act and how amused they were that they had filched her from London.

The manager told her that he thought it wise for her not to play breeches parts before their Majesties.

'This is not for His Highness the Prince of Wales, Mrs Jordan,' he said. 'His Majesty believes in stern propriety so these are the plays in which I think it would be wise for you to appear.'

Dorothy looked at them: *The Country Girl, The Maid of the Oaks, The Sultan, The Poor Soldier* and *The Virgin Unmasked*.

She would have enjoyed playing Sir Harry Wildair.

'You should have had Mrs Siddons,' she told him.

'Oh, no. Her Majesty the Queen thinks that a little *light* entertainment would be better for His Majesty. If you can amuse him, Mrs Jordan, you will please Her Majesty.'

'I'll do my best,' said Dorothy. 'But I'm sure a breeches part would have been more likely to.'

But the manager did not agree.

It was not until Dorothy arrived in Cheltenham that the King and Queen honoured the playhouse with their presence and from their royal box they looked down with approval at the actors, and Dorothy had the satisfaction of hearing the King laugh at her antics.

This pleased the Queen and when Dorothy made her final bow they expressed their pleasure by inclining their heads for her alone.

It was not the gracious acknowledgement she had had from the Prince of Wales, but this was the King and his bulbous eyes which still looked a little wild were kindly, and so was his smile.

'Very good,' Dorothy heard him say. 'A pleasant little actress, eh, what?'

And the Queen replied that Mrs Jordan's performance had given her great pleasure.

That was triumph and Dorothy was delighted to have contributed to the King's pleasure.

The people of Cheltenham were pleased too. The famous London actress had brought a change to their town. They were grateful to her and almost as pleased that she was with them as they were to have royal visitors.

All the same she was glad when the time came to return to London.

She came back to change.

Dr Ford – who should have been her father-in-law – had made his decision to retire and leave London. He had bought a house in Wales and since he would be far from the metropolis he had no further interest in the theatre. He was therefore going to sell his share in Drury Lane.

For some time there had been a certain amount of friction between Sheridan and Tom King; they could not agree on policy and their tastes differed widely. Sheridan had done his best to curtail King's power and at the same time had himself shown a greater interest in affairs outside the theatre. This was understandable in view of the King's illness and what had seemed a few months earlier a certain Regency. But King resented Sheridan's attitude. If he wanted to be a politican and a man about town he insisted he should give up his theatrical commitments.

When he knew that Dr Ford wanted to sell out, King had hoped to buy his shares and thus gain a stronger influence at the theatre; unfortunately in attempting to raise money for this he gambled and lost heavily so that he was worse off than he had been in the first place. He went to see Dr Ford and told him that although he could not produce cash he had some securities and if Dr Ford would accept these he was eager to buy.

King's hope was that the ever impecunious Sheridan would

certainly not be able to raise the necessary capital, but he had reckoned without Sheridan's friends. The Duke of Norfolk came to the rescue and lent Sheridan the necessary cash with the result that, with his father-in-law Thomas Linley, he became the proprietor of Drury Lane, and as Linley had nothing but a monetary interest this gave Sheridan complete control.

King declared his intention to leave and go to Dublin and work there. He had had enough of Sheridan and Drury Lane.

This was the state of affairs when Dorothy returned from Cheltenham.

It did not greatly perturb her that King was going. He had been fair to her but she knew that he, being an old man, did not care for her style of acting. He did not see comedy as the romp she made of it. He believed it should be more refined; and for that reason he had never held the high opinion of her that Sheridan had held, while at the same time, as manager, he must respect her ability to fill the theatre.

It was when King's successor was appointed that she began to feel uneasy. For Sheridan had chosen none other than John Kemble to act as manager; and Kemble, as the brother of Sarah Siddons, could scarcely be a partisan of Dorothy Jordan.

No sooner had Kemble taken over than trouble began. He made it clear that in his opinion the greatest draw at Drury Lane was Sarah Siddons and every other actress must be subordinate to her.

Sarah immediately suggested that her salary was not enough and Kemble arranged to pay her thirty pounds for each performance. This meant that if she only played once a fortnight she would be more highly paid than Dorothy who might be playing every night, for she was still getting only her twelve pounds a week.

This rankled and Dorothy had made up her mind not to accept it.

Since the birth of Dodee she had suffered from minor indispositions and there had been occasions when she had found it impossible to appear. Kemble always made the most of this and set a rumour about that Mrs Jordan was becoming so autocratic that she would only appear when she felt in the mood to do so and made the excuse of illness.

This was accepted by the public who had been disappointed once or twice, hoping to see Mrs Jordan and being fobbed off with some lesser light.

Kemble was determined to show Dorothy in what little esteem he held her and that although he was prepared to accept that she had a certain following he regarded her as in no way the equal of his great sister.

One night when she was playing, her brother George went behind the scenes and Kemble, finding him there, demanded to know what he was doing. Was he playing? George was not. Then what right had he to go behind the scenes while the play was in progress?

'You've forgotten my sister Mrs Jordan is playing.'

'I had not forgotten and that does not give you a right to be there. You are fined five shillings.'

Kemble strode off and George was discomfited to hear the titters of Sarah's adherents. The incident would be talked of in the Green Room that night and be all over Town by tomorrow. It was an insult to Dorothy. It was hinting that she was of no more importance than the humblest player, and her friends and family had no right to be anywhere but in the front of the stage and in a seat for which they had paid.

Dorothy paid the five shillings but the matter became an issue in the press which was forming itself into factions for and against one or the other side in the Jordan–Kemble dispute, and it was becoming quite clear to Dorothy that she would have to make a stand or leave Drury Lane. Harris of Covent Garden, who had done his best to denigrate her, would doubtless change his tune if she showed her willingness to work for him; but she had no desire to do so. She could not forget the insults he had flung at her and was certainly not going to forgive him for the sake of expediency if she could help it.

She could of course appeal to Sheridan who was her partisan, but he was so little in the theatre and so completely absorbed with his own affairs and his grand friends – and it must be admitted very often a little bemused by too much wine and spirits.

She would fight her own battles. And they were arising on all sides. Most important was her relationship with Richard, who was so content in their present circumstances he made no effort to change them. His father had retired from the theatre to his comfortable country establishment with a fortune – so rumour had it – of £100,000, and surely now was the time to tell him of their desire to marry.

'No,' cried Richard vehemently. 'He'd be so incensed he would cut me right out of his will.'

'Let him.'

'My dearest, do you understand what this would mean? He would cut off my allowance and what I get from my briefs wouldn't go far.'

'You must get more briefs and I must get a higher salary. I'm a bigger draw than Siddons. I'll not endure this much longer.'

Richard tried to evade the question at issue by going on at length about the injustice Dorothy suffered at the theatre, but she would not allow this.

'It's true,' she said, 'and I shall not endure it much longer. But there is no reason why we shouldn't marry. The Kemble set are starting rumours about the immoral life I lead and that might harm me with audiences.'

'Not a bit of it. They like their idols to have a bit of excitement in their lives.'

'You call this exciting! I have all the responsibilities of marriage without the standing that goes with it.'

'I've been happy. I couldn't have been happier.'

'I could have been . . . if I had been married.'

'My poor darling, as soon as the old man agrees . . .'

'Which he never will.'

'He can't live for ever, Dorothy. Then I shall have all his money . . . providing I don't displease him in the meantime.'

'To hell with his money,' cried Dorothy. 'We'd manage.'

Richard shook his head. She looked at him and tried to see him afresh – not as the man she had loved and still did love, though in a different way from that in which she had at first. She saw him now in all his weaknesses. Weak! that was the word that best described Richard. He was weak – content for her to be humiliated; content for her to provide the bulk of their income – anything rather than that he should face an irate parent and possibly incur the loss of his father's money.

She was nervous and touchy and she gave way to her disappointment in him, her anger against circumstances. She had to fight her way through life and the man she had chosen to stand beside her was a weakling.

There were tears and reconciliations, but that did not alter her opinion of him.

'It's these Kembles,' she said. 'They're determined to plague me.'

'They can't harm you,' he soothed. 'It's you the people come to see. You're twice as popular as Siddons.'

'It's true,' she admitted. 'But they feel they ought to like Siddons and there are many people who will insist they like what they ought to like. To weep and moan is somehow intellectual; to laugh is vulgar. They've got this fixed in their silly heads and Kemble and his crowd are going to see that it sticks there.'

'We'll fight it, Dorothy,' he said, stroking her hair.

He'd fight it! she thought. When had he ever fought for anything? Even in his own profession he couldn't make his mark.

But she did not want friction; she was still deluding herself that one day they would marry.

'And I'm worried about Mamma,' she said. 'She hasn't looked well lately.'

Yes, that was a period of great uneasiness.

Dorothy decided that she could no longer accept the position into which Kemble was thrusting her when it was suggested that she appear in *The Romp* on the same evening as Mrs Siddons played in *Macbeth*.

Dorothy laughed aloud when she heard.

'I understand,' she cried. 'The people come to see me and it will be said that they have come for Mrs Siddons. Oh, no, no. She'll play one night and I'll play on another – but I'll not draw the people in for her to get the praise for doing it.'

'You over-estimate yourself,' said Kemble.

'Then it'll make up a little for your under-estimation.'

'So you refuse to play in *The Romp*.'

'On the same night as your sister plays her tragedy, yes.'

'What is it going to be this time – indisposition?'

'By no means. It's simply that I won't be the draw for her to get the praise . . . and the money.'

The last word was ominous but Kemble shrugged his shoulders and turned away.

The next day a paragraph appeared in the *Morning Post* which ran:

'Mrs Jordan and Kemble, according to Green Room reports, are not on the most amicable footing. It is supposed that the lady takes advantage of her popularity to be ill when she pleases and has refused to perform in a farce when Mrs Siddons performs in a play and for this modest reason "that she will not fill the house and let Mrs Siddons run away with the reputation of it". If this be true it is proper to tell this lady that this higher province of the drama will prevail when dowdies and hoydens are forgotten or despised.'

When Dorothy read this she had no alternative but to see Sheridan, and as soon as she had an opportunity she presented herself to him.

He was a little absent-minded. His thoughts were outside the theatre. The Prince of Wales was now relegated to a position without great influence; and although he continued in affection for his dear Sherry, there was no great political advantage on the horizon. Sheridan's dreams had been too rosy; he had thought longingly of the Great Seal; and he knew that there came a moment in a man's life when it was possible to seize the coveted prize and that if that moment passed without bringing the reward it might never come again. The King could not last for ever; the Prince must come to the throne; but where would Sheridan be then?

It was a sobering thought.

And here was Dorothy Jordan – dissatisfied, as all actresses always were. Not getting her dues. When did they ever believe they were? She was not being treated fairly. Was it not the perpetual cry?

'I won't endure it,' she was saying. 'Kemble is a fool. I know Sarah Siddons is his sister and a little bias is natural, but in his efforts to ruin me he's ruining the theatre. He's going to turn away people to Covent Garden if he's not careful.'

'Eh!' cried Sheridan, coming out of his reverie at the mention of his rivals. Whatever his dreams of grandeur he had to face reality now and then – and the theatre was his reality. So were the bills which came every day with wearisome regularity. He had his debt to Norfolk. He had to make the theatre pay. And one of the people he depended on in this was this little actress.

Quarrels between manager and performer were common. He'd had them himself although less than most. He was adept at flattery and thought how skilfully he'd handled the troublesome Perdita Robinson. But Dorothy was not like her. She had a real grievance.

'You saw the paragraph in the *Morning Post*? "The drama will prevail when dowdies and hoydens are forgotten." What a fool your manager is. He's decrying the stuff he is trying to sell.'

'You think he's responsible for this!'

'I know he is.'

'You *have* disappointed the public on several occasions.'

'Only when I was too ill to appear. Would you have me go on and collapse on the stage?'

'It might not have been bad publicity. And you've refused to play the same night as Siddons.'

'I certainly have. I am not going to bring them in and let her get the credit for it. What! At her thirty pounds a performance against my twelve pounds a week.'

'Ah, money. It all comes back to money. The love of money is the root of all evil, my dear.'

'You should tell Sarah that. There's no doubt she loves it dearly.'

'And you?'

'I love it to the extent of thirty pounds a week. That is what I want and that is what I intend to have. If not . . .'

'If not?'

'I'll say good-bye to Drury Lane.'

Sheridan looked at her obliquely. Did it mean an offer from the Garden? Kemble was a fool! They couldn't afford to let Dorothy Jordan go. True, his sister had a reputation. The greatest actress of the day and that was generally accepted as a fact. But it did not mean that although the public liked to *talk* of the Divine Sarah they didn't prefer to *laugh* with Dorothy Jordan.

Sheridan thought of those mounting bills, of disappointed

hopes. God in Heaven, he thought, we mustn't lose Dorothy Jordan.

'You have a case, my dear,' he said. 'I shall consider it. There's no doubt that you should be paid more.'

'Thank you,' replied Dorothy. 'And a quick decision . . .'

'Will be appreciated, I know, my dear.'

'It will be not only appreciated, Mr Sheridan,' retorted Dorothy, 'but necessary.'

Theatre news always interested the public and there were spies all over the theatre ready to supply it.

The quarrel between Kemble and Dorothy Jordan, her refusal to work for her present salary – all this was soon communicated to the audiences. Dorothy wanted to bring herself in line with Sarah. Dorothy Jordan – who *called* herself Mrs Ford – was going into battle supported by Richard Ford and her family, who depended on her, against Sarah and the Kembles.

Gleefully the public waited for what would happen and took bets on which of their favourite actresses would emerge victorious.

There were letters in the press.

'Take Mrs Jordan – who calls herself Mrs Ford – out of hoyden rusticity and what is she? Will the public sanction her in opposing the Manager and for demanding an increase because she can at present excite a little curiosity when perhaps in a little time her attraction may be wholly exhausted?'

But those loyal members of the public who supported Dorothy were not going to allow the other side to get away with that.

'When the salary of performers is below the rank of their talents and the advantages rising from their labours, the public should interfere.'

The battle persisted and Sheridan conferring with Kemble pointed out that all prejudice aside it was absurd that Sarah – dear, excellent, wonderful Sarah – should take thirty pounds a performance whereas Mrs Jordan, who – comic though she might be and not in the same category for one moment as the Divine Sarah – King would have to admit, had the same pulling power as Sarah – some said better – should receive so much less. This was not, he hastily added, passing judgement on the quality of the acting of either lady . . . yet, it was not exactly *just* that two actresses with equal pulling power should show such a discrepancy in the manner in which they were paid.

'In fact, Kemble,' he went on, 'you should never have paid Sarah so much. Now we have no alternative but to offer Jordan thirty pounds . . . but we'll make it a week, not a performance.'

'And if she feigns illness and plays but once a week?'

'Then, my dear fellow, she will be in line with your sister.'

'So you're going to pay Jordan thirty pounds a week.'

'No alternative. It's thirty pounds a week and Jordan or no Jordan.'

'We can't afford to pay her thirty pounds a week.'

'It's true. We can't afford it. But the theatre is a matter of compromise, my dear fellow. We can afford still less to lose Jordan.'

So the battle was won. Dorothy must play at least three times a week; she must appear in both plays and farce; and the public applauded. They wanted more of Dorothy Jordan and providing she did not disappoint them by not appearing when she was billed to do so they were on her side.

The first night she played after the news was out that she was to be paid thirty pounds a week, all seats were filled and people stood in the gangways.

They cheered so loudly that Sheridan declared he was afraid the roof would fall in.

'You see, my dear Kemble,' he said, 'one must always please the public however much, in doing so, one displeases oneself.'

Kemble accepted his defeat as gracefully as he could. He had to admit that whatever he thought of Dorothy Jordan as an actress, the public had a very high opinion of her and she could fill a house as no other actress could.

Dorothy was not vindictive and Kemble realized his mistakes and seemed ready now to advance her career.

There was one concession she did ask of him; this was to take on her brother George and rather to her surprise he did so. So George started at Drury Lane with a salary of five pounds a week, which caused great rejoicing in the family.

Grace had watched the battle with indignation and delight;

and when Dorothy received the large salary of thirty pounds a week she could not contain her joy.

Dorothy remarked to Hester that she looked almost her old self; and that was an admission that Grace was ill.

George was delighted and eager to prove himself. He accepted the smallest parts with enthusiasm – and they were small and usually consisted of walking on and perhaps saying a line or two. But he could do this with an air and was already beginning to be noticed, but perhaps that was because he was Dorothy Jordan's brother.

Not long after her battle with Kemble, Dorothy found that she was pregnant again.

Royal visit

The company was doing *Love for Love* and Dorothy on this occasion was not playing, so she took the opportunity to have a night at home in Gower Street where the rest of the family had moved in with her and Richard. It made it so much easier for Hester to look after the children. Young Frances was giving them some cause for concern; she was a naughty child and jealous of little Dodee. Dorothy could not look at her without remembering the child's father and wondering whether she had inherited his characteristics. Hester, however, was an excellent guardian and with Dorothy so much at the theatre this had become a full-time occupation.

Hester declared that she had never felt the urge to act which, seeing Dorothy, she realized a true actress should feel.

'If I had been a true actress,' she would say, 'I should never have dried up on that first appearance.'

'Poor Hester. You never forgot it. You let it haunt you for ever.'

'Some things do,' said Hester.

And remembering her experiences with Daly, Dorothy supposed it was true.

After the show George came in full of excitement.

It had been a most interesting evening at the theatre. The Duke of Clarence had been in the audience.

'Let's see,' said Dorothy. 'He's the third son, I believe.'

'Yes – and jolly . . . a regular sailor. They said he was only home for a brief leave, and so he came to the theatre. I'm surprised he didn't wait until you were on.'

'Or dear Sarah,' said Dorothy. 'But why all the excitement? We've had Dukes in the audience before.'

'He was in the Green Room, you see, and young Bannister who was playing Ben went in all ready for the stage. He was meeting some girl there and going to show himself off and who should he find in there but the Duke. The Duke said to him: "Hello, young fellow, what are you supposed to be – a sailor?" "Why, yes, Your Highness," said Bannister, "I'm Ben the sailor." "Then you won't do, Ben, my boy." He laughed a great deal, and his language is not what you'd expect from royalty, because royal he is and the brother of the Prince of Wales.'

'Naturally,' said Hester, 'if he's the son of the King. Go on.'

'The Duke said "No sailor wears a handkerchief that colour round his neck. You want a black one. I won't accept you as a sailor, Ben, with that colour handkerchief. Oh, no. I shall protest. If you're going to be a sailor you must look like one." Well, by this time several people had come into the Green Room and someone ran and fetched Kemble. You should have seen him bowing and scraping and Your Royal Highness this and Your Royal Highness that. It was something not to be missed. And then Kemble sent someone for a black handkerchief. Bannister put it on and the Duke said it was not tied as it should be. And he tied it himself . . . with the right sort of knot. "I ought to know," he said. "I used to do it myself when I first went to sea as Midshipman Guelph." And everyone laughed and he laughed with them and he said that young Bannister at least looked like a sailor now. The play was late in starting and there was nearly a riot and then Kemble came on the stage and said His Royal Highness the Duke of Clarence was honouring them and told them that he'd tied Sailor Ben's knot for him and the audience roared and cheered and there was the Duke taking the bow – not like the Prince – but jolly and friendly. And it was an evening I wouldn't have missed.'

'Well,' said Dorothy, 'I hope next time His Royal Highness, the obliging Duke, condescends to visit the theatre, I'll be there to play for him.'

Shortly after that George played Sebastian to Dorothy's Viola in *Twelfth Night*. The critics were not very kind to him. He lacked his sister's genius, they said; and he was too much like her to play with her. But George had shown himself to be an actor.

The first one to congratulate him was Maria Romanzini. She herself was already half way up the ladder to fame and fortune, but she followed George's progress with intense interest.

'Was I good?' he asked her.

'You were very good.'

'You wait,' he said, 'very soon now they'll be crowding in to see me.'

'It'll be wonderful,' she said; she knew that once he felt secure he would ask her to marry him.

With the spring it was necessary to go on tour again and Dorothy was uneasy; she did not like to leave Grace who had grown more feeble in the last weeks; Hester stayed behind to look after her and the tour began.

Now that she was pregnant once more she thought longingly of the home life. To play occasionally at Drury Lane would always be a pleasure, but the exhausting tours with all the difficulties of travel and facing provincial audiences was something she would gladly abandon.

It was necessary, though. She needed the money. It was amazing how even her salary was swallowed up. Thirty pounds a week had seemed affluence at first but with so many calls on her purse it did not go far. Richard's briefs were infrequent; his father, in spite of his vast fortune, had not increased his allowance; and the bulk of the expenses must be met by Dorothy. She simply could not afford to give up these tours even though, as now, she was expecting a child.

She passed through Leeds and Harrogate and went on to Edinburgh playing all her roles to which she had added Nell in *The Devil to Pay* which had become one of the most popular. Rosalind in *As You Like It*, Roxalana in *The Sultan*, Lucy in

The Virgin Unmasked, Peggy in *The Country Girl* were among others and of course she included the most popular of them all, Sir Harry Wildair in *The Constant Couple*, Miss Hoyden in *A Trip to Scarborough* and Priscilla Tomboy in *The Romp*.

She was playing to big houses in Edinburgh when news came from Hester that Grace had taken a turn for the worst and was constantly asking when Dorothy would be back. Hester thought that if she wished to see her mother alive she should return without delay.

In the middle of the season Dorothy left Edinburgh and returned to London.

The sight of her mother's wasted frame appalled Dorothy and she was glad that she had ignored the threats of an irate manager and come home.

'You came, then,' said Grace, tears filling her eyes.

'Of course I came. What did you expect?'

'And the theatre . . .'

'Can do without me for a while.'

'So you are going to stay with me till the end.'

'Oh, Mamma, do not say that. You are ill and will get better.'

But Grace knew differently.

'I'm proud of you,' she said. 'You've been a good girl to me, Dorothy.'

'We belonged together. You were good to me . . . to us all.'

'I tried,' said Grace. 'I never forgave myself for bringing you into the world without a name . . . but when I think of what I should have been without you I know that the best thing I ever did was to give my Dorothy to her public.'

'Oh, Mamma, don't think of all that now. It's no use reproaching ourselves for what we do.'

'I feel happy to leave them all in your hands. You'll look after them.'

'I would, Mamma, but they don't need me. They can look after themselves. George is doing well. He'll be marrying soon, I expect.'

'Ah . . . marriage . . .'

'I know, Mamma, and I'm sorry, but Richard says one day . . .'

'It was what your father said, Dorothy. "One day, Grace," he

103

said, "my father won't have the power to stop me." But he never really did have the power, did he? And then he went away and married that woman . . . leaving us all.'

'It's long, long ago and best forgotten.'

'He would have been proud of you, Dorothy.'

'I hope so.'

'Well, we came through, didn't we? Do you remember when we heard you were to come to Drury Lane?'

'I shall never forget it, Mamma, nor shall I forget your help and love. Throughout my life nothing has helped me more than that.'

Grace nodded, smiling. 'I'd like to think it's so,' she said.

They were silent for a while.

Then she said: 'Dorothy, you're going to have another child.'

'Yes, Mamma.'

'It's so like . . . so like . . .'

'Don't fret, Mamma. Rest. I'm here with you. Hester's near, too. We can send for all the children if you wish.'

Grace closed her eyes. 'I'm happy,' she said. 'I've come to the end . . . and I'm happy. Richard's a good man. He'll marry you, Dorothy . . . one day.'

'One day,' repeated Dorothy and her mouth curled a little cynically; but she did not allow Grace to see this.

Let her die happily believing that one day her daughter would reach that status which she had always longed for her to possess.

Dorothy was inconsolable for some months after the death of her mother. She was almost unaware of the threats of Jackson the Edinburgh manager who sued her for breaking her contract. This was one of those occasions when Richard could act for her. He dealt with Jackson to her satisfaction and although she declared that she would never perform in his theatre again the matter was settled without too much expense.

The imminent birth of her child meant an absence from the theatre and the coming of the baby – another little girl whom she named Lucy – did much to console her.

That autumn Richard Daly came to London. Naturally he was in the theatre to see Dorothy act.

Maria Romanzini came into Dorothy's dressing room to tell her.

'He's here,' she said, her lovely dark eyes round with horror. 'He's actually in the theatre.'

When she was told to whom Maria referred, Dorothy too felt a tremor of alarm. Foolish, she told herself. What harm can he do me now? She turned to Maria. 'You look as though you're afraid he's going to carry you off,' she said.

'He used to terrify me,' Maria replied, shivering.

'You're a big girl now, an important actress at Drury Lane Theatre, How can an Irish manager harm you?'

'I don't like to think of him here, Dorothy.'

'George will protect you now as your mother did before. Not that he'd be such a fool as to attempt to harm you. Everything is changed for us both, Maria.'

That was true and yet she had to remind herself continually of it, and when one of the theatre servants came to tell her that Mr Daly from Dublin was in the Green Room and was requesting her to meet him there she said sharply: 'Pray tell Mr Daly that I cannot see him.'

She had never thought for a moment that that would silence him. He called at Gower Street but she had guessed this would happen and her servants had been warned that she was not and never would be at home to Mr Daly.

He wrote to her. He wished to see little Frances. She could not deny him a sight of his own daughter.

She was terrified. She gave instructions that Frances was to be closely guarded. The doors were to be kept bolted all day and Mr Daly was never to set foot inside the house.

Now she realized how deeply he had scarred her youth. She dreamed of that horrifying experience in the attic; she would awake from nightmares of fleeing from Dublin, recalling it all – the cold of the boat, the nagging anxieties that no one would employ her in England, the humiliating experience of carrying a child of a man she hated.

All this came back vividly from the past and she cried: 'Never, never will I tolerate him near me.'

He did not give in easily. He wrote congratulating her on her success. He had always known she had a talent that was near to genius. He offered her large sums of money if she would appear in Ireland. Her answer was No. Never again will I accept Richard Daly as my manager, she kept assuring herself. Never again will I willingly speak to him.

And at last even he had to accept her answer and he went back to Dublin without having spoken to Dorothy or having had a glimpse of his daughter.

When he had left Dorothy laughed at her fears. There was no need to have been so frightened. He was the evil genius of her youth; he could not harm her now.

Another year. More parts to be played. More triumphs to be won.

She was going to play Letitia Hardy in *The Belle's Stratagem* and a new piece had been offered to her – a short play to be performed after the main event. It was one of the farces which the public had come to expect from her called *The Spoiled Child* and the main part was Little Pickle, a schoolboy, which seemed to have been written for Dorothy. It was the sort of part the public liked best from her; in the first place it put her into breeches; in the second it allowed her to do all sorts of clowning, some of which she thought up on the spur of the moment; and there were some catchy songs – the sort she sang with such verve that in the space of a few moments she had the audience singing with her.

Dorothy threw herself wholeheartedly into rehearsals for *The Spoiled Child* for she knew that this was the piece which would bring in the crowds. As a play it had no merit; it was sheer knockabout farce; but in Dorothy's hands it was a masterpiece. She knew she would have the audience shrieking with laughter over Little Pickle's pranks, such as sewing a courting couple together with a needle and thread while they were unaware of it; and putting his aunt's parrot on the spit in place of the roasting pheasant, and pulling chairs away when people were going to sit down. It was the sort of practical joke type of humour which could send audiences wild with delight.

Dorothy knew she had a winner here. Nor was she mistaken. The whole town was talking of Little Pickle. 'Have you seen Pickle? You must see Pickle. It's the most utter farce, but it makes you ache with laughing. You must see the Jordan's Pickle.'

She was referred to in the press as Little Pickle. When the audience came to see a play they would shout for Pickle afterwards. Dorothy was at the height of her fame, and well might Mrs Siddons shudder and the whole Kemble family ask each other and their supporters what the theatre was coming to. The fact remained that the majority of London theatregoers wanted Pickle and were determined to take no other.

One night when Dorothy was to play in *The Spoiled Child* George came to her dressing room in a state of some excitement.

'The Duke of Clarence is in the house,' he said.

'What! Come to see Pickle!'

'It's going to be a good night. It always helps with a bit of royalty.'

A good night. She often thought of that afterwards. She was to remember that night vividly for the rest of her life.

William, Duke of Clarence

The royal nursery

When the Duke of Clarence fell in love with Dorothy Jordan he was by no means an inexperienced young man. A few years younger than Dorothy – he was twenty-five, she twenty-eight – he had been at sea for eleven years.

When he was born in August 1765 he already had two brothers: George, Prince of Wales, aged three, and Frederick, Bishop of Osnaburgh and Duke of York-to-be, aged two. Horace Walpole had cynically remarked that if it were not for the Queen's supplying the country with dukes the peerage might well become extinct, though he had not known then that there would be more to follow.

So William entered a nursery which was dominated by his brother George, already something of a despot, being not only the eldest but the cleverest, most handsome and most charming of the children. George, who was adored by his mother and idolized by the servants, knew exactly how to wheedle concessions or to demand them, and how to wriggle out of trouble if the need arose. There was only one person whom George could not charm, and that was the King, their father. It was natural that a young brother should admire George, and George liked admiration more than almost anything else. Frederick was already his devoted henchman and young William immediately fell into line. George was the kindest of brothers and although William was younger he was never allowed to feel an outsider. George was always there to explain, advise and collect admiration. George was the god of the nursery and his younger brother accepted the situation as naturally as the sunrise. If they were in difficulties they went to George – large for his age, pink-cheeked, flaxen-haired, blue-eyed George, the little Prince of Wales, whom people cheered whenever he was seen driving out with their nurses, who already knew how to smile and wave in a manner which was both cordial and royal and made watchers smile and marvel at his precocity.

When their mother came to the nursery and took William on her knee because he was the youngest and talked to him, her eyes would be on George the magnificent. William had seen the wax figure of a baby on her dressing table. She had had it put there so that she could gaze at it while her women did her hair. It was George as a baby – the bonniest, healthiest, most beautiful baby in the world. There was no jealousy in the nursery. George was George and his benign dictatorship was acceptable to all – except the King, who would often come in with a cane to correct arrogance, disobedience or greed.

Yet, as Frederick once remarked to William, if it were not for Papa there would be no one for George to fight against. It would be like having St George without the dragon.

William had slowly grasped the point. He was not so quick as his brothers and often did not understand what they were talking about, particularly George, though when George realized this he would always explain with the utmost patience.

The royal nurseries at Kew were presided over by Lady Charlotte Finch and the King had laid down very rigid rules on diet and discipline; the children were to eat no fat with their meat and meat was not to be eaten every day. They were not to eat pastry and if there was fruit pie they had only the fruit, but they might have as many greens as they cared to eat. 'But who wants greens?' cried the Prince of Wales. 'I want pastry. I want fat.'

William remembered the day of the rebellion when George had demanded meat instead of fish and had picked up the fish and thrown it at the wall; and Frederick who always did what George did picked up his and did likewise, while Lady Charlotte was speechless with horror as a chuckling William did the same.

Lady Charlotte did not punish them herself; she must always report their bad conduct to their Majesties and this of course brought a red-faced bulging-eyed parent to the nursery to mete out justice. They were all to be caned by His Majesty himself, this being a serious offence. William watched George's face grow as red as his father's because there was one thing George hated more than anything and that was to be caned. It was not the pain, though this was considerable, but the loss of dignity which worried George.

'Discipline,' said the King. 'I will have discipline. I will beat discipline into you boys. You will not eat meat for a week and you will all be caned by *me*.'

The Queen was there too; and she tried to protest but the

King looked at her in amazed surprise that she dared. She hated the boys to be beaten – particularly George.

George said: 'But I was the one who started it. Your Majesty should not blame Frederick and William.'

St George and the dragon!

The Queen had looked fondly at her first-born but if the King approved of the sentiment he pushed it aside and the canings began. George yelled so they all yelled and the Queen stopped her ears and tried not to look and the King's face grew redder as he said between strokes: 'I . . . will . . . have . . . discipline in the nursery.'

When he had gone George told them that he had not cried because it hurt but because he wanted to shame Papa. He hated Papa and when he was King – which he would be one day – he would not be a bit like Papa, who (whispered low and with great daring) was a silly old fool and a lot of people thought so too – people in Parliament, for George had heard the servants talking. And because he hated Papa they must do so too and find ways of plaguing him and having disobedience in the nursery which should be ruled over by the Prince of Wales not the King of England. Thus the friction between George and his father began at an early age; and William and Frederick were staunchly behind George.

They were all high-spirited and while the King was busy preparing to lose the American Colonies and the Queen bearing children they managed to have a great deal of their own way. But always they stood together – the band of brothers – and it was the same when the other children joined the nursery.

William often remembered the occasion when George had jumped on a drum and broken it and they had thought what fun it would be to turn it into a carriage, and they wanted one of the young women attendants to sit in the drum that they might drag her round the floor.

'Nothing of the sort, Your Highness,' she said to George. 'You had no right to jump on the drum.'

'I have every right to do as I will here, Madam,' said George, regally arrogant as he well knew how to be. 'And now you will be seated in your carriage so that your three fine steeds can do their duty.'

'I'll do no such thing.' William who had not yet learned that his brother did not approve of violence to ladies tried to push the attendant into the drum. In her efforts to evade him she threw him off with the result that he slid across the floor and cut his head open.

Lady Charlotte Finch hurried to the scene, demanding an immediate explanation. Prince William had attempted to strike her, the woman said, and she had merely tried to protect herself. She had not struck Prince William and he had only himself to blame for the cut on his head.

'She did strike him,' said George.

'I did not, my lady,' said the attendant. 'He fell of his own accord after attempting to push me into the drum.'

But George knew that this incident could very likely result in a caning for William, but if the women struck him – which was forbidden – he could not be blamed for showing resentment.

Lady Charlotte Finch called another servant who had been a witness and who declared that the attendant did not strike Prince William; he had pushed her and in doing so had fallen and cut himself.

'This is nonsense,' cried George rushing in to protect William. 'You did strike my brother. *I* say so. These maids will say anything to favour one another.'

What could Lady Charlotte do? She could only warn all concerned that there must be no more such trouble. It was said at Kew that if an attendant offended one brother he had offended them all; and it was clear that they would lie to defend each other if necessary. The point was that trouble for one was trouble for the others, and although Prince Frederick and Prince William might be dealt with, the Prince of Wales, with his charm, his quick wits and his ability to twist the truth to suit his own ends, was a formidable adversary.

Therefore many misdemeanours of the nursery were overlooked.

William had always been fascinated by the sea, just as George and Frederick were by the army. When his two elder brothers played with soldiers, William wanted ships.

The Queen reported this love of ships to the King who approved for once and said that when the time came William should go into the Navy and Frederick into the Army; as for George he would have to learn to be a king.

The Queen often doubted that the manner in which the boys were being brought up was most suited to a future monarch. The discipline the King insisted on was surely certain to produce rebellion in a character like that of the Prince of Wales. He grew more headstrong every day; and it was clear that when he at last broke free he would be like a frisky young horse who is determined to gallop anywhere . . . as long as he could revel in his freedom.

The Queen saw this, but the King could not, and ever since she had arrived in England – a plain little German princess in her teens who could scarcely speak a word of English – she had been made to realize that her duty was to bear the children; everything else might be left to the King, his mother and her lover Lord Bute. A frustrating state of affairs, but what could a humble princess do but bide her time. She lacked beauty, brilliance and all the graces it seemed, her only asset being her fecundity.

There was no doubt of that. The children had continued to arrive at regular intervals – in time fifteen of them, two of whom died in their infancy; but thirteen was a good number.

Both the King and Queen would have been happier in a less exalted position; and they tried to turn Kew – their favourite place of residence – into the home of a country gentleman rather than a royal palace. The King often wished he had been a farmer, for farming interested him more than state affairs. They were very depressing at this time in any case, with the colonists raising their voices against the mother country and half the House of Commons calling for stern methods to bring them to order and the other half advising placation. The King, with his firm ideas of the divine rights of Kings – and teaching his sons to have the same – could not understand why there should be any need to give the colonists what they asked. They were attempting to be disloyal to the crown, said the King. Let them feel the full weight of England's displeasure.

There had been trouble with John Wilkes who had fought for free speech and whose actions the King had deplored. 'Wilkes for ever!' was a cry which made his eyes bulge with anger; yet it had been heard very frequently in the streets – and in the nursery too.

One day the King and Queen had been together – the Queen at her tatting, the King making buttons, a pastime from which he derived great pleasure and which his people derided as an unsuitable occupation for a King – when the door was thrust open by a very bold young Prince of Wales, with Frederick beside him and little William bringing up the rear.

It was rebellion against the lack of freedom in the royal nursery; it was the Prince of Wales, heedless of consequences, in revolt.

'Wilkes for ever!' cried the young childish voices.

And as the King hurried to the door he was just in time to see William being dragged out of sight by his brothers.

It was difficult to know how to punish such an action, said the King. It showed an interest in affairs which was commendable; it showed certain spirit; but it showed disrespect to their parents, which was disrespect to the crown.

The Queen said she thought that as the incident had made His Majesty smile perhaps this was an occasion when he might consider being lenient.

Leniency was not always advisable, said the King ponderously, and went on to deliver a lecture on the bringing up of children.

The only time he ever explained his actions to her was when it concerned the household; if she dared mention state affairs he was displeased and Wilkes, with all the trouble he was making, was a state affair.

He said he would tell one of the tutors to do the caning. It would give it less weight than if delivered by the King himself.

He gives more thought to caning his children, thought the Queen resentfully, than he does to state affairs. And one of these days they'll grow up to hate him.

It was not all punishment at Kew. The King was fond of his children and, it had to be admitted, proud of them. It was his pride in his eldest son which made him stern. The boy was too handsome, too clever, too spoiled by those who surrounded him – and his mother would be included in this if the King did not keep a firm hold on her – and for this reason he must be periodically caned, watched over and kept in constant restraint.

Both he and his brother Frederick were allowed to have their little patch on which they were to grow wheat because the King wished to instil in them his own love of growing things. That they loathed it, particularly George who could not bear getting his hands soiled, was of no consequence. The wheat must be taken through its various processes and, when ready, made into bread which the King sampled with great discrimination, passing judgement on the boys' skill as wheat growers.

William remembered George's fury. 'Are we farmers, then? What do people think of a king who believes that part of the training of kings is tilling the soil!'

Frederick agreed and so did William and Edward, Ernest, Augustus and Adolphus. The nursery was fast filling at that time.

There were happy occasions. William enjoyed those times when the public came to Kew. The King had made it a rule that sightseers should be admitted every Thursday; and the band used to play on the Green. The people loved to see the royal family, but in particular the children, and George bowed and smiled and received their admiration with such pleasure that he was the most popular member of the family.

Frederick, William and the other brothers looked on, content that this should be so. In fact they would have been astonished if anyone had not been delighted with George and would have thought there was something wrong with any person who could not appreciate their brilliant and flamboyant brother.

There was always plenty of music, for the King was eager that his sons should understand and love it. George had a quick ear and could sing well but William had little understanding of it and could not appreciate the genius of Handel of whom the family was particularly fond. The King would sit beating time while the musicians played and the children were all expected to remain in awed silence and to be able to talk knowledgeably with their father on the subject of oratorios and operas – which George could do with ease. William feared he was not very musical. In fact he was beginning to fear that he was not nearly as clever as his brothers. Fred was of course a pale shadow of George but he could joke with his elder brother and they could be quite witty together. William was too slow. Never mind. He knew he could never compete and so did they and they accepted this.

In any case he did not have to attend the Queen's Drawing Rooms every Thursday which the two elder boys did because he was not considered old enough. George grimaced when he talked of these.

'Lucky William,' he said. 'At least you escape that.'

And William grinned sheepishly but wished that he went all the same, because nothing seemed right unless he shared it with his brothers.

Cards were played but not by the Princes, of course, who must stand beside the Queen and receive the guests and then listen to the music which was played in the next room, with the King sending out instructions as to what was to be next on the programme.

It was all very dull, said George, and when he was King he would have everything very different.

William did enjoy some of the parties which their parents arranged for them. There were birthday entertainments when the most magnificent firework displays were given. William would stand beside his mother and be unable to suppress his excitement, especially when, because it was his birthday, there was to be a cake in the shape of a ship.

'Where is our Sailor William, eh?' the King would say, his eyes protruding, trying to be gay and jolly; but William was never sure of his father and he could not forget the canings – not his own, oddly enough, but those which had been administered to the Prince of Wales.

In those early days of his life Kew was like a little village with its houses scattered about the Green. There was the royal farm where the butter, milk and eggs for the royal household were produced. This was personally supervised by the King, who liked to take his children round to watch the butter being made – and to give a hand now and then – and to tickle the pigs with a long stick until they grunted and fell down in a state of bliss, little guessing that in a short time they would be served up as pork or bacon on the royal table.

There was Lady Charlotte Finch with her own house and her own little garden, the Queen's house and the house where the children were lodged.

It was an orderly life. They must be up early for the King

believed in early rising; they must retire early too. The Queen herself superintended their baths which took place every morning at six. She and the King had a habit of looking in now and then during mealtimes so that the children were never sure when they were coming. The Queen sometimes looked on during lesson times, and their father worked out their curriculum.

That was how it was until William was eight years old and then his world was shattered. The Prince of Wales and his brother Frederick were to have a separate establishment as they were considered too old to be with the younger children. A governor was appointed for them and a new household, and William remained behind in the nursery.

Life was easier then. There were not so many inspections and rigorous laws. William had always realized that the important member of the family was his brother George who was destined to be King. Once he had left the nursery it could not be the same again.

They met now and then and George was unfailingly kind to his young brother. If William were in any difficulty he knew he only had to go to George.

When William was in his thirteenth year the King became very concerned. Nothing was going right. The trouble between England and the American colonies was working towards a climax. Burgoyne's defeat at Saratoga had raised a storm in Parliament. The impossible was happening. The English were being beaten by the American Colonists, and there were rumours that France was sending aid to the rebels. The King conferred with his Prime Minister, Lord North. It was a question of 'Conciliate or fight on'. Lord North wanted to resign, but the King would not let him; he wanted to show himself a true ruler and he believed that the best way of doing this was to preserve a stubborn resistance. He was anxious and uncertain and determined not to show it; and his mind was torn between events at home and abroad.

The Prince of Wales was sixteen and chafing against his lack of liberty. There were rumours of his sentimental attachments to women. There had actually been a scandal at Kew where he had been meeting a maid of honour in the gardens and had seduced her – aided and abetted by his brother Frederick, and possibly William.

The Prince of Wales was contaminating his brothers.

'We shall find we have a family of libertines,' the King declared to the Queen. 'Something will have to be done. Frederick has a will of his own. It's William I fear for. Besides, he's so young, but he's constantly in their company. Why shouldn't William go to sea?'

'In due course,' said the Queen placidly.

'Who said anything about due course, eh? I mean now. Let him learn to be a sailor before George makes a knave of him.'

The Queen was horrified. 'William is thirteen,' she reminded the King.

'I am aware of his age, but other boys go to sea at thirteen. It's the right age. There's no reason why he should be any different from anyone else.'

'He . . . he's only a child.'

'Hm,' replied the King not unkindly. She was a mother and wanted to keep them all children for ever. 'Just the time. Thirteen. Right age for a midshipman.'

'Midshipman!'

'You don't think he can be an admiral right away, do you? He's going to start as a midshipman and he'll work his way up. It'll be a hard life, but hardship never hurt anyone. That brother of his has had everything too easy.'

'He has often been somewhat severely caned,' the Queen reminded him with some resentment.

'And that has prevented his being worse than he is, you may depend upon it. It will do William a power of good. I shall go down to Portsmouth myself and see the Commissioner there.'

'I would beg you to consider his age.'

'Stuff,' said the King; and added as though he had had a brilliant idea: 'And nonsense.'

'Thirteen years old and a Prince . . .'

'Old enough, and princes have their duty more than ordinary men.'

The Queen knew that once the King had made up his mind nothing would make him shift it, for one of his most persistent characteristics was his obstinacy. She was alarmed for William

120

who, although disciplined, had enjoyed the luxuries of a royal existence. How would he fare as a sailor – for the King intended him to have no privileges. It was to be part of the rigorous training, the discipline, the hardening process.

My poor William! thought the Queen.

When William heard the news he was horrified.

He wanted to be a sailor, yes – but not yet. And when he had dreamed of going to sea it was as an admiral – at least a captain – not a midshipman.

He went at once to see his brother.

George was writing a letter to one of his sisters' ladies-in-waiting. He greatly enjoyed writing letters for he had a way with a pen and he wept as he wrote of his emotions and undying affection for the lady.

He laid down his pen in concern at the sight of William's face.

'You haven't heard, then, George, that they're sending me to sea?'

'Oh yes, but not for years.'

'Soon. Our father has gone to Portsmouth to get it all arranged and I'm to go off at once.'

'It's madness,' cried George. William felt better. One could rely on George.

'But our father is determined.'

'Our father is an ass, William,' said George sadly. 'Here am I a man . . . and treated like a boy. But no matter. You are in a worse plight. Sent to sea! How can that be? You're not old enough to command.'

'I'm to go as a midshipman.'

'How dare he! *My* brother . . . a midshipman.'

'I've been studying geometry for months and I'm to go . . . so he says. He doesn't want me here.'

'He's afraid I'll contaminate you. It's time he saw what a fool he is. Everyone laughs at him. The Royal Button Maker! Farmer George! Are they names for a king? Stab me, William, if I were King you would not be forced to do anything unless you had a mind for it.'

'I know, George, but you're not King. He is. And he's our father and he says I'm to go to sea.'

121

The brothers regarded each other sadly. They both knew they had to obey their King and father. As yet, thought George rebelliously. But although he might rage about the restrictions which hemmed him in the problem was William's. Poor William, to be sent to sea like a common sailor.

What could he do to comfort him?

'You'll have leaves,' he said. 'And you can't treat a sailor as a child. If he wants you to live like other people he'll have to give you some freedom, won't he? I'll tell you what, William, when you are on leave we'll meet. We'll disguise ourselves. We'll go to Ranelagh . . . We'll enjoy life.'

George could always comfort him. Listening, William tried to think ahead to those leaves for only by doing so could he forget temporarily what had to come first.

It was characteristic of the King that he should be much happier arranging the departure of William than he was managing state affairs. In his family he was the complete despot; in the country he was plagued by his ministers. So energetically he personally set about the preparations for William's departure.

He himself had gone to Portsmouth to see Sir Samuel Hood, the Commissioner of the Dockyard, and had taken the opportunity to meet Rear-Admiral Robert Digby with whom William was to sail.

'Now,' said the King, 'no concessions, eh? He's to be with the others . . . treated like the others. Make a man of him.'

Rear-Admiral Digby said that His Majesty's orders would be carried out.

'If he does wrong, he's to be punished. Never believed in sparing the punishment. Bad for them. He'll be with the others . . . eat with the others . . . live with the others. That's understood?'

The Rear-Admiral understood perfectly.

'He's a bit wild,' said the King. 'Brothers!'

Growing used to the King's staccato methods of conversation, Digby grasped that he was referring to the wildness of the Prince of Wales and Duke of York of whom there had been certain rumours.

'Life at sea. Good for the lad. He's a good boy. Don't want him spoilt. Now what's he to bring, eh?'

Digby asked if His Majesty would care for a list of Prince William's requirements to be sent for His Majesty's secretary.

The King's eyes bulged slightly. 'Secretary! No. He's my son. I want to see that he comes as he should. I'll have the list now.'

Digby was somewhat surprised at such unkingly methods. He was, however, not so conversant with the sartorial requirements of his midshipmen as the King supposed; he would have the list compiled, he said, and it should be handed to His Majesty before he left Portsmouth.

'Very good. Very good. I think you'll like the boy. Cheerful lad. Always had a feeling for the sea. Right stuff for a sailor. Good boy, but . . . brothers.'

Rear-Admiral Digby said he understood; and was extremely grateful to His Majesty for giving him his instructions in person.

It was the night before William was to leave for Portsmouth and the family were gathered together to say good-bye to him. The King, the Queen, seven brothers and four sisters – the only exception being Baby Sophia who was too young to appear. The Queen was tearful and as resentful as she dared be. She thought it was very wrong of the King to send his young son away like this. Who ever heard of such nonsense? A boy not yet fourteen and a Prince, to be sent to live with common sailors. She was thankful it was not George who was going. That she could not have borne. He was so sensitive, so fastidious. Fortunately William was more amenable, slower, dull when compared with George and so might be able to adjust himself better, but it was a shameful indignity all the same. She often felt resentful against the King. When she had come to England from Mecklenburg-Strelitz she had thought she was going to rule with him as Queen; but quickly she discovered that the only decisions she was allowed to make was what embroidery her daughters should do and who should walk the dogs. Even her children's diet had been arranged by the King. And now her son William – against her wishes – was to be sent away to live among common sailors! There were times when she hated her husband. And she sometimes thought of that strange illness of his which had occurred twelve years before when he had frightened her so thoroughly.

It had been a fever but something more than that. Once when in conference with his ministers his face had become very red and he burst into tears. That had been very odd – but only she knew of the alarming manner in which he had rambled on when they had been alone together. 'They're all against me,' he had said. 'Everyone in the cabinet is against me.' And he would go on saying it until she had wanted to scream to him to stop.

'I am insulted by the people,' he had cried. 'I can't sleep for thinking of them and my ministers. They hate me. They won't let me alone.'

And so on in such a strain that she had feared he was losing his mind. He had feared it too. 'Sometimes,' he said to her, 'I fear I'm going mad. There should be a Regency Bill. George is too young . . .' George had been three years old at the time. 'A Regency Bill . . . a Regency Bill . . .'

And at that time he had developed that urgent repetitive manner of speaking which had stayed with him; and often she was reminded of that terrible time when she, a newcomer to England at that time with a three-year-old George, a two-year-old Frederick and William on the way but not yet arrived, had wondered what her fate would be if her husband went mad.

He had recovered; but such an illness left its scars and often she asked herself: Is he going mad again?

And this notion of sending young William to sea seemed a form of madness.

William sat at the supper table next to his father in the place of honour so that the King might talk to him and give him advice, which he did incessantly.

'I've sent off a hair trunk, my boy, with two chests and two cots done up in a mat. You'll settle in. You'll soon be telling us that there's no life like that of a sailor. Yes, a hair trunk . . .'

George looked at Frederick and said slyly: 'Papa, how many hair trunks?'

The King's white eyebrows shot up and his blue protuberant eyes regarded his eldest son. The young fellow always seemed to him too arrogant and he resented that air of languid elegance about him.

Frederick suppressed a guffaw and their mother trembled while the others looked on in admiration of the Prince of Wales who dared mock their father.

'A hair trunk, I said.'

'I see, Papa, I thought there were several.'

'One hair trunk,' said the King, 'two chests and two cots done up in one mat.'

'William is lucky to have Your Majesty *nurse* him like a . . . like a . . . nursemaid.'

'H'm,' said the King, never sure of George, suspecting that he was trying to be insolent but determined not to have friction with his eldest son on the eve of William's departure.

He turned his attention to William. 'I shall give you a Bible before you go. Read it every day.'

'Yes, Papa.'

'You are about, my dear boy, to leave your home and to enter into a profession in which, I will not hide from you, you will be obliged to undergo many hardships and be surrounded by danger. You understand, eh, what? Your first duty is to your superior officers. If you are going to command you must first learn to obey; and you should not think that your rank absolves you from any menial task which may be demanded of you. Don't think that because you are the son of a king you will be treated differently from officers of the same rank. The same discipline and routine will be yours. You will not be known as a prince but as a common sailor. Understand?'

The Prince of Wales shuddered and put a hand over his eyes as though to conceal his emotion; the Queen frowned; but the King was rambling on, having said what he had prepared himself to say and now repeating it.

William was almost glad when the party broke up.

'Retire early,' said the King. 'A good night's sleep. You'll need all your wits about you tomorrow.'

George embraced his brother with tears in his eyes. George wept easily and effectively.

'Don't forget, William,' he said. 'You'll soon be home. Then we'll enjoy life . . . together.'

George could offer more comfort than the King with all his homilies and the Queen with all her fears.

Midshipman Guelph

The next morning William left for Portsmouth to join the *Prince George* at Spithead, a vessel of ninety-eight guns under the command of Rear-Admiral Digby. He was dressed in plain blue jacket, sailor's trousers and a low crowned hat. The Prince of Wales suppressed a shudder as he looked at his brother for he did not wish William to know how humiliating he considered it even to *wear* such clothes.

Final farewells were said and William trying not to cry set off in the company of Mr Majendie, his tutor, who, in spite of the King's determination to make the Prince live as an ordinary midshipman, must accompany him to give his daily lessons. Although the boy was to be a sailor he must not be uneducated; and as he was not yet fourteen it could not be said that his education was complete. It was only when he was jogging along those country roads in his unfamiliar garments that he was overcome by the strangeness of everything and he felt this was indeed the most wretched moment of his life. He yearned for the old nursery days with George in command; he longed to be anywhere but on the way to join the *Prince George*. The only comfort was in the name, but even that only reminded him of his beloved brother.

Still, as George had said, he was not the most imaginative of them and this did enable him not to dwell too much on what the future might be but to wait and see what it was like; and he kept telling himself he had always wanted to go to sea.

He tried to think of great battles with himself directing actions from his flagship. Admiral Prince William . . . but he was supposed to forget he was a prince, of course.

Arrived at Spithead there was no welcome for him. Instructions had been that he was to be treated like any midshipman. He was not without courage and as he descended the ladder into the steerage he felt a lifting of his spirits. After all, this was adventure such as George himself had never had; and he thought of those leaves when he would tell his brothers all about this and they would listen enthralled because it was something they had never experienced. He must act like a king's son although he must never remind anyone that he was.

He looked about him; what an airless place. Surely the King with his passion for fresh air would never have agreed to his sleeping in such quarters.

This was where midshipmen slept, ate and spent their leisure he supposed. He could not imagine anything less like the royal apartments at Kew, St James's, Windsor or Buckingham House.

Peering into the gloom he made out a table covered with a stained table-cloth; he wrinkled his nose with disgust at the odour of cooking grease and onions, and wondered what was the horrible smell which dominated everything else and discovered later that it came from the bilge water.

How was he going to eat in such a place, sleep in that narrow berth? How could he live here in between leaves? Going to sea was not what he had thought it would be. He had dreamed of commanding from his flagship, winning great victories – not living in quarters like these. Then with a start he realized he was not alone in this dark place. He was surrounded by silent watchers.

There were other boys down here all wearing the same kind of jacket and trousers and low crowned hats. They were staring at him.

Seeing that he was aware of them, one crept forward and peered into his face. William knew at once that they were conscious of his identity and did not like him the better for it. He knew too that they would have been told: Treat him as one of yourselves. That is the wish of the King.

He thought of George and wondered what he would have done in such circumstances. But George would have refused to wear these clothes in the first place; he would have come here in velvet coat and diamond shoe buckles and no one would have dared look at George as these boys were looking at him now.

'Have you come to sail with us?' called a voice from a berth, and a cloud of evil-smelling tobacco came from the same direction.

'I have,' said William.

'You have, have you,' was the comment. 'And what's your name?'

'I am entered as Prince William Henry,' said William, 'but my father's name is Guelph.'

'Guelph, is it? We are not to bow three times every time we see you, you know.'

William laughed. 'Why should anyone bow three times?' he asked. 'You must call me William Guelph, for I am now nothing more than a sailor like you. Which is my berth?'

There had always been something natural about William; his fellow midshipmen sensed it now. They had been expecting a swaggering arrogant young coxcomb whom they had determined to put in his place since the orders had gone round that he was to be treated like the rest of them.

But how could they put William in his place when he had already put himself there?

'I'll show you,' said the young man who had asked the questions, leaping from his berth and coming up to William. 'What do you think of it, eh? It's not St James's Palace, you know, and it's not Windsor Castle.'

William laughed – a rather fresh innocent laugh. He had always had an ability to make friends which his brothers lacked. His was so natural and at heart modest.

The atmosphere changed suddenly. William's shipmates had decided that although they had a king's son among them he was not very different from themselves.

A few days after his arrival the *Prince George* set sail for Torbay and from there went to join the Channel Fleet, the immediate task of which was to prevent the French fleet joining up with that of Spain. This, however, the British fleet failed to accomplish and the combined ships of France and Spain sailed boldly up the Channel as far as Plymouth causing consternation all along the south-west coast of England. The Spanish and French commanders stood on their decks looking through their binoculars at the land and deciding that it would soon be theirs. When they saw the wooded hills of Devon and the rich red soil their eyes glittered greedily, but when they saw too the guns trained on them and heard that Sir Charles Hardy, who commanded the British fleet, was on his way they lost heart and retreated.

William had believed that he was about to see his first action and was surprised on arriving at Plymouth to find that the enemies had fled. The *Prince George* docked there and William was given a brief leave of absence. His parents wished him to set out for Windsor without delay.

William was delighted although not as eager as he had thought he would be. After a few weeks at sea he had quickly adjusted himself to a midshipman's life and he found it not as restricting as the schoolrooms of Kew. He had become a man; he listened to men's talk; he had already engaged in fisticuffs after an argument with one of the midshipmen.

'If you were not the King's son,' he had been told, 'I'd teach you better manners.'

'Don't let that be a hindrance,' William had retorted.

But his adversary had said it would not be fair for he was older and stronger; but William would not take that for an answer, and they had fought and William had not come out of the fray too badly. The rest of the company liked him because he did not seek special advantages. They forgot half the time who he was and as they knew him as Guelph he seemed exactly like one of them.

Now he was on his way to Windsor and when he arrived he was told that Their Majesties wished to see him without delay.

There were tears in the King's eyes as he embraced him.

'I've had good reports,' he said. 'Digby tells me you've done well. Good lad. Glad to hear it. Must remember to set an example.'

The Queen embraced him in her somewhat detached manner; she never showed much affection for any of them except George, and only to him by the way she looked at him and listened intently when he spoke.

The King wanted to know all about his adventures, how they had sailed up the Channel and put the French and Spanish to flight. He was clearly proud to have had a son involved in such an action and William felt pleased with himself; and decided that after all a sailor's life was a good one and it was more satisfactory to be a midshipman on board *Prince George* than a child in the nursery.

He saw his two elder brothers who had come down to Windsor for the express purpose of being with him.

George was horrified at his uniform and the oaths which he had picked up, but also amused.

'They've toughened you, William,' he said, 'but by God they've made a man of you.'

'It's an improvement in a way,' added Frederick.

And they took him into their confidence and told him of George's latest conquest and how assignations were made in the gardens at Kew while Frederick kept guard for his brother.

They talked with more frankness than they had ever shown before, and William knew that his brothers considered that in becoming a sailor he had become a man.

When he returned to the *Prince George* it was to a somewhat chilly reception.

'His Highness has returned,' declared one of the midshipmen. 'But of course he had to go home to see Mamma.'

'What do you mean?' demanded William.

The boys continued to talk over his head.

'No leave for the likes of us. Oh, but it's different with His Royal Highness. He's not old enough to leave his Mamma. So he has to run home to her and tell her what a rough lot he's been put with.'

'Nothing of the sort,' cried William angrily. 'It wasn't my mother who said I was to go, anyway. It was my father.'

'Ho! His Majesty's command, eh?'

'That's about it,' said William.

'And while Master Guelph was going to balls and banquets, Sam here asked leave to go because his father was dying and did he get it? No. But it's different with His Royal Highness.'

William turned to Sam, real concern showing on his face. 'I'm so sorry. I wish I'd known. I'd never have gone. I'd have said you must go in my place. How is your father?'

'Dead,' was the laconic reply.

There was silence. William turned away. George would have wept and said something moving; but William could say nothing; yet his silence was more effective than words would have been.

Then someone shouted, 'Wasn't your fault, Guelph.'

William answered: 'I have to do what they tell me. I get more freedom here on board than I ever did at home.'

The tension was broken. Someone laughed. 'Who'd be a Highness? Never mind, Guelph, you can forget all about that here.'

They had realized once more that they really did like their young princeling.

*

It took only a day or so to adjust himself to life in the cockpit of *Prince George*. His brief stay with his family had made him forget how coarse the language could be – half of which he did not understand – how airless the cramped quarters, how nauseating the mingling odours and what it was like to live in the semi-darkness with only the constantly burning lamp swinging from the ceiling to relieve the gloom.

His fellow midshipmen were still ready to pounce on the slightest show of royalty; they laughed when he was relieved of duties to study with Mr Majendie. They watched him, when they remembered, for what they called airs and graces.

'Avast there, my hearty!' was a constant cry. 'The son of a whore is as good a man here as the son of a king.'

'I'd agree with that,' was William's good-humoured comment. 'It's the man himself we have to work with, not his father.'

Although he could be hot-tempered his anger died quickly; he was more likely to resort to fisticuffs – at which he was quite accomplished – than words. He was not quick-witted but he was good-natured; and if he could help anyone he would.

Resentment grew into an amused tolerance. Willie Guelph was not a bad sort and as long as he kept his royalty to himself they would not complain.

He learned to swear like the rest of them. When they went ashore he would go off in the company of his friends and like theirs his greatest interest was in the girls of the town.

He was a regular fellow, this Guelph; he was accepted; he was an example of the truth of the saying that one man was as good as another.

The *Prince George* was at Spithead once more and Christmas was approaching. A message was sent to Admiral Digby that Prince William was to return to Windsor where he would pass a few days with his family.

Some opposition had been expressed to the Prince's absences of duty – there had been several of them since he had joined the Navy – and the Earl of Sandwich had actually spoken to the Queen on the subject. Such favouritism could not add to the popularity of His Royal Highness, he pointed out; at which the Queen looked at him very coldly and replied that she thought his son's career was a matter for His Majesty to decide. Sandwich, who prided himself on his bluntness, retaliated with 'If Your Majesty does not know your duty, I know mine!' which made the Queen very angry but because her word carried no weight with the King she allowed the insult to pass. However, William still continued to enjoy frequent leaves from duty.

This was a sad occasion, for during this one he was to say good-bye to Frederick who was to be sent to Germany to learn how to be a soldier.

The Prince of Wales was in despair. He and Frederick were inseparable. What was he going to do without Frederick? Who was going to help him to meet the ladies of his choice? In whom was he going to confide? And if Frederick was to become a soldier why could he not do so in England? Why did the King believe that only the Germans knew how to train soldiers? The Prince of Wales wanted to be a soldier too. If Frederick had to go he would like to go with him. 'A Prince of Wales cannot leave the country,' said the King. 'Then let us train in England,' retorted the Prince, which so shocked the King that his eyes bulged and he called his son a young jackanapes whose insolence was growing beyond endurance.

So it was not a very happy occasion.

The King was very solemn, full of advice and maudlinly sentimental, for since the Prince of Wales had started to cause so many scandals Frederick had become his favourite son.

His Majesty made all the arrangements in detail just as he had with William and the last day arrived and the family gathered for the last evening as they had for William.

William was unhappy because of George's grief. George had been sorry to lose William but he knew that William would be frequently returning to England and have his spells of leave. It would not be so with Frederick. He would stay in Germany perhaps for years.

George wept and embraced Frederick; they mingled their tears. It was most affecting.

'And to think,' said George to William, 'that the old fool could have let him train in England – then we need not have been separated.'

*

'William must stay with us for my birthday celebrations,' declared the Queen. 'Frederick has gone, so William must stay.'

William was delighted. Although he had now grown used to life at sea he found the complete change stimulating. The contrast between his exquisite brother George and his shipmates was overwhelming. They seemed rougher when he returned to them, and George seemed to grow more and more elegant. But perhaps this was the truth for George was becoming increasingly interested in his clothes and had even invented a new style of shoe buckle which was being worn everywhere and known as 'the Prince of Wales's Buckle'. The young women – William's prevailing passion – were different too. He liked the girls he met in taverns but he liked fine ladies too; and now that he was a man he could discuss his adventures with George which was interesting. George's approach was entirely romantic – very different from that of the sailors. George had to adore the object of his passion; she had to be perfect, angelic, an ideal of womanhood. It was a new outlook and a fascinating one; and was more satisfying to William's nature – which was not unlike that of George in this respect. To be in love was an ecstatic experience. Without it, to George's fastidious mind, there was no great pleasure to be found in associating with women.

He converted William to this point of view.

And thus it was when the brothers attended the ball at St James's which was held to celebrate the Queen's birthday, William fell in love for the first time.

She was the Hon. Julia Fortescue and when William saw her he understood fully the doctrines of the Prince of Wales. He danced with her; they talked. He was no longer shy but in her presence he felt a little tongue-tied. He was not yet sixteen – very young, of course, but then so was she and he had been living like a man. They could not make a man of him one minute, he thought, and expect him to be a boy the next.

He danced again with Miss Fortescue. He told her that he had had many adventures during his life at sea but he had never met anyone like her before. She thought he was charming, because he was so modest and humble in spite of being the son of the King.

The Queen was aware that he was dancing with Miss Fortescue

more than he should. He ought to remember his duty. There were other ladies – not such young ladies – with whom he should be stepping out. But Her Majesty was not so concerned with him as she was with the Prince of Wales who was showing marked attention to Lady Sarah Campbell.

After the ball he and George talked of their divinities and it was George who suggested that they should marry.

'Marry!' cried William ecstatically. 'It is what I wish for beyond all things.'

He called on her. Her family lived in Piccadilly in a big house facing Green Park, and naturally the son of the King was welcome there.

Every day he visited the Fortescues; people were talking and Julia and he began to make plans.

'We will marry,' declared William.

'Could we?' she asked. 'Is it possible?'

'Of course it is.'

'There is the Marriage Act.'

William wrinkled his brows; he had not concerned himself much with Acts.

'The King and Queen would never consent.'

'Why not?'

'They'd want a princess for you.'

'You're better than any princess. They must see that.'

But of course the King did not think so; and when he heard that William was dancing attendance on Miss Fortescue, calling on her at her home and was talking of marriage, he sent for his son.

'What's this, eh? Courting a young woman. What are you thinking of, eh?'

'Marriage, Sir,' said William.

'Are you mad?'

'Only in love, Sir.'

The King's eyes bulged and his face grew red but he was momentarily silent. He couldn't help thinking of his own youth. He had been only William's age when he had been so wholeheartedly in love with a young Quakeress that he had acted in the most foolish way. And he had been Prince of Wales.

He softened a little. Mustn't be too hard on William.

'Look here, my son, you cannot marry this young woman. You must know that.'

'Why not? She is of good family. I met her at the St James's ball. You speak as though she were some innkeeper's daughter.'

The King shuddered. An innkeeper's daughter was not very different from a linen-draper's niece; and he would be haunted for ever by his love affair with Hannah Lightfoot. Just William's age . . . he was thinking. It's not easy to be a young man.

'My boy,' he said gently, 'you are a prince, a king's son, and as such you owe your duty to the State. It is the Parliament which decides whom you marry. You have to obey the Parliament, my boy. It's something all your family have to learn sooner or later. Make no mistake about it.'

'Why should Parliament decide whom I marry?'

'Because, my dear boy, you are in the line of succession for one thing. You have two elder brothers it is true, but you could one day be King of this realm – that is not an impossibility and because of this you must marry the bride who is chosen for you.'

'I could refuse.'

'You are wrong, my son. You could not refuse. And you must have my consent to marry. If you married without it your marriage would not be legal.'

'A marriage is a marriage . . .' began William stubbornly, amazed that he should for the first time in his life dare to contradict his father. It was his love for Julia Fortescue which was driving him on to do so.

'When legal,' interrupted the King. 'Now listen, William. Have you ever heard of the Royal Marriage Act, eh? I'll tell you. It was my Act so none could tell you better, eh! You know how your uncles Gloucester and Cumberland displeased me. Not received at court. You know that. Well, they married without my consent . . . unsuitably. But they are married. It was after their marriages that I brought in my Act. And in that Act, my boy – and it will be well for you and your brothers to remember this – no member of the royal family under the age of twenty-five may marry without my consent. They can go through a ceremony of marriage, yes, but it is no marriage – because that is what it says in my Marriage Act.'

William's face had grown red; he was angry; but the King was surprisingly lenient.

He laid his hand on his shoulder.

'Young women,' he said. 'Very attractive. Want to protect 'em ... marry 'em. Yes, yes. I understand. But king's sons have their duties, eh? It doesn't do for kings' sons to make promises of marriage.'

William went to Julia and told her what his father had said. They wept together but they knew they would have to obey the King.

'We'll wait,' said William. 'You must write to me when I go to sea.'

And he did go to sea very quickly.

'Mischief they get into at home,' said the King to the Queen. 'Boys – always trouble with them. Different from the girls. William's not a bad boy, though. Now George ...'

And while the King gave himself up to his major irritation and preoccupation – his son George – William returned to sea to dream of dancing at St James's and riding out in the park with Julia Fortescue.

Julia wrote to him and he received some of her letters. He thought of her as he went through his duties on board; for several weeks he dreamed of flouting his father, the Parliament and Julia's family and marrying her whatever they said.

Why should Parliament tell me whom I should love? he asked himself.

And then he went ashore and carousing with some of his friends he met other girls. Girls were irresistible and he struggled to be faithful to Julia; but she was so far away and so different; and the friendship of these girls involved him in no trouble except perhaps a fight or two with another midshipman who was a rival for their favours.

There was so much to do. There were after all enemies afloat. There were constant skirmishes with French and Spaniards – and life was too full of exotic incidents to brood on romance at home. He was not like George – an elegant lover of beautiful women, who could write flowery letters and concern himself only with romantic love. He had to be a sailor at the same time; he had to

136

do his watches and his other duties. Life was arduous when there were no concessions to royalty.

The King thought it best that William should not return home for a while, so he stayed at sea and the King decided it was not a bad idea for him to visit New York.

William was delighted to see the world. He had been farther afield than any member of his family and that seemed a distinction. Even George had not travelled; not that George would have wished to visit uncivilized places; but there was no doubt that travel added to his knowledge.

New York was exciting. The conflict between the colonists and England was over – with victory for the colonists – but there was great interest in the arrival of William. He was the first member of the royal family to set foot in America and he received a warm welcome: but the mere visit of a boy member of the family could naturally not stop the flow of events.

It was an exciting period although William did not learn until afterwards how exciting. He was to discover that a certain Colonel Ogden had with the help of George Washington planned to kidnap him and hold him as a hostage for bargaining with the Mother Country. The plan went awry but William was thrilled when he heard it. He wondered what would have happened if the colonists had succeeded in carrying him off.

It was small wonder that leading such a varied and exciting life he forgot in time what Julia Fortescue looked like; and he became more and more eager to win the favour of any attractive girl he met.

William had never taken kindly to his lessons; poetry he despised; he did not even have the family's love of music. But he was passionately fond of the drama. He like to visit the theatre and to play parts himself. This had not been possible in the nurseries at Kew. George might have acted and delighted in it, and Frederick would have followed George, but there was no one else to take parts so it had not occurred to them to play.

But here on board there were plenty to take parts and William did not see why they should not spend some of the time at sea in staging a play.

When he explained how they could use the orlop deck for their theatre and how they could improvise their costume he did not have much difficulty in arousing enthusiasm. They were clamouring for parts. He had decided they would play *The Merry Wives of Windsor* which he had seen at Drury Lane. He thought they would have some fun with the men dressing up as women, and characters such as Falstaff offered great opportunities. There was a great deal of amusement on the orlop deck and some of the senior officers came to see the play.

It was an excellent way of keeping the men contented during long periods at sea.

When William returned home he was determined not to cast aside his newly-won manhood and looked for the same adventures in London as he had found abroad. He saw clearly the folly of incurring scandal for the sake of Julia Fortescue. He could not marry her and her family would not consent to their forming an irregular union. He must seek excitement elsewhere.

One of his shipmates who was in London at the same time suggested they go together to one of the masked fêtes at Ranelagh which were so popular and which offered numerous opportunities for adventure. The gardens were notorious; there ladies roamed in order to lose their reputations among those who had already lost theirs; and everyone was looking for pleasure.

William and his friend in their sailors' uniforms could be in fancy dress; they had only to put on their masks and they were ready to mingle with Venetian noblemen, shepherdesses, and lords and ladies in the colourful costumes of courtiers. Their masks hiding their features, William and his friend strolled to the Rotunda past the Chinese Temple, the Grotto and the Temple of Pan; they listened to the al fresco orchestra; but they were soon tired of the sights and decided to explore the winding narrow paths, which gave such opportunities, in search of girls. They quickly found them – and William was attracted by one who wore the habit of a nun which was very intriguing because it was obvious that her costume was chosen out of contrast to her way of life.

This seemed a great joke and they were planning how to escape from their companions and go off alone to that part of the gardens which had been carefully cultivated to appear like a natural forest, when they came to a seat under a tree where William's sailor friend suggested they sit down for a while.

This they did and as the young sailors chatted to their ladies and made sly attempts to remove their masks up strolled a group of men led by one in the costume of a Spanish grandee. There was something arrogant about that grandee; he walked with a swagger and looked through his mask, which was even more concealing than most, as though he not only owned Ranelagh but everyone in it.

He glanced at the group under the tree and his eyes rested on the nun.

'Charming!' cried the grandee, and held out a languid hand to the nun.

William was on his feet.

'Begone, you insolent dog,' cried William.

'How dare you address me so, puppy,' retorted the grandee.

'Do you think an officer of His Majesty's Navy will accept insults from a Spaniard?' demanded William.

'If he is forced to,' was the reply, 'and you will be, my little sailor boy.'

William had learned to use his fists; he was on his feet and delivering a blow which would have felled the grandee if his companions had not rallied round him as though he were a person of some consequence.

But he did not wish to be protected. He demanded satisfaction; a commotion ensued and someone called the constables.

'Who started this?' demanded the officer of the law.

The grandee's friends said it was the sailor, and William and his declared it was that overdressed popinjay, the Spanish grandee; and as a result the constables arrested both the grandee and William and marched them off to the watch-house.

When they were brought before the constable of the night they were ordered to unmask.

When the grandee and William took off their masks they stared at each other.

'Eh! William, is it you?' cried the grandee Prince of Wales.

'Eh, George, is it you?' echoed William.

There was loud laughter. The brothers embraced, while the constables looked on. Here was a pretty state of affairs when they arrested the King's two sons.

The Prince of Wales was never at a loss for a gesture.

'You did good work,' he told the constables and presented

them with a guinea apiece, at which, astonished and delighted, they accepted their rewards and joined in the general amusement.

Then George linked his arm through that of William. They must be together; they must talk; George wanted to hear all about William's adventures and he would tell William his.

There could be no greater pleasure for George than to be with his brother.

So, Ranelagh forgotten, they went back to George's apartments in Buckingham House and there they talked far into the night. And William thought how good it was to be home and that there was no one in the world who meant so much to him as his brother George.

When the King heard of the night's adventure, he fretted to the Queen.

'Arrested by the Watch! Bribing constables with guineas! It won't do. It won't do. He'll be just like the others. Hear stories of Fred. Wild . . . just like George. Can't have William following in their wake, eh, what?'

When the King talked in that breathless jerky manner the Queen was fearful. It was reminiscent of that alarming time which she tried to forget and never could.

'William is a good boy,' she reminded the King. 'You've had excellent reports from his superior officers.'

'Sometimes I wonder . . . Sometimes I think I don't get the truth.'

'Admiral Digby would not distort the facts. As for that man Sandwich . . . he would soon have something to say.'

'It's the influence of George.' The very mention of his eldest son's name made the King's veins knot at his temples. 'He shall go back to his ship . . . without delay,' he added.

So William's leave on that occasion was considerably shortened and the plans he had made to tour the town incognito in mask and fancy dress with George could not be put into action.

The return of the sailor

The pattern was set for the next years of William's life, but it was an adventurous life. None of the royal family had seen the world as he saw it. He had become weatherbeaten from sun and storm; his muscles had developed; he had grown to love the sea and no matter what happened he would always think of himself as a sailor.

His journeys took him to many foreign ports and he delighted in seeing these exotic places, but most of all he was interested in the women. He followed the ways of his brothers and when the King suddenly decided to recall William from the sea for a few months to do the Grand Tour of Europe and he went to Hanover he found his brother Frederick almost as skilled in the art of seduction as George.

The exciting adventures he encountered in the countries he visited, the reunion with Frederick, the entertainments which were given in his honour compensated him for being recalled from the sea. There were romances in plenty, the most serious perhaps with the beautiful Maria Schindbach with whom he was seen daily throughout the whole of one winter. They drove around together in a train of sledges; they danced together whenever possible and would take no other partners during an entire evening. The Prince was in love, said everyone. It was an explosive situation for although Maria was not exactly a beauty she fascinated many, and being such a highly desirable young woman she was scarcely likely to settle for anything less than marriage.

Captain Merrick, a fellow sailor, who had accompanied the Prince was also attracted by the young lady, and having served at sea with William and having treated him on board as no different from any other member of the crew, he was not going to withdraw from the pursuit of Maria simply because his rival was the son of the King.

Maria was amused and delighted by the rivalry; but besides being beautiful she was wise. She knew that there could be no marriage with William; she had learned all about that awkward Marriage Act which prevented ambitious young ladies like herself entering the royal family. Captain Merrick could offer what Prince William could not: marriage.

So she accepted Captain Merrick.

William suffered the pangs of disappointment for a few weeks before going in search of fresh adventures. He found one with a passionate young woman who was to bear his son, but he did not know this at the time. He had passed on before his mistress was aware of it.

Such was his life. Excitement, gaiety, adventure; and after the Grand Tour, to sea again.

William was eighteen when he formed an important friendship.

He had been transferred to the *Barfleur* which was lying in the Narrows off Staten Island at the time and was doing watch duty on deck when a barge came alongside in which was a young man in the uniform of captain. The Captain came aboard the *Barfleur* and was received by Admiral Lord Hood who brought him over to William.

It was one of those occasions when William's rank was remembered for Lord Hood said: 'Your Highness, I would like to present Captain Horatio Nelson.'

William thought Nelson the youngest captain he had ever seen, and as they talked together an immediate liking sprang up between them. It was to be the first of many meetings.

Nelson talked with more earnestness than any man the Prince had so far met. He was ambitious in the extreme, not for wealth but for the glory of the Navy. William had never known anyone who had such knowledge of ships and war and how the former should be the means of bringing the latter to a satisfactory conclusion.

When Nelson was at hand there was a marked change in the Prince's behaviour; he did not care so much for roystering in foreign ports. He became imbued with the Captain's ideals; he listened earnestly to Nelson's plans for reform in the Navy; he learned of wrongs which had not occurred to him until this moment; he was informed of the unhappy effects of nepotism which appointed the wrong men for certain posts at crucial moments in history.

Nelson talked with a firmness which was infectious.

William grew to love the Captain, and his happiest days at sea were when he was under his command.

*

In due course William received his commission. This had meant passing an examination before the Board of Admiralty and the King announced beforehand that there were to be no special concessions for his son. However, no one on the board had the slightest intention of declaring the Prince unfit to receive a commission in the Navy and Lord Howe reported to the King that Prince William was a true sailor, and he became third lieutenant on the frigate *Hebe*.

The King declared himself pleased with William's progress and as soon as he had passed the Board sent for him to come to Windsor to spend a few days with the family before taking up his new position.

George, who had now acquired Carlton House and his independence, insisted that William join a breakfast party at his town residence and it was certainly pleasant to be his magnificent brother's guest of honour. The sojourn at Windsor was not so pleasant, being excessively dull; however, that meant that he was glad when the time came to set off for Portsmouth.

Hebe toured the British Isles calling at various ports in Scotland and Ireland; and in a short time William had become second lieutenant; and in less than a year he was made a captain and given the command of the *Pegasus* which he took to Canada and afterwards to the West Indies. It was in Antigua that he found Nelson who was the commanding officer on the Leeward Island Station, which meant that the Captain of *Pegasus* was under his command.

Nothing could have delighted William more, and he was determined that Nelson should have nothing of which to complain in his command of *Pegasus*.

William began to grow more serious under Nelson's influence; he learned of the reforms Nelson was seeking to introduce; and they had many discussions about ships and the sea.

William regarded Nelson as his greatest friend, and the most brilliant sailor it had ever been his good fortune to meet. He did not think so much of Nelson as a lover, however, and he told him so; for Nelson had met the widow of a physician who was serious, intelligent and delightful in every way and was considering marrying her.

The Prince wanted to hear all about Mrs Nisbet and would

laugh at the calm and judicious manner in which Nelson described her.

'My dear Horatio,' he said, 'you talk more like a man who is married than a man who is about to be.'

'And what does Your Highness mean by that!'

'That you show more enthusiasm for reforms in the Navy, seem more enthusiastic about tackling an enemy than marrying this lady.'

'It is a different matter.'

'Oh, you don't deceive me. You are married already. Only a married man could be so calm.'

'As Your Highness has never married . . .'

'I know what you are going to say. How could I be sure? But I am sure. I have never married because I'm my father's son. Many times I have been on the point of marrying but have been unable to because of the Marriage Act.'

'Then perhaps we should be thankful for the Marriage Act.'

William laughed. 'Oh, I doubt not that had I married I should have settled down happily enough. Happily enough . . . yes . . . as you are now, my dear Horatio. Calm, contented but not ecstatic. That is why I say you are more like a man who is already married than one who is about to be.'

Nelson laughed at his friend which was because, said William, Horatio knew more of the sea than the ways of women.

'Nonsense,' retorted Nelson. 'I am morally certain that Frances Nisbet will make me a happy man for the rest of my life.'

'Spoken like a married man,' mocked William. 'And I tell you this: I shall insist on giving the bride away when the occasion arises.'

'We will take you at your word,' replied Nelson.

On a March day in the year 1787 Nelson was married and, true to his word, William gave the bride away. William was twenty-two, a little envious of the young Captain who could marry as he wished and did not have to suffer the restrictions put on princes.

Frances Nisbet – now Nelson – was a charming woman and he hoped his dear friend would be happy. He realized that serving under him had been the most rewarding period of his life. He had come to idolize the Captain and to feel differently about him than

144

he had about anyone else in his life. He marvelled at Nelson's genius as a commander coupled with his care for his men. He considered the welfare of the lowest rating. 'How can you have an efficient ship if the men are not as well and happy as you can make them?' He had asked. 'Discipline yes, but a discipline the men can accept as justice. Then you'll have no need to enforce it.' Although they had visited pestilential ports they never lost a man through disease, which was due to Nelson's rigorous rules on hygiene which, because he explained them in detail to his men, they accepted.

No one had had such an influence on his life as Horatio Nelson.

That was why when Horatio and his bride sailed for England and William received orders to sail for Jamaica he had never before felt so depressed.

With Nelson gone and orders to report to the nearest commanding officer William was suddenly in revolt.

Why should he be ordered here, there and everywhere and have no say in his own actions? It was bad enough not to be able to marry where he would. Every common sailor had that right. He wanted to be home. He wanted to see his brother George and discuss his situation with him. George was the most sympathetic person in the world for while William was fond of and greatly admired Nelson, the sailor had rigid ideas of duty which the Prince of Wales lacked. George knew how to get what he wanted from life. He had captured Maria Fitzherbert and was extremely happy with her. Everybody seemed to be able to do what they wanted except William.

On impulse, instead of obeying orders and reporting to the nearest ship, he set sail for Halifax.

Here he was received with dismay and when he could give no satisfactory explanation of his arrival there when he was expected in Jamaica was sent to Quebec there to remain for the winter.

This was not what he wanted and still in rebellious mood he set sail for England.

When his unexpected arrival was reported to the First Lord of the Admiralty a message was sent to the King without delay telling him of William's action.

The King heard the news in horror. He went to the Queen; he

was confiding in her more than he ever had and the reason was that he was sometimes afraid of talking to his ministers because he was apt to lose the thread of what he was talking about and ramble on vaguely of other matters.

The Queen had noticed disturbing signs during the last months and she was worrying more about the King than ever.

There were rumours about George and Maria Fitzherbert and the question of whether or not they were married was being raised everywhere. Frederick was home from the Continent and no sooner had he returned than George had grown more wild than he had been recently, for the influence of Mrs Fitzherbert had been a good one and for a time he had appeared to live a quiet and domestic life with her; but with the return of Frederick there had been wild parties, practical jokes, drinking and gambling – the sort of activities to set the King worrying.

And now William. She had thought William had settled down; he had had his wild moments, of course, and had at times been uncomfortably involved with women. She remembered a time when he had deserted his ship to come home and tell her that he had fallen in love with a young woman in Portsmouth – was it Portsmouth? some such place! – and pleaded with her to intercede with his father to allow him to marry this young woman. The King had quickly had William transferred to Plymouth, she believed. The places were unimportant. It had only been necessary to remove him from the young woman.

Now here he was back again, disobeying orders, having forgotten that lesson which they had once believed that he had learned so well – that as a sailor he was no different from any other man.

What a trial the boys were! She would make sure – and so would the King – that the girls did not give their parents the same sort of trouble.

'You hear this. You hear this?' demanded the King. 'The young fool. Deserted his ship. Come home . . . without permission. What next, eh, what?'

'Where is he?' asked the Queen fearfully.

'In Cork Harbour. He's to sail to Plymouth without delay. Young jackanapes. What does he think, eh? Who does he think . . . ? Sons! Who'd have them? Fred's the best of the bunch. Hope of the house. As for George . . .' The King's face grew more scarlet merely to think of his firstborn. 'Arrogant young dandy! Prancing about. That woman . . .'

'She seems to be having a good influence.'

'Good influence! Aping at marriage. Disgusting. Nice woman. Too good for him. Fine state of affairs.'

'Your Majesty should calm yourself.'

He looked at her quickly. What was she suggesting, eh? But he knew. She was frightened of what would happen if he continued with his tirade. She thought he might start to rave, and was afraid that he might do something . . . violent.

So was he.

William had committed a grave indiscretion for which any other captain of a vessel would have been court-martialled.

When he brought the *Pegasus* into Plymouth badly damaged, for on the way from Ireland they had encountered a bad storm and the mainmast had been struck by lightning, he found orders awaiting him there. He was to remain in Plymouth, supervise repairs to the *Pegasus* and await orders to sail again.

The trip to London which he had no doubt promised himself was not to take place. If he had thought to have a pleasant reunion with his family he was mistaken.

He was depressed and angry. For the first time in his life he was in revolt, but when he considered what he had done he was appalled. He had been eight years in the Navy during which time he had conformed to discipline and now some spirit had got into him and he had flown straight into the face of authority.

What would they do to him? He did not care much. Perhaps he was tired of never being at home for long; perhaps he wanted an end to the wandering life. He had seen a great deal of the world. Was he to roam all his life?

And now here he was confined to Plymouth with none of the amusements he had promised himself. It was as bad here as it would have been in Quebec. He might as well have stayed there and prevented all the fuss.

While he was brooding on his wrongs and studying the accounts of the damage to the ship one of his men came to tell him that visitors had arrived and were asking to see him.

He grimaced. No doubt Lord Chatham, the First Lord; or some such dignitary come to lecture him, or worse still.

'Bring them in,' he said.

They came. He stared; then he gave a cry of joy; he flung himself into their arms.

'If you could not come to London,' said the Prince of Wales, 'there was only one thing for Fred and me to do. So we did it, didn't we, Fred? We came to Plymouth.'

The brothers were laughing and hugging each other. William felt suddenly emotional, and seeing this the Prince produced his ever-ready tears.

'Of course we came. We weren't going to let you be bored to death in Plymouth. Have you forgotten the old motto?'

'I haven't,' cried William.

Frederick grinned. 'United we stand,' he said.

There were gay occasions in Plymouth. Surely it was a time for celebrations with three princes in the city, and one of them the heir to the throne.

The Prince of Wales with his brothers made a tour of the dockyards much to the delight of the people of the town who flocked out in their thousands to welcome them.

In the suburb of Stonehouse where the assembly rooms were situated gala balls and banquets were arranged. Wherever the Prince of Wales appeared there was elegance, and Plymouth wanted to show it could entertain royalty as well as Brighton or Cheltenham, Worthing or Weymouth. In the Long Room at Stonehouse the Prince danced with the ladies, and Frederick and William did their duty with him. There was racing and gambling and for three days Plymouth was as gay and famous as Brighton and London.

William, happy to gain what he had come home for and what he had feared would be denied him – his brothers' company – was full of high spirits. He was more at home in Plymouth than his brothers were, being the sailor of the family. He could talk of ships in a manner which amused the Prince of Wales while it won his admiration.

Accompanied by his brothers George drove his phaeton through the town and into the surrounding country and it was

148

touching to see how delighted the people were to have a glimpse of their future King. George was in his element, gracious, charming, courteous and witty.

They were three exciting days.

During them William fell in love. She was a pretty girl named Miss Wynn and they immediately called attention to their feeling for each other because at the Long Room they were together throughout the ball and neither danced with anyone else.

The poet Peter Pindar who invariably brought out verses to suit every occasion wrote:

'A town where, exiled by the higher powers
The Royal Tar with indignation lours;
Kept by his sire from London and from sin,
To say his catechism to Mistress Wynn.'

The verses were circulated and everywhere the revelries of the three brothers were being discussed. When they were brought to the King's notice he ground his teeth in anger and wept with frustration. His sons flouted him, he complained; and he could not sleep at night for worrying about them. It seemed to the Queen that he was moving towards some fearful climax.

The Prince of Wales and Duke of York were accorded a royal salute as they rode out of Plymouth, and when they had left Captain Horatio Nelson sailed into the harbour where to William's delight he spent a few weeks.

It was very pleasant to be in the company of this brilliant sailor, though it was very different from that of the Princes. With Nelson to listen to, William's friendship with Miss Wynn began to wane; he became very interested in the Navy once more and was fired with enthusiasm to follow Horatio Nelson.

The Admiralty thought it was high time some action should be taken and William was transferred to the *Andromeda* and ordered to sail for Halifax.

The Queen was growing more and more worried about the King's health although she sought to hide her fears from him and everyone else. While he was aware of his affliction he could to some extent control it but the Queen's dread was that he would become unaware of it and be unable to hide his growing aberrations.

He was in a continual state of anxiety. Ever since the loss of the American Colonies he had been fretful; he blamed himself for this colossal blunder – and not without reason; the conduct of his sons was a perpetual source of worry. He would wake in the night and cry out: 'Is he married to that woman? Is it true that she's a Catholic, eh, what?' Almost everything he said was in the form of a question ending in 'eh, what?' which his listeners found most disconcerting for they never could be sure whether or not an answer was expected.

The Queen thought that it might relieve the King to see a good play but she hesitated to suggest a visit to the theatre. She was terrified every time the King appeared in public; but some diversion was necessary so she hit on the idea of inviting a few actors and actresses to Windsor Castle to perform for the King.

The leading actress at Drury Lane was Mrs Siddons and she would suggest to Mr Sheridan that a little troupe headed by this lady should come to perform before herself and the King.

Mr Sheridan with his usual grace declared that nothing could be simpler and that Mrs Siddons and her fellow actors and actresses would be overwhelmed by the honour.

The actors came and the play was performed. The King sat through it smiling, applauding, and when it was over he asked that Mrs Siddons be brought to him for he had something to say to her.

Sarah entered the anteroom in which he was to receive her as only Sarah could. She made a drama of the most insignificant happening, but no one could say that being personally thanked by the King – which she was sure this was to be – was insignificant.

She prepared to declaim in her wonderful voice the speech which she had prepared – and rehearsed – when the King began to mumble something she could not understand and thrust a paper into her hand.

'For you,' he said. 'For you. For you. Very good, eh? Gratitude, what? Very good.'

She was dismissed clutching the paper and when she looked at it she found it was blank except that he had signed it.

She stared at it in amazement for some moments and then she

said aloud as though it was the last line of a scene before the curtain fell: 'The King is mad.'

The Queen sat holding the piece of paper. Mrs Siddons had brought it to her with a display of distress, declaring that she believed it her duty to do so.

'I have wrestled with myself,' said the actress, striking her left hand against her breast. 'I have asked myself what I should do. And my conscience tells me that I should bring this to Your Majesty. His Majesty presented it to me as though it were some insignia of honour. Your Majesty, I greatly fear that the King is ill.'

The Queen thanked Mrs Siddons. She had done right in bringing the paper to her, she said. There was some mistake, of course. At a convenient time she would ask His Majesty what his intentions were.

And when Mrs Siddons had gone she sat down wearily.

Was this the end of her endeavours to hide the state of his health? Was the truth to be betrayed at last?

It seemed so, for events moved quickly after that. The King was acting strangely and the whole royal household knew it. The Princesses whispered together and sat silent in the presence of their mother, working at their embroidery, filling her snuff boxes and taking care of the dogs – which was, they complained bitterly to each other, all their lives consisted of.

But something was about to happen.

Frederick sent urgent messages to the Prince of Wales in Brighton; he should be at hand, for the King was very ill indeed – not only physically ill, although he had high temperature and a chill, but strangely ill.

The Prince came at once, driving his phaeton from Brighton at a great speed; and that night at dinner the King rose suddenly from his seat and approaching his eldest son seized him by the throat and tried to strangle him.

There could be no disguising the fact.

The King was mad. His doctors must be called and the almost certainty of a Regency discussed.

*

The struggle over the Regency Bill began, with the Queen and the Prince of Wales in opposing camps. The Queen who had doted on her eldest son, who had had a wax image made when he was a baby so that she might remember for ever his perfections and gaze on them every day – for it stood on her dressing table – had been consistently flouted by him and shut out of his life. Because of this her love had changed. If he had given her the slightest consideration she would have been ready to love him; but hurt and humiliated by his neglect she forced herself to hate him. Her emotion towards him – love or hatred – was the strongest in her life.

Pitt, who had stood with the King, found himself in opposition to Fox who stood for the Prince. Fox declared in Parliament that since the King was unable to govern, the heir to the throne must be Regent. Pitt brought all his powers to oppose this, knowing that a Regency in the hands of the Prince of Wales could mean the fall of the Tories and the substitution of the Whigs under Fox.

Pitt sought the help of the Queen by offering her something which all her life she had been denied: Power. The country was split between those who supported the Prince of Wales as Regent and those who wished for a Regency committee. The royal family was divided. The Queen and her daughters (who dared do nothing else) for Mr Pitt and the constitution, and the Prince and his brothers for a single Regent who would be the Prince of Wales.

The Prince had strong backing in Fox, Burke and Sheridan, but Fox made the tactical error in the House of Commons of referring to the Prince's *right* to the Regency which gave Pitt his opportunity to challenge the right of any to such a post in a constitutional government and asked slyly whether Mr Fox had not meant 'claim'.

Because of this unfortunate choice of a word Pitt had his opportunity to play a game of delaying tactics which infuriated the Prince and his supporters and widened the rift between Fox and George. Twice Fox had offended him; once when he had denied his marriage to Mrs Fitzherbert in the House – and Mrs Fitzherbert had been so incensed that she had broken off her relationship with the Prince and had never forgiven Fox – and now by the use of this word 'right'.

As Fox said to his mistress Mrs Armistead, perhaps he was getting too old for politics and should retire. He did not blame himself for that denial in the House because in view of the circumstances there had been nothing else he could do, but the use of the word 'right', in the hearing of a brilliant politician like Pitt, was a terrible blunder.

So Pitt had his opportunity to present his Regency Bill which restricted the powers of the Prince Regent so that he would be no more than a cipher; but no sooner had it passed through a fevered House of Commons that the King's doctors declared that he had recovered and the conflict had all been unnecessary.

When William came back to England he found a state of war in the family.

The King – a changed man – nervous, uncertain, often incoherent, clearly relied on the Queen to whom previously he had denied all say in matters outside the domestic circle – and even there he had laid down his laws. The change was obvious. Mr Pitt during the King's aberration and the conflict over the Regency Bill had allied himself with the Queen and any ally of Mr Pitt was a person to be considered.

The Queen accepted her new role with restrained pleasure but the change in her was as apparent as that in the King.

She had lost no time in acquainting the King of the villainies of their sons, and in particular the Prince of Wales who had sought to get power into his hands and would, of course, as soon as it was possible, have replaced dear Mr Pitt with that villain Fox, while Frederick had been staunchly behind him and the other boys, she regretted to say, had stood firmly with the Prince.

William! Well, William was at sea, but she had no doubt – knowing his devotion to George – that had he been at home he would have been every bit as disloyal to his father as his brothers had been.

William heard the story from George and Frederick.

There was madness in the King, said the Prince. Didn't they know it! He might have made some semblance of recovery but he would go mad again. The Prince of Wales was twenty-seven years old. Wasn't that old enough to be a ruler? The King had been King long before he was that age; and surely if their simple old father was capable, it was an insult to say that the brilliant, erudite Prince of Wales was not.

'That devil Pitt,' said the Prince. 'He's the real enemy. You can be sure our mother would not have had the wit to stand against us if she had not had his support.'

William joined whole-heartedly with his brothers and declared war on that devil Pitt.

The King sent for William and when he was ushered into his presence and saw the change in him William felt a twinge of pity. The King embraced him and there were tears on his cheeks.

'You, boy . . .' he stammered.

William felt repentant for all the wild adventures, the flouting of discipline; and wished at that moment that he could have been the son his poor old father hoped for.

Kings seemed to be the most unfortunate men on earth as far as their families were concerned. They either longed for sons whom they could not get, or had too many of them who caused so much trouble.

'Well, William,' said the King. 'You're growing up, eh? Quite a man, what?'

'Twenty-four, Sir.'

'H'm. Time you had some title, eh? Clarence . . . that's what you'll be. Duke of Clarence; and they've voted you twelve thousand a year. All right, eh, what?'

Twelve thousand a year! It wouldn't keep the Prince of Wales in shoe buckles and neckerchiefs, but it sounded like a fortune to William.

'Thank you, Sir.'

'All right, eh, what? And a place, eh . . . place of your own. Richmond Lodge on the edge of the Old Deer Park, eh?'

'Well, Sir, I'd like it very much. It'll be something to come home to after voyages.'

'H'm,' said the King. 'Can't have you away all the time, eh? King's son. Duke of Clarence. Two elder brothers . . . yes . . . knaves! George always was. But Fred . . . I thought Fred would be different. Hope of House. Don't like it. What are they coming to, eh, what?'

William said: 'Richmond Lodge will be much appreciated, Sir. Thank you.'

'H'm. Not often I get thanks from my sons. You've got to take care, boy. Keep away from women . . . and drink . . . and gambling . . . understand, eh? Mostly women. They can cause trouble . . . great trouble. Might be a good woman. That woman of George's . . . Good woman, beautiful, nice woman. But they cause trouble. Could be Quakers . . .' The King's eyes filled with tears. What am I saying? he asked himself. All long ago. All over now.

William left his father thinking: The old man may have recovered but madness is still lurking there. And then: Richmond Lodge and twelve thousand a year!

Settling into a new house was a great pleasure. He was satisfied to be home and have a rest from the sea.

Twelve thousand pounds was a great deal of money but not when George and Frederick showed him how to spend it.

He enjoyed being a householder; he took great pride in his new possession; he engaged the servants himself and laid down the rules and made sure that he locked up every night to ensure that they did not stay out late. He took an interest in them; he was discovering that the quiet life appealed to him. He would have liked to be a landowner – if he were not a sailor – looking after his tenants, living in conjugal bliss with the wife of his choice and rearing a family. He fancied that the Prince of Wales felt the same for he was very happy with Maria Fitzherbert – if occasionally unfaithful – and liked to know that cosy domesticity was awaiting him when he cared to return to it.

In spite of all William's care Richmond Lodge, which had been renamed Clarence Lodge, was damaged by fire one night and while the damage was being repaired William took another house close by called Ivy House and himself superintended the repairs to Clarence Lodge.

He was restive. He thought nostalgically of life at sea; he was already tired of being the country squire and nothing could compensate him for the feel of decks beneath his feet and the rock of a ship, the arrival at strange exotic places, the adventure of the sea. They had made a sailor of him. They could scarcely expect him to settle on land.

But apparently they did.

'Not fitting,' said the King. 'Go to the Admiralty. On the

Board, give advice . . . Yes . . . still in the Navy. But a King's son should be at home. Besides, you broke discipline. That sort of thing, frowned on. Favouritism. Not right. Bad feeling. Stay where you are . . . for a while.'

So he must stay. He found a very pretty and diverting young woman named Polly Finch of very obscure origin who delighted him and made few demands and agreed to come along and share Ivy House with him.

It was in a way the domesticity he hoped for. Polly never let the fact that he was a royal Duke affect her. She abused him in the manner of the streets and made love with a careless abandon. He was delighted, never having known anyone quite like Polly.

She was interested in the repairs to Clarence Lodge, for she thought they would live there. William dreamed of their living in obscurity and raising a family and himself going away to sea for periods and coming home to find Polly waiting for him.

It was a sentimental dream. Polly was not that sort of girl.

He talked to her about the sea. The rank of Rear-Admiral had been conferred on him and he would soon be an Admiral. It was inevitable. One could not be a royal Duke and not in the highest position.

'But don't imagine, Polly,' he explained, 'that I shall not deserve my promotion. But I must be ready for it.'

He wanted her to stay at home in the evenings while he read to her from the *Lives of the Admirals* which he regarded as a most fascinating document. Polly would sit at his feet yawning and nodding while he read of the decisions of these great seamen and their adventures at sea.

It might have been enthralling to him but it was more than Polly could endure.

Before Clarence Lodge was ready for occupation she had left him for a more congenial companion.

There was an uneasy tension throughout the country. Mr Pitt and his Tories did everything in their power to vilify the Prince of Wales and his brothers. It was not difficult. It was true that the Princes indulged in wild living, their gambling debts were enormous and their amours the main theme of court and town gossip. The cartoonists and lampoonists delighted in these and exaggerated and ridiculed them to public pleasure and their own good profit.

Every little indiscretion was exaggerated. Every prominent person was pilloried it was true, but the most profitable cartoons were those which libelled the royal brothers and in particular the Prince of Wales.

John Walter of *The Times* was known as one of the most scurrilous writers of the day. His comments on the conduct of the King's three eldest sons were outrageous, and exaggerated beyond all endurance. They were having an effect on the public and as the Prince of Wales was the principal target and he was constantly being held up to ridicule, he was becoming increasingly unpopular. It was no new experience for him to be treated to a hostile silence in the streets but when his carriage was pelted with mud and rotten fruit it was the time to take some action.

A prosecution was brought against Walter for libelling the Duke of York; he was found guilty and sentenced to a fine of fifty pounds, an hour in the pillory at Charing Cross and a year's imprisonment in Newgate. There was another charge to be answered – a libel this time jointly on the Prince of Wales and the Duke of York which brought a further fine of one hundred pounds and another year in Newgate. The Duke of Clarence had not escaped, for Walter demanded of his readers why it was that the son of the King was allowed to desert his ship and return home to be rewarded with a dukedom and twelve thousand pounds a year.

The heavy sentences imposed by the judges on John Walter angered the public. Mr Pitt, delighted at any circumstances which brought criticism to the Prince of Wales, declared that he was astonished that he and the Duke of York should have brought their cases against Walter; he believed that the Prince of Wales had declared himself for the freedom of the press. Was it a different matter when he himself was attacked?

Never had the unpopularity of the Prince of Wales been so great. It was incredible that this was the same man who had once delighted the people with his charming manners, his elegance and romantic adventures.

It was particularly alarming when it was considered what was happening on the other side of the Channel. The Bastille had fallen; it was said that the French Monarchy was tottering; an unpopular Prince, such a near neighbour, could not help feeling somewhat uneasy.

The only place where the people seemed to have any regard for him at all was Brighton, which had every reason to be grateful to him since he had turned the remote village of Brighthelmstone into the most fashionable town in England.

The Prince affected not to care and continued to concern himself with his tailor, his beautiful houses – Carlton House in London, the Pavilion in Brighton – with art, music and literature, gambling, horse racing, his own stables and women.

He liked the theatre and one day drove his phaeton down to Clarence Lodge to tell William about the play he had seen the evening before.

'*The Constant Couple* – very amusing,' he said. 'Dorothy Jordan takes the Wildair part as I never saw it played before. She looks well in breeches. You should go and see her, William.'

William told his brother about the plays they had put on on board ship and what fun they had had.

'We had a fine fat Falstaff,' said William. 'I think his name was Storey . . . That's it, Lieutenant Storey. We had to improvise quite a bit and I remember in the bucking scene we used a hammock for the basket. The river was represented by a heap of junk and we were to topple our fat lieutenant out of the hammock and into the junk. It was a sight to be seen, I can tell you. This fat fellow sprawling there. It was the most successful moment of the play.'

The Prince said he could well believe it. He liked a good practical joke himself and had once contrived it that Sheridan was challenged to a duel by a Major Hanger and he and his fellow jokers had gone to great pains to put dud bullets in the pistols and Sheridan had fallen down and pretended to be dead. The Prince often said it was the best joke he ever remembered seeing played on anyone; and even Major Hanger had thought so too and because of it had become one of the Prince's special cronies. So he laughed heartily at the joke William and his friends had played on his plump Falstaff.

'We threw a lot of pitch over the junk heap,' said William. ' "We must be realistic," I said, "for if Falstaff were tipped into a muddy river he would not come out unsoiled." Well, we tipped him into the junk heap and you should have seen him – rubbish of all sorts sticking to him and to our young two middies who played Mistress Page and Mistress Ford.'

The Prince laughed and told of his own experiences in the theatre, but he said nothing of his love affair with Mrs Perdita Robinson, because that matter had so humiliated him when she had threatened to publish his letters, and still rankled.

Perhaps he should warn William, he pondered for a while. There was something innocent about William in spite of his travels and adventures.

The Prince hesitated and the moment passed. And talking of the theatre filled William with an urge to see a play; and he decided there and then the very next night he would go along to Drury Lane.

He went and that night Dorothy Jordan was playing Little Pickle in *The Spoiled Child*.

Dorothy and William

Royal courtship

Dorothy Jordan had no idea on that autumn night in the year 1790 that it was going to be the most significant of her life. Strangely enough she was feeling depressed and was heartily wishing that it was one of her free nights. Nothing would have pleased her more than to stay at home with the children.

While she sat before the looking glass in the bedroom she shared with Richard her eldest daughter came in and started playing with the articles on her dressing table.

'Fanny, dear, pray don't touch my rouge. You will make such a mess.'

Fanny scowled. She looked remarkably like her father when she did so. She had a quick and vindictive temper and Dorothy was rather afraid she was unkind to Dodee who was only three. Fanny was eight. Was it only nine years since that dreadful time when she had been the slave of that odious man? It seemed longer. But then so much had happened. An obscure actress had become a famous one and the mother of three little girls as well.

She thought of darling Lucy just over a year old and wished once more that she might have a quiet evening at home instead of facing an audience.

Fanny was dabbing rouge on to her cheeks and Dorothy looked at her daughter and burst out laughing. 'You don't need it, my precious.'

'Why not?'

'Because you're young and pink enough without it.'

'Why aren't you?'

'Because I am not so young and not so pink.' She bent over, took the pot from the child and kissed her. She always felt she had to be especially gentle with Daly's daughter.

'Mamma, what are you playing tonight?'

'Henry Wildair.'

'Is that a breeches part?'

'Oh, Fanny, where do you hear such talk!'

'From all the people who come here. Shall I go on the stage? I want to go on the stage. Would I be a good actress?'

'I should think it likely. You have the theatre in your blood.'

'Have I? Has Dodee?'

'You are both my little girls,' said Dorothy quickly. But it was more likely she thought that the daughter of Richard Daly should become an actress than Richard Ford's.

And neither of them legitimate! she thought, with sudden bitterness. Since her mother's death she had often considered her position. It was humiliating, for although most people accepted her as Richard's wife it was widely known that she was not.

And for what reason? Why did Richard live with her openly and yet shy away from marriage every time she broached the subject? What could the reason be except that he did not consider her worthy to be his wife? And yet he was not averse to using her money. He had pleaded his father's wrath as an excuse. He had said that he would be disinherited. He might as well have been for all he got from his father; he was not too proud, though, to live on *her* salary!

For she was rich – or she would have been if there had not been so many calls on her purse.

Her sister Hester came in carrying Lucy, with Dodee clinging to her skirt. Dodee flung herself at Dorothy.

'Mamma is going to read to us.'

'Not tonight, my darling, Mamma has to go to the theatre.'

'Naughty old theatre,' said Dodee.

'Don't be silly, Dodee,' said Fanny. 'It's a good old theatre.'

'It isn't. It isn't. It takes my Mamma.'

'And gives her lots of money for us.'

Dorothy laughed. 'You think that's a good exchange, Fanny?'

'Well, of course it is,' retorted Fanny. 'It gives us plenty of money so that Papa can have a new velvet coat and we can have sweetmeats – one after our dinner every day.'

'So now you see, Dodee,' said Dorothy.

'I don't want the theatre to have my Mamma,' said Dodee, her lips beginning to quiver.

'Don't be a cry-baby, Dods,' said Hester briskly. 'I'll sing you a song while you're having your supper.'

I ought to be here with them, thought Dorothy. *I* ought to be singing a song to them while they have their supper.

Hester sat on the bed and said; 'It's Wildair tonight, I suppose.'

'Wildair followed by Pickle.'

'And you'll come straight home after?'

Dorothy nodded.

'Richard will be in the theatre.'

'Yes, I suppose so.'

'You seem tired.'

'Oh, no. Just wishing that I could have an evening at home.'

'You'll feel differently when the curtain rises.'

'It's strange, Hester, but I always do. Now I feel depressed, and when I'm waiting my cue I'll have that fluttery feeling inside. I never fail to get it; but once I'm on . . . I forget all about it and enjoy myself.'

'There speaks the true professional.'

Fanny was listening eagerly to the conversation; she was vitally interested in everything connected with the stage. Dorothy thought: I don't want that life for them. I'd like to see them all married happily and settled down in comfort. Would she ever realize that dream? In the first place they would have their illegitimacy as a drawback. Damn Richard! Why should he be such a coward? Why shouldn't he defy his father for the sake of his family?

She would want dowries for the girls; and she would provide them if she could. But would she ever be able to? However much she earned she seemed to need it for her family's expenses. She was beginning to realize that not only did she keep the children but Richard as well.

Hester was dependent on her; but what would she do without Hester, particularly now? Hester scarcely ever appeared on the stage because she was devoting herself to the children, and they looked upon her as a part of the household. They relied on Aunt Hester more than they did on their mother.

Richard came in and said: 'You'll be leaving shortly, I suppose?'

She looked at him with faint irritation. He was anxious for her not to be late at the theatre and was always worried when the quarrels between her and Mrs Siddons and the Kembles flared up. At the back of his mind was the fear that that powerful family might oust her and that if she were turned out she wouldn't be able to command the salary at Covent Garden, say, that she was getting at the Lane. Oh, Richard had his eyes to her salary. There was no doubt of that.

Hester seemed to be very sensitive regarding the atmosphere in this house. When she guessed trouble was rising between Richard and Dorothy she always endeavoured to be out of sight and earshot.

Now she said: 'I'll take the children off for supper. Come along, Fan.'

Fanny said she wanted to stay and talk to Papa and Mamma; but Dorothy said sternly that she was about to leave for the theatre and Fanny must go with the others.

Fanny pouted and stamped her foot, but Hester had a way with fractious children.

'Now, Fanny,' she said, 'we don't want to make a little idiot of ourselves, do we, before a famous actress?'

Fanny accepted the fact that her mother was a famous actress who had her name on play-bills and at whom people stared in the streets and to whom they often called out a greeting and added that they had seen her in such and such and enjoyed her performance. She differentiated between her mother and that actress and while she displayed her temper to the one she was in awe of the other. Hester seized the opportunity to remove her.

When they had gone Richard said: 'You spoil that girl.'

He often referred to Fanny as 'that girl' – and Dorothy resented this because it implied that he was remembering she was not his.

'Poor child!' said Dorothy. 'Poor Dodee and poor Lucy! I wish to God they had a right to their name.'

'Oh dear,' sighed Richard, 'are we on that old theme again?'

'We are and we shall continue to be until you do your duty by those girls.'

'Look here, Dorothy, we've gone over and over this. I can't marry you. You know what the old man is. Are we going to throw away a hundred thousand pounds?'

'Yes, gladly,' said Dorothy, 'for the sake of the girls.'

'It's for their sake that we want it and they're perfectly happy now.'

'Now they are because they don't realize the position they're in.'

'Oh, nobody cares for those things.'

'*I* care,' said Dorothy. 'When we set up house together you said we were to be married.'

'And so we are as soon as it's possible.'

'I have a feeling that that moment will never come and that you are determined that it never shall.'

'What a ridiculous thing to say!'

'I suppose it is ridiculous to want a name for one's children, to hate the insults which are thrown at me . . . constantly.'

'Who throws these insults?'

'You know very well how I am pilloried in the press. It is frequently happening.'

'My dearest Dorothy . . .'

'I am certainly not your dearest Dorothy. If I were you would grant me this small concession.'

'My dear Dorothy then, you know that all famous people are pilloried. Look at the Prince of Wales, the Duke of York and young Clarence. They've only recently had this action against Walter.'

'There is no reason why I should be humiliated for this cause.'

'Oh, for heaven's sake, Dorothy, you are spoiling for a quarrel. I saw it in your face as soon as I came in. So did Hester. That's why she left.'

'She knows and you know that I have very good cause for my grievance.'

'Listen, my dear, as soon as . . .'

'As soon as it's possible we'll be married. You've been saying that for how long . . . ever since . . .'

'Ever since we met and I fell in love with you and knew I couldn't live without you.'

'Providing it was not in wedlock.'

'Oh, Dorothy, where is the difference?'

'If there is no difference why do you hold out against it?'

'You know my father . . .'

'I know you. You are spineless, gutless . . . and I'm sorry you're the father of my children.'

'Two of them,' said Richard. 'Don't forget you already had one before we met.'

She could have wept with rage and frustration; and this was no mood in which to go on the stage and play the debonair Harry Wildair.

'Oh, go away,' she said. 'I'll be late for the theatre.'

'I'll take you,' he said.

'Thanks, I can do without company.'

She stalked out of the room. She had been a fool, she told herself. She should never have agreed to live with him. She had loved him once, madly, passionately; and now that had altered slightly, but she still had an affection for him. He was weak, but perhaps she was fond of him for that very reason. Perhaps he had presented such a contrast to the brutal, bestial Daly.

She was unhappy. At the pinnacle of success she lacked what she most wanted: the warm cosy security of marriage. She was well aware why Grace had always wanted it for her.

If Richard would marry her; if she could feel that she was in truth his wife and the children were legitimized she would be happy. She would be able to face the jibes of the very respectable Sarah Siddons who never failed to remind her that not only was she superior to Dorothy Jordan on the stage but in her private life.

Life was niggardly; it offered freely with one hand and held back with the other.

Kemble was anxiously waiting for her when she reached the theatre.

'I feared this was going to be one of those nights when you were too indisposed to act,' he said with sarcasm.

'I am in good health,' she retorted.

'I know that. But I still thought . . .'

She cut him short. 'What's the fuss about?'

'You're a little late.'

'I'll be on the stage in time, don't worry.'

'I hope so. We have a royal visitor.'

'Oh?'

'His Highness the Duke of Clarence.'

Dorothy felt disappointed; she had hoped for the Prince of Wales. On the nights he came it was a real gala evening.

She went into her dressing room; and while she was dressed she was thinking of Richard, his weakness and his obstinacy and her feelings towards him were so mixed that she found it difficult to analyse them.

From the moment she came on stage she was aware of the young man in the balcony box; he led the laughter when she played for laughs; he leaned forward to get a closer look at her; he applauded vociferously at the end of *The Constant Couple* and in accordance with custom she turned and curtsied especially for him. She was accustomed to appreciation but there was something more than usually ardent in the young man's manner. Such enjoyment as he expressed and from a royal visitor was stimulating and she looked forward more than usual to playing Pickle.

It was a silly little farce really and yet played by her it never failed to amuse the house. It was an excellent idea to do it after the play so that the audiences went home laughing. It was something that had to be seen by the fashionable world; they called it a trifle, but if anyone had not seen Mrs Jordan as Pickle they were out of touch with London life.

Both Kemble and Sheridan knew that it would have been little use putting anyone else in the part. It had been written for Dorothy and only Dorothy had that special gift for clowning with a certain youthful abandon which alone could make the part possible.

The farce consisted in fact of one practical joke following on another which were all played by Little Pickle, the schoolboy hero. Dorothy's small, neat and shapely figure was entirely suited to the costume which showed off her femininity to perfection and the very sight of her appearing on the stage in the Pickle costume set the audience cheering.

The Duke of Clarence leaned over his box and laughed at Dorothy's antics until the tears ran down his cheeks.

He was heard to say: 'George said I must see it, and, by God, he was right.'

Dorothy took her calls, made her obeisance to the royal visitor and retired to her dressing room, all depression gone. She had forgotten her anxieties for the girls and her quarrels with Richard.

Sheridan was at the door, smiling, slightly intoxicated. He could not take his drink as his cronies could. He was neglecting the theatre less nowadays and not leaving so much of the business to Kemble. He had had great hopes of political fame when the Regency Bill was being discussed, for a Regent Prince of Wales would have been a great fillip to his fortunes. As it was that avenue was closed temporarily, and the concerns of the theatre were once more a matter of urgency to him.

'His Highness the Duke of Clarence wishes you to be presented.'

Dorothy grimaced. 'I was hoping for an early night.'

Sheridan laughed. 'His Highness is most excited. He's been babbling to me about your performance. Now he wants to babble to you.'

'I suppose I must.'

'My dear, are you mad? Of course you must. We have to treat our royal patrons royally.'

Sheridan was smiling secretly. It was obvious that the young Duke's admiration was great; and he had something of a reputation for his affairs with the ladies – not quite as great as that of the Prince of Wales or the Duke of York, but coming along very nicely. And a royal romance in the theatre was always good for business. Sheridan's thoughts went automatically to Mrs Perdita Robinson. Dorothy was more of a business woman, with her eye to the cash. She had to be with all the hangers-on whom she kept about her – the children and Ford, who would never make a fortune, he was sure. No, Dorothy would not be as foolish as Mrs Robinson.

But His Highness was waiting.

'I'll bring him to your dressing room,' said Sheridan. 'He's very impatient.'

He was standing in the doorway – smiling, young and rather charming with the unmistakable Hanoverian stamp on his features. Not as handsome as the Prince of Wales, not as tall as the Prince nor the Duke of York, but of medium height. There was a certain innocence about him which was appealing.

'Your Highness,' said Dorothy with a sweeping curtsey which she had perfected through many parts, 'this is such an honour.'

'No,' he said, advancing and taking her hand, 'the honour is all mine.'

'Your Highness is gracious as well as kind.'

'I was so enchanted by your performance. I never laughed so much as I did at your Pickle. Those tricks . . . reminded me of my days as midshipman. We were up to all sorts of pranks. I must tell you about them some time.'

Some time! So there were to be other times? Dorothy felt a twinge of alarm. These royal profligate brothers believed that actresses were fair game for a brief adventure. She would have to disillusion the young man quickly.

She guessed him to be about twenty-five; she herself was twenty-eight. But the brothers had always liked women older than themselves. Oh, yes, she would have to be very careful with Master Clarence and the best way of doing this was to disillusion him as soon as possible.

'May I sit down?'

'If there is anywhere suitable,' she replied.

He laughed at that. Sheridan said he would send for a chair for His Royal Highness.

'Don't worry, Sherry. This stool will suit me very well, providing it is near enough to Mrs Jordan.'

Sheridan laughed. 'If Your Highness will excuse me, I have theatre business.'

'Certainly, certainly.'

Sheridan went out and they were alone.

'I felt I had to tell you how much I enjoyed your performance.'

'Your Highness did that in your box. I was most gratified. It was a wonderful house and that was due to Your Highness's pleasure and appreciation.'

'No, no. It was the beauty and genius on the stage.'

He was eyeing her with pleasure.

'Stab me,' he said, 'you look no more than a schoolboy though I never saw such a pretty one.'

She smiled faintly and said: 'It is surprising for I am the mother of three children.'

'Then you are even more wonderful than I had thought possible.'

'Your Highness would be surprised if you saw me in my home in the heart of my family. Mr Ford and I are a very domesticated couple.'

'You are not only the most beautiful woman I ever saw, you are a good and virtuous one too.' His eyes were softly sentimental. 'You must know how I admire you.'

'I do not think I am worthy of so much of Your Highness's attention.'

'That's not true,' he said. 'It is I who am not worthy to ask it. I knew as soon as I saw you that you were no ordinary actress. I want you to know that as soon as you came on the stage I was aware of this.'

She laughed; it was the merry sort of laughter she used in her tomboy parts. It was difficult, she thought, for an actress to get away from her parts. One played them off stage as well as on and these little theatrical gestures had often proved very useful in a difficult situation.

'So kind,' she said languidly. 'So kind.'

'Tell me,' he said, 'where is your residence?'

'In Somerset Street, Portman Square. It is not really near enough to the theatre. But I have a tiny place in Richmond. The children are often there. I think the air at Richmond is particularly beneficial.'

'The air of Richmond is excellent,' he said delightedly. 'I have a place there. So we are near neighbours.'

'I am more often in London,' she reminded him. 'Except of course when I play in Richmond.'

'Yes, yes,' he cried delightedly. 'This is all so interesting.'

'I am surprised Your Highness finds it so.'

'But everything concerning you is of the utmost interest to me.'

'That surprises me even more; but you will find your interest is misplaced. I am only interesting – at least I hope I am – on the stage. Outside that I am an ordinary mother and . . . wife.'

'It is so . . . charming,' he said. 'And I long to know more of your interesting life. Could we have supper together?'

'Your Highness is so gracious it seems churlish to refuse but . . .'

'But?' There was no hint of arrogance, only bitter disappointment.

'My family is expecting me. I know Your Highness will understand.'

'You would be anxious if you came, you would be thinking of them?'

'I fear so – and no fit companion for such a gay young Prince as yourself.'

'I shall be far from gay without you.'

'So Your Highness excuses me.'

'My dear Mrs Jordan, my *dearest* Mrs Jordan, I want you to know right from the start that your will must always be mine.'

He had charm, she had to admit it. She had heard that the Prince of Wales was the same; when *he* pursued a woman he subdued all arrogance and was the humble lover. The young brother evidently took his cue from the elder; but even if the humility was assumed, it made for smooth communication.

'If Your Highness would excuse me . . . I must be leaving now.'

It was unheard of, she guessed – an actress to dismiss a Prince after refusing to sup with him. He must be furious beneath that charming grace. At least it would show him right from the start that she could not accept his advances. And she need not fear that he could harm her career. She was too firmly established with the theatre-going public for that.

'Perhaps you would allow me to take you home. My carriage is waiting.'

'Your Highness is insistent on showing me kindness which I do not deserve. Mr Ford is doubtless in the theatre having come to take me back to our home.'

He bowed. 'Then I can only thank you for allowing me these few moments of pleasure.'

He did escort her to the Green Room where she was pleased to see Richard was waiting.

The Duke bowed and she curtsied. Then he left her and she went to Richard who was watching in some surprise.

'We had the Duke of Clarence in the house tonight,' she said. 'He came back-stage to compliment me on my performance.'

'Good,' said Richard.

She went out with him to her carriage and she thought angrily: I played the virtuous matron to the young man tonight; and Richard could so easily give me the satisfaction of being exactly that in reality.

Was she a promiscuous woman? She most certainly was not! Yet she had three illegitimate children. One forced on her by Daly; the others the result of her union with Richard who had sworn he would marry her.

She felt angry with this man to whom she was ready to be the devoted wife, whom she had loved whole-heartedly and whom she now helped to keep in a comfortable if not completely luxurious manner.

And yet he would not do this one thing for her which he knew she craved.

He was cowardly and selfish; and for some reason her encounter with the Duke of Clarence had made this more apparent.

At least, she promised herself, she would have no more overtures from that young gentleman.

In that she was mistaken, for the next night the Duke was again in the balcony box and it was clear that he had come for the sole purpose of watching Mrs Jordan.

He came each night and afterwards back-stage. They talked as they had on the first occasion and then she would tell him that Mr Ford was waiting to take her home. He will soon be tired, she told herself. He is no doubt accustomed to easy conquests. But he did not get tired; he greeted her always with adoring looks and made no complaint that she refused to have supper with him. She could not be unaffected by his attentions and was aware that her performances were even more vivacious than before. She even wondered whether she was playing more to please the young man in the balcony box than the whole of the house.

One night, after the show, he said to her: 'Do you find me not persistent?'

'The most persistent playgoer in the house, I believe.'

'It is not in my playgoing that I am persistent but in my admiration for you.'

'I am honoured.'

'And yet you will not have supper with me?'

'Your Highness, I wish you to understand my position.'

'I do understand it. I have discovered everything I can about you. I know of your attachment to Mr Ford and that you have been faithful to him for many years.'

'Then you will understand that I am of the faithful kind.'

'I would not have it otherwise. I would be also.'

'I have proved my fidelity,' she said with a smile. 'I shall go on doing so.'

'I wish you would give me a chance to prove mine.'

'Your Highness must understand . . .'

He put his hand over hers almost reverently.

'I can remain silent no longer,' he said. 'I am in love with you. I have been ever since the first night I saw you. If it were possible I would ask you to marry me, but I cannot do this. I have to ask my father's consent and he would not give it.'

Dorothy could not help smiling ruefully. It was the same story;

but in his case it was true. As the son of the King he was in the line of succession to the throne and if the Prince of Wales and Duke of York did not marry and have children, this young Prince could be the King. It *was* different from Richard's case. She granted him that.

'But,' he went on, 'while I cannot marry without my father's consent I can refuse to marry at all – and that I should do. With us it would be a marriage . . . as my brother's with Mrs Fitzherbert. I want to live respectably . . . as married, and be faithful to one woman all my life; and now that I have met you, I know that there is only one woman who could fill that role in my life – and she is you.'

'You are charming,' she said, 'but I am committed.'

'Richard Ford is not your husband.'

'We shall marry in due course and two of my children are his.'

'We could have children, you and I.'

She shook her head. 'I shall never forget the honour you have done me, but I consider myself married to Mr Ford and as you have said: I am faithful.'

'I shall never stop loving you,' he assured her. 'And I shall not give up hope. Will you have supper with me tonight?'

'I must say no,' she said with a smile, 'for I must go home to my family.'

William called at Carlton House and George received him in the library with his windows looking out on to the gardens.

'What a lovely place you have here, George!' cried William, throwing himself into a chair and gazing disconsolately out at the gardens.

'It didn't grow of itself,' the Prince reminded him. 'It has taken me quite a time, the advice of architects and the skill of artists, but I flatter myself I now have a worthy dwelling here and at Brighton. You haven't been to the Pavilion lately, William. You must come. How is Clarence Lodge progressing?'

'Very well, but I did not come to talk about houses, George.'

'No? Then what?'

'Women. Or rather a woman.'

'Mrs Dorothy Jordan.'

'How did you know?'

The Prince laughed. 'My dear William, didn't you realize that we are watched by a thousand eyes; we are listened to by a thousand ears and a thousand pens a day are taken up to ridicule or libel us in some way. I have been reading snippets concerning a certain exalted young gentleman and Little Pickle. I couldn't help knowing to whom that referred. So you took my advice and went to Drury Lane and there you saw the delectable Mrs Jordan.'

'You think she is charming?' William smiled beatifically.

'I think she is utterly delightful.'

'I always said there wasn't a man in England with better taste than you.'

'I am inclined to agree with you. And I will say this, that if I were not so entirely and absolutely committed to my dearest love, my Maria, I would be your rival.'

'Oh, don't say that. I should be terrified. She would never be able to resist you as . . .'

'As she is resisting you?'

William nodded wretchedly. 'That's what I wanted to see you about. I want your advice. You see, George, she is a wonderful woman. She considers herself married to this man Ford. And there are children. Two of his and one of Daly's – some theatrical brute who forced his attentions on her. You see I have learned all about her. And because she considers herself married to Ford she is faithful to the fellow.'

'What sort of fellow?'

'A barrister of a sort . . . not very successful. Dorothy keeps the home going with her salary, so I hear.'

'She is a good woman,' said the Prince, 'and believe me, there is nothing so important to a man – and to Princes like ourselves – as a good woman. If I could have married Maria openly I should have been the happiest man on Earth.'

'But are you absolutely faithful to Maria?'

'That is not the point. I would never leave Maria. She knows that. I should always go back to her and although I might stray now and then – for as you know I find it very hard to resist a pretty woman and there are so many of them and all so charming in their different ways – it is Maria whom I regard as my wife. I could not live without Maria nor she without me.'

'That is how I feel about Dorothy, but I should always be faithful to her.'

'But then you see, my dear William, I am a married man of some standing whereas you are about to be married. That is the difference in our points of view.'

'About to be married?'

'Well, in a manner of speaking.'

'George, she refuses me. Every time she tells me that she will be faithful to Ford.'

The Prince smiled reminiscently. 'Maria would not consent for a whole year . . . and more. She went away . . . abroad . . . and I was faithful to her. I wrote the most heartrending letters.'

'I haven't your power with the pen.'

'Nor do you need to have because she is here.'

'But I can get no further with her.'

'I had to attempt suicide for Maria.'

'Do you think I should for Dorothy?'

'Not at this stage. But don't give up. Try to think what would appeal to her and you will win in the end. You have your royalty, and royalty is an asset which few women can resist. In addition you are young, tolerably handsome; you are not without charm; and I am sure you could please the lady more than this . . . what's his name?'

'Richard Ford.'

'More than he does. Persistence is your line. Never give up. Now, since I knew of your interest in the lady I have been considering her and I have found many little items in the gossip columns about her. Actors and actresses are considered fair game for gossip – just as we are. I have gathered that there are often stormy scenes between Mrs Jordan and Mr Ford. I cannot believe he can offer as much as you can.'

'But she is not to be *bought*.'

'Everyone is to be bought by one thing or another. It may be love; it may be money; it may be fame. But there will be something. She has children. She is a good mother. Now if I were in your place . . . But then I am not. Through my tribulations I have come to happiness with my Maria and our circumstances were different from yours.'

'George, you were saying . . . if you were in my place.'

'If I were in your place I should ask myself where she was most vulnerable. It is through her children. It is because she is anxious for the welfare of her children that she clings to Richard Ford.

They are his; he accepts them as his. Perhaps this is the reason. Suppose you were to agree to shoulder those financial burdens. Suppose there was some agreement . . . a real agreement drawn up by lawyers say . . . in which you undertook to provide for the children.'

'Could I do that, George?'

'Why not?'

'But I should need money.'

'Money!' said the Prince of Wales, wrinkling his charming nose in the manner which was famous. 'My dear William, Princes do not concern themselves with money.'

'You and Fred are in debt to thousands, I know. I couldn't be.'

'Why should you? Just by providing for these children? My dear William, you are the King's son. *My* brother. I think you forget that at times.'

'Perhaps I do. It was all those years at sea when I was treated like a common sailor.'

'How revolting!' said the Prince with another wrinkle. 'But don't worry about money. It always comes from somewhere. Continue to see her. Let her know that you are sympathetic, that you love children, that you are concerned for hers. Win her confidence and let her see that all Richard Ford can do for her you can do – for it seems that he does not marry her.'

'I think you are right, George. I knew you would be. How can I thank you.'

The ever-ready tears filled George's eyes. He regarded his brother with affection.

'There is one way you can thank me – by winning the delightful lady and being happy with her.'

Dorothy and Hester had put the children to bed. It was one of Dorothy's free nights.

'What are you playing tomorrow?' Hester asked.

'Beatrice in *The Panel*.'

'I suppose *he* will be there.'

'You mean the Duke of Clarence?'

'Whom else?' asked Hester.

'He is always there when I play.'

'You speak with some complacence.'

'Well, it is not a matter for congratulation when the King's son comes to the theatre every time one appears.'

'I wonder where it is going to end.'

'He will grow tired.'

Dorothy had seated herself in an arm-chair and Hester had taken the stool at her feet. It was a position they had occupied in those long ago days in Leeds when the whole family had looked to Dorothy's skill – as they still did. But in those days it had had to be proved; now it was.

'You will be sorry when he does.' Dorothy hesitated and Hester added quickly: 'You are growing fond of him.'

'He is charming and he never shows anger because I continually flout him. He always tries to please me . . . far more than Richard ever did.'

'Has Richard said anything?'

'About marriage?' Dorothy's lips curled. 'He has not changed his mind if that is what you mean.'

'The Duke could not marry you.'

Dorothy laughed aloud. 'Here I am between the two of them. One who swears he would if he could and one who could if he would. A fine state of affairs, Hester. And I think of the girls. What will happen when it is time for them to marry? Oh, Richard is cruel. After all, they are his children.'

'All but Fan.'

'And Fan . . . what will become of her? I worry about them, Hester. I know how Mamma felt about us. She longed for marriage and it was denied her. How odd that my position should be so like hers. She wanted marriage for me so much; and in the same way I want it for the girls. It will be a great hindrance to them if they cannot have their father's name. Look at me: Mrs Jordan. A name given to me by Wilkinson! A name to which I have no legal right! I don't want that for the girls. Surely Richard must understand this.'

'He does and I am sure he would marry you if . . .'

'If he were not afraid of his father! What sort of a man is he?'

'What does he say about the Duke's attention?'

'Nothing. Precisely nothing.'

'Perhaps it will force him to some action.'

'I find the situation quite humiliating. I might . . .'

Hester was alert, but Dorothy did not go on.

Hester could not help visualizing what changes might be in store for the household.

Dorothy's brother, George, called at Somerset Street with Maria Romanzini. George was doing fairly well and had had one or two minor parts; he was now a qualified actor but without pretensions to greatness, while Maria Romanzini's fine singing voice was her great asset and made up for her somewhat squat figure and unfashionable swarthiness.

Dorothy guessed what they had come to say as soon as she saw them and she could not suppress a pang of envy although she was pleased for George's sake.

'Dorothy,' said George solemnly, 'we have come to tell you something.'

Hester laughed and said, 'I don't think you need to, George.'

'So you've guessed,' cried Maria, opening her great dark eyes which with her plentiful rippling black hair was her only beauty.

'It's written all over your faces,' Dorothy told them. 'So you decided to marry at last.'

'At last!' cried George. 'It hasn't been so very long.'

Dorothy kissed the bride and groom and told them that she wished them every happiness, and Hester brought out a bottle of wine so that they could drink the health of the newly married pair.

'Neither of us is doing so badly now,' said Maria almost apologetically, 'so we thought that there was no sense in waiting.'

'We want a family,' added George.

'Of course,' agreed Dorothy. 'It's all very natural and God bless you both.'

They drank and talked excitedly of the future. George would not be playing small parts for ever; and Maria might go into opera. There was a growing popularity for opera, she believed. They would manage in any case.

They talked about parts and the theatre and how Drury Lane was doing better business than it had for years.

'It's your Pickle that brings them in, Dorothy,' said George. 'It must be wonderful to get on that stage and see that big audience and know that it has come to see you.'

Dorothy smiled. Yes, she thought, but there are more wonderful things. If Richard would marry her as George had married Maria that would give her more pleasure than all the full houses in the world.

Yet she was not in love with Richard any more. He had disappointed her. In the beginning she had felt as Maria and George so obviously did, but he had failed her. Solemnly he had promised. It was absurd to say that his father would object. He was not a boy any longer. They would do without his father's money and approval.

Maria was looking at her with envy. Maria, who was a good actress, a fine singer, but who knew she would never rival the talents – some called it genius – of Dorothy Jordan. Dorothy was at the top of her profession; a royal Duke was in love with her; she was the mother of three children. And the one thing she wanted – respectable marriage, security for the girls – was denied her, and by the man who was supposed to love her and could so easily have given her what she wanted.

Her brother's marriage had affected her deeply. It had made her consider the hopelessness of trusting Richard Ford.

The Duke was in her dressing room, humble, adoring as usual.

'You are too kind,' she said.

'I want you to know that the only thing I ask in life is to be kind to you.'

'I am grateful. How I wish that I could give what you ask.'

'You do wish it?' He was eager.

'I could not help but be moved by such devotion.'

'I shall go on waiting . . . and hoping. But I fear I weary you.'

He fancied he saw a faint alarm spring into her eyes. Did she think he was hinting that *he* was growing tired? Then although she would not give in she did not want him to give up trying. There was hope in that.

'When I leave every night I think of you going home to your children. How I should love to be there! I am so fond of children. They are little girls, I know. Little girls are particularly charming, although I confess I should like a son.'

She told him of the children, of her anxieties over Frances, who was inclined to be wayward; she was less alarmed for Dodee and Lucy.

'Dodee is named for you?'

She laughed. 'We could not have two Dorothys in the family.'

'I shall call you Dora,' he said. 'It shall be my name. You are Dorothy for the multitude of your admirers – you shall be Dora for this one.'

He told her about Petersham Lodge where he was now living. He should like to show it to her.

'The gardens are splendid. Are you fond of gardens? I should like your advice about the flower-beds I am having planted. It's large but not too large . . . and an ideal place for children to play in.'

What was he suggesting? That he would take her *and* the children?

'One day,' he said, 'I hope to meet them. I hope to make them fond of me.'

'So you really are fond of children?'

'I adore them. I should like to have a large family and give them the happiness which I missed as a boy. We had a very strict upbringing, you know. Our father was a martinet. He believed in discipline and many were the canings we had to endure – particularly George, my eldest brother. He was so proud and so determined to have his own way. You will love him as I do – he's the best fellow in the world.'

'I doubt,' she said, 'that the Prince of Wales would be eager to . . . to . . . accept me.'

'My dearest Dora, you are wrong. Absolutely wrong. I have talked to him of you. He thinks you are delightful. He longs to meet you. He bids me say that you would be very welcome in the family. He is interested too in your children. He says I should set your mind at rest concerning them . . .'

'The Prince of Wales said that?'

'Certainly he did. Did I not tell you he is the best brother in the world? Oh, my dear Dora, you have been reading these wicked scandals about him. Don't believe them.'

'I don't need to be warned against the scandalmongers. I have suffered enough from them myself. But you say that the Prince of Wales . . .'

'We discuss everything together and I have naturally spoken to him of what is the most important matter in my life. He says I should refuse to give in; that I should make you see that your children would lose nothing. He says that as you are a good woman this would be a matter of concern with you. He is right, is he not, my dear love?'

She was moved. He thought: George is right. Trust George. This is the way.

'I am deeply moved by the Prince's concern. I did not think . . . I did not know . . .'

He embraced her and for the first time she did not repulse him.

Oh, blessed George, who understood the ways of women as well as he did the cut of a coat and the arranging of a neckcloth!

She withdrew herself and said: 'But I must go home now.'

He did not seek to detain her. The first battle was won – thanks to George, Prince of Wales.

'George has married Maria Romanzini,' said Dorothy sitting at her dressing table and combing her long beautiful hair.

'I guessed he would,' said Richard, yawning from his pillows.

'He was determined that there should be no gossip about their relationship.'

'Who would gossip about them?'

'Certainly it would not be the same as it is about me.'

'I'm tired,' said Richard. 'Come to bed.'

She stood up and threw the hairbrush on to the dressing table.

'I'm tired too,' she said, 'tired of waiting for you to fulfil your promises.'

'Oh, Dorothy, not tonight.'

'Why not? Tonight is as good as any time. I want a plain answer. Are we to be married or not?'

'Of course we are.'

'When – on Judgement Day?'

'In due course.'

'The same thing,' she said. 'Listen, Richard, I have had enough. I want a plain answer to my question: Are you going to marry me or not?'

'I will marry you as soon as I can conveniently do so.'

'And what of the children – two of them illegitimate and all because you have failed to keep your promises.'

'They will be all right. I'll see that they're all right.'

'That is a promise. As reliable, I daresay, as that you gave me when you said we'd be married.'

'I suppose,' he said, 'it is His High and Mightiness who has put this notion into your head? You've been ten times more difficult to live with since you started your friendship with royalty.'

'The Duke of Clarence is in love with me.'

'And promised to marry you?'

'Don't be absurd. You know that's impossible.'

'And you accept that?'

'I have accepted nothing from him because I consider myself married to you in every way except by signing my name on marriage lines.'

'Well, of what importance is that? You and I are together for the rest of our lives. In spite of your wearying insistence on that ceremony and your rages because of it, I still want to go on as we have been.'

'Well, I don't. I want that ceremony – for the sake of my children. And if you won't give it . . .'

'You will go to His Highness?'

'I have not said that. I am uncertain what I shall do. But I will not go on in this way. I want a definite answer. Will you marry me, Richard Ford? Will you marry the mother of your two little girls or not?'

'I'm tired,' he said. 'We'll talk of it later.'

She lay at one end of the bed, he at the other. He was soon asleep, but she was not.

She knew that the moment of decision was at hand; and she thought of the advantages of living with a royal Duke. If he gave security to the children, if there need not be this continual preoccupation with money . . . how restful that would be. She would not be married, of course, but then she was not married to Richard – and she was beginning to wonder whether she ever would be.

William felt more hopeful than he had since Dorothy had refused to have supper with him. The Prince of Wales was right. Persistence was what was needed. He had to show her that he was determined, that he loved her completely, that he would do anything in the world for her except marry her and even that he would do if it were in his power. The Prince of Wales was on his side; and the Prince of Wales would one day be King. If she came to him she need have no more anxieties; she wanted a peaceful happy life with the knowledge that her children were secure.

He would give her that. He could give her so much more than Richard Ford could; and when he looked at that insignificant fellow he felt angry that he should have been accepted while he, Royal William, was not.

He met him one night back-stage and gave him a look of contempt. Ford did not seem to mind. Of course he did not. Dorothy shared his home – or he shared hers, for it was her money that paid for it – and she regarded him as her husband.

The Duke was jealous of the insignificant barrister.

He went to find Sheridan.

'I say, Sherry,' he said, 'I don't like that fellow prowling about back-stage.'

'What fellow has dared offend Your Highness?' Sheridan wanted to know.

'That fellow Ford.'

Sheridan nodded. 'He's always had the run of the theatre. His father once had a very large holding of the shares.'

'His father?'

'Yes, rich old devil. Very careful with his money. Retired on a fortune and living in the country.'

'And one day this fellow will inherit, I daresay.'

'I daresay, if he behaves himself and keeps in Papa's good books.'

'Well, stop him going back-stage, will you, Sherry?'

'I humbly crave Your Highness's pardon, but I have no power to stop him.'

'You're the manager of this theatre.'

'There are rules in the theatre, Sir, which have to be regarded. Tradition, they call it. Mr Ford has as much right to go back-stage as Your Royal Highness has. You see, he is . . . attached to one of our leading actresses. I can tell you,' added Sheridan slyly, 'that he comes to see Mrs Jordan. Perhaps if the lady liked him not to . . .'

William turned away, roused from his usual good humour.

Well, it would not go on indefinitely. He was not going to be kept from his desire by a second-rate barrister.

*

Dorothy was well aware that her affairs were moving towards a climax. So much depended on Richard. He had only to offer to marry her and she would accept . . . even at this stage. He had humiliated her by his constant refusals, but her main concern was the children. She wanted above everything else to legitimize them; and if she could not do that she wanted to make their futures secure.

She talked it over with Hester continually; and she knew that Hester believed in her heart that she should abandon Richard and accept the Duke. Richard had proved beyond doubt that he was a weakling. It was true that love-affairs with royal princes were of notoriously short duration. And yet there was something innocent about William. There was no doubt that he was sincere at this time. He believed his love would endure and because he did so wholeheartedly he had begun to make her think so too.

She was not in love with him. Sometimes she wondered whether she was capable of being in love again. Daly had disgusted her, had made her shrink from men until she met Richard, and Richard had disillusioned her. Between the brute strength of Daly and the weak indecision of Ford, she had lost the power to love passionately and exclusively.

They had between them turned her into a calculating woman; but at least she was not calculating for herself. Always her concern was for the children.

Then came the news that she was to play at Richmond.

She would stay in the little Richmond house with Hester and the children; Richard would stay in London. This, she believed, would give her the opportunity she needed to come to her decision.

William was delighted that she was to play at the Richmond Theatre. He immediately went down to Petersham Lodge, a delightful villa which he had recently bought from Lord Camelford. His father had helped him to do this, having had twelve thousand guineas assigned to him to be used for this purpose. 'Must have a proper residence,' said the King. 'Eh? What? Good air. Pleasant. Not far from Kew.'

Residence at Petersham Lodge enabled him to be in attendance at the theatre on Richmond Green every night Dorothy played.

The theatre was full but not so much to see the play as to watch Mrs Jordan and the Duke of Clarence, for his pursuit of her was now common knowledge.

Every day there was a piece in one of the papers about the progress of the Duke's courtship. Has she submitted or has she not? It was the great question of the hour; and all were certain that it could only be a matter of time.

'Little Pickle has been besieged at Richmond by a certain exalted youth whom at present she has managed to keep at bay.'

ran one paragraph.

'The Duke of Clarence is in Richmond. He comes to compliment Mrs Jordan. His Highness has for some time been enamoured of Little Pickle's playful frolics.'

'We hear from Richmond [said one of the London papers] that an illustrious youth has at length passed the Ford, yet is not likely to be pickled by a legal process.'

Dorothy read the papers and discussed them with Hester.

'At least,' consoled Hester, 'it is bringing matters to a head between you and Richard.'

'I don't think he cares, Hester. He is too lazy to care. I'm sure if I went off with the Duke tomorrow he would let me go without a regret.'

'He is so . . . timid,' agreed Hester.

Meanwhile William was growing bold, being certain of eventual success. The Prince of Wales had suggested that he give a fête for the fashionable world of Richmond to which he should ask Mrs Jordan and show her quite clearly that she was the guest of honour.

'Capital idea,' cried William, and set about making preparations.

Soon there was another announcement in the paper.

'The Duke of Clarence is to give a fête to all the Fashion. Little Pickle is to be of the party.'

Dorothy was alarmed. To attend a fête openly was to some extent to commit herself. She was growing more and more fond of the persuasive young man; and yet more than anything she wanted marriage with Richard, and the girls when they grew up to have a father, their own father.

A way out of her dilemma came to her in the form of an invitation to play in two benefits at the Haymarket.

Sheridan had long decided that Drury Lane was an antiquated building and not suited to modern theatrical requirements. He had planned to have it rebuilt and operations were started that summer; he had taken a temporary lease of the Haymarket Theatre while his new Drury Lane was being constructed; and it was in the Haymarket that Dorothy was to play.

When the Duke called at the theatre and told her of his plans for the fête, she said: 'I am sure it will be a great success.'

'If you are there it will be for me,' he replied ardently.

She opened her eyes wide and acted surprised, for he had not formally invited her but had simply taken it for granted that she would be present.

'I did not understand that I was to be a guest.'

'My dearest Dora, there could be no other reason for having it.'

'But . . . I shall not be here. I am playing at the Haymarket.'

His disappointment was so acute that she felt almost inclined to cancel the benefit. She must be growing fond of him.

'But the fête was for *you*.'

'How very generous you are to me! But you see, I have my career.'

'You won't need a career, when . . .'

'I have a family to support. I shall always need a career.'

'*I* am going to take care of your family.'

She closed her eyes. In that moment she was near to surrender. But she must be cautious. Men had treated her badly; she must not make another mistake.

She opened her eyes and smiled at him. 'Oh, I have learned to rely on myself.'

'There shall be settlements on the children,' he said. 'It shall all be arranged. They shall go short of nothing. They shall have dowries when they marry.'

She turned away. It might be the answer, she thought. But not yet. She must wait. She must talk it over with Hester. She must give Richard another chance. Perhaps when he knew she was on the point of leaving him he would relent.

'But you understand,' she said, 'that I cannot attend your fête.'

'There will be no fête,' he said. 'It is all cancelled.'

'Just because I have to be at the Haymarket?'

'And because I have to be there, too.'

'You, but . . .'

'Where you are,' he told her, 'I have to be. That is how it is going to be from now on.'

Richard came driving over to Richmond. When she saw him she gave a cry of pleasure for she thought he had been reading of the Duke's constant attendance at the theatre; but it was nothing of the sort. She might have known it. Richard had come to tell her that there was a letter from Wilkinson which was urgent and this doubtless meant an offer to play at Leeds or York.

'Wilkinson should pay you well,' said Richard. 'I shouldn't accept less than Sarah Siddons did when she was up there. I hear Elizabeth Farren had the same, too.'

Richard was very good at making arrangements for her to bring in the money; he could draw up her contracts and insist tenaciously on the best terms. Oh yes, Richard was very good at getting her to work for more and more money so that they could all live in comfort.

She was unhappy. She felt that she had treated William badly by making him cancel the fête; and yet if she could get away from him for a while she believed that she would be able to make her plans.

She read Tate Wilkinson's letter.

'Yes,' she said, 'it's a good offer. One hundred and fifty pounds for a week's work.'

Richard's eyes sparkled and she gave him a contemptuous look. But she was glad of the opportunity to get away. When I come back, she thought, I shall know what I have to do.

The northern tour was the most unhappy she had ever had.

The strain of the Richmond tour and the emotional turmoil of trying to come to a decision had exhausted her. She was in no mood for work.

Moreover, it was several years since she had played in York and the audience was inclined to be critical of the smart London actress she had become. They were not going to applaud an actress just because she was popular in London. In fact they were going to be hypercritical for that very reason.

On the opening night she was to play Peggy in *The Country Girl* and Nell in *The Devil to Pay*, but she felt disinclined to play the two.

'I can't do both,' she told Wilkinson, 'I feel too ill. They'll have to be content with Peggy.'

'They won't like it. They've been promised *The Devil to Pay*; and this is not a London audience, you know. *The Country Girl* doesn't always go well up here. They're inclined to think it immoral.'

She laughed.

'You've forgotten them,' said Wilkinson. 'But they'll love Nell.'

But she insisted and as a result the theatre was half empty and the audience unresponsive. She was fully aware of the sniggers of provincial actresses who demanded of each other, 'Who does she think she is? It's only luck that she's where she is. First she got round Daly, then Richard Ford whose father almost owned Drury Lane and now the Duke of Clarence. We know how she "got her place".'

There was nothing worse than playing to a listless house; she would almost have preferred a hostile one. When the applause for Peggy was luke-warm and she came off-stage in a fury she found Wilkinson waiting for her.

'If you'd go on and sing for them, it might be different.'

'Why should I? I'm tired. They're not worth it, anyway.'

Wilkinson took her hand and said, 'Do you remember when you all came to me in Leeds . . . you and your family, and I gave you the chance you wanted?'

'I'll never forget it.'

'Do something for me now then. Go on and sing.'

So because she could not resist such an appeal she went back and sang some of her songs; and as Wilkinson had expected the response was immediate.

They may not have cared for her Peggy but they loved her songs. Wilkinson, smiling in the wings, heard the thunder of the applause and the cries for more.

So the situation was saved.

But York was indifferent to her acting; she was affected by this and was glad when the week was over.

John Kemble was to play the following week in York and it was arranged that during that time Dorothy should take his place in the company which John's brother Stephen was bringing to Newcastle.

Dorothy left York for Newcastle feeling depressed, but when she arrived at Newcastle it was to run into further trouble.

Stephen Kemble's company was not there. Richard immediately busied himself in making inquiries and a cool note was received from Stephen Kemble to the effect that as his brother John had not consulted him about substituting Dorothy Jordan for himself, he had made other plans for the company which he could not break. He could not in the circumstances bring them to Newcastle.

To think that she could be so insulted infuriated her.

What were they trying to do? To tell her that in spite of her success on the London stage they cared nothing for her?

'We shall leave at once for London,' she told Richard.

'There's nothing else to be done.'

'I have never been so humiliated in my life. It's deliberate, I know. John Kemble knew exactly what would happen when he asked me to substitute for him.'

'They're jealous,' said Richard. 'It's obvious.'

So back to London, her problems unsolved.

When they arrived at Somerset Street she had made up her mind that she would give Richard one last chance.

'Richard,' she said, 'tell me honestly, do you intend to marry me?'

'You are tired out with this disastrous tour,' he replied.

She laughed at him. 'That tells me all I want to know,' she retorted.

'But I don't understand.'

'You will,' she told him. 'I am going to bed now. I am too tired to argue with you.'

And she lay in bed thinking: I will let the Duke of Clarence know that if he will provide for the children I will become his mistress.

Prince's mistress

William lost no time in bringing his schemes to fruition. Dorothy had given in. Now they could begin to plan their lives together. He wrote to the Prince of Wales:

'Allow me now to return you my sincere thanks for your friendship and kindness on this occasion, and believe me I shall ever be grateful for your advice. You may safely congratulate me on my success. They never were married. I have all proofs requisite and even legal ones. I have as quiet, full and ample possession of the house in Somerset Street as if I had been an inhabitant for ten years. No letter could possibly contain the particulars: Suspend then judgement until we meet. On your way to Windsor come here Sunday . . . I am sure I am too well acquainted with your friendship to doubt for a moment you will, my dear brother, behave kindly to a woman who possesses so deservedly my heart and confidence . . .'

He was so happy. He brought her to Petersham Lodge. She should never have another care in the world, he promised her. Everything – yes, he meant everything – was taken care of.

He was a most appealing lover. Neither of the others had had such concern for her. He could be both passionate and tender and in every way played the husband. He acted always as though theirs was to be a permanent relationship. He did not seek the so-called gay life, he told her. Did she? His idea of bliss was to live at home, graciously it was true, in the utmost comfort, but in a home.

She told him that they were of one mind. She had been his mistress only a few days when she began to love him. It was impossible not to do so, she told Hester. He was charming and modest, but there was an inherent dignity about him – the dignity of royalty, and it was different from anything she had ever known before.

She continued to play at the theatre; he was there every time she performed, waiting to take her home in his carriage. But, he said, they must settle the tiresome legal side for he knew how she felt about the dear children.

He met the children. Fanny, on her best behaviour, tried to charm him and he was ready to be charmed by anything that belonged to Dorothy. Little Dodee and Lucy were naturally charming and he knelt on the floor and played with them, having brought little models of ships for them which he sailed in a tub of water and shouted orders as they pushed the boats around to the excited pleasure of the children.

Later in the little house at Richmond Dorothy talked over the future with Hester.

'Well?' she asked.

'He's charming,' agreed Hester. 'I couldn't believe we were entertaining the King's own son.'

'He makes you forget it, doesn't he?'

'Oh, Dorothy, the things that happen to you! Everyone is talking about it.'

'Let them. They must talk about something.'

'What about the children? You won't want them with you.'

'But I do want them with me.'

'You can't embark on a love-affair with a royal Duke and a ready-made family.'

'Why ever not?'

'It is not fair to him. No, Dorothy, you want this to last, don't you? It would be awful if you've given up Richard just for an affair of a few months.'

'Hester! You think it will be like that?'

'Not if you're wise. He doesn't believe it possible. Nor must you. You must keep it like that. But he will want your full attention. You have your work. Are you going to have the family at your heels, too? No. I have a suggestion to make. I'll stay here and look after the children. You go with him to Petersham Lodge or wherever he wants you to. Start afresh. It's the best way. And then if you have children . . . his children . . . they'll naturally be with you both; but you can't expect him to take on Fan, Dodee and Lucy. It's too big a strain. Believe me, Dorothy.'

'Richard might claim them.'

'Not Richard. He'll be glad to be rid of the responsibility.'

'Oh, yes,' she said bitterly, 'Richard is always glad to be rid of responsibility.'

'Think about it. Leave the children with me.'

'I know you've looked after them so much in the past, but you have played occasionally.'

'I was never much of an actress. I'll give that up to look after

193

the children. You can pay me for it. He's going to treat you very handsomely, I suppose.'

'I'll talk it over . . . with him. I'm sure he will do what I wish.'

'He's different from Richard,' said Hester with a smile.

Dorothy's lips tightened for a while, then she smiled.

'Very different,' she said. 'I think I am going to be very fond of him.'

William agreed that it was an excellent idea for Hester to have charge of the children.

'And I know you won't object to my seeing them very often.'

'We will see them together.'

'You are so good to me,' she said earnestly.

Hanoverian eyes filled with ever-ready Hanoverian tears. She was to learn that almost all the royal brothers were excessively sentimental. While they were in love they loved whole-heartedly and were not afraid to say so; it was the great secret of their charm and they were loved for it almost as much as for their royalty.

She was to have an allowance of a thousand pounds a year from him.

'It is too much,' she declared.

'Good God,' he cried. 'It should be more.'

Then she would sign over six hundred pounds of her own for the present support of the girls under Hester's care, and she would immediately transfer every penny she owned into a trust for their future.

'It shall be as you say. I'll get my lawyer William Adam to look into these things. Then it will all be signed and sealed and you'll have not the slightest cause for anxiety.'

'I only hope,' she said, 'that I shall be worthy of you.'

He was so happy, he told her, and all that happiness was centred in her.

It was perfect bliss for him; and for her? She had never in her life felt so secure before. She had never been treated with such generosity and courtesy; she had never been so loved; Richard had said he loved her; but Richard was not a demonstrative man. To be loved by a Prince was exhilarating, exciting and filled her with joy. For the first time in her life she did not have to worry about money; she felt free, without responsibilities; it was astonishing how lighthearted she could be.

For a while at any rate she would give herself up to romantic love, for that was what the Duke was leading her to believe this was.

'I'm happy,' she told Hester, 'really happy . . . for the first time in my life.'

The press was delighted. The royal brothers gave them constant cause for pleasure. If it was not one knee deep in scandal, it was one of the others. The liaison of the Prince of Wales with Mrs Fitzherbert would always be a *cause célèbre* for the all-important question 'Did he or did he not marry her?' had never been satisfactorily answered. But that did not mean there was not a good deal of attention to spare for Clarence and his actress.

'The comic syren of Old Drury has abandoned her quondam mate for the superior attractions of a Royal Lodge to which Little Pickle was long invited.'

was one comment. Another was:

'A favourite comic actress, if old Goody Rumour can be trusted, had thought proper to put herself under the protection of a distinguished sailor who dropped anchor before her last summer at Richmond.'

Let them write of her. What did it matter? They had always applauded her or ridiculed her. An actress had to accept this. The famous were out in the arena to be shot at. She had long ago learned that.

In response to his brother's request the Prince of Wales called at Petersham Lodge on his way to Windsor. Dorothy was nervous. It was one thing to play on the stage before this gorgeous personage; to receive him as a guest in the house of which she had recently become the mistress was quite another matter.

But she was soon put at ease.

'George, I want to present my dearest Dora to you.'

He bowed – the famous bow which was said to be the most elegant in the world; his eyes were alight with admiration.

'You are even more beautiful than William has been telling me,' he said.

'Your Highness . . .'

'Oh, come, we are brother and sister now. William would wish it. Is that not so, brother?'

William, beaming love and good nature, was, he said, the happiest man in the world to see that the two whom he loved beyond any others had taken to each other on sight.

'Not,' he declared, 'that I conceived it possible to be otherwise. Two such good and charming people! It was George who put me on the right lines, you know, Dora. But for him I should not have won you yet.'

'Then we must both be grateful to His Highness.'

'You flatter me . . . both of you,' said the Prince lightly. 'But I forgive you because it does me so much good to see two people as much in love as you two are. It is exactly so with my own dear Maria, whom you shall meet.'

The Prince's eyes filled with sentimental tears and Dorothy was surprised because she had heard that he kept Mrs Crouch whom she knew slightly, for the woman was an actress who had played at Drury Lane and she had boasted of having a place in Berkeley Square and some £5,000 of jewellery which he had given her. Rumour had it that Mrs Fitzherbert was furious because of the liaison and it was only when she threatened to leave him that he had broken it off. There were even now rumours about Lady Jersey who seemed to attract him in the oddest way. She fascinated yet repelled; she was an extremely sensuous woman, wicked, some say, and as different from Maria Fitzherbert as it was possible for two women to be. It was true that the Prince wanted to keep Mrs Fitzherbert; but he was by no means faithful to her as he was implying now. But he did so with such a show of sincerity that it seemed he must believe it to be true.

Considering all she had heard of him Dorothy felt uneasy, fearful that William who seemed to have such a high opinion of his brother might take his cue from him.

But now the Prince was determined to be charming; he was completely at ease; he talked to Dorothy of the theatre and plays and playwrights of which he was very knowledgeable.

He told her how he admired her voice and begged her to sing for him; and she amused them both by singing the song which she often sang after playing *The Spoiled Child* with its line:

'What girl but loves the merry Tar?'

196

The Prince sang it with her. His voice was good, quite strong and very pleasant. He was rather proud of it and said that as she had sung for him he would sing his favourite sentimental ballad for her.

It was *Sweet Lass of Richmond Hill* – a tribute to the absent Maria.

Then they all sang together and Dorothy forgot the high rank of her visitor, for indeed he behaved like an affectionate brother-in-law.

When he rose to go he expressed his regrets that he must do so.

'I have to go to Windsor,' he explained to Dorothy. 'You can imagine nothing more dull.'

And he spoke as though she were indeed a member of the family.

When he had gone, William seized her hands and cried: 'Well, what do you think of him?'

'He is charming . . . even more so than I had expected.'

'He is the best brother in the world. And he is fond of you already. I told him he must be or I should never forgive him.'

'It is good to see such affection between brothers,' she said; and she thought: he is affectionate by nature. I believe I am a very lucky woman.

But the lampoonists and the cartoonists were not going to allow Dorothy to enjoy her happiness if they could prevent her doing so. There was scarcely a day when some piece about her did not appear in the papers. Behind her back her fellow-actors and actresses called her 'The Duchess'.

There was veiled criticism of her desertion of her children. One of the morning papers came out with the statement:

'To be mistress of the King's son Little Pickle thinks respectable, and so away go all tender ties to children.'

This was something which upset Dorothy more than all the coarse allusions to her life with the Duke.

She took the paper to Hester when she went to see the children and asked if she had seen it.

Hester had.

'What if the children were to? I know Dodee and Lucy are not old enough, but what if Fanny should?'

'Fan is bad enough now,' said Hester. 'She talks of you and the Duke constantly and is piqued because you have not taken her to live with you. You know Fan's temper.'

'That's what I fear – that they should see these comments . . . and heaven knows they are everywhere.'

'What of Richard?'

'I haven't seen him.'

'He has taken it all very calmly.'

'I never thought he would do anything else. I do believe he is glad to be rid of me.'

'I think he was sorry to see you go, Doll, but he's relieved that someone else is going to look after his children.'

'I'm well rid of him. I often wondered how I could ever have wanted to marry him.'

'It was not Richard you wanted, Doll. It was marriage.'

'Mamma instilled that into us, didn't she? And now I think it is something I shall never have.' She sighed. 'But I'm not going to allow this to be said. Richard will have to do something. He will have to make it publicly known that I have *not* deserted our children, that I am the one who is caring for them and that he is the one who has freed himself from his responsibilities.'

'How can you make him do this?'

'I am sure William can.'

William did.

He went to his lawyer William Adam and pointed out how the papers were abusing Mrs Jordan. He wished Adam to watch the papers and if anything was said which was actionable to be ready to take it on his behalf.

Adam's advice was that Richard Ford should write to Mrs Jordan a letter in which he set out fully all that she was doing for their children. He would go and see Ford and advise him that it was a moral duty to do this without delay.

Ford agreed and Dorothy received a letter from him.

It ran as follows:

October 14th, 1791

To Mrs Jordan.

'Lest any insinuations should be circulated to the prejudice of Mrs Jordan in respect to her having behaved improperly towards her children in regard to pecuniary matters, I hereby declare that her conduct has in that particular been as laudable, generous and as like a fond mother as in her present situation it was possible to be. She has indeed given up for their use every sixpence she has been able to save from her theatrical profits. She has also engaged herself to allow them £550 a year and at the same time settle £50 a year upon her sister. 'Tis but bare justice to her for me to assert this as the father of these children.

Richard Ford.'

She showed the letter to William who took it and gave it to William Adam. Adam promptly sent it to the *Morning Post* who published it.

When Richard Ford saw it he was astonished; he had written for Dorothy alone and was embarrassed for people to know that it was Dorothy who had taken on the responsibility of arranging their children's future. But it was now clear to all that Dorothy, while becoming the Duke's mistress, had by no means neglected her children, and it was said that had Ford married her – and after the respectable life they had led together he owed it to her – she would have remained faithful to him.

Opinion was veering round. Ford was going to be the scapegoat now.

He took action at once and left the country for France – scarcely the most peaceful of retreats at this time, with the monarchy dangerously tottering and where no person who did not wear ragged breeches and red cap was safe to go abroad.

Once Richard had gone the public lost interest in him. The famous actress and the King's son were far more amusing than Richard Ford.

The lampoons began to appear thick and fast. There was never a day which did not bring an allusion to them.

There were pictures of Dorothy and Mrs Fitzherbert together. 'The pot,' ran the caption, 'calling the kettle black.'

The favourite story was that of the King sending for his third son and when he arrived at Windsor saying to him: 'I hear you keep an actress.'

'Yes, Sir,' William is reputed to have replied.

'Eh, what, how much do you give her, eh?'

'A thousand a year, Sir.'

'A thousand, eh, what? That's too much. Five hundred . . . quite enough . . . quite enough.'

The story went on that the Duke wrote to Mrs Jordan telling her what the King had said, to which she replied by tearing off the bottom of a play-bill on which was written:

'No money returned after the rise of the curtain.'

People pretended to believe the story; it was just one of the many coarse comments which were made about the lovers.

Domestic bliss

This was the happiest time of her life. She often wondered what her mother would have said, had she been alive to see her now. Would she have been satisfied? Perhaps. The Duke behaved in every way like a husband. He *wanted* domestic happiness; he was most content when they were alone together; and there was nothing he enjoyed more than to sit with her in the evenings and talk to her about his life at sea.

'I missed it you know, Dora,' he told her. 'I was badgering my father to let me go back to sea. But now that I have you it's changed. Rather a life ashore with my Dora than at sea, I can say to myself. Of course I could take you with me. Oh, no. Too many dangers. A storm blows up, men are swept overboard . . . Stab me, I couldn't let my Dora face that. I'd die of fright.'

He liked to hear her stories of the theatre.

'Always attracted me,' he said. 'I reckon that if I'd not been born the son of my father I'd have been an actor. The footlights . . . the rise of the curtain . . . and that moment when the audience are quiet . . . waiting. It never fails to thrill me. And I'll never forget that moment when you came swaggering on the stage in your breeches . . . Sir Harry Wildair. I was yours from that moment. No one else in the world would ever do after that. I was determined, you know. I wasn't going to stop pestering you until you said yes.'

He smiled at her tenderly – the lover, the husband, the protector.

Oh, God, she thought, I'm happy. Let this last for ever.

'There's no one to touch you on the stage, Dora. George said so. And George is the connoisseur of the drama . . . literature . . . oh, of everything. He says they go to see Siddons because they think they should; but they go to see you because they want to. You can trust George to put his finger right on the point.'

'The King and the Queen favour Mrs Siddons, I believe,' she reminded him.

That made him laugh. 'Now you're one of the family I shan't mince my words about *them*. My father is less like a king than any king has ever been. Now, George when the time comes will be a king every inch of him. But my father . . . If you could know what life at Kew is like. The little farm there . . . and all the fuss he makes about how the butter is made and the dairy run. Oh, God, he's like a petty landowner. He's carried away by little cares about where a chair is and how much fat you eat or how much exercise you take, and he's prudish in the extreme.'

'Then what does he think of us?'

'Even he sees it's inevitable. He spoke kindly of you. He knows we can't marry and he sees that since we can't, this is the next best thing. If George hadn't been the Prince of Wales he would have thought it all right for him to settle down with Mrs Fitz. But you see George will one day be King. As for the rest of us . . . there are so many of us that we need not marry.'

'And if you had to . . .'

He was at her side, taking her hands, kissing them. 'There is only one woman on Earth I would marry – and I consider myself married to her already. Dora, my lovely Dora, if it had been worth anything I should have gone through the ceremony with you, we'd have taken our vows before a priest. But it would not count. My brother Augustus's case proved that. It would be called no marriage in the eyes of the State. That is the only reason why we have not gone through our ceremony.'

Dorothy said: 'I do understand these things – and I don't know how I can deserve your love and devotion to me.'

'It's simple,' he replied. 'Go on loving me. It's all I ask. It's all I command.'

So it was a perfect union, she thought – at least as near perfect as that between an actress and a Prince could be.

Yes, even her mother would be satisfied.

There was a feeling of expectancy among the Drury Lane Company.

Every ambitious young actress who thought she had a comic genius to compare with Dorothy Jordan's but merely lacked opportunity and good luck was surreptitiously studying the Jordan parts and in many a little room in dingy lodgings near the theatre rehearsals of Wildair and Little Pickle went on.

The mistress of the King's son could not possibly continue with her career as an actress.

She was referred to ironically as 'Her Grace'.

'Has Her Grace been in the theatre today?'

'Oh, yes, she came with His Grace. They have been in Mr Sheridan's office. If you meet her you must curtsey right down to the ground because you have to stoop lower for a jumped-up Duchess than a high-born one.'

'I saw Her Grace's carriage yesterday.'

'Her Grace's tailor is in the theatre. He wants to measure Her Grace for Little Pickle's breeches.'

They were envious of her happiness with a Duke and at the same time delighted that there was a possibility of stepping into her shoes.

Sheridan shook his head over them. It was no use their clamouring to him to play Little Pickle. There was only one Little Pickle in the world and that was Dorothy Jordan.

He was not at all sure that he was going to lose his actress; he fervently hoped not.

He called at Petersham Lodge to see her when he knew the Duke was not there. He kissed her hand and congratulated her on her good looks.

'This life suits you, my dear,' he said.

She bade him be seated and sent for refreshment. He watched her in his inimicable way and she secretly wished that she could have complimented *him* on his healthy looks. There were darker shadows under his eyes and in spite of his rakish appearance she knew he was concerned. He was constantly on the edge of financial disaster and the rebuilding of Drury Lane with its delays and set-backs was giving him many a disturbed night – when he returned home from his carousals.

'I have been wondering what your plans are . . . theatrically speaking, of course.'

'I have not yet discussed them with the Duke.'

'An actress like you, Dorothy, has a duty to the public.'

'Don't you think I have done my duty now, Sherry?'

He was Sherry to William and the Prince of Wales and so to her now. He was aware of the change in her manner towards him. It amused him and reminded him of her elevation. He was a friend now as well as her theatrical manager. All to the good, he thought.

'To your public yes, but what of yourself and the girls?'

'It is all taken care of.'

'There is the future.'

'What do you mean? It is the future I'm thinking of.'

'How can one plan for the future? How can one know what will happen? I know you, Dorothy. Improvident spendthrift that I am, I know you – and all the better because you are so completely different from myself. You can command high salaries in the theatre . . . none higher, even our Sarah. Are you going to throw it away? Why don't you go on working? If you don't want the money yourself, you have a family. There are those three girls.'

She was thoughtful.

'I talked in this way to another young actress. Mrs Robinson. I said to her: "Now the public wants you. It will pay to see you *now* . . . and go on paying, no matter what happens. But if you stay away for a year or so . . . five years perhaps . . . ten years . . . there is no coming back. Or perhaps I should say that it is rarely one can come back." The public will go on being faithful as long as an actress remains faithful to it. You understand me.'

Of course Sherry was a cynic. He did not believe her romance with the Duke would last. Of course he would not. What a romantic young man he must have been when he eloped with the lovely Miss Linley and no doubt swore eternal devotion to her. They had believed he was going to be the greatest playwright of all time. He had written *The Rivals* and *The School for Scandal* among other plays . . . and then he had become a theatre manager, a politician and the friend of Princes. He had thrown everything away for the sake of gay company; he had drunk too much, spent too much, had too many passing affairs with women. So that he had besmirched his marriage, not developed his genius and lived in constant fear of the bailiffs. It was natural that Sherry should take a cynical view of life.

And yet . . . she thought of the money she had been earning; she thought of special Benefit nights. The Duke was the kindest and most gracious of men, but like all the royal brothers he had little understanding of money. He would give her all he had, but he was too generous, not business-like enough. She would have to be the one who looked to the girls' futures. She wanted them all to make good marriages and she would have to make up for their illegitimacy with big dowries.

'I believe you are right,' she told Sheridan. 'I will talk it over with the Duke.'

Sheridan left smiling to himself. Something told him that all the second-rate actresses who were busy studying Jordan roles were going to be disappointed because he was not going to lose his biggest draw after all.

The Duke made no secret of his devotion. When *The Country Girl* was put on at the Haymarket with another actress in Dorothy's place, the lovers occupied a box together and their tender exchanges during the performance were noticed. In fact the majority of the audience took no notice of what was happening on the stage; their entire attention being focused on the box.

They went out together, walking arm in arm through the streets like any devoted couple.

In the press the Duke was called 'Pickle's infatuated lover'. He sent for Romney to paint her. The artist had already done a portrait of her as *The Country Girl* but the Duke wanted a new one of her.

The excitement and pleasure of those few months were marred only by the envy of her fellow-actors and the frequent unjust comments in the press. But Dorothy decided to ignore them. They could not touch her now.

She had broached the matter of her continuing to play at the theatre and William considered it gravely.

'And what do you wish, my love?'

'I think I should do it. It may not be possible to resume later if I want to. And I would like to make sure of a good dowry for all three girls.'

'You know you can leave these matters to me.'

'You are the most generous man in the world, but you are a Prince and must live like a Prince. I have heard talk of the debts of the Prince of Wales.'

'My God,' cried William, whose life at sea had addicted him to strong oaths which he attempted to curb in Dorothy's presence. 'His debts are astronomical. Why, it was because of them that there was all that trouble in the House when Fox denied he was married to Mrs Fitz. and she nearly left him because of it. Yes, George is in debt . . . up to his ears now.'

'And you too?' asked Dorothy.

'Well, to tell you the truth, my love, I haven't given the matter much thought.'

That made her smile. 'You have answered for me. I will go on acting providing you have no objection.'

'I want to do everything you wish.'

'You mean you will leave this decision to me?'

He took her hand and kissed it – a courteous gallant gesture. How different from brutal Daly, from indifferent Richard Ford.

'Then I shall go on,' she said. 'And I shall try and save money so that in case you should be financially embarrassed when the girls come of age they will be sure of their dowry.'

'You are a wonderful woman,' said William.

So to Sheridan's delight Dorothy agreed to appear again. The crowds packed the Haymarket to see her, and on the first night of her appearance after the brief lapse during which the papers were filled with accounts of her love-affair with the Duke, so great was the crowd trying to get into the Haymarket that a man was trampled to death and one woman was badly injured.

The Duke was present every night she played. He went backstage and sat in her dressing room. He watched her all the time she was playing and scowled at any man who deigned to glance at her.

The public was amused. He seemed mightily pleased to see her perform. Was it because he was anxious to share in the profits?

205

Everyone knew that the royal brothers were in perpetual debt.

The latest rhyme ran:

'As Jordan's high and mighty squire
Her playhouse profits deigns to skim;
Some folks audaciously enquire:
If he keeps her or she keeps him.'

Dorothy did not care; nor did William; they told themselves that they must expect these spiteful shafts. People were jealous because they had found what everyone was seeking: perfect happiness.

When Dorothy called to see the children she found Hester in a state of excitement.

'Richard has been here,' she said. 'He says that he does not see why he should be kept from his own children.'

'So he is back from France,' replied Dorothy. 'And having done nothing for his children he has now decided he wants to see them.'

'Dodee at least. Lucy has forgotten him. But Dodee hasn't.'

'And you are suggesting that I should allow them to visit him?'

'He is their father,' Hester reminded her.

'I am sure the Duke would not hear of it.'

'But the Duke is not their father.'

Dorothy flew into a rage.

'Listen, Hester, Richard had every opportunity of giving my girls a name. This he refused to do in spite of all his promises to me in the first place. I should never have agreed to live with him if he had not promised to marry me. And he failed me. He lied to me and betrayed me. I have finished with him. I am happy now and I am determined to remain so. I am not going to allow him to poison me in the minds of my children.'

'He would never do that, Doll. He feels kindly towards you in spite of the fact that you have left him.'

'You speak reproachfully.'

'Oh, no. I wouldn't presume to do that. But you did regard him as your husband and you have left him for the Duke.'

'Oh, not you too, Hester! Isn't it enough with the press! They are my children. I am providing for them. I want nothing more of Richard Ford.'

'I think you are being a little hard.'

'Hard! You don't know what you're talking about.'

'I do. I am bringing up the children.'

'Well, Hester, if you feel so critical of me and of the Duke perhaps I had better find someone else to look after them.'

Hester looked stunned and Dorothy's anger subsided as quickly as it had arisen.

'Oh, Hester, I didn't mean that. Don't let us be at cross purposes for heaven's sake. The future of Dodee and Lucy . . . and Fan, means so much to me. I have to give them a good start in life. I want them to have all the advantages that we didn't have.'

'We had our mother with us all the time.'

'They will have you and me, too. Both of us, Hester – to love them and care for them.'

Hester said somewhat mollified: 'It is such a complicated household. One never knows what is going to happen next.'

'Oh, why didn't Richard stay in France. It would have been so much more comfortable if he had.'

'I don't think it would have been very comfortable for him. He said that the country is in a fearful state of revolution. No one is safe. He thinks that soon they'll murder the King and Queen.'

Dorothy shuddered. 'God forbid that such things should ever happen here.'

She was afraid suddenly. She thought of the King and Queen of France with their family being subjected to humiliation; she could well picture the mob roused to anger. She had seen a hostile audience which was not pleased with the play that was being presented to it; a pale shadow of course of what was going on across the Channel; but she knew the fury of mob violence. And to think that what was happening to the French royal family could happen to the English one. She was part of that family now. It was strange but it was true. She could not bear to think of William in danger, of contemplating losing him.

She was loving a man as she had thought she never would; she would not have believed that she had so much affection to give. Everything must go right now. Nothing must spoil this. She had waited so long for happiness and suffered so much, but if she could remain as happy as she was now everything would have been worth while. Richard Ford must not be allowed to disturb her.

'So he has come back,' she mused, 'and discovered that he has some feeling for his children after all. Well, Mr Richard Ford has made his discovery just a little too late; and I suspect that he has made it now that he knows he will not be expected to support them.'

Hester lifted her shoulders.

'I only want to do as you wish,' she said. 'And I do think of the welfare of the children.'

'I know you do, my dear Hester. But all will be well with them. I merely want them brought up in quiet, peace and respectability; and I want to work hard so that when they come of age I can give them a good dowry. Dodee and Lucy are babies yet, but Fan is not so young.' A shadow passed across Dorothy's face. 'And how has Fan been behaving?'

'She has her tantrums.'

'I'll go and see her now. I expect she knows I'm here.'

'Oh, yes,' said Hester, 'there is very little Madam doesn't know.'

Fanny was just a little like her father and when Dorothy caught that likeness as she did now and then, it always depressed her faintly; it repelled her; she could not help but remember him, with his lecherous face close to hers, demanding submission.

For the very reason that Fanny reminded her of him made her feel that she must be especially kind to her eldest daughter.

In the nursery she found Fanny dressed up in one of her own Harry Wildair costumes. It was quite a good fit for Fanny was almost as tall as her mother.

She was acting for the little girls who were seated on stools watching her.

She stopped when Dorothy entered.

'So you are playing Wildair, eh?'

'Oh, yes, Mamma. I wish I had a proper audience . . . not just silly Dodee and sillier Lucy.'

'My darlings!' Dorothy knelt and embraced three-year-old Dodee and two-year-old Lucy.

'Mamma going to stay?' Dodee wanted to know.

'Yes, Mamma is going to stay for a while.'

'Then you'll go away,' said Fanny. 'I wish I could come and live with you. Shall I?'

'One day, perhaps.'

'*Now!*' pouted Fanny; and Dodee took up the cry.

'Now I am here,' said Dorothy. 'And I will play Little Pickle for you, shall I, and you shall all be my audience?'

Playing Pickle was the greatest fun and even Fanny lost her sullen looks, for Dorothy thought up all sorts of ridiculous tricks Pickle could play in the nursery and soon the children were shrieking with the same rollicking laughter that she was accustomed to hearing in the theatre.

'When I'm big,' announced Fanny, 'I'm going to be an actress.'

'Me too,' added Dodee.

'Perhaps you will, my darling.'

'I'm going to marry a Duke,' said Fanny.

And Dorothy asked herself: What do they hear?

Hester came and took the younger children away and when Fanny was left alone with her she took her mother's hand, examined the diamond which the Duke of Clarence had recently put there and said that she wanted to live in a grander house than this and instead of having Aunt Hester to look after her she wanted to be with her mother and the Duke.

'My dear, you couldn't do that. You must live here and I will come and see you sometimes.'

'Where is our father? He came here the other day. He wanted to see Dodee and Lucy . . . not me.'

'Well, you see, darling, they are his and you have another father as I told you long ago.'

'I know he was your first husband, and Dodee's and Lucy's papa was your second.'

Dorothy did not answer. There were going to be complications as the children grew up. If Richard had married her it would have been so much easier. Not that she regretted that now that she was in love with William and had her new life. She could face the complications.

She decided then that the children should no longer be known as Ford; they should all be Jordans.

Fanny said good-bye to her with great reluctance; she was petulant and inclined to sulk. They would have trouble with Fanny if they were not careful. When she reached Petersham Lodge she found the Duke at home eagerly awaiting her.

He embraced her with fervour as though they had been separated for a month. He was always afraid, he said, when she was out of his sight.

He had been to see Adam again, he told her. 'An anonoymous book is being sold in which you are mentioned . . . scandalously.'

'In what connection?' she asked faintly.

'In connection with the Irish manager Daly. It's supposed to be written by Elizabeth Billington, the singer. She declares she knows nothing of it and is taking proceedings against the publishers. I have authorized Adam to buy up all the copies he can find and if necessary I shall take action against the publisher.'

'You are so careful of me,' she said.

'My darling, it is my pleasure to protect you from these . . . these villains.'

'I wish they would stop persecuting me,' she said. 'I wish they would let me be happy.'

'I'll not let them stop that.'

She felt tired and tears came to her eyes.

'Foolish of me,' she said, 'but I am not used to being so tenderly cared for.'

Life had formed itself into a pattern – pleasant and comfortable. Those people who had predicted an early end to the love-affair between Mrs Jordan and the Duke of Clarence now sneered at them because they seemed to have settled into a cosy domesticity.

As William said to her often: he needed no one else but her. To be with other people meant that they could not talk together, be close to each other. Now he preferred his own fireside.

She was working at the theatre and he must be there to watch her play and to bring her home. When he saw Richard Ford at the theatre he was angry and once again tried to prevent his going back-stage. He was afraid that the fellow, having lost his prize, would do anything to regain it; and if he were to offer Dorothy marriage, which was the only thing he himself could not give her that Ford could, he was afraid her desire for respectability and her sense of duty towards her children might make her accept.

He told her of this fear and she laughed at him.

'Nothing would make me go back to him,' she declared. 'Even if I was not in love with the best of men, I would never go back to Richard Ford.'

That contented him.

His brothers smiled at him indulgently. Frederick, Duke of York, was married unhappily. He and his wife did not live together and in fact could not bear the sight of each other. Frederick had his mistresses and the Duchess of York her animals. Her place at Oatlands, William told Dorothy, was more like a zoo than a ducal manor.

As for the Prince of Wales, he was going through a difficult time emotionally. But then he invariably was; but this time there was serious trouble, for he had become so enamoured of Lady Jersey that there was real danger of a breach with Mrs Fitzherbert.

William discussed the matter with Dorothy, expressing his concern.

'Poor George, he loves Maria. I have always known that.'

'But if he loved her surely he would want to be faithful to her?'

'He is under some sort of spell. I don't know what that Jersey woman has but George cannot resist her. Maria is a proud woman.'

Dorothy conceded that she was. She believed that Mrs Fitzherbert had not been as friendly towards her as the brothers had hoped because she feared they might be compared. Mrs Fitzherbert was very anxious that no one should regard her as the mistress of the Prince of Wales, although if she were his wife it was enough to abolish George's hopes of the crown.

The affairs of the Prince of Wales and the Duke of York shifted the spotlight a little from William and Dorothy, and this increased their happiness.

But for his new experience of settling down as a husband William realized that he would have been restive. After a life at sea it was not easy to reconcile oneself to staying on land. He had hoped for a position in the Admiralty now that he had been made a Rear-Admiral but the Admiralty did not want him. He had a sense of duty which his brothers lacked, and was in fact more like his father than any of them.

He was often seen in the House of Lords and decided to take up the cause of the slave trade and work against the abolitionists. His speeches were long and verbose and when he rose to his feet a groan would go up throughout the chamber. He lacked the eloquence of the Prince of Wales, and his support of the slave trade brought him a certain amount of odium from those with more humane feelings.

'I have seen the plantations,' he had pointed out. 'As a sailor I have visited these far off places. In Jamaica and America I have seen the system at work. To abolish the slave traffic will disrupt the plantations and will mean higher prices for certain commodities here.'

On and on and on with members promising themselves that when the Duke of Clarence was present they would make a point of slipping out.

William was no orator, no politician; and his understanding of state matters was not great. But because he wanted to be the family man, he must work. He was denied a place in his own profession, so he must do something.

He did not want to spend his time at the races, building extravagant residences like Carlton House and the Pavilion; he did not want to give fêtes and balls. He wanted to live quietly and peacefully like a respectable country gentleman with one woman – as his father would have wished to do. But his father had his interest in the farm at Kew; he made his buttons; he had his duties as King of England, and much as he liked the homely life at Kew he must appear at St James's when duty demanded that he should.

William, however – the third son – who, it was hardly likely would ever reach the throne, had had his career as a sailor brought to an end. He must do something. Therefore he decided to make his voice heard in the House of Lords.

Dorothy listened to his opinions, heard him rehearse his speeches. She knew the effect she was having on him. The gay young sailor he had been was being transformed into the uxorious husband; even his language had changed and the rather coarse oaths which he had picked up at sea were gradually disappearing. William was indeed settling down. And what could be more desirable than this cosy domesticity? Even George, the elegant adventurous Prince of Wales, had told William he envied him his peaceful existence.

William and Dorothy grew happier every day, and then Dorothy became pregnant.

During that spring Dorothy continued to play; her benefit was one of the most successful not only of hers but in the history of the theatre. She received £540 for one night's performance and Sarah Siddons had only received £490.

William was delighted at her ability to earn money. When he remembered the pay he had received as a captain it seemed strange that his little Dorothy could earn so much in one single night.

'And deserve every penny!' he declared when he went back-stage to collect her.

There would be comments about this benefit in the press, he knew. The scribblers would sneer at him and suggest that Dorothy was keeping him. It rankled. He was constantly wanting to sue them. George had said he should try and forget it. It was the penalty of royalty; and if he had seen some of the lampoons on himself and Maria he would think these concerning himself and Dorothy very mild.

Then the irritation was forgotten, for Dorothy was ill. She had been working hard at the theatre and the pregnancy was proving a difficult one. Five months after conception she had a miscarriage.

William was in despair. He sent for the doctors. She would recover, he was told. She needed rest and care – that was all.

He was at her bedside throughout the day and night.

'You must not fret, my darling. There will be more children . . . but only if you wish it.'

Dorothy was sad. She had wanted so much to have his child. And so she should, he assured her. But she must get really well first.

'Oh, William,' she said, 'I feared I was going to die and I wondered what would become of the little girls.'

'My darling, haven't I given you my word to care for them? Besides, you have taken care of that.'

'I worry about them, William. But this little one would have been yours, too. That would have been different.'

'Don't talk of such depressing things. You are going to get well. I am planning to take you to the Isle of Wight. The sea air is so beneficial. George swears by it. And I daresay you would like to see the children. I thought so. So I have told your sister to bring them here.'

They came with Hester. Dodee and Lucy happy to see their mother, Fanny taking in the details of Petersham Lodge.

'Oh, Mamma,' she whispered, 'it's so grand. When I grow up I want to live in a house like this.'

Fanny's eyes hid secrets. What does she hear? wondered Dorothy. How could one shield children from the world? There was the gossip of servants, those pernicious paragraphs in newspapers.

But she must not fret. She must get well. William expected it of her.

George and Maria Bland came to see her and brought their twins – two healthy children; but Dorothy sensed Maria's impatience with George. She was so much more successful than he was in the theatre and this was making a rift between them.

She was anxious. Since her mother's death she had felt herself to be the guardian of the family and she could see trouble ahead for George.

Happiness was so elusive. How grateful she should be for William!

They did not go to the Isle of Wight for the Duchess of Cleveland offered them her house in Margate and they went there instead.

It was so pleasant to be by the sea and to live in the large and comfortable mansion as a simple country gentleman and his wife.

William was happy. His great task was to look after Dorothy; to make sure that she did not exert herself; it was, she believed, the happiest time of her life.

And when they returned to Petersham Lodge she did not take on any new engagements for a while. It was so comforting to be away from the competitive atmosphere of the theatre and while they remained out of the public eye the comments on them ceased to appear.

The Prince of Wales was the great target of attack on account of his debts, his love-affairs and the extravagant profligate life he led.

Dorothy was again pregnant and in the January of the year 1794 she gave birth to a boy.

He was big and healthy; and William was delighted with him. He carried him about the apartment insisting on calling every-

214

one's attention to his perfections; Dorothy from her bed smiled on them both. It was a picture of conjugal bliss.

They called the child George – after his uncle the Prince of Wales – and he was known from then on as George FitzClarence.

It was so pleasant to be simply a mother; and that was all she was for the following months. Her life was filled by William and the children, for she was soon driving over with young George to see the household at Richmond.

The three girls loved their half-brother, though Fanny was inclined to be jealous of him.

Why should he, silly little thing, be allowed to live in Petersham Lodge while they had to live in this little house with Aunt Hester?

Because Petersham House belonged to his father.

'Oh, why wasn't the Duke my father?'

How she wished that had been so. How happy she would be now if they were all William's children. But life was not as simple as that. There was so much to be suffered before one reached happiness.

Sheridan called. He was in trouble. Drury Lane had not yet been rebuilt and he could not use the Haymarket this season because it was already leased to the Opera Company.

'It's the devil of a business,' said Sheridan.

Dorothy was sure it was; but she could not greatly concern herself. Little George was proving to be a robust child, imperious and demanding. She adored him. So did William.

'The New Drury Lane will be opening in April, I hope,' said Sheridan. 'Then, I trust you will do us the honour of coming back.'

'The Duke insists that I take a *long* rest,' she told him.

He grimaced and thought: We shall have to come along with some very attractive offers.

'We shall doubtless open with an oratorio or something solemn,' he told her, 'and I hope for the attendance of Their Majesties.'

'And the Prince of Wales?'

'We don't want a riot on the first night.'

'Is he so unpopular?'

'They've turned against him. That's the mob all over. There

was a time when he couldn't put that charming nose of his into the streets without cries of Hurrah. It's a different matter now. And then his Mamma and Papa are rather cross with him, you know. There's always the big quarrel in progress. It's handed down from generation to generation in the family.'

'A pity,' said Dorothy, and thinking of her beautiful little George she wondered how any mother could possibly quarrel with her son.

'A great pity! There's some anxiety because of the behaviour of our neighbours.'

'Our neighbours?'

'Across the Channel. Since they've cut off the heads of their King and Queen I don't think those of ours rest any happier on their pillows.'

'It couldn't happen here.'

'It happened there.'

'But our King is so . . . so . . . He's such a *good* man.'

'Farmer George the Button Maker! There's a certain tolerant contempt for him, it's true. And Charlotte. They never liked her, though she has done no harm – except provide them with thirteen mouths to feed. I'm sorry, Dorothy. You're one of the family now. William behaves with decorum since you've set up house with him. But George . . .'

'The Prince of Wales, you mean.'

'I'm sorry. I spoke disrespectfully. His unpopularity is a little . . . alarming at this time. Mobs are inclined to follow an example without knowing why. Debts! Building! Balls! Banquets! These were the grievances that were brought against the Queen of France. But I am depressing you, Dorothy; and you looked so charming when I arrived. So much the happy young matron. Don't give what I'm saying another thought. I'll just say there's one thing which could make everyone happier . . . everyone except George himself, perhaps. And that's if he married.'

'Married . . . but isn't he . . . ?'

'Maria! Well, he is and he isn't. In the eyes of the Church but not those of the State. It's the State that counts, Dorothy. If he takes a wife the people will be pleased. They prefer wedding celebrations to riots, I do believe. Then there will be children. And the people love children. They loved George when he was a

216

child. Besides, he should marry. He's no longer so young. He has to get an heir.'

'I'm sorry for Mrs Fitzherbert.'

'She's been sorry for herself for a long time. You should be pleased if he married. Has it occurred to you that if he didn't and if Fred doesn't get children – and he's not living with his Duchess, you know – your William might become a very important member of his illustrious family.'

She looked alarmed and he was quick to soothe her.

'Don't worry. It won't happen. I'll whisper a secret. Marriage is in the air . . . for George.'

'But what if he refuses?'

'He won't. He'll be caught in the net. It's closing round him. Debts, Dorothy. They can govern a man's life as certainly as any king ever did. I speak from experience . . . of the most bitter nature. George will be pressed into marriage by a gang of creditors. You see. Only not a word to William. It would distress him. I talk too much.'

'You're letting your imagination run on, Sherry.'

'A habit of mine. It used to be a profitable one. Which brings me back to the theatre. It's going to be sad at the Drury Lane without its comic genius. But you'll come back to us.'

'You're very prophetic today, Sherry.'

'In my profession it's a useful gift,' he told her.

She thought of what he had said after he had left. William . . . third in succession to the throne. The thought alarmed her. The Prince of Wales would be expected to marry; the people expected it. And if he refused and Frederick had no children . . .

William. No! No one ever thought that William could one day be King of England. And she refused to.

It was so much more comfortable to forget.

She called for her carriage to be brought to the door. It was a plain yellow one and no one would guess when they saw it who rode inside. She had made an appointment to call on her milliner, Miss Tuting, in St James's Street. She would take little George with her. The airing would be good for him and the girls in the shop would enjoy seeing him.

It was a lovely day. Sunshine brightened the buildings and the trees seemed greener than they did during other years. It was foolish to be depressed by Sheridan's gossip. William was the third son. If he were the second, there might be cause for alarm; but George and Frederick made a comfortable barrier between William and the State.

The carriage stopped before the milliner's shop and Miss Tuting herself came out to welcome the important customer.

'Mrs Jordan, this is a great pleasure. The girls have been excited all the morning. Your new hat is ready. It looks wonderful. And you have the baby. The girls will be beside themselves . . .'

And so into the shop where everyone was twittering with excitement. The news was carried to the work rooms. 'Mrs Jordan is here. She has brought the baby!'

Miss Tuting went to the foot of the stairs which led down into the basement. 'Girls, you may come up two by two to see Master George. I rejoice to say he is quite the bonniest child I ever saw.'

So Dorothy sat holding the imperious George who expressed lively interest in those who came to look and worship.

Miss Tuting's right-hand, a middle-aged woman, was allowed to hold him while Dorothy tried on the hats which were being made for her and everyone turned their attention from young George to her.

'I think the blue ribbon more becoming than the pink,' twittered Miss Tuting. 'And the roses . . . and the veiling. What does Mrs Jordan think? The young rascal is getting impatient for his Mamma. Oh, but how pretty she will look in her new hat, Master George. You will like that, eh? And the velvet . . . this silver colour gauze is most fetching.'

It was a pleasant morning. She was completely at home.

In an awe-inspiring silence she changed Master George's linen in the shop and he, more comfortable, chuckled with glee as he was carried back to his yellow carriage by one of her grooms and carefully handed to his Mamma.

Riding home Dorothy felt that her life was pleasantly domesticated. She refused to consider Sheridan's suggestions. Poor Sherry, he was perhaps a little envious. He had made such a failure of his life; while she had at last come to real success, which was not to be found in the applause of an audience, the glitter of jewels, the luxury of riches, but in a home – the shared love of a husband and wife and the family which between them they would raise.

A royal marriage

The Prince of Wales came to Petersham Lodge to talk over the disaster which was about to overtake him.

He sat in his chair, elegant even when he sprawled, one highly polished boot crossing another; his buckskin breeches moulded to his well-shaped though fleshy thighs; his green cloth coat of the most fashionable cut; his neckcloth a masterpiece of ingenuity to hide the swelling in his neck, the symptom of a distressing complaint which must always be hidden by the neckcloth which he had specially designed for the purpose.

He liked to talk to them and lately had become a frequent visitor to Petersham Lodge, where William and Dorothy were living in retirement because Dorothy was pregnant again.

The Prince was saying: 'They have caught me. I have to marry. It is the condition they demand if my creditors are to be satisfied.'

'How much do you owe?' asked William.

The Prince waved his hand. 'My dear William, I never keep account of figures. They bore me. Suffice it to say that I owe such a sum that these tiresome people will wait no longer for the settlement of their accounts and refuse to supply me and moreover will take action against me. What can I do? I have an intimation from our father of what is expected of me.'

'Marriage?' asked William.

'You say it complacently. Oh, I am not surprised. You have made a very comfortable home for yourself with our dearest Dora. How fortunate you are!'

'I always thought that you and Maria ...'

'Yes, yes. I was happy for a while. But Maria has the most devilish temper, you know. I did not want to leave her. It was she who made the decision. I have always regretted it. But I could not be ... commanded. You understand?'

William understood perfectly.

'My dear Dora,' said the Prince, 'I am going to ask you to sing for me presently. In the meantime you must forgive me if I weary you with the repetition of my so tiresome affairs.'

'I am only sorry that Your Highness is grieved.'

'Pray come and sit near me. It comforts me to see you. Oh,

William, how fortunate you are! There is nothing like a happy home. And you have young George. How is the rascal? And why is he not here to see his uncle?'

'I will send for him,' said Dorothy.

'Not just yet, my dear. I want to talk of this disaster which is about to overtake me.'

'Perhaps it will prove a blessing,' said Dorothy.

'What a comforter you are! Is this how she comforts you, William?'

'She is a great comfort to me,' said William solemnly.

'I have a choice of two – Germans both. The King's niece or the Queen's.'

'And which are you choosing?' asked William.

'You don't think I would give our mother the gratification of choosing hers?'

'So it is to be the Princess Caroline of Brunswick,' said Dorothy.

The Prince lightly touched her hand. 'How delightful of you to concern yourself with my wretched affairs. Yes, the Brunswick one. What does it matter? One German *hausfrau* is very like another.'

'I am sure Your Highness will be agreeably surprised.'

'It would be churlish of me not to be comforted when you make such efforts to please me. What about our little song now. And I will join with you.'

Dorothy said it would delight her to sing for and with His Royal Highness.

She was sorry for him – Prince of Wales though he was. She was sorry for anyone who did not enjoy the domestic bliss she had discovered.

What should she sing? There was one song which would certainly not do. No *Sweet Lass* today. She was sure the ballad would reduce the poor Prince to regretful tears.

On a bleak March day Dorothy's second son was born. Like his brother George he was young and lusty. He was named Henry; he was exactly a year and two months younger than his brother George, and his parents were delighted with him.

'We now have our little family,' said William fondly. 'Two sons.

I declare I'm a proud man. I wonder if I'm going to have as many children as my father had.'

It was so pleasant at Petersham Lodge, looking after her boys. Dorothy felt she could be happy living like this for the rest of her life. She found she was rather pleased to have an excuse to rest from the stage for a while, although of course when she was recovered she must go back.

These little FitzClarences would be well cared for, she had no doubt. They had royal blood in their veins; but she must not let her delight in them blind her to the fact that she had daughters.

Little Henry's birth was scarcely noticed in the press. It had another matter with which to occupy itself. The coming marriage of the heir to the throne.

Events were moving too quickly for the Prince of Wales. Once he had agreed to marry preparations went ahead and by April Caroline of Brunswick had arrived in England.

Lady Jersey – the mischievous and malicious mistress of the Prince of Wales – went to Greenwich to meet her. She had learned that Caroline was much less likely to please the Prince than his mother's niece, Louise of Mecklenburg-Strelitz, and it was for this reason that Lady Jersey had done everything possible to persuade the Prince to take Caroline for she did not want him to have a wife for whom he might feel some fondness and who might lessen the influence of his mistress. She was delighted therefore when she saw Caroline, who was surely like no other Princess. Her head was too big; her neck was too short, she was plump and without grace; her complexion was florid and her teeth bad. She was overdressed, laughed too loudly and was none too clean. Lady Jersey felt hilariously gay when she considered the effect this female would have on the fastidious Prince of Wales. She had even taken the precaution of having a dress made for Caroline which would be as unbecoming as possible and persuaded the Princess to change into it for her meeting with the Prince of Wales. Caroline was foolish enough to do this but she rebelled against the hideous white turban which Lady Jersey had brought for her.

The meeting between the Prince and his future bride had been disastrous. He had taken one look at her and called for brandy to help him sustain the shock.

After that he was beside himself with indecision. He had promised to marry because Mr Pitt and the King said he must. The Princess of Brunswick had been brought over for him; she was already married to him by proxy; and the proper ceremony was to take place shortly.

He came to Petersham House. He paced up and down beating his forehead; he threw himself on to a couch and wept. Everything else must be set aside that they might talk of this terrible disaster which had befallen him.

'I will not marry her,' he cried, 'and if I do not they will not pay my debts. Was ever a Prince in such a dilemma for . . . money?'

They were sorry for him; they wept with him. Dorothy was learning to weep whenever tears seemed the only polite response. Her years of acting enabled her to play a part as well as the Prince of Wales whom she recognized at once as an equal in the art.

'My life is in ruins. I would die rather than marry this . . . creature. She is offensive to my sensibilities . . . to my heart, to my mind and . . . nose.'

'Dear me,' said William, 'Is she as bad as that?'

'Every bit as bad, brother. Every bit.'

What could they do to comfort him? There was nothing except to listen sympathetically when he told them that he knew he would never be able to go through with the ceremony.

And when he had left them, they congratulated themselves yet again on the felicity of their own position.

Throughout the royal households bets were being taken. Just as after the scandal of Mrs Fitzherbert it was a gamble on 'Are they married or are they not?' now it was a matter of 'Will he or won't he?'

On the eve of his wedding the Prince of Wales begged William to come to him.

'Poor George,' said William to Dorothy. 'How sorry I am for him!'

'Do you think he will go through with it?'

'I really don't know. But there'll be such trouble if he doesn't.'

'And if he does,' sighed Dorothy.

'I wish you could come with me. You always cheer him.'

'I doubt whether anyone would cheer him tonight. I daresay he wants to confide in you, William. Perhaps he is going to refuse at this late date.'

'He daren't. His debts are so great that if I told you the figure you wouldn't grasp it. He must get Parliament to pay his debts and their condition is . . . marriage.'

Dorothy shivered. 'I can imagine nothing worse than being forced into such a relationship.'

She thought of Daly who had forced her, but in a different way. She would never forget that man; he was like a menacing shadow over her life even now.

'I shall convey your affection to him and tell him of your sympathy,' said William. 'I will tell him that you wanted to accompany me and if you had been well enough would have insisted.'

So while William drove to Carlton House Dorothy remained in the nursery to play with little George and to gaze with enraptured admiration on eleven-day-old Henry.

The Prince received his brother with mournful pleasure.

'I knew you'd come, William.'

'Of course. United we stand.'

'And did you find it so hard to tear yourself away from that family of yours?'

'My dear George, the family wanted to come and would have done . . . all four of them if Dora had been well enough.'

'Thank her for me, William. Tell her I appreciate her goodness.'

'She is most unhappy for you, George. She says she knows exactly what it is like to be forced into such a relationship. That man Daly, you know.'

'Poor girl, poor girl! William, I don't know which way to turn. I really don't think I can marry that woman.'

'My poor, poor brother.'

'She is completely repulsive to me.'

'Then refuse.'

'Is it possible?'

'Why not? If you refuse to take her they can't force you to.'

'They can't exactly force me into marriage but they can force me into bankruptcy.'

'Well, Parliament will pay up. Don't they always.'

'That fellow Pitt insists on marriage. He was always against me.'

'I know.'

'And our father supports him; our mother supports him; although she is going to hate this woman as much as I do.'

'Perhaps you should have taken our mother's niece instead.'

The Prince sat down on a couch and dramatically buried his face in his hands. 'I should have done anything . . . anything rather than have been brought to this pass.'

'You have till tomorrow to make up your mind.'

'What can I do, William? What can I do?'

'You can either marry her or refuse to do so,' said William as though he was offering a bright idea.

George looked at him with veiled exasperation. Really, William was very like their father at times. He was not very bright. But one must not be annoyed for he was a good and loyal brother.

'I cannot think what to do. Oh, William, how I wish that I might talk this over with Maria.'

'With Maria Fitzherbert!' cried William aghast. 'Why, she is the last one . . . considering she thinks you're already married to *her*.'

'My dear William . . . it is precisely because they are trying to marry me to this . . . this . . . creature that I want to turn to Maria.'

'But you couldn't let it be known that you are married to Maria, George. There might be a revolution.'

'Do you think the people care enough about me for that, William?'

'No,' said William. 'But they care about the monarchy and they'd never have a Catholic Queen.'

George sighed. 'Oh, what trouble I am in! To think of marrying that woman, going to bed with her. I feel sick at the very thought.'

'Once she's pregnant you can leave her alone.'

The Prince shuddered. 'You express yourself somewhat crudely, William. It's that seafaring existence of yours. But I know you feel for me just the same.'

'I'd do anything for you, George. If I had the money to pay your debts . . .'

'I know. Money! It's such a sordid affair. Why should I be pestered like this on account of . . . debts.'

The Prince began to weep silently but effectively, and William sat disconsolately watching him.

'George, if there is anything I can do . . .'

'There is, William. I sent for you that you might do this for me. This evening I went to Maria's house. I drove past. I expected she would make some sign. She must have been aware of me. Someone in her household would have known I was there. I drove past and back again and I repeated that. Then I did it again. I gave her every opportunity.'

'And what happened?'

'Nothing, William, precisely nothing.'

'And if she had come to the window; if she had called you in . . . what then?'

'Why then, William, I believe I should have said I would not go through with this marriage. I would have asked Maria to take me back. I thought she would have had some sympathy. I thought she would have come to the window.'

'Perhaps it is because you are still with Lady Jersey.'

'It's different, William, Maria should know that. Imagine yourself fascinated by some unusual woman – a wild and passionate creature who is different from all others, whom you do not exactly love but who fascinates you, so that you could not turn your back on her. Surely Dorothy would understand.'

William wrinkled his brows.

'Wouldn't she?' demanded the Prince.

'It could never happen. Dora and I are like a man and his wife.'

'By God,' cried the Prince. 'So was I with Maria. But Frances Jersey . . . she was irresistible. Surely Maria could have understood that. But she was too virtuous, my Maria. It meant that she had little understanding. But what a devil of a temper. She was magnificent in her rages. And she was always so damned independent. It was always If you want to go, Go. But I never did want to go, William.'

'But you did,' persisted William. 'You left her for Lady Jersey.'

'This is not the time to remember it.'

'Perhaps it is not the time to remember either of them.'

'Oh, God, now you have reminded me of that . . . creature.'

'I don't think,' said William, 'that she has ever been far from your mind.'

'William, what am I going to do?'

'Either marry her or refuse.'

The Prince laughed aloud. 'My dear William, you are brilliant, brilliant! But I have asked you to come here tonight for a reason. I want you to go to Maria. I want you to tell her that you have been here tonight. I want you to tell her what state I am in. And say this to her: "Mrs Fitzherbert, he asked me to tell you this: 'You are the only woman he will ever love.'" Perhaps then she will have some regrets. Perhaps she will wish she took the trouble to come to the window, to comfort me in this nightmare, this terrible ordeal.'

'I will take your message to her,' said William. 'And tomorrow ...'

'Tomorrow,' said the Prince, 'I shall have come to my decision. Good-night, William. Thank you for coming. Lucky William, with your happy home, with your dear Dora, your delightful children. Have you ever thought, William, what a lucky man you are.'

'I often think it,' said William. 'And if you had kept with Mrs Fitzherbert ...'

Dear William, best brother in the world, thought the Prince of Wales, but singularly lacking in tact.

The next day the Prince was married. He had fortified himself with brandy to face his ordeal and once during the ceremony he rose from his knees and made as if to walk away. But the King was beside him, forcing him to kneel again, determined that having gone so far there should be no turning back.

William discussed the ceremony with Dorothy and told her that it broke his heart to see dear George in such a melancholy state.

'He was so drunk that it was hard to keep him standing, so Bedford told me, and he should know for he was one of the Dukes who stood on either side of him ... very close, I can assure you, to prop him up. His eyes were quite glassy and he didn't look at her once.'

'Poor Princess,' said Dorothy. 'I wonder how she feels.'

'Glad to have escaped that little place she comes from, no doubt. It's a bit of a madhouse there, I hear; and she herself seems tainted with the family complaint. I can only hope that she'll be pregnant in a few days and then he'll be free of her.'

'It makes one glad one is not a Princess,' said Dorothy. 'Not that I should wish to be anyone but myself.'

They heard the rumours later. The Princess Caroline of Wales let it be known that her husband had spent their wedding night under the grate, so drunk that he was oblivious of the world.

William called at Mrs Fitzherbert's London house where her friend and faithful companion, Miss Pigot, took him into her pleasant drawing room with the blue satin-covered walls and told him that her mistress would attend on him immediately.

William bowed as Mrs Fitzherbert came into the room. His eyes filled with tears; he had always been fond of her, and like his brother, Frederick, had deplored the breaking up of her relationship with the Prince.

'My dear William, how good of you to call on me.'

'He asked me to come.'

'The Prince!' Her face hardened and the colour in her delicately tinted complexion, one of her greatest attractions and which owed nothing to rouge and white lead, deepened slightly.

'He has been most distressed.'

'To marry when one already has a wife would be disturbing to most people, I'll swear.'

'He looks upon you as his wife, Maria. He always did.'

'I suppose,' she said, 'that is why he is living with Lady Jersey and marrying the Princess Caroline. But pray sit down, William. I will send for some refreshment. You must tell me how life is with you.'

'I came to talk of him . . . at his request.'

'You mean he sent you.'

'He asked me to come and tell you that you will always be the only woman he ever loved.'

She was moved but attempted to hide the fact. 'He always loved drama.'

'He meant it.'

'Of course he did while he said it. He always means his parts. That is why he plays them so well. He should have been on the stage.'

'He is suffering,'

'If he is it is due to his folly.'

'But that doesn't make him any the less pitiable.'

Maria Fitzherbert thought: William is growing up. The crude sailor was disappearing; it was the effect of his life with Mrs Jordan, she supposed. Poor woman, how long did she think that would last? How long could Princes be expected to be faithful?

She said, 'I heard you had another son.'

'Henry. You should see Henry. And Master George is just a little jealous. He is at pains all the time to remind us that he is our firstborn.'

She smiled. The family man! And he was content. She sensed that in him.

Well, had not George been the same in the first years? These royal brothers had a certain charm – even William had – although he was not nearly as elegant, fastidious and civilized as George; but there was an unworldliness about William which was not unattractive. Perhaps he might settle into the life of domesticity which he had chosen to live with his actress. He would in any case not have to face the same temptation for he was, after all, not the Prince of Wales.

'I am sure you are very proud of your little boys,' she said; and she thought: If we had had children would it have made any difference? He was still the Prince of Wales and would have had to marry for State reasons.

'You illuminated your house last night to celebrate the wedding,' said William.

'What did you expect me to do? Plunge into darkness so that all should say I had gone into mourning for the loss of a husband? Though in truth I had already lost him. He left me, you remember, for Lady Jersey.'

'He is most unappy. He talks of you continually.'

'To the Princess Caroline? Or to Lady Jersey?'

'He never talks to the Princess. He cannot bear to be near her and I am sure he would never discuss you with Lady Jersey.'

She turned to him. 'My dear William, you have always been a good brother to me and I thank you for coming along to me today. You thought to comfort me, I know, but I have finished with him. He has gone from my life. I have started afresh and it is as though I had never known him.'

He looked at her disbelievingly. How could that ever be? Whenever romantic affairs of the Prince of Wales were discussed the name of Mrs Fitzherbert would always arise.

'I could not tell him that now when he is in need of comfort.'

'Dear William,' she replied. 'I will leave it to you to say what you will.'

When he took his leave he decided to write to his brother who was on honeymoon at Windsor – poor George, what a dreadful ordeal!

Maria Fitzherbert stood at her window watching his carriage drive away and Miss Pigot came into the room. This lady was no ordinary companion; she had been with Maria since the beginning of her relationship with the Prince of Wales and had suffered and rejoiced through all their vicissitudes. She loved them both and it was a great tragedy to her when they had parted.

'So the Duke of Clarence came to see you. Did he bring a message?'

Maria turned round. 'Of course,' she said. 'It's like him, don't you think! He sends his brother after the ceremony to tell me that I am the only woman he ever loved.'

'It's true,' said Miss Pigot.'

'We have had such proof of it,' put in Maria sarcastically.

'Yes, we have.'

'Lady Jersey for instance. And now this marriage?'

'Now, Maria, be sensible. The marriage had to be for State reasons.'

'And Lady Jersey?'

'Well, he wouldn't have left you for her. It was you who left him.'

'Did you think I was going to remain to be . . . insulted.'

'No, I didn't. But he would have come back.'

'I don't wish to discuss him and his affairs. Let him go to Lady Jersey. Let him marry. I'm just sorry for this poor Princess. I wouldn't be in her shoes for anything.'

'Nor would I . . . from what I hear. And seeing that he's in love with another woman.'

'Romantic old Piggy,' said Maria affectionately. 'I wonder how long it will last for Mrs Jordan?'

'He's a nice boy – William.'

'They're all nice boys, but not faithful boys, you know. They have another son – did you hear?'

'Yes, and living very quietly there at Petersham Lodge.'

'And she acts now and then for large sums of money so perhaps she'll keep him out of debt.'

'They say that her money keeps the establishment going.'

'He'll get into debt, never fear. It's a family habit. Frederick will be the next. They were brought up to grow wheat and do worsted work. Did you know that? George told me about it once. I think all that discipline decided them to run wild when they had a chance. Perhaps that should be blamed.'

'Well, I hope the poor Prince is not *too* unhappy, and that William goes on being as contented as he is now.'

'My dear Pig, you alway hoped for the impossible, didn't you!'

'You're crying, Maria.'

'Oh, leave me. I didn't want you to see. I could have burst into tears when William told me. Then I should have had him weeping too. Living with the Prince taught me, I always thought, to restrain my tears. He shed enough for both of us, but his could be turned on and off at will and they never meant anything. He always wept so effectively, didn't he? Oh go away, there's a good woman.'

Miss Pigot lifted her shoulders and left.

She's still in love with him, she thought. And he with her. He'll come back one day.

The Queen came into the King's study unannounced. It was something she would not have done before his illness. He was aware of this but he did nothing to stem the change in their relationship. It was inevitable. That terrible experience five years ago had left a mark on him which would never be eradicated. He faced the fact that for a few months of his life he had been insane. It was not the first lapse; and he lived in constant fear that there would be others.

It was a fear which the Queen shared with him; and such an emotion shared must bring them together. It was not out of affection for him that she worried; it was a case of what would happen to her and who would seize power. He understood a little of what had happened when they had thought he would never recover. There had beèn the battle in Parliament over the Regency Bill and the conflict between the Queen and the Prince of Wales. Then he had recovered and there was a return to normality – at least a show of normality. But the King's mind was not so impaired that he did not know that nothing would ever be the same again.

There she was, the mother of his fifteen children – two had died so only thirteen were left to them – a woman whom he had never loved but by whom he had done his duty. He often remembered their marriage, when he had been in love with the beautiful, mischievous and inconsequential Lady Sarah Lennox and could have married her, he supposed, had he insisted. After all he had been the King at the time. But he had been under the rule of his mother and her lover, Lord Bute, and they had pointed out the need for him to marry a Princess and had chosen Charlotte of Mecklenburg-Strelitz. He knew why now. It was because she was so plain, so unattractive that they believed she would never cast a spell on him and therefore would have no power to influence him; that she could not speak English was another point in her favour. They had been determined that he should not have Sarah, because in spite of being the most seductive creature for whom, as he wrote to Lord Bute, he 'boiled' she was related to the Foxes – that ambitious politically minded family who would have been ruling the country before long. Charles James Fox was her nephew – and the King was well aware of the mischief that fellow had done. He believed he had ruined the Prince of Wales, teaching him about drinking, gambling and women, and incidentally politics – Whig politics. So they had snatched Sarah from him and married him to this plain German Princess and meekly he had complied and they had lived together for more than thirty years, but he had never allowed her to have a say in anything; even in the nursery he had been the one to lay down the rules.

He had never really known her. He had thought her meek and content with her lot, bearing child after child; she had always seemed to be giving birth to a child or preparing to do so. But when he was indisposed, when he lost his reason, she had thrown aside her docility; the real woman had stepped out from behind the mask of meekness and disclosed an ambitious schemer. Pitt –

the great Pitt himself – had been on her side, against Fox and the Prince; and she had shown herself formidable.

So now she did not wait to be summoned; she did not wait for her opinions to be asked: she volunteered them.

'I'm hoping everything will go well with the bride and bridegroom,' she said. 'I thought he was going to refuse right up to the last.'

'H'm,' said the King. 'Nearly did. Was on the point. At the altar. I had to act quickly. Otherwise . . . what would have happened. I don't know. I don't know.'

'He had a shock when he saw her,' said the Queen; her wide mouth turned up at the corners in a sardonic smile. 'I could have told him. In fact I tried to. My niece would have been so much more suitable.'

'Caroline seems quite a handsome young woman.'

The Queen looked at him as scathingly as she dared. Was he a little attracted by his daughter-in-law? He was attracted by women and had been all his life, in spite of his fidelity. She suspected that he confined his erotic adventures to the imagination. She had little to be grateful to him for. But they must of course stand together against the Prince of Wales, the Whigs and the King's threatened instability.

'Settle down perhaps,' said the King. 'See reason. I was afraid he was going to say No . . . right there at the altar. Dreadful moment. Think of the scandal.'

'I do hope,' said the Queen, 'that now that he is married he will realize his responsibilities. We don't want scandal.'

'No,' said the King. 'Dangerous. Lot of trouble. People protesting. Low wages. High price of food. Thank God for Pitt. Good young man . . . but arrogant . . . very arrogant, eh?'

'I think we should be grateful for Mr Pitt,' said the Queen.

'Keep George in order. Seems to have lost some of his love for Fox, eh?'

'Yes. He upset George in the House over the Regency Bill.'

The King winced. He hated references to the period when he had been unable to govern.

'Mustn't have scandals,' he said. 'Very bad. Can't help thinking of what happened in France. The King and the Queen . . . executed. I dream of it sometimes.'

'I will tell the doctors to give you something to make you sleep.'

'Can't sleep . . . thinking of those boys. Ten sleepless nights in a row I've had worrying about them. Did you ever know such boys for getting themselves into trouble? It's always women . . . and money. I can't think why. Eh? I've brought them up strictly . . .'

'Perhaps too strictly,' said the Queen coldly, but the King did not hear her. His mind was wandering back to the past.

The Queen said suddenly: 'I've been thinking about William and his actress.'

'That Jordan woman. They have another child. It's disgraceful. They are living like a married couple in Petersham and she is acting on the stage and they are beginning to raise a family. Shouldn't you speak to William?'

'What could I say to him?'

'You could tell him that it must stop. Isn't it time that he settled down with a wife . . . a Princess whom we should find for him.'

'He seems to be living . . . respectably.'

'Respectably! Unmarried! And with an actress who appears in male costume on the stage for everyone who has the price of a seat to watch!'

The King's mind had gone off again. He could see a very young man riding out to a lonely house in which there lived a beautiful Quakeress. They had loved each other tenderly; she had borne his children; and he was a young Prince of Wales and later a King. He understood William's position. He did not want to be too hard on him.

The Queen was saying: 'George lived with Maria Fitzherbert and no one knew whether or not they were actually married. Then he had love-affairs with other women and now he is married to Caroline. But I fear they have not settled down. There is Frederick who won't live with that wife of his who keeps a zoo at Oatlands; I believe he has a host of mistresses. And now there is William . . . Whichever way we turn we are knee-deep in scandal. George is at last married; Frederick is married. It is time William was married.'

'There's George and Frederick. One of them is bound to provide some heirs. Eh?'

'Do you think so? George already hates his wife; Frederick will not live with his. Who is going to reign when we are all gone?'

'Everything will depend on what happens between George and his wife.'

'You mean that if they have sons ... daughters will do ... if they have *children* then you will leave William in peace with his actress?'

'I don't see why not.'

'So then everything depends on George's wife giving us an heir to the throne.'

'A great deal depends on it,' said the King.

'I tell you this,' said the Queen. 'I shall never stand by and applaud an illicit union of a royal prince with an actress.'

'What do you propose to do then, eh, what?'

'I shall choose the moment to rescue William from that woman. Obviously he must marry.'

'We'll wait and see,' said the King.

Very soon news reached them that the Princess of Wales was pregnant.

The Prince of Wales rejoiced and made it quite plain that he would have nothing more to do with his wife.

The King was pleased that his daughter-in-law had shown such early signs of being productive. He was still less inclined to interfere with his son William's arrangements.

But the Queen kept her eyes on all her sons; and she had determined that she would not tolerate for ever even a third son's liaison with a play-actress.

Perdita's *Nobody*

Dorothy was amazed to receive a letter signed by Mary Robinson, who requested the pleasure of a visit from her that they might discuss Mrs Robinson's new play in which she hoped Mrs Jordan would play the principal part.

Dorothy was surprised and a little curious for she knew this lady to be none other than that Mrs Robinson who had been known as Perdita when she had enslaved the Prince of Wales, and about whom there had been a great scandal.

She decided she could not refuse to see the lady and went along to her house where she was ushered into her study by her daughter.

Mrs Robinson held out a hand to Dorothy and begged to be excused for not rising.

'I have to be lifted from my chair because I am paralysed with rheumatism.' She glanced upwards in a most pathetic manner as she said this and Dorothy immediately recognized the tragic actress.

'It is so good of you to come,' went on Perdita. 'But I knew you would. I have heard of your kindness. Ah, it does not seem so very many years ago that I was in a position similar to yours. So similar. The people used to flock to see me as they now do to see you.'

'I know,' said Dorothy. 'Who has not heard of Mrs Robinson?'

Perdita fluttered her lashes. She was carefully painted and her gown was made of satin and lace – delicately coloured and very feminine. She must have been a very pretty woman in her youth, Dorothy decided.

'I was known as Perdita because it was in *The Winter's Tale* that I scored my big success. *He* was there in the box . . . the balcony box, you know. I shall never forget it. The Prince of Wales, and he had eyes for no one but me. How good it is to speak to someone of the theatre! I think so often of those days. And now you see me here, crippled. Thank God I have my daughter to care for me. You have daughters, Mrs Jordan. What a blessing! When we are alone . . . deserted . . . there is no one who can comfort one like a daughter.'

Dorothy said: 'You seem to be so well looked after. But you wished to speak to me about your play.'

'I am going to give it to you to read. My writing is very important to me now. We live on what I earn . . . with my pension of course. And you see we are not uncomfortable.'

'That is a blessing,' said Dorothy.

Perdita gave one of her theatrical shrugs. 'You know how it is with us theatre folk. We learn to be extravagant and then we find ourselves alone, in debt,' She shivered. 'I feel I can confide in you, Mrs Jordan . . . because I was once on the stage.'

'You think there is a part for me in your play?'

'Undoubtedly. It was written with you in mind . . . and Sarah Siddons and Elizabeth Farren. There's a part for Mrs Pope and Bannister too, so everyone should be satisfied.'

'Good parts for all?' asked Dorothy.

'Excellent. This is a play with a purpose. I want to call attention to the terrible habit of gambling and do my small part in helping to abolish this vice.'

'Do you think the audiences will like that?'

'They will have to *learn* to like it. It is a lesson in itself. You look doubtful, Mrs Jordan.'

'It is merely that audiences come to be entertained, not to learn lessons. And it is the players and the playwrights who have to please them rather than expect them to learn to like what they are given.'

'Ah, my dear Mrs Jordan, I have advanced ideas. I have written a play on gambling and Mr Sheridan must put it on for me. I am sending a copy to him too, but I wanted to see you . . . in person. I felt a great desire to see you.'

'That was kind of you.'

'Perhaps it was curiosity. I have read so much about you.'

It was Dorothy's turn to grimace. 'I hope you have not believed all you heard about me?'

'Ha! ha!' Perdita's laughter was stage laughter, high–pitched and artificial as everything about her. Dorothy felt as though she were playing a scene with this woman – perhaps it was because they were two actresses together. 'You can tell *me* nothing about the scandal sheets. My dear Mrs Jordan, no one . . . but no one . . . has been libelled and slandered so much as I. You would be too young to remember . . .'

'I was probably not in London. I did not come here until ten years ago.'

'Ten years,' she murmured. 'Ten years. It seems but yesterday. I believed him, you know. When he wrote eternal faithfulness I was young and romantic to believe him. That is what we poor women do, is it not, Mrs Jordan?'

'I suppose so,' said Dorothy. 'Do you want me to speak to Mr Sheridan when I have read the play?'

'Only to tell him that you will enjoy playing the part. I thought it would go on for ever. I gave up the stage. The *friend* of the

Prince of Wales could not go on playing, I was told. Sheridan said that if I left I would never come back. He said the public was fickle. They forget and will not welcome you when you return, he said. How right he was! And when it was over . . .' She laughed. 'Of course there were offers. So many offered. Mr Fox was my good friend and helped me to get my settlement. And then he went off with my maid, that Mrs Armistead. They say he has married her. Is it true, do you think? Do you think a man like Mr Fox would marry a lady's maid? And how strange that she . . . who used to wait on me . . . should be Mrs Charles James Fox! Life is strange, Mrs Jordan.'

'It is very strange,' agreed Dorothy. She rose. She had a great desire to get out of this room. She felt uneasy. This woman was trying to say something to her. 'You are looking at yourself in fifteen years' time. The woman who gave up everything for love. The woman who did not consider the cost.' But that was not true. Mrs Robinson had considered the cost. She had her settlement. She had bartered his letters for it. Everyone knew the story of Mrs Robinson and the Prince of Wales.

'Pray do not go yet. I have asked my dear daughter to bring us in a dish of tea. It is not often that we have the pleasure of entertaining the famous Mrs Jordan.' She called, 'Maria! Maria, my dear. Pray bring in the tea.'

The daughter came at once.

'Oh, Mrs Jordan, I am so pleased you are staying,' she said. 'Mamma gets so few visitors and she does love to talk. Are you comfortable, Mamma?'

Perdita smiled at her daughter. 'You see how I am looked after, Mrs Jordan? Sit with us awhile, my dear. Mrs Jordan has promised to stay and talk to me.'

But it was Perdita who talked; she talked of that high-light in her life when for a brief time she had been the mistress of the Prince of Wales. She made Dorothy see the romantic meetings on Eel Pie Island, the entreaties of the Prince before she would give way. 'And I gave all for love.' She spoke in dramatic clichés. 'And you will understand that, Mrs Jordan. I should have been wise, should I not? But who ever was wise in love? I loved not wisely but too well! And I did not count the cost. But I have my dear daughter and we manage to get along, do we not, my pet?'

'We manage very well, Mamma. Have you talked to Mrs Jordan about the play?'

'Mrs Jordan is going to speak to Mr Sheridan about it and she wants to play the main part. This play must run for years. There will always be those who need to be warned against the sin of gambling. It was gambling which ruined him, you know. Oh, he was handsome in those days! He has grown a little gross now . . . but still elegant . . . and of course, magnificent. But he could never be faithful. We heard so much of Mrs Fitzherbert.' Her lip curled in contempt, but the envy showed in her eyes; she was not actress enough to hide that. 'But she did not last, either. And this poor woman he has married. But it never lasts! It never lasts with princes.'

She is telling me to beware, thought Dorothy. What does she expect me to do, to keep his letters to use them as she used George's?

' "Princes, princes," ' went on Perdita, ' "put not your trust in princes." '

Dorothy said the tea was delicious. She must discover their tea merchant. And now she must go. She would give Mrs Robinson an early report on the play.

'It was good of you to come,' said Perdita. 'I *had* to see you. An actress like myself . . . It reminded me so much . . .'

Driving to her house in Somerset Street Dorothy could not shake off the mood of depression.

For the first time she felt insecure. She could not get out of her mind the memory of that poor woman with her painted face and her exaggerated gestures; she could imagine so clearly how beautiful she must once have been; she could picture so vividly her romance with the young Prince of Wales.

And then . . . the disillusionment and the end.

'Put not your trust in princes.'

It was like a chilly wind blowing up on a lovely warm summer's day.

Somewhat against his better judgement Sheridan decided to put on Mrs Robinson's play which was under the uninspiring title of *Nobody*. The sentiments expressed, he knew, would anger many, for the theatre was patronized by gamblers and were they going to sit meekly in their places and listen to a diatribe against their favourite pastime? There would be a hostile reception, he feared. Besides, Mrs Robinson was no genius. On the other hand, she had been the central character in a famous scandal, and the fact that the principal actress was the mistress of a prince and Mrs Robinson had been the mistress of his elder brother did have a certain value. Moreover, he was desperate for new plays. The old favourites had been repeated so many times and although an audience would call for Little Pickle when he offered them something else – he did need to replenish his repertoire. Who knew, the controversial subject might catch on.

Nobody went into rehearsal and Sheridan promised himself that with such a cast it would have every chance of success.

It was impossible to keep its subject secret and the news went round theatrical circles that Sheridan was going to give them some tract against gambling. It would be drink next. Before they knew where they were they would be living in the sort of puritan society which had occurred after the Civil War and which, having once tasted, the people had decided they would never have again. They preferred their extravagant kings and their mistresses to that.

Sheridan was not only a theatre manager, he was a politician. Did this play reflect his own feelings? Impossible! There wasn't a bigger gambler in the country unless it was the Prince of Wales. They had both been schooled in the art by Charles James Fox who had gambled several fortunes away. Sheridan was in debt – up to his eyes. He had reformed? Was it the case of the devil being sick and wanting to be a saint?

Whatever it was they were not having plays against gambling.

When Dorothy went into her dressing room after rehearsal there was a letter propped up on her dressing table.

She opened it and read: 'Damn *Nobody* or you will be damned.'

She took it at once to Sheridan who shrugged his shoulders. 'You're not the only one who has such a letter. We're all getting them.'

'What are you going to do?'

'Do. We're in production. We can't take any notice of lunatics like this.'

'Lunatics can wreck a performance.'

He laid his hand on her shoulder.

'We'll have a full house,' he said with a grin.

But she was afraid. She was immediately sensitive to the mood of an audience and hostility unnerved her. It had always been so. She lacked the absolute confidence of Sarah Siddons who could go on and forget everything but the magnificence of Sarah. Dorothy must have a friendly audience, an audience who loved her.

'I don't look forward to it,' she said; and began to brood on it.

She stayed in London and did not go down to Petersham Lodge. The Duke wrote to her. He had expected her, he said with mild reproach.

She wrote and told him that she was concerned about *Nobody* and she felt she would be a hot-tempered irritable impossible-to-love creature, so she preferred to stay away. She knew the babies were well cared for, with him and the nurses.

She went to Hester to talk to her about it. It did not matter if she was irritated with Hester.

Hester thought she should make some excuse not to play. 'After all,' said Hester, 'you could plead sickness.'

'I could, but I keep thinking of that woman. I could see what it means to her. She wants this play to go on. She longs to be some sort of pioneer. It's a kind of expiation for the past.'

Hester shrugged her shoulders. 'The Prince of Wales didn't feel the same need for repentance and he was the one who deserted her.'

'But she threatened to publish his letters and this settlement was arranged. One would feel ashamed of that. I was sorry for her. She was so obviously living a part. I think she suffers a great deal in her private thoughts and that is why she plays this part . . . unconsciously.'

'Some people can't stop acting.'

'I can't get her out of my mind.'

Hester looked at her sharply. 'Is all well between you and the Duke?'

'Of course.'

Hester did not speak for some time but Dorothy knew what she was thinking. How long would it last? Already it had lasted longer than the affair between the Prince of Wales and Perdita.

240

It was a different sort of relationship. Cosy, almost respectable. They already had two little boys and the Duke doted on them. He was meant to be a father and she a mother.

It is different . . . quite different, thought Dorothy.

She said resolutely: 'No matter what happens, I shall play my part.'

When she returned to the theatre she learned that Elizabeth Farren had decided to give up her part in *Nobody*. A friend of hers had been libelled in it and she could naturally not give her support of it. In fact her lover, the Earl of Derby, had warned her that there would be trouble and she must not play.

As the first night of *Nobody* grew nearer Dorothy grew more and more nervous.

William called at Somerset Street in the morning of the day *Nobody* was to open.

'We hoped you would come to Petersham Lodge,' he told her coolly. 'George was most disappointed.'

'Darling George! Did you explain to him that I was so busy rehearsing?'

'I did not. Do you think he would have understood? But he might have if I'd told him that you had been to see the girls.'

'Understood?' she stammered.

'That you had time for the girls but not for the boys.'

'But that is absurd.' The terrors of the coming night were like dragons closing in on her, breathing fire and wrath; and she had to face them. She would forget her lines. She knew she would. It was going to be a nightmare; and her family for whom she was suffering all this, because always at the back of her mind was the need for money, were carping because she needed a little respite, and had wanted to talk things over with her sister – herself an actress who had known the terrors of going on a stage when one was overcome with fright.

'That be damned,' said William. 'It's a truth. Did you not go to see them?'

'I went to see Hester to talk about this . . . this nightmare of a *Nobody*. And if you can't understand what I'm going through now I don't want to talk to you. I don't want to talk to anybody.'

'Is that dismissal?'

'If you have come to reproach me about something of which you are entirely ignorant, yes.'

'I know something of the stage.'

'The deck of the *Pegasus* is somewhat different from Drury Lane.'

Her face was flushed and angry. He had never seen her like this before.

'All right,' he said. 'Go to your precious girls and leave the boys to me.'

With that he left her.

She could not believe it. It was the first time he had spoken to her in that way. She thought: It was my fault. I lost my temper – and I always had an Irish temper. I wish I'd never heard of *Nobody*. That woman had been like a sinister prophetess sitting with her rouge and white lead covering her wrinkles and those bows and ribbons which were too young for her.

From the moment she had seen Perdita Robinson the doubts and fears had come – and not only for the play. She passed the day in a state of nervous tension; and was almost glad when it was time to go to the theatre.

There she found the atmosphere explosive.

Sheridan was prepared for trouble. The house was full but several employees from the gambling houses were there and clearly they had come for a purpose.

As soon as the curtain rose and the play started the audience made its disapproval clear. Rotten fruit was thrown on the stage. Even the fine ladies hissed behind their fans, and comments – derisive and abusive – were shouted at the players.

Dorothy struggled through. It can't last forever, she kept telling herself. This nightmare will end.

She was thankful for the support of her fellow actors on that night. Whatever petty rivalries took place behind the scenes once they were in action they were real professionals. They acted as though nothing was happening. She was grateful to them on that night.

How they stumbled through to the end, she was not sure, but they did; and the curtain fell to a storm of hissing and booing.

Poor Mrs Robinson, thought Dorothy, this is the end of *Nobody*.

She felt sick and ill. Perhaps she had acted too soon after her confinement. Perhaps this life she was living was too much for her. The life of a popular actress was enough in itself; one could not be the mistress of an exacting prince and the mother of young children at the same time. Perhaps she should retire. As Perdita Robinson had?

Only if a woman had a docile partner – like Will Siddons for instance – could one combine such careers as that of prominent actress and prince's mistress.

Is this the beginning of the end? she asked herself; and she remembered his face cold, almost hating, as he had reminded her that she had been to see the girls.

She opened her dressing room door and as she entered someone stepped from the shadows and held her.

'William!'

'Of course I came,' he said. 'That dreadful play! The audience was in a nasty mood.'

'You were out there?'

'No! I was back-stage. I was going to get on to that stage and carry you off if anything started.'

She felt limp with relief and happiness.

'Oh, William . . . and I feared . . .'

'There is nothing to fear,' he said.

'But you thought . . .'

'Jealous,' he said. 'Jealous fool, that is your William.'

It was over. Sheridan put on *Nobody* for the two following nights; the audience were hostile. On the third night he ran down the curtain on *Nobody* for the last time.

Dorothy was happy.

There was no rift. Everything was as it had been in the beginning between her and William. But she must remember that there must be no jealousy between her two families. She wished that she could have had them under one roof. But although she assured herself that William loved her and wished to give her everything she desired, that was something for which she dared not ask.

The attempted fraud

She waited for William to suggest that she give up the theatre, but he did not.

He expressed a great interest in all her parts; and although this necessitated her often staying in London while he, with the boys, was at Petersham, he accepted this too.

The money she earned was important. She was commanding the highest salary of any living actress; and always in her mind was the household presided over by Hester. She could not ask William's support for the girls, particularly now that they had their own family. His delight in the boys was great; and although he raised no objection to her seeing the girls and even taking the boys to visit them and allowing the girls to come now and then to Petersham, it was obvious that he would not have wished them to be under the same roof.

She could understand that. It would be a constant reminder to him of her relationship with Daly and Ford, both of whom were still alive.

She needed the money her profession brought to her; and William, who had his brothers' disinclination to consider the cost of what he wanted and was unable to come to terms with money, was constantly short of it.

She must work. She must make sure that her children were cared for.

It was a shock to learn that Richard Ford had married. His wife was a woman of some property and he had become a city magistrate. His father had approved of the marriage and Richard was on his way up in the world.

Dorothy was angry.

For all those years he had lived with her, enjoyed the comforts her salary had brought them and their children, and had evaded marriage – which was the one thing she had asked of him. And now . . . shortly after their parting he had married.

He was an opportunist. He was weak. Why had she ever believed she loved such a man? And he was the father of her two little girls!

It was humiliating – and only the devotion of William could comfort her.

*

One day soon after the *Nobody* fiasco, a visitor called at Petersham and asked for an audience with the Duke of Clarence and Mrs Jordan. It was on a matter which he was sure would be of great interest to them both. His name was Mr Samuel Ireland which they would not know, but when he imparted to them the news of his discovery he was sure they would welcome his visit.

His curiosity aroused, the Duke ordered that the man should be brought in to the drawing room where he and Dorothy were alone.

'Your Highness! Mrs Jordan!' said Mr Ireland, with a bow. 'It is good of you to receive me. I will get to the point without delay. My son, William Henry Ireland, has made a great discovery. An old trunk has come into his possession which he is certain was once the property of the late William Shakespeare, and in this trunk are certain plays and deeds which, since they were placed in this trunk by William Shakespeare himself, have not seen the light of day.'

'This is incredible,' cried Dorothy. 'Where is this trunk?'

'It is in the house of my son, Madam. He believes it to be the greatest discovery of the age. He said I should come to you, Sir, as a patron of the theatre, and to you, Madam, as our greatest actress.'

'But when can we see these . . . plays?' asked Dorothy.

'If Your Highness would give me an appointment, I and my son would bring one of the plays to wherever you wish.'

'There should be no delay about a matter like this,' said the Duke. 'Bring them to my apartments at St James's Palace tomorrow morning.' He smiled. 'You will be with us there, my love?'

Dorothy said she certainly would. She was filled with excitement about this great discovery.

So the next day in the apartments of the Duke of Clarence in St James's, Mr Samuel Ireland arrived with his son William Henry, and they brought with them a folio inscribed *Vortigern and Rowena* by William Shakespeare.

'You will observe,' said William Ireland, 'that the play is in the style of Shakespeare. I was inclined to think that someone might be playing a hoax, but as soon as I read on . . . I was convinced.'

The interview was interrupted by the arrival of the Prince of Wales who had heard the news and wanted to see the discoveries.

Dorothy had not seen him since his wedding and thought he looked less healthy than he had before. She had heard from William how eagerly he was awaiting the birth of his child and though he hoped for a son, a daughter would do, because it was freedom from his wife that he wanted more than anything; and if she could give birth to a healthy child he need never see her again.

'This is fascinating,' cried the Prince. He turned to William Ireland. 'Pray tell me how the trunk was discovered.'

'My father is a writer and engraver, Your Highness. His work took him to Stratford upon Avon, for he is producing a book called *Picturesque Views of the Avon* and he went there to make his engravings. I accompanied him and there made the acquaintance of an old gentleman whose name I have given my solemn word not to divulge. He showed me this trunk and gave me his permission to bring the papers therein to the notice of the public.'

The Prince had picked up a document which was signed by William Shakespeare in a handwriting similar to that of the poet. It was sealed in the Elizabethan manner; and the Prince declared the parchment to be that which was used at the time.

A page came in to say that Mr Sheridan was without and asking leave to come in. He, too, had heard of the play and had come to see it.

'Bring him in,' said the Prince.

When Sheridan glanced at the play, he saw that it was very long and written in blank verse in the style of the existing plays; the language was similar, and he decided that forgery or not he would have to have it or Covent Garden would get it and that would be a great calamity. In any case it was so long – he'd have two plays there for the price of one. He declared there and then that he would put on *Vortigern and Rowena*.

The whole theatrical world was excited about the discovery and the play went into immediate production with Mrs Jordan in the part of Flavia and John Kemble as Vortigern. At the first rehearsal Sheridan suspected it was a forgery; and as the company ploughed through their turgid lines it became increasingly clear that it had never been written by the Bard of Avon.

Sheridan considered the position. He had paid a good price for the play. The audience would flock to the theatre to see a new Shakespeare piece. Was he going to let the manager of Covent Garden laugh at him? No. They had been duped; they would feign ignorance of that and see if it were possible to dupe the audience.

Mrs Siddons failed to arrive for rehearsals. A message came to the theatre that she was indisposed and was so ill that she was afraid she must abandon her part.

The play was not going well. Dorothy was aware of that. The memory of *Nobody* was still fresh. Not another night like that, she prayed.

The actors were cautious. Kemble would doubtless have liked to throw in his part, but as Sarah had already done so, for him to follow in her wake would have proved disastrous.

The uneasy first night arrived. People waited in the streets for hours, all determined to get in to judge *Vortigern and Rowena* and the house was more than crowded; it was overflowing; many of those who usually went to the pit, finding it full, bought boxes; and discovering them to be already filled climbed down into the pit. Quarrels ensued over the possession of seats. It was a noisy, eager and excited audience when the curtain was raised on the first act.

The theatre audience knew its Shakespeare and did not take long to recognize the fraud. Lines of other Shakespearean plays were recognized with shouts of derision.

'Be quiet!' cried a man in one of the boxes who was obviously under the influence of drink. 'Don't you know you are insulting Shakespeare.'

There were howls of derision. Someone threw an orange at the man in the box and very soon he had to duck down to dodge a shower of them.

Kemble went on reciting his lines without fire, without enthusiasm or belief, while the audience laughed, jeered and hissed. Dorothy came forward and tried to make herself heard.

'Take it off!' screamed the audience. 'It's a miserable fraud!'

'Fraud! Fraud! Fraud!' chanted the audience. 'Shakespeare – my foot.'

Back-stage William Ireland was almost fainting with fear.

'Cheer up,' said Dorothy. 'They are sometimes like this.'

'Little Pickle!' cried the audience. 'We want Pickle.'

It was as bad as *Nobody*; and she could never face such audiences with the nonchalance some could. She felt sick and ill and had to keep running off stage to prevent herself retching.

There was pandemonium; and when the curtain went down on *Vortigern and Rowena* it was never to rise again on that play.

Dorothy could not help feeling sorry for the frightened boy she found cowering in the Green Room. He dared not go home to his father's house; he dared not go into the streets. He feared the people would tear him to pieces for what he had done.

He looked so young – not much older than Fanny – and Dorothy said he could have a night's shelter in her house in Somerset Street and the next morning he would have to disappear and hide himself where no one could find him.

He slipped out of the theatre and when Dorothy returned home she found him already there.

'You'd better tell me all about it,' she said. 'Why did you believe you could get away with such a thing?'

'It seemed as if I would. My father believed me. Everybody believed me at first. Mr Sheridan bought the play.'

'But did you really think you could hoodwink us all?'

'People like what they think they ought to like,' said young William stubbornly. 'They go to see Shakespeare and sometimes sleep through the performance, but they feel some merit because they've been to something good. Then they will go to a farce and laugh themselves hoarse and apologize for it.'

'It's true,' said Dorothy.

'I wanted to show that it was Shakespeare's name they admired as much as his plays.'

Dorothy was thinking of what William had said about the King who when he went to the theatre invariably saw Shakespeare because that was what the people expected, but secretly he thought it was 'sad stuff'.

'Tell me how you did it,' she asked. 'I suppose we could say it was a clever hoax.'

'My father was a great admirer of Shakespeare and I wanted to give him a gift. There was nothing he would like so much as a relic of Shakespeare whom he admires more than any man. I had nothing, so I forged a document and put a seal on it from an old

248

one. I work in a lawyer's office and I can get old parchments and seals easily – and I made up this Shakespeare relic and gave it to him. He went wild with delight. And I thought if I could produce a document like that why not a Shakespeare play? So I wrote the play on paper I got from the office . . . and I knew it was the right sort because we have documents in the safes going back two hundred years and more. Then I made up this story about the trunk and everyone was so excited. I almost believed it was true myself.'

'And now you are heartily wishing that you had not been so foolish.'

'It didn't prove what I wanted to prove.'

Dorothy looked at him sadly. Poor boy. She did not know what action would be taken against him. Fraud such as this was surely criminal; but Sheridan might not take action because he was going to look rather foolish if he did, and the last thing Sheridan the politician must do – even if the theatre manager did not mind – was to look foolish.

She told the boy this to comfort him. And he went on to tell her how he hated being a lawyer's clerk; how he longed to be a writer. He had read about Thomas Chatterton the poet who had taken his own life at a very early age. Why? Because he was not appreciated. What chance had people to prove their ability? It was only after they were dead that they were appreciated.

'And so what you wanted to do was to prove that it was not quality which won approval; that the public likes what it is told to like. Then I would say that you have learned a valuable lesson tonight. If you want the appreciation that is given to Shakespeare you must produce work like his.'

'Why are you so kind to me, Mrs Jordan? Why do you shelter me here?'

'Perhaps because you are young, and it is hard for the young. Perhaps because I have a daughter who is headstrong like you and wayward and envious . . . Who knows?' She yawned. 'It has been a tiring night. When you are rested I should leave this house. Go out of Town for a while and then when the affair is forgotten, which it soon will be, go back to your father's house, confess everything and be a good lawyer.'

'I shall never forget your kindness to me, Mrs Jordan.'

But she laughed wearily and said she was going to bed.

The next morning young William Ireland had left and she never saw him again.

An important birth

As the summer passed into autumn everyone was eagerly awaiting the birth of a child to the Princess of Wales, but none more eagerly than the Prince. In his anxiety he was often at Petersham Lodge and would pace up and down in a state of the most desperate tension.

'She must succeed, William,' he would cry. 'I do not know what I shall do if this fails. I cannot go near her again, and yet they will insist. Oh, how fortunate you are! You don't know how fortunate. No one could who had not had to marry that . . . monster.'

He played with little George, his namesake. The child was excited by colourful Uncle George who had no objection to being climbed over and who answered the childish prattle of his nephew with an amused good temper.

'The Prince loves children,' said Dorothy to William. 'He will be much happier when the child is born – not only because he so badly needs an heir, but because he will have a child of his own.'

A startling event occurred that November.

The King was on his way to open Parliament and the people lined the streets to see his carriage pass. It was not exactly a loyal crowd for many had gathered there to protest about conditions in the country and to remind the King that wages were too low, the price of bread too high. The King might be parsimonious in his household but he had the inevitable debts which had to be met through taxation. The Prince of Wales was notoriously extravagant. The amount of his debts which had been disclosed just before his marriage had shocked everyone deeply.

There was too much high living on one side; too much poverty on the other. The tragedy across the Channel was too close to be ignored. It was never far from the King's mind and he could not help wondering how far it was from his people's.

There were shouts of 'Down with Kings' as the King's coach trundled along. He made no sign of having heard. He had never been lacking in courage and at the time of the Gordon Riots had appeared among the people in person and had himself taken the bold action which had quelled that mob violence. King George would always do his duty. His trouble was that he rarely knew what it was.

As the carriage passed an empty house a shot was fired. It missed the carriage but the King was aware of it.

He continued to sit upright, looking neither to the right nor the left.

'Your Majesty,' said his equerry who was riding with him in the coach, 'do you think we should turn back?'

'What for, eh?' asked the King. 'Because of a shot. Why, if my time has come then it has come. God disposes of all things and I trust Him to save my life. If he does not wish it to be saved then it will not be.'

His calm was an example to all and he went on to Parliament, performed the ceremony as though nothing had happened to disturb him and started on the journey back.

This was even more stormy. Stones were thrown at the royal carriage, one of which caught the King on the arm. A bullet whizzed past his ear and buried itself in the upholstery of the coach.

The King glanced at it.

'A few inches nearer,' he said, 'and that would have been the end of George III.'

When he returned to St James's, it was to find the Queen and her daughters in a state of agitation. News that the King had been shot had reached them and they had expected to see him carried home.

'You see me unharmed,' he said. 'It was not God's will that I should die yet.'

The Queen sent for William and when he arrived embraced him without much warmth. There was nothing unusual in that. The Queen had little affection for any of her children except the Prince

251

of Wales; and although she insisted on spending a great deal of time in the company of her daughters it was because she liked to have them in constant attendance.

She was critical of William. William had to some measure escaped from the family. He was living a non-royal existence in that house of his at Petersham; and no one would guess that he was one of the King's sons. He seemed to be perfectly content to live this life, hardly ever came to court unless summoned and behaved like a simple country gentleman.

It was due to that actress, thought the Queen – a connection which, as his mother and Queen of England, she deplored.

'You have heard, William, that His Majesty suffered an unfortunate experience on his way back after opening Parliament?'

'Yes. Everyone is talking about it. I trust His Majesty is not suffering from the shock.'

'His Majesty will always do his duty and his duty in this case is to ignore the action of a maniac. I wish every member of the family were as conscious of his duty.'

'Oh, I think we all are, Mamma, when the occasion arises.'

'I am glad to hear you say so, for it could very well arise . . . for *you*!'

William looked uneasy.

'Yes,' she went on. 'If your father had been killed by that bullet . . .'

'God forbid!' cried William.

'Indeed yes. It could have been disastrous . . . and even now . . . in your father's state of health . . .'

'He is ill?'

'Come, William, let us be frank within the family. Your father's derangement six years ago gave us all great cause for anxiety. And you must know, as we all do, that he has never been the same since. It could happen again . . . and then . . .'

William was growing worried. It was a subject to which his mother had never referred before. There was some purpose behind this.

'This child should soon be with us. If all goes well I shall be greatly relieved. If not . . .'

'But surely, Mamma, all is well. I heard excellent reports of Caroline's health.'

'Child-bearing is always uncertain. I pray that Caroline will be delivered of a healthy boy . . . or girl. But if anything should go wrong . . .'

'Please don't mention it.'

'You are a superstitious sailor! Don't be foolish, William. We have to face facts. If something should go wrong, George will never live with her again. I can't say I blame him. The creature is . . . impossible. Mad, I think. There cannot have been a Princess in the whole of Europe less suited to your brother. If he had listened to me . . . But it is too late now. He says he has done his painful duty. If this attempt fails there will never be another. And it would be heartless to expect it of him.'

'Perhaps he will change his mind.'

The Queen's burst of laughter was far from mirthful.

'Frederick's wife is barren and he won't live with her. I wanted to remind you that you are the next in line. If Caroline fails, you will have to do your duty, William.'

'I have other brothers . . .'

'You are the next in seniority.'

'I am sure one of the others . . .'

'Why do you think you get a pension from the State, my son, if it is not for services which will be demanded of you? Your private life is a matter for scandal. Is there not one of you who can live decently?'

William flushed hotly. 'I can assure you that I do that with my family.'

'Your family! An actress who was never married but had children before you took up with her. Bastard children!'

'Your Majesty, I must ask you to refrain from speaking of this lady in this way.'

'Sentimental as well as superstitious. Very well, William. Be sentimental. Be superstitious – as long as you remember that if it is necessary you will be obliged to do your duty. That is really all I have to say to you.'

'I should like to see my father before I leave.'

'What? To ask him if it is necessary to pension off your mistress and seek a suitable bride?'

'To ask after his health.'

'He is not well enough to see you.'

'I thought you said that he had suffered no ill effects from the shooting.'

'My dear William, he is often unwell. These bouts appear at all times. I know my duty. And that is to preserve him from the anxiety the very sight of his sons sometimes arouses in him. No, William. You cannot see the King. But go away and think of what I have said. If Caroline fails to produce an heir to the throne you will have to consider your position very carefully.'

William bowed abruptly and left her.

Dorothy noticed that he was worried. She knew that he had been to see the Queen and she guessed that there had been some criticism of their relationship.

'You had better tell me what it is, William,' she said. 'It concerns us, doesn't it?'

He nodded glumly.

'The Queen is urging you to break off our relationship?'

'It is not quite that. She doesn't approve, of course. She merely pointed out my duty to me. Even if Caroline miscarries George has sworn he won't go near her again. Nothing will induce him to. There will be no hope of an heir. And it is the same with Frederick. He refuses to live with his wife. My mother pointed out that the country needs an heir to the throne . . . and there can't be more delay. She says that I . . .'

'William . . . but your two brothers come before you.'

'George will refuse and so will Fred. That leaves me.'

'Why should you not refuse?'

'Because . . . one of us will have to . . .'

'You mean that if there is no child . . .'

'It would be my duty. I should have to do it . . . for George.'

'What about Frederick?'

'They believe the Duchess of York to be barren.'

'But the Prince must live with his wife. It's what he married her for.'

'He won't. He will expect me to make the sacrifice . . . My parents expect it. It was what my mother wished to say to me.'

'And us . . .' she asked blankly. 'Our children, George, and little Henry . . .'

He began to kiss her frantically. 'I would always care for you,' he said. 'But it won't happen. Caroline *must* bear a child.'

'And if she fails . . .'

Dorothy thought: It would be the end. I know it. He wants me to know it. He wants to prepare me. And yet not so long ago he said that nothing would induce him to marry. If they cannot let me marry whom I wish, he said, at least they cannot force me to marry if I don't want to.

He had changed. She could see that if pressure were brought to bear on him by his parents and his brothers he would give way.

She was sad; he had changed. He was no longer the passionate lover to whom she had meant everything; he was devoted to her and the children; he would be a good husband and father if he were allowed to be. It was not quite the same.

She was afraid. The pattern was changing. Just a little here, just a little there – and by and by everything would be different.

My children, she thought – my three little girls, my two little boys. I must care for them and particularly the girls for surely he will always provide for his own.

She must continue to work. She must never lose touch with her audiences. She must build up a fortune so that her girls would never want.

She thought of that life of ease and comfort of which she had sometimes dreamed: living at home in the heart of her family, far from the smell of greasepaint and the candles, the triumphs and disasters, the applause and the catcalls, the compliments and the jealousies. Would it ever be hers?

She must be careful over money; she must bargain that she was paid the highest prices, and she must never give up; for how could she be sure when she would be without a protector and her girls in need.

William was a boy of nature. A little naïve and wanting to be honest, he had reasoned with himself that it was only fair to warn her; and having done so he now wished to dismiss the subject.

'There is nothing to worry about. Caroline's pregnancy is going just as it should. There'll be a healthy boy, you'll see.'

Perhaps, she wanted to say; but that will not alter the fact that you could contemplate a marriage of State. And if you did, what would become of us?

He wanted to forget the unpleasant subject. He had done his

duty; that was the end of it. She refused to dwell on it. He did not wish to be depressed; he had been upset enough by his mother's implications.

It was better to pretend to forget it, to pretend all was well.

On a cold January day the Princess of Wales gave birth to her child. It was a girl and they called her Charlotte.

They had hoped for a boy, of course; but there was no Salic law in England and girls could inherit the throne as easily as boys. There had been two great queens to prove that women rulers were no bar to a country's greatness; under Elizabeth and Anne the country had expanded as never before. Charlotte was the heir-presumptive to the throne. If her parents had no more children one day she would be Queen.

She was a lusty young creature right from the start. The Princess of Wales was almost hysterical with joy to have a baby of her own; the Prince was delighted because he had done his duty; the country rejoiced for it had no prejudices against girls, and in fact preferred their rulers to be feminine.

Dorothy breathed more easily. There would be no plan to marry William off now. Strange to think that she owed her peace of mind to that infant at Carlton House who lay in her cradle all oblivious of her importance.

It was fortunate that the child was healthy for when she was three months old the Prince wrote a letter to his wife in which he suggested that they part amicably for he had no intention of living with her again.

There was one ominous phrase in the letter:

'Even in the event of any accident happening to my daughter, which I trust Providence in its mercy will avert, I shall not infringe the terms of the restriction by proposing, at any period, a connection of a more particular nature.'

William was aware of this clause in the letter which his brother had sent to his wife. He told Dorothy of it. They both understood what it meant. If any accident befell the baby Princess Charlotte and she were to die, William would be obliged to marry.

It was an uneasy thought; but Dorothy knew that the period of complete happiness was over, that they had passed through the honeymoon and now the harsh realities of life had to be faced.

How right her mother had been when she had warned her daughter to marry. Security was very necessary to peace of mind.

I shall never have it, thought Dorothy. But I must see that my daughters do.

Theatrical conflicts

Money! She must earn it; she must save it; it must be there for the girls when they married. They would need a bigger dowry than most to offset their illegitimacy.

She had a benefit night coming along and hoping to do well out of it decided that she would play Ophelia. This was a departure from her comedy roles, but she was sure she could do justice to the part; and made her announcement that she had chosen it.

She was unprepared for the storm this decision aroused.

When she arrived at the theatre it was to find John Kemble raging in Sheridan's office. As she had received a message to go along there as soon as she came in she knew that something was wrong.

Kemble was shouting. 'Ophelia! It is ridiculous! It's quite out of her range.'

She cried: 'Are you afraid I shall take attention from your Hamlet?'

Kemble drew himself to his full height and struck a pose which might have been Hamlet's own. 'Such fear has not occurred to me, Madam. I have not yet come to terms with the absurdity.'

'And why should it be absurd? I am an actress. I believe there are few parts which would daunt me.'

'One could not introduce *comedy* into *Hamlet*, nor could Ophelia rise from her watery grave to sing a ditty and do an Irish jig.'

'I have no intention of doing either on my benefit night, as you will see.'

'I shall not see, for you will not play Ophelia on your benefit night.'

'And why not, pray, since I have chosen it? Is it not the custom for players to choose the plays for their own benefits? Mr Sheridan, I beg of you, explain this custom to Mr Kemble.'

Sheridan, who remained aloof from the quarrels of his actors and actresses, sat glumly, his arms folded; his mind was far from the theatre where he feared he would never make his fortune. He wondered what would happen if there was another attack on the King's life and this time it was successful. A change in government, with the Whigs coming into their own and high place in that government for Mr Sheridan?

'Eh?' he said, rousing himself.

'Mr Kemble is of the opinion that since he has chosen to play Hamlet for his benefit, I cannot play Ophelia for mine.'

Sheridan stood up. 'I have work to do,' he said. 'This is a matter for you two to settle between yourselves.'

The antagonists glared at each other.

'I am determined to play Hamlet,' said Kemble.

'I am determined to play Ophelia,' retorted Dorothy.

When the two *Hamlets* were announced the public was interested and very soon news of the dispute between the leading actor and actress was well known. As usual sides were taken, but as Dorothy was more popular than Kemble the majority was with her.

Kemble dramatically threatened to resign and there was uproar throughout the theatre. Mrs Siddons supported her brother and declared there would be trouble if Dorothy insisted on playing Ophelia.

Sheridan could no longer close his ears to the dispute. He was after all the manager. It was absurd to play two benefit *Hamlets*; and he called the antagonists to his office and told them that they must both choose another play.

'I *must* play Hamlet,' declared Kemble.

'My dear sir,' replied Sheridan. 'This dispute is over. You will not play Hamlet in my theatre. And if you are wise you will go away at once and make up your mind what you will play, for it will do you no good to resign as you well know. As for Mrs Jordan, she will go away and choose her play. Anything I say . . . anything you like . . . as long as you don't both choose the same play.'

They were glad of his compromise. Kemble chose *Coriolanus* and Dorothy, rather unwisely, *Romeo and Juliet*. Whereas Ophelia would have been less demanding and she could have adapted her talents to the fey half-crazy girl, the young innocent Juliet was not suitable to an ageing woman who was the mother of five children.

But the benefit was profitable and if her Juliet was not highly praised by the press – it commented that she was not young enough nor was her figure, which had widened with the years of childbearing, quite suitable – she was actress enough to give a good performance.

But the public wanted Dorothy as *The Romp*. With Little Pickle it was the name she was known by. They wanted her to go on being just that.

It was not easy for a woman of thirty-five.

So the passing of the years was another anxiety.

Dorothy had received an offer to play in Dublin; as soon as she saw it she knew from whom it had come and she was as uneasy as the very thought of that man could always make her.

How dared he! she thought. Would she never be free of him?

She slit the envelope and read his terms. He would pay her more than she had ever been paid before if she would pay a return visit to Dublin.

Never, she thought. Not for all the money in the world.

She did not tell William of the communication but went to see Hester.

Fanny was fourteen now and she had a look of her father. She was wayward, vivacious but far from handsome. She had a talent for acting and was longing to go on the stage. It was not the life Dorothy had wanted for her. She had dreamed of her living quietly, the step-daughter of a lawyer, meeting others of that stratum – barristers, doctors or even army officers. Desperately she wanted for Fanny a good steady man who would marry her.

Every time she saw her daughter she doubted whether this would be achieved; and in any case it was well known that she was Daly's daughter; there had been so much gossip about them all.

If Richard had married her and Fanny had taken the name of

Ford it would all have been forgotten. But she was glad he had not now, for she had her happiness at Petersham.

'I've had an offer from Daly,' she told Hester.

Hester looked at it and whistled.

'Are you taking it?'

'Hester, what do you think!'

'I know – but such an offer! The children all need new shoes and prices are rising. I think I'll have to ask you for a bigger allowance.'

'You shall have it.'

'I daresay Daly would like to see Fan.'

'I should never allow it.'

'I hear he is doing very badly in Dublin. Philip Astley has opened at the Amphitheatre and is taking all his business.'

'Serve him right.'

'I daresay he thinks that you would set him on his feet again.'

'He can think again.'

'But all this money . . .'

'It doesn't tempt me at all. And William would never allow it.'

Hester grimaced. She was not very fond of William. She would have liked to live at Petersham Lodge with the girls; and it seemed to her that by keeping them in a separate establishment they were being slighted.

'He might be interested in the money,' she suggested.

'What nonsense!' said Dorothy sharply. 'He would never consider it for a moment.'

Was that true? wondered Hester. Her sister with her vast earnings was a good proposition for any man – even a royal Duke, for like all royalty William was in debt.

Dorothy saw the children and listened to Fanny's complaints. When was she going on the stage? Shouldn't she begin soon? Did her mother remember that she was fourteen? Dodee and Lucy wanted to hear about George's latest exploits and little Henry. And after an hour with them she left.

Daly wrote again begging her to reconsider, but she tore up his letter.

If I were starving, she thought, I would never go back to that man.

*

The Duke was excited. He had decided to move from Petersham Lodge which was hardly large enough for his growing family, and Dorothy was once more pregnant.

He had sold Petersham Lodge some time before – being in need of money – but had continued to rent the place and now that his father had offered him Bushy House he decided to leave the Lodge.

Dorothy must come with him and see the new place, he said, and this she was delighted to do. These pleasant domestic touches were the greatest happiness he could give her; and when she saw Bushy House she was charmed by it.

It was close to Hampton Court and situated in Bushy Park; it had magnificent gardens which would be ideal for the children to play in. Young George was such a strong little fellow; he was into everything.

'George needs plenty of space,' said Dorothy laughingly.

It was the perfect house. Gracious, red brick, it had been built in the reign of William and Mary, and the main central building was flanked by lower wings on either side.

'Come, I want to show you,' William said, excited as a boy and reminding her of young George in that moment as he drew her along.

She was enchanted by the gracious drawing room with its beautifully moulded ceiling and the pillars which supported it.

He took her over the main house and then they explored the two pavilions on either side – one of which consisted of a spacious ball-room, the other the chapel.

This was their new home, he told her. He hoped that they would be as happy in it as they had been in Petersham Lodge.

'My father has presented me with this house because he has made me Ranger of Bushy Park – and as I'm also Chief Steward of the Honour of Hampton this place will be ideal. I shall be right on the spot.'

'It's wonderful,' cried Dorothy. 'The sort of house I've always dreamed of.' Then she said: 'It will need a fortune spent on the furnishings.'

'Oh, I'm taking care of that,' he told her easily.

She was momentarily alarmed. He had no idea of the value of money. She had her house in Somerset Street which was necessary for when she was working; he had his rooms in St James's Palace; there was the separate establishment she must maintain for Hester and the girls – and now Bushy House. The cost would be great.

But this was not the day to worry about such matters.

Bushy House with its rural situation, its spacious rooms, its charm and grandeur was the ideal family home. The children would love it.

She said: 'I know I am going to be happy here.'

Mrs Siddons in distress

And she was happy at Bushy House.

Almost immediately she settled in to prepare for the birth of her child, and this time she had a little girl, Sophia.

How pleasant it was to rest after her confinement; to sit in the garden with the baby on her lap and the little boys playing on the lawns. Young George was getting remarkably like his uncle, the Prince of Wales. He swaggered about, sure of the approval of nurses, parents and younger brother.

'You'll have to watch young George,' was the constant admonition. 'He has the strength of two boys of his age, and the mischief.'

When his father came he would clamber all over him and fight him with his fists because the Duke wanted to make a fighter of him. William delightedly declared that he did indeed have to defend himself.

Young Henry stood by watching with admiration.

If only we could go on like this for ever! thought Dorothy.

But there was always anxiety about money and the fact that William did not greatly concern himself tended to make her more anxious.

Her brother George was not happy in his marriage. His wife Maria, who was so much more successful in the profession than he was, bullied him and was unfaithful to him. He was constantly short of money and naturally turned to Dorothy. Her brother Francis who was in the Army, and whom she had believed to be happily settled, had also run into debt. He wrote to his sister, knowing her strong family feeling, and when he had heard of the vast sums of money she was paid merely for appearing a few hours on a stage, he had been sure he could rely on her to help him.

What could she do? How explain? She could say: I do earn large sums of money but I have so many dependent on me.

Even William was embarrassed now and then.

'A fellow demanding payment of a paltry four hundred pounds or so. I can't lay my hands on it for the moment.'

So she must provide it. And all the time she was thinking of the girls and the dowry she must have ready for them. She had set her heart on ten thousand pounds apiece. It was expected of her. She was a famous actress and the mistress of a prince. She could never make them understand how difficult it was to keep the money she earned – although she spent so little on her own needs.

But she was happy at Bushy House. Happier, she kept telling herself, than she had ever been. If it could only go on like this for the rest of my life, she thought. Living here in this gracious house, with the children gradually growing up around me, I would ask nothing more.

The domesticities of life were so happily uncomplicated. If only she could have devoted herself to being a wife and mother! Wasn't it what her mother had always wanted, what she had taught her to want for herself?

The baby began to cry. Little Sophie was not so contented as the boys had been. Dorothy rocked her to and fro and watched young George attempting to climb one of the chestnut trees. He could come to no harm for he could not possibly climb it.

She would write to William and tell him all the news of the children. He was at St James's now; he was most concerned about the country's affairs. She knew that he longed for a command at sea and very much resented the fact that the King would not give it to him. The country was at war, and he was powerless. But she was glad he must stay at home. What anxiety if he had been at sea at such a time!

But it was natural that he should wish to serve the country and he had been brought up to be a sailor so he would want to do it in the manner in which he could be of the greatest use. It was no desire to leave his family that made him long to fight for his country. He was devoted to them. Since they had come to Bushy House there had been an even closer unity. When he was not at home he wanted constant news of the children and took a great interest in the smallest details concerning them. When she had to go away to play in London he contrived to be with the children at Bushy. The children should always if they could possibly manage it have one parent with them.

She thought of the royal brothers. Edward, Duke of Kent, was faithful to his mistress Madame de St Laurent; they were devoted to each other and an aura of respectability surrounded them. There was William and herself, and even the Prince of Wales had been happy with Mrs Fitzherbert for a few years – and he had had so many temptations. There were rumours now that he was tiring of Lady Jersey and was writing impassioned letters to Mrs Fitzherbert begging her to take him back.

So perhaps there was a streak of fidelity in the brothers – and she had been fortunate indeed to have William.

He had shown her a letter he had written to Thomas Coutts, his banker, in which he had said:

'I have long known Mrs Jordan's generosity but have never had so favourable an opportunity of making her merits public. In short, I may be permitted to be partial, but I cannot help thinking her one of the most perfect women in the world . . .'

That after seven years together! He had watched her read it with an almost boyish pleasure.

'There, you see how I speak of you when you are not present.'

He did love her – sincerely, deeply; and if he was not forced for State reasons to marry they could go on happily together for the rest of their lives, rejoicing in their children and their grand-children.

It was a pleasant dream, to picture them on this lovely lawn – growing old together. The theatre would be a part of her past. She would not wish to go on playing when she was old. Her parts in any case were young parts.

Thinking of it she could almost wish she were old with all the tribulation behind her.

She laughed at her thoughts and said: 'Come, George, my darling. Come, Henry, my pet. We are going in because I have to write to Papa. He will want to know what you have all been doing while he is away.'

'Will you tell him that I jumped down four steps?' asked George.

'Yes, I will.'

'And I did one,' said Henry.

'I shall tell him everything. So come along in now.'

So she went in and wrote to him.

'I hope I need not say how I wish your return . . . The children are as well as possible. I shall wean Sophie tomorrow. George's new boots are excellent ones. I expect the others to arrive tomorrow. Sophie has been very cross but now she is composed and easy.'

She smiled. George had come to kneel on a chair beside her.

'Is that a letter to Papa?' he asked.

'It is.'

'When is he coming to see me?'

'As soon as he can, I am sure. Will you put a kiss in this letter for him?'

'Yes I will,' said George, and bending over spat on to the paper.

'Do you call that a kiss?'

'Yes,' said George, 'It is a kiss for Papa.'

She kissed him; and taking his hand guided it for him to make a cross. Then she wrote:

'I asked George if he would put a kiss into this for you. He immediately spat in it.'

William would be amused. It would remind him while he was in London of his family; and she knew that he would be eager to return to them.

With Sophie weaned and debts mounting Dorothy could not linger in idleness at Bushy House. Her audiences were demanding that she return and reluctantly she did so, dashing home to Bushy whenever possible, sometimes arriving at midday and leaving again in the afternoon for the evening performance.

Monk Lewis had written a new play in the Gothic tradition entitled *The Castle Spectre* and Dorothy had the part of the heroine, Angela. The play was an immediate success largely because of an unusual ghostly scene in which Angela's mother rose from the grave to bless her daughter. The lighting effects were such as the playgoers had never seen before. They applauded madly and Sheridan was inundated with requests for more of *The Castle Spectre*. Dorothy's portrayal of Angela pleased audiences and they would have no one else in the part.

Sheridan was delighted to have such success in the theatre again; but he was so deeply in debt that he made excuses not to pay his actors and there were often angry scenes in the theatre. He had never attempted to withhold Dorothy's salary. He was too fearful of losing her; nor did he want the Duke to talk of his deficiencies in this respect to the Prince of Wales. More and more Dorothy thought longingly of retirement to her family in Bushy. She was once more pregnant; this always meant that she grew very tired and after a performance would sink into bed and wish that she could stay. But in the morning if it were possible she would be riding out to Bushy if only for a short glimpse of the children.

She was now often helping William financially.

In spite of the comparatively quiet life he led at Bushy he was always short of money and because of the intimacy between them he had no compunction in using hers. He had taken to reading all her contracts; he was at the theatre as often as possible to see her perform; he would criticize her performance and that of the other players, and was beginning to think of himself as a theatre critic. He was a constant visitor to the Green Room. 'Royal patronage,' Sheridan called it slyly; but Dorothy was delighted; it pleased her that he should take such an interest in her career, and she refused to consider the fact that the money she earned was so important not only to her but to him. Often she had to go away on tours but she made them as brief as possible. These were the most unhappy times of her life.

She would ask him whether or not she should accept certain engagements; if it was out of London he would always shake his head although he gave in later when she reminded him how much they needed the money. She would write to him 'I received fifty-two pounds' – or whatever the sum – 'for tonight's performance. Let me know whether you need it before I spend any of it.'

Sometimes she remembered the rhyme:

'*Does he keep her or she keep him?*'

But she put it from her mind. There was nothing mercenary about William. It was simply that he could not keep within his income.

It was their hope that one day she would be able to leave the theatre and devote all her time to her family. It was what she longed for; and William assured her that he did, too. She might be one of the leading actresses of her day, but she was first of all a wife and mother. Her own mother had been the same, which was the reason why she had been so eager for Dorothy to marry.

It had been an exhausting day and she had been looking forward to leaving London on Friday morning and going down to Bushy House for a few days. Tomorrow night she must work and then there would be that brief respite.

As she was about to leave her dressing room a messenger came to her to say that Mr Siddons was at the theatre and asking if she would see him for a few moments.

'*Mr* Siddons!'

That was correct, she was told.

'Then tell him I will see him in the Green Room in five minutes.'

He was waiting there when she arrived. She was always rather sorry for poor Will Siddons. Sarah was so brilliant, so dominating, that she made him seem even more insignificant than he actually was.

'You wished to see me, Mr Siddons?'

'Ah, Mrs Jordan. I have come on behalf of my wife.'

What trouble now? wondered Dorothy, for she could not imagine it was not trouble between herself and the queen of tragedy.

'We are in great distress, Mrs Jordan. Our second daughter, Maria, is dying.'

Dorothy was immediately sympathetic.

'The doctors are with her now. They hold out no hope. She may pass from us this very night . . . or she may live for a few more weeks.'

'I am so sorry. Pray convey my sympathy to Mrs Siddons. Tell her I understand her feelings.'

'You are a mother yourself, well I know; and it is for that reason that I come to ask this favour.' He hesitated miserably. 'I know there has been little friendship between you and the family . . .' Poor little man, thought Dorothy, it was not his fault that the Kembles had treated her so badly.

She shrugged her shoulders. 'It is but the usual rivalries of our profession,' she said. 'What favour did you wish to ask?'

'Mrs Siddons has committed herself to play on Friday night. She cannot refuse to play unless someone will take her place. You understand that she cannot bear to leave our daughter, and in the circumstances hesitates to face an audience.'

Dorothy nodded. She was thinking that instead of driving down to Bushy she would have to stay in London to play.

'Sarah sent me to ask ... oh, I know it is asking a great deal ... but if you would take her place on this occasion she would be most deeply grateful.'

'Tell her I will do it,' said Dorothy. 'And give her my sympathy.'

'Thank you, Mrs Jordan.' There were tears in his eyes.

'Pray think no more of it. It is the least I can do.'

When he had left and she was driving home to Somerset Street she could have wept with disappointment.

What is the matter with me? she asked herself. It was due to the fact that she was pregnant, she supposed. But she felt weary and longed poignantly for Bushy, the children and William.

Soon it will be time for my confinement, she promised herself, and then I shall go to Bushy; and when the new baby comes I shall be forced to rest awhile.

And tomorrow? Perhaps she would go down to Bushy in the morning and come back for the evening performance. And Friday would be a day of rehearsal to enable her to play that night.

The children would be disappointed; but they were accustomed to her frequent absences. William would be, too. Was she right to leave them all so often? Yet she must for the money was so important to them all.

Oh for that day when she would say goodbye to the stage and spend day after peaceful day in beloved Bushy House.

She wrote to William:

'2 o'clock. I have just returned. You will be surprised to see me advertised to play on Friday night, but I trust not angry when you know the reason. Mrs Siddons has bound herself to play that night, but since she is in constant fear of losing her second daughter, Mr Siddons came here to request I would play otherwise Mrs Siddons would be obliged to quit her child. On such a serious occasion I thought it would not be humane to refuse and hope you will agree with me . . . I got fifty pounds last night . . . If you want this money let me know that I may not dispose of it . . .'

She lay on her bed and thought about the family at Bushy and the girls with Hester; and greatly she wished that she could gather them all under one roof and never leave them.

The child was born in November – another girl. This one was Mary. There were now four little FitzClarences as well as her three girls.

This was a happy time. It was no use thinking about money and the theatre. She simply must rest awhile until the baby was ready to be weaned.

'I am growing fat,' she thought, 'and lazy. I shall have to give up soon. I'm too plump now for *The Romp* and *Little Pickle*.' It was strange how audiences still demanded those parts – and her in them. It was no use trying to give them solemn characters – although they loved her Angela in *The Castle Spectre*. It was all very well for Sarah Siddons. Her roles did not demand a youthful figure. In fact Sarah was far fatter than Dorothy, only being tall she could carry her weight better. But the Tragedy Queen was finding it difficult to get out of a chair once she had sat in it and was demanding that she be helped out; and lest this should call attention to her bulk all females on the stage must be helped out of their chairs as though it was some new fashion invented by the author.

The arrogance of Sarah was supreme. But Dorothy was sorry for her at this time for she had lost her little daughter who had that October died of congestion of the lungs.

The girls came over to Bushy to see her. Fanny was now sixteen, Dodee eleven and Lucy nine. Fanny was the one who worried her – Fanny always had. Conceived in hatred, Dorothy thought. Was that the reason? If so, she must make sure that she gave more care and attention to Fanny than to any of the others. Fanny frightened her. Was it because she could never forget her father? She was quick-tempered, could not learn as easily as the others and was vain and selfish.

Four-year-old George was delighted by his half-sisters. Dodee and Lucy adored him, but Fanny of course cared for no one but herself. Young Henry followed George in everything so he was always pleased by the girls' visits.

What was so pleasant was that William did not resent them as much as he once had appeared to, although she sensed that he was always rather pleased when they left. It was good of him, she told herself, not to put any barrier in the way of their visiting her.

Those days would have been perfect but for Fanny.

'Mamma,' she would demand, 'why can't we live here? Why do we have to live in a little house while you and the boys have this lovely place? There's room for us all here.'

It was difficult to explain. 'Well, you see, Fanny, this house belongs to the boys' Papa.'

'Is he not our step-father?'

'Y ... yes.'

'Well then he should look after us, too.'

'He does.'

'But he doesn't let us live here.'

Oh, dear, what could one say? Then Fanny would behave towards William in a way he did not like. How could one say to her: You must be particularly careful how you treat the Duke for he is the King's son and used to special deference.

One moment he was the King's son and another he was their step-father.

Fanny declared that he was a selfish old beast and she hated him because it was quite clear that if Mamma could have arranged it they would all have lived at Bushy House.

There was another matter which put Fanny into a sulk.

'Why can't I be a famous actress?'

'Because there is no need for you to be.'

'Why not. You are?'

'I had to earn money when I was a girl. You do not.'

'Then what am I supposed to do?'

'When you are old enough I will give a big coming-out ball for you. I hope you will love someone and marry and live happily ever after.'

Fanny was mollified – but only temporarily.

Hester said Fanny would never be satisfied. Nor it seemed would Hester. She, too, would have liked to live at Bushy House.

Now that she was getting older she asked herself – and Dorothy

– what sort of life she had had. She had been subservient to her famous sister all the time. She was perpetually being obliged to ask for more money to run the household. Dorothy was ready to provide it – if she had it. William, though, had now overcome all his scruples. She realized that as in the case of his brothers, money was merely a symbol that passed from hand to hand; whose it was did not matter as long as it was there.

The need for money was like a heavy cloud always likely to appear and overshadow the sunshine of Bushy Park.

But chiefly she was happy when she could be with the children and William in that pleasant state of domesticity enjoying a brief rest from the theatre and caring for the latest babies. They were arriving regularly, and no sooner was one weaned than another was on the way. Frederick was born in December 1799 following exactly a year and a month after Mary.

Five little FitzClarences and the three girls. Eight children in all.

'No wonder I am getting too fat to play Pickle,' she remarked to William.

William laughed at her. 'You still look the same as you did when I first saw you romp on the stage as Pickle.'

That made her laugh with contented derision. So it was when one was observed through the eyes of love.

Danger in Drury Lane

Since the birth of Princess Charlotte the tension within the royal family had considerably lessened. It was true that the Prince of Wales had grown most unpopular. The situation between him and his wife was considered to be unnatural and he was blamed for it. The Princess of Wales was a heroine who was cheered wherever she went; and the people always loved a child. Indeed the little Princess Charlotte was a bright engaging child and although little was seen of her there were anecdotes about her quaint sayings and her charm which pleased the people.

The King doted on his granddaughter and although he deplored the fact that George and Caroline did not live together he had to admit that George had done his duty and provided the heiress to the throne. As long as the little girl continued to thrive the brothers need not be harried into marrying.

Money was a subject which recurred constantly in the royal household, where expenses always exceeded income. The Princes – every one of them – were in debt. Every now and then there would be a piece in one of the papers about the Prince of Wales or one of the royal Dukes having to be dunned for money.

Money! It was the need for it which had driven the Prince of Wales to marry Caroline, and that was a disaster, if ever there was one. The Queen could never think of it without a certain smug satisfaction because George had ignored her advice and taken the King's niece Caroline of Brunswick instead of her own, Louise of Mecklenburg-Strelitz. At the same time she realized that it was a disaster which she should deplore. Caroline was eccentric to madness – and there would most certainly be more trouble there. As soon as Charlotte was a little older she should be taken from her mother's care and put under that of the governess and tutors chosen for her by the King or her father.

'We are not seen in public enough,' said the King. 'We should perhaps go to the theatre now that they've opened this new Drury Lane.'

'Well, you know how you always disliked Mr Sheridan.'

'I always disliked Mr Sheridan and I always shall,' said the King. 'He is a profligate, eh? He is a man who drinks too much, gambles too much, spends too much and is unfaithful to his wife. Do you expect me to admire a man like that, eh, what?'

'I do not. But George is fond of him and thinks him very clever.'

'Hand-in-glove,' said the King. 'It was that fellow Fox. He was the one. Between him and this Sheridan they made George what he has become. And I say I don't like Sheridan and you understand that, eh, what? But I shall not go to Drury Lane to see Sheridan. I shall go to see a play. And the people expect us to go. They like to see us. We should all go . . . you and I and the girls.'

'That woman of William's will doubtless be playing.'

'Well, well, I hear she's a good actress.'

'You would sit in a box and watch William's mistress?'

'I would watch a good actress in a play and I hear she is that.'

'But to live as they do.'

'They live in the only way they can be expected to. I hear they are very respectable there at Bushy, that William does not drink to excess and I have noticed he no longer uses those coarse oaths he came back from sea with. I know he should be married to some German Princess – legitimately married – he should produce a son or two . . . but not too many to be a drain on the exchequer . . .'

The King looked worried. Once it had seemed so admirable for Charlotte to produce a child every year or so. And now look at them – all these sons living dangerously on the edge of some scandal that could erupt suddenly like an active volcano, all in debt, all leading irregular lives with women – and the girls no longer young, spending their lives waiting on their mother, fretful because they were not allowed to go out into the world. Too many of them, thought the King; and passed his hand over his brows. Too many worries, eh, what? But where were we. Theatre!

'Yes,' he said, 'We should go to Drury Lane. The people expect it.'

'To go would be in a way to show our approval of William's . . . connection.'

'You think William should marry?'

'He's the third son and George will have no more legitimate children and Frederick will have none. Shouldn't William have a family . . . in reserve.'

'Think of the cost of bringing a German Princess over for him? Our ambassador to go to negotiate . . . a wedding . . . And for a third son! No. It's not as though this actress of his costs him a great deal. She's a rich woman herself . . . earns large sums, so they tell me. And some of these have paid William's debts.'

'So in Your Majesty's opinion Mrs Jordan is a good financial proposition?'

'Has to be considered, eh, what?' said the King. 'Seems a good woman . . . All those children. Never hear of a scandal. As for William, better for him to be living like a husband at Bushy than racketing around with George and Fred.'

'I see the point of that,' said the Queen. 'But it keeps him from court and he scarcely lives like a royal Prince.'

The King looked a little sad. These days his mind took strange journeys into the past which often seemed more real to him than the present. He tried to hide this from the Queen, but there were occasions when he lost track of time and was not sure whether he was in the past or the present. Now he was thinking of the beautiful Quakeress whom he had loved secretly and often it seemed to him that he had been happier then than ever since; and if he could have lived quietly like a country gentleman in a house like Bushy Park with a good woman whom he loved and their children about him he would have been a very happy and contented man. No ceremonies, no state occasions, no pressing responsibilities. Colonies! he thought. Gordon Riots! Mr Pitt and Mr Fox! Addington and Burke, Canning and the rest . . . all like a lot of wild beasts snarling at him behind the courteous homage they paid to the King. And sons to plague him . . . with their debts and their gambling and their erotic adventures with women which he had never been able to enjoy and which he might have done . . . as well as they did. There were the girls, his girls, with whom he would never part. He would keep them all, particularly Amelia, the youngest, the best loved, his darling, affectionate Amelia who sometimes made everything seem worth while. But even she added to his anxieties with her delicate health. What had life brought him: a crown that was too heavy for him, a plain German Princess whom he could never love but by whom he must do his duty, a family of fifteen with thirteen now living who plagued him and gave him sleepless nights.

Where were they? The theatre.

'Yes,' he said, 'we will go to Drury Lane and take the eldest girls with us. They shall send me a programme and I will choose the play.'

William was amused.

'Dora,' he said, 'you are to be honoured, my darling.'

'What is this?' she demanded to know.

'My father is coming to see you play.'

'Why William . . . is that really true?'

'Yes, he has sent for Sheridan and he is choosing the plays. He will pay several visits and every one is to be a play in which you perform.'

'What does it mean?'

'It means that he does not think badly of us, I suppose.'

She was elated. Somewhere at the back of her mind had always been the fear that there would be some royal command to whisk William away from her. She knew that William's brothers were sympathetic; the Prince of Wales never failed to treat her as a sister; but she could not expect approval from the King and Queen. But now it seemed she was to have, if not that, acceptance.

When she arrived at the theatre it was to find Sheridan in a merry mood, and she guessed the reason.

'Royal Command performance,' he told her with a bow.

'I know. The Duke told me the King and Queen were coming.'

Sheridan nodded. 'They have chosen three plays – and all in which you appear. Now that seems significant to me. Oh, Mrs Jordan, you are rising in the world! To have won the approbation of a Royal Highness is an achievement, I grant you. But of a Majesty – that is very rare. This is the wish of His rather than Her Majesty, I'll guess.'

'It is good news. I confess I shall be a little nervous.'

'Not you, my dear. Believe me, His Majesty is more easily pleased than any of their Royal Highnesses. He has accepted your situation. I don't doubt for a moment that he will be enchanted with your person . . . and your acting, of course.'

'What has he chosen?'

'Three plays, if you please. *The Wedding Day*, *Love for Love* and *She Would and She Would Not*.'

'I should have thought he would have chosen Shakespeare.'

'On this occasion he has clearly chosen what he likes, not what he thinks he ought to like. Which gives a pleasant family flavour to occasions, do you agree?'

He looked at her sardonically and wondered whether even at this time she was carrying a little grandson or granddaughter for His Majesty.

Playing Lady Contest in *The Wedding Day* she was conscious of the pair in the royal box. The watery protuberant eyes of the King were on her all the time – kindly and benevolently.

She would have been surprised if she could have read his thoughts. Pretty woman, he was thinking. Lucky fellow, William.

Fine figure . . . a little plump but all the better for that. And they live there at Bushy with those children. I hear little George Fitz-Clarence is a fine young rascal. Like to see him. Shouldn't send for him, though. The Prince of Wales goes and sees them. Takes presents for the children, Why should he have everything? Making a mess of it, though. Back with that Mrs Fitzherbert now. Wishes he'd never left her. Did he marry her? Good woman. Lovely woman. Catholic, though. What a mess, eh, what? He must remember he was in public. Must think of what was happening on the stage. Must watch William's woman. Not difficult. Easy to watch. Good actress. Pretty creature. Small and womanly. Charming. Lucky fellow, William.

He glanced at the Queen's sour face beside him. Why should they have pretty women while he had to remain faithful to Charlotte?

The play was over. Pretty little Mrs Jordan was taking the bow. She curtsied charmingly at the royal box. The King smiled, nodded and clapped; and everyone cheered. They liked him for liking their Mrs Jordan.

The Queen clapped perfunctorily.

But the evening was a success.

'The King thought you a first-rate actress,' William told Dorothy delightedly. 'He sent for me to tell me so. He said: "Pretty woman, charming creature . . ." and I answered: "The best in the world, Sir." '

Yes, that was triumph.

Love for Love went off with equal success and the next month the Command performance of *She Would and She Would Not* was scheduled to take place.

On the morning of the day an unfortunate incident occurred in Hyde Park. The King was reviewing a battalion of the Guards when one of the spectators who was standing quite close to him was hit by a ball cartridge. After assuring himself that the victim was not fatally wounded and giving orders that he should be attended to without delay, the King continued with the review. But speculation was great. The attempt had evidently been made by one of the soldiers who had fired the volley but it was impossible to discover which one.

The King's cool courage made it possible for the incident to pass off lightly, but it seemed certain that the cartridge had been intended for him.

That evening there was a full theatre. The people might laugh at Farmer George, the Royal Button Maker, but he had an aura of royalty and that was enough to give glamour to any occasion.

But the fact that he had escaped assassination that very morning made people all the more eager to see him.

Sheridan rubbed his hands together gleefully and remarked that the would-be assassin could not have timed his attempt more to the advantage of the theatre.

Dorothy was playing the role of Hypolita in the play and it was one of those which she had made very popular. In her plumed hat, with her quizzing glass and her breeches she was still attractive, although her increasing weight did worry her and, dressed as she was, she could not help wishing that the King could have seen her in this costume as she had been when she had first made the role popular; but she must console herself with the truth that although her figure might not nowadays fit so well into such a costume she could make up for that by the finesse of her acting.

The King and Queen with the four eldest Princesses were in the foyer. Sheridan was greeting them, bowing, smiling, murmuring that the whole company was honoured.

The King glared at him, his face slightly redder than usual, his eyes seeming as if they would pop out of his head.

The Queen acknowledged Mr Sheridan's greeting unsmiling. The man who had helped lead George to his downfall – not, she was ready to admit with something between exasperation and admiration, that George needed a great deal of leading. George would always go his own way; and if Mr Sheridan had not been there to lead him someone else would. But she did not like this clever gentleman who was reputed to be the greatest wit in London.

The four Princesses could not take their eyes from him. The wicked author of *The School for Scandal*, the man who created scandals of his own, who had eloped with his beautiful wife and then betrayed her a hundred times with other women, and above all was the friend and confidant of their fascinating brother the Prince of Wales – who was even more startling in his adventures than Mr Sheridan.

'If Your Majesties will allow me to conduct you to the royal box...'

'Lead the way,' said the King.

When Sheridan threw open the door of the box, bowed and stood aside for the family to enter, shouts and cheers rang through the theatre.

The King, always moved by a show of affection from his people, went to the front of the box and stood there bowing and smiling.

Then suddenly a man stood up and pointed a horse-pistol straight at the King.

There were shouts of: 'Stop him!' And at that moment the shot was fired.

The Princesses screamed; the people in the theatre shouted and leaped to their feet; the man with the pistol was seized by some members of the audience and the orchestra. Everyone was crowding round him.

The King stood erect.

'I am unhurt,' he said.

Pandemonium had broken out in the theatre. The man who had tried to kill the King was hustled away but the noise continued until Mrs Jordan came on to the stage.

'Your Majesties,' she said, holding up her hand for silence. 'Ladies and Gentlemen. The man who fired the shot has been taken away. There is nothing more to fear.'

The Queen said: 'Perhaps we should leave.'

'Nonsense,' said the King, 'we came to hear the play and we shall stay to hear it.'

Mrs Jordan was looking at the royal box. No doubt waiting for the royal assent for the play to continue.

He nodded to her smiling; she curtsied and cried: 'Your Majesties, Your Royal Highnesses, ladies and gentlemen, we shall now play for your enjoyment *She Would and She Would Not.*'

It was an evening to be remembered. No one could help but admire the cool courage of the King. He looked younger and in better health after the shooting than he had been before. In such a situation he had full confidence for he knew how to act. Courage was a quality he had never lacked; it was statecraft that baffled him.

Dorothy played as well as she ever had. She held the audience which was not easy after such a scare. Everyone wanted to talk about it, to ask who the man was, why he had shot at the King, how near he had come to killing him. It all seemed so much more interesting than the fate of characters in a play.

Behind the scenes the Duke of Clarence was waiting for Dorothy when she came in between playing. It was a man called John Hadfield, he told her. He was obviously another of those madmen who got it into their heads from time to time that they should kill the King.

'His Majesty is magnificent,' said Dorothy emotionally. 'I feel tonight that I have indeed played before a King.'

Sheridan said that such an event in his theatre must not go unnoted. When the last curtain calls had been taken he came on the stage to say how happy everyone present was that there had been no tragic outcome of that unfortunate affray. No one need be alarmed. The culprit was under arrest. But they were a happy house tonight because they had His Majesty the King and Her Majesty the Queen with them and what might have been a tragedy had turned out to be merely an incident. His Majesty's cool courage was an example to them all and he believed that they should all stand up and sing the national anthem with special fervour.

Because they would all wish to show their loyalty and devotion to His Majesty he had this very evening composed an extra verse which he was sure every man and woman present tonight would feel, and want His Majesty to know they felt, so he had had the new verse printed and it would now be handed round that they might all rise and sing another verse to the national anthem.

They rose and sang and the King stood up, tears falling from his eyes while his loyal subjects expressed their delight in his escape by singing from the bottom of their hearts the national anthem with Sheridan's additional verse:

'*From every latent foe,*
From the assassin's blow,
God save the King!
O'er him thine arm extend,
For Britain's sake defend,
Our father, prince and friend,
God save the King!'

People were weeping openly, embracing each other and smiling up at the royal box.

The King had not been so happy for many years. His people loved him. A madman had tried to shoot at him and because he had failed his dear people were rejoicing. Pretty little Mrs Jordan – William's woman – was on the stage leading the singing in her enchanting voice; even the Queen was touched.

It was an inspiring evening and he would not let them be too hard on the man who had shot at him. A madman, they said; he had a great desire to be kind to madmen.

And when he returned to St James's it was to hear that the Princess Amelia when she had heard that he had been shot at had fallen into a fit and could not be comforted until she saw for herself that her dear father was safe.

He went to her at once. He embraced her – his darling, the best loved of them all.

'I'm safe,' he said. 'No need to fret. I'm back. All went well. Mrs Jordan is a delightful woman. Plump and pretty. Acts well, sings even better. And even that villain Sheridan composed a very nice addition to the national anthem and they all sang it most loyally. Nothing to fret about, eh, what?'

So in spite of what might have been tragedy the night the King saw Dorothy in *She Would and She Would Not* was a great success for all except poor John Hadfield.

After that incident the relations between the King and his sons improved. They had all called at Buckingham House the following morning to take breakfast with their parents and to congratulate them on their lucky escape.

'We don't see enough of you, William,' said his mother. 'You must not forget your position entirely, you know.'

William thanked her for her kindness. He wanted to say that it was difficult for him to appear as much as he would wish when the lady whom he considered his wife could not be received at court as such.

The Queen understood perfectly and was implying that he should come without her.

The Prince of Wales was also affable to his father and the King to him, but the Queen could not help wondering what her son's real feelings were. She had a notion that his fingers were itching to take the crown. And the poor King's mental state was not improved by incidents like that of last night, however bravely he might stand up to them.

William was thoughtful as he left Buckingham House. He would go to some functions; he owed it to his parents and to his position. As long as it did not interfere too much with life at Bushy. George was happily reunited with Mrs Fitzherbert and was enjoying one of those honeymoon periods during which he was promising himself that they would never be parted again.

He was not very good company at such times.

William left his brothers and went down to the House of Lords where Lord Auckland's bill on divorce was being discussed. He made one of the long boring speeches for which he was becoming notorious, full of allusions and quotations which made him feel he was indeed a statesman.

He spoke against divorce and everyone listened to him in amazement for they knew that when he left the House of Lords he would drive down to Bushy to live in comfortable domesticity with the kind of woman to whom he referred in his speech as 'lapsed'.

It was scarcely likely that this would pass unnoticed. His speech on that day gave rise to a fresh spate of lampoons which once more called attention to his irregular union and the affairs of all the brothers, so that the popularity which had risen through the incidents in Hyde Park and Drury Lane was forgotten.

The royal family was making itself ridiculous again.

On the road to Canterbury

Dorothy was worried about Fanny, and William was a little irritated because of her preoccupation over the girl.

'I declare,' he said petulantly, 'that in your eyes Madam Fanny is more important than the rest of us put together.'

She assured him that it was not true. But he was often sullen about Fanny.

She had to think of Fanny's dowry and when he needed money she became, as he said, almost a usurer, making a bond with him, so that she might be sure that the money was paid back by him when Fanny would need her dowry.

'It's simply that I feel I must do the best for poor Fanny,' she said.

'Poor Fanny!' grumbled William. 'I'd call her rich Fanny.'

How could she make him see that Fanny had always been the outsider? Richard Ford had loved his two little girls – not enough to marry their mother but still he had cared for them. As for the FitzClarence family they were petted by everyone. Their father concerned himself with them; their uncles came to see them; and the Prince of Wales himself was particularly fond of young George, his namesake. The point was, she tried to make William understand, Fanny did not get the attention that the rest of them did.

'I always feel I have to make it up to poor Fanny.'

Fanny had taken a great fancy to Gyfford Lodge, a house on Twickenham Common, which stood in pleasant gardens surrounded by a high wall. It had belonged to the Marchioness of Tweedale before her death and it was now empty and to let. The rent was fifty pounds a year. Not a large sum. And how pleasant for Fanny to have a house which she could call her own!

She should choose her own decorations and they would select the furniture by degrees. It should be Fanny's own house and she should live there with a servant or two; Dorothy guessed that she would want to invite her sisters to stay with her now and then, but the invitation would come from her.

Fanny was enchanted with the idea and for a while she was happy with Gyfford Lodge.

William did not like it, though.

'Damned unnecessary expense,' he said, and a quarrel flared up before Dorothy realized it.

'It happens to be my money.'

William was angry because he had lapsed with the allowance he had pledged himself to pay her.

She was talking like some low scribbler, he said. He'd be damned if he'd ever ask her to lend him another penny, even though he was prepared to pay back anything he had from her. Did she ever consider what she'd had from him? What he'd given up for her? Why he was cut off in a way from his own family. He ought to be going to court; he ought to be serving with the Navy. Why did she think he was denied a place in the Navy? Because he was out of favour with his father. And why? Because he had upset them all by living with an actress who displayed herself on a stage in breeches for anyone who had the price of a ticket to gloat over.

This was too much for Dorothy.

'Did I want to go on acting? I should have been happy to give it all up. Why do I have to go on? Because we'd be in debt ... more than we are already ... if I didn't. You may be a royal Prince but you still need money ... *my* money!'

It was too much. The Duke walked out to the stables, took his horse and rode off in a rage, while Dorothy sat down and wept. Her head was aching, her eyes ablaze with anger. And when she saw her reflection in the mirror, she said: 'I'm growing old and fat. He no longer cares for me.'

She lay on her bed and wept until he came in and found her.

He saw the traces of tears on her cheeks; she saw those on his. Like all the brothers he shed tears when disturbed, though not as readily – nor as elegantly – as the Prince of Wales.

She rose from the bed and went to stand close to him. He put his arms round her.

'We must not quarrel, Dora,' he said.

'It was my Irish temper.'

'It was my arrogance.'

'Oh, my love. What is there for me without you and the little ones?'

'And for me? There would be nothing in my life without you.'

'You are a King's son. You could be at court. There could be a great future for you.'

'My future is here. You are a successful actress. Without us you could be rich, fêted. You need not work so hard.'

'I would throw it all away – all the success and applause – if I might live here in peace for the rest of my life.'

They laughed and clung to each other.

'I could not believe that we were really quarrelling. It was like the end of the world.'

'It would be the end of my world if we could not mend our quarrels.'

'What was it all about? Something silly . . . something of no importance.'

'So it is over.'

'It is over.'

And afterwards she thought: It was money. It's always money . . . money and Fanny.

She was back to the old routine. Working at Drury Lane, snatching what time she could to go down to Bushy. Now and then doing provincial tours because they were profitable and they needed the money.

She was soon pregnant again.

'I must be the most fertile woman on Earth!' she told the Duke.

'I know one to equal you – the Queen!'

'She had fifteen, I believe.'

'Elizabeth was your sixth.'

'You're forgetting Fanny, Dodee and Lucy. Nine with them.'

It was often that he forgot those three, she thought a little resentfully and then chided herself inwardly. It was natural. It was his own little FitzClarences who counted with him.

'And this new one will make ten. Not a bad tally.'

'It's time I stopped having children. It's time I gave up the theatre.'

'It won't be long now. We'll work towards it. I look forward to it, too. How pleasant it will be when you're not constantly running away from us.'

'I long to be home more. Just think, little George is eight now. I feel they are growing up a great deal of the time without me.'

But when the time of birth grew near it meant an enforced rest and how happy she was to drive down to Bushy and say to herself: Now for a few months I shall be with the family.

She came down in January of that year to await the birth of the child and on a bleak February day the seventh little FitzClarence was born – another boy to delight his father. They called him Adolphus and caring for him, having the others about her, with frequent visits from the girls, Dorothy was happy again.

*

But she could not enjoy the peaceful existence for long. There were more engagements to be filled; and two incidents in the next months made her wonder whether she and William should not try to make some arrangement whereby their expenses could be cut by half and to save her from having to work so hard and continuously.

He was deeply in debt, she knew. He was going more often to Windsor and appearing in court circles as his mother wished. He visited the Prince of Wales in Brighton and he as the Prince's brother must be as fashionably dressed as others. There were fêtes at Carlton House. To these Dorothy would be invited for the Prince of Wales never treated her as anything but the Duchess of Clarence.

It always came back to a question of money.

I will give myself another year, Dorothy would say to herself. I will complete this contract. Then we must cut expenses. Fanny was now twenty, most certainly of a marriageable age; Dodee seventeen and Lucy sixteen. It could not be long now before they were married; and then once their dowries were paid she would be relieved of great expense and anxiety. This would be the turning point – when the girls married.

One of the most profitable engagements she was getting was to play in the theatre at Margate – a pleasant seaside resort which though small was becoming more and more fashionable. Like all such towns it sought to emulate Brighton but without the personality of the Prince of Wales that was not possible. Yet Margate was growing more populated every year; houses were being built and rapidly sold; and its great advantage was that if it lacked the high fashion of Brighton it was less costly. It had a good theatre and Dorothy had had several successful visits there.

William was always uneasy when she went on what she called her 'cruises' and he had prevailed on her to take with her as companion the Reverend Thomas Lloyd, one of the chaplains he had taken into his employ when he moved into Bushy House.

Dorothy was paying the Reverend Thomas four hundred pounds a year to teach the children but now that the girls were growing up she felt that he could well be spared – and they left to their governesses and tutors – and could act as companion to her.

The chaplain was an interesting and amusing companion and Dorothy was always glad of his company.

This was particularly so when she received the first of her frights.

The journey to Margate was taken in easy stages; she was to play in Canterbury for a few nights before going on to Margate. They had changed horses at Sittingbourne and were within a few miles of Canterbury when Lloyd looked out of the window and said: 'I think we are being followed.'

Robbery and violence were commonplace on lonely roads; and as dusk was falling it was very alarming to be followed. She looked out of the window. She had seen the two black-clad figures gradually gaining on the carriage; there was no other vehicle on this lonely road but hers – and she was here with the chaplain, the post boys and one man, Turner.

'Speed the horses,' she said.

'I fancy I see lights ahead. It could be Canterbury,' said Lloyd.

One of the men had ridden on ahead of his companion and was now level with the carriage. He glanced in. Dorothy shivered; she thought: This could be the end. Did he know who she was? Did he expect that she would be carrying large sums of money? If they had waited until she was on her way home she would certainly have been carrying a great deal.

The man in black had ridden up to Turner and struck him. Turner's horse reared and threw him. The carriage had come to an abrupt halt which threw Dorothy and the chaplain out of their seats.

'Are you hurt, Mrs Jordan?' cried Lloyd.

The man in black was looking into the window and staring at Dorothy. For a few seconds she believed she was looking into the face of death for he carried a blunderbuss.

It was strange how in such a moment she could think of nothing but Bushy House and the children who would now be in the nursery, the younger ones in bed, George protesting that it was not his time to go and leading Henry and Sophie into rebellion. She pictured their receiving the news . . . and the girls . . . would they get their dowries? All this in the space of a terrifying second.

She had closed her eyes, and when she opened them the man in black was still staring at her.

Then he acted very strangely. He bowed to her and said: 'I am a gentleman.' And turning he went to his companion who had now come up and whispered something.

Then they both rode off in the direction from which they had come.

Turner had picked himself up and was rubbing his head.

'Are you hurt, Turner?'

'No, Madam. Just a few bruises, I expect. He got me before I saw it coming.'

'Then get up and we'll go with all speed to Canterbury.'

She lay back in the carriage. Lloyd looked at her anxiously.

'A close thing,' he said. 'It was lucky they recognized you.'

'You think that's what it was?'

'I can't imagine anything else. They were all set for robbery . . . perhaps murder. And then they suddenly changed their minds. How do you feel?'

'Very shaken. And you?'

'The same,' he said. 'There was a desperate look about them.'

'We must never travel after dark again.'

'I do agree it is most unwise.'

They came into Canterbury and while she was washing off the grime of the journey before going down to eat the meal she could smell being prepared – 'something special in honour of Mrs Jordan,' said the host – it occurred to her that the post boys and Turner would be talking of their adventure and that news would reach London and in the nature of such news it would doubtless be greatly exaggerated. It would probably be rumoured that she had been murdered – or at least so mutilated that she would never walk again.

So before anything she must write to William and tell him exactly what had happened and that she was alive, well and only suffering from the shock of it all.

'Canterbury, half past ten.

. . . We got here about half an hour ago safe after a very narrow escape of being robbed . . .'

She tried to describe it all – the lonely road, the growing darkness, the moment when the Rev. Thomas had first been aware that they were being followed.

'I feel the effects of the fright now more than I did at the time. My hand shakes and I can scarcely hold the pen. It has determined me to stay here the night and never travel after dark. Lloyd and Turner behaved very well. God bless you all. Kiss the dear children for me. I would not have mentioned this but I feared you might have heard it with additions. Be so good as to write to the girls for the same reason. They may be alarmed. I'm afraid you will hardly be able to read this – but I am a good deal agitated – but this a good night will remove.

'I set out tomorrow at seven for Margate. Once more God bless you all.'

She played for two nights in Margate to appreciative audiences but the weather was hot and the theatre stifling and she was glad when a violent thunderstorm broke up the heatwave. From Margate she made the short journey to Canterbury to do *The Belle's Stratagem* there and return the next day for another brief spell in Margate.

These journeys were tiring but so very profitable; and it was necessary to work when there was no London season.

She played to a house so full in Canterbury that she knew it was going to be more than usually profitable and she thought gleefully of telling William how much she had earned on this 'cruise'. Half the proceeds of the house were to be hers and part of the pit had been turned into boxes to bring in higher prices. There was no doubt that the theatre-goers of Canterbury were delighted to have Mrs Jordan with them.

To play before such an audience, to step on to the stage and sense the thrill of excitement that ran through the audience, to throw oneself into the part, to take the audience into one's confidence, as it were, and know that one was in theirs, was a thrilling experience and one for which she would always be grateful. But she wanted to know how the children were. She could not help imagining all sorts of accidents that might have befallen them. George and Henry were far too adventurous and Adolphus too young to be left.

But while she was paid so highly for her work she knew she must go on. There were so many – too many – purposes for which the money could be used.

Before leaving Canterbury that morning she had a happy hour buying presents for the children: a writing case for George, a

288

lanthorn for Henry and a very pretty work-box for Sophie.

It would not be long, she kept reminding herself, before she was back with them.

Had Death determined to catch her? It seemed so.

She was playing Peggy in *The Country Girl* in the Margate Theatre when a draught blew the train of her dress over one of the lamps. The flimsy material caught fire immediately and one side of her dress was in flames.

There was uproar in the audience and several people rushed on to the stage. In a matter of seconds the flames were extinguished.

She was shaken; she knew that she might easily have been burned to death. But there was only one thing to do since she was unharmed apart from the shock and that was to go on playing.

When the play ended she was given an ovation such as she had never had before. But she was trembling, and as soon as the curtain finally fell felt ready to collapse.

Back in her lodgings she lay in bed and thought of the night's misadventure. It was only two weeks earlier that she had faced the highwayman on the Canterbury Road.

It was strange – twice in such a short time to have come close to disaster.

It seemed like a warning.

Enjoy life while it is left to you. Time is running out.

The brief intrusion of Master Betty

Everyone was talking about the Delicate Investigation, that inquiry which the Prince of Wales had set in motion in the hope of proving that his wife Caroline had had an illegitimate child. Sir John and Lady Douglas, her neighbours, had brought this accusation against her and since Caroline had a child, William

Austin, living with her, on whom she doted and treated as her own, the Prince had hoped he would find reason for divorce.

William talked often of the matter to Dorothy. He hoped his brother would get his wish and prove his wife guilty that he might divorce her and marry again. If he did, he would have more children doubtless; and the one hope of the House would not be young Princess Charlotte.

Dorothy knew that William hoped for his brother's release not only for the Prince's sake but for his own. While there was but one young heir in the family the position of the brothers was uncertain.

William wanted nothing, he told her, but to go on as they were. Bushy was his home. She was his wife and with the FitzClarence children made up his family.

The Prince of Wales, however, did not get his wish. Adultery could not be proved. A woman named Sophia Austin came forward to testify that William Austin was her son and that the Princess of Wales had adopted him. The Prince fumed and cursed the woman he had been trapped into marrying; but there was nothing he could do about it.

But Princess Charlotte existed in health, vigour and high spirits to plague her aunts, her grandmother and her governesses and provide that bulwark between the brothers and their duty to the State. Life went on as before. Playing at Drury Lane, going for strenuous provincial tours, bringing in the money and spending it on ever increasing expenses. The FitzClarence family grew every year – or almost.

Molpuss, as Adolphus called himself, was no longer the baby. Augusta had been born a year after Adolphus, to be followed sixteen months later by Augustus. There were now nine Fitz-Clarences and George was only twelve years old.

As they grew up so did they become more expensive. Such a large family needed servants and tutors, a constant renewal of wardrobes and quantities of food. They were a healthy, lusty brood, with the exception of Sophia who was apt to be fretful; and in addition there were the three elder girls.

Fanny continued to be the chief cause for concern. Dorothy had given at Gyfford Lodge a great *fête champêtre* for her coming out and in spite of the fact that it had poured with rain it had been well attended. But Fanny did not make friends easily. She was without the good looks of the rest of the family, lacking in charm and overloaded with self-pity; in addition she was quick-tempered, not as intelligent as the other girls and inclined to be coquettish in a way which sent men scurrying from her side.

Dorothy was often in despair about her prospects. She was no longer very young and there had been no offers of marriage. This was, she had to admit, a mixed blessing, for she had lent William the money which was to provide the dowries and if Fanny had wanted to marry she would have had to ask William for it.

Then oddly enough an elderly gentleman named William Bettesworth offered marriage to Fanny. He was a theatre-goer and Dorothy had been long aware that he came often when she was playing. Sometimes he came to the Green Room and if he could have a word with her was very happy indeed. He admired her greatly; he was in fact in love with her; and one day when Fanny came to the theatre to see her mother he was introduced to her, and since she was Dorothy's daughter, he was deferential and extremely attentive.

He seemed to have come to the conclusion that since he could never aspire to being Dorothy's lover, her daughter was the next best thing, as he desired above all things to be connected with the genius of his favourite actress. He proposed to Fanny and was accepted.

Dorothy was uneasy; but then she would always be uneasy about Fanny.

She would have to produce the dowry which fortunately would be paid over a number of years. This would mean broaching William to honour the bond he had given her, She hated doing this because she knew that William was getting deeper and deeper into debt with each passing year. He had suffered some bad attacks of gout and this had depressed him, so she did not want to ask him for money.

Then Mr Bettesworth died suddenly, but before his death he had made a will in which he left a little money to Fanny providing she would take his name.

So Fanny became known as Fanny Bettesworth which gave rise to rumours that William Bettesworth had in fact been her father and that she was not the daughter of Daly as had been supposed. Another rumour was that Dorothy had had two illegitimate daughters before she met Ford – Daly's and Bettesworth's.

It was all very unpleasant but the press could not let such an opportunity pass.

One blessing was that Dorothy did not have to provide the dowry; but she very much wanted the girls to marry. Like her mother she was becoming obsessed by the idea of marriage. She felt it was the only secure and respectable way of life.

There were also Dodee and Lucy to be considered.

The theatre world was startled into incredulity by the sudden appearance in its midst of a boy of about thirteen to fourteen years who after playing briefly in the provinces came to London and took over many of the tragic roles. He was hailed as a genius and people flocked to see him.

Dorothy first met him when he was brought to her dressing room by his father. She was immediately struck by his unusual good looks and charm of manner; he had a certain diffidence about his abilities and seemed not greatly impressed by all the clamour which his acting aroused.

His name was William Henry West Betty known generally as Master Betty, the young Roscius; and no other actor nor actress on the stage was in such demand as he was.

The whole theatre-going world seemed to dote on him. When he began playing Kemble's Shakespearean roles, Kemble was furious. No one wanted to see Kemble any more; they preferred Master Betty in his roles. When Kemble attempted to speak a prologue he was hooted off the stage with cries of 'We want Betty'. Kemble retired temporarily on a plea of ill health; it was beyond his dignity to stay and be looked upon as inferior to a mere boy. The dignity of Sarah Siddons was also impaired. A pleasant state of affairs, she grumbled, when a mere boy came in and all the years of service were forgotten.

Dorothy was the only leading actress who was not affected. Comedy roles were not for Master Betty.

He might enchant all with his Hamlet but he could not play Peggy in *The Country Girl* nor Nell in *The Devil to Pay*, and the public continued to want these parts.

But when Betty played the streets were filled with people trying to get into the theatre; many people fainted and inside the theatre there was chaos. People paid for boxes and when they arrived found that others who had paid pit prices had climbed into them and taken possession. There was pandemonium throughout the theatre.

Sheridan was delighted, for Betty had saved him from ruin. In the month the boy played at Drury Lane he brought in more than seventeen thousand pounds.

The public was mad for Betty. Everything he did was wildly applauded. His father managed his affairs and demanded high prices for him which were readily paid. There was no actor or actress in London who could fill a house like this wonder boy.

William went to see him and was enchanted by his acting like everyone else. Dorothy sat with him in his box and was not so sure of young Betty. It was true that he had passion for acting; he lived the part, but her professional eye could detect faults and she doubted whether when he lost his youth he would seem so wonderful. It was in fact his youth which made him a phenomenon. He could not play Hamlet as Kemble could. His tragedy could not be compared with that of Sarah Siddons. The public were in fact worshipping youth and the ability of a boy so young to act as he did – which Dorothy was prepared to admit was remarkable. But William declared the boy to have genius and Dorothy, not wishing to be accused of professional jealousy, did not protest. William sent for him to come to the Green Room and then invited him to St James's Palace. Such genius must not be set aside, he declared to Sheridan, who listened sardonically.

Really, Clarence was an old fool, he thought. Just because he lived with a famous actress he thought he had a place in the dramatic world. And he was deluded like the rest. Let him be. The more young Betty was fêted the better for Drury Lane; and Sheridan had no illusions at all – he had lost them all twenty years before. He saw quite clearly that what Master Betty had which greater actors lacked was that most desirable and transient gift of Youth.

'We will have young Betty's portrait painted,' declared William. 'He must be painted as he is now . . . at this stage. I will arrange it.'

And he did and even went to James Northcote's studio to watch him at work.

For the whole of that winter season there were few the public wanted to see but Master Betty.

But the next year when he came back the play-goers had lost interest. Master Betty was a little older; he was no longer a novelty.

They preferred Kemble. They no longer crowded the streets to get in to see Betty. They were critical of him.

Betty was wise. He had made a fortune. He retired to obscurity to enjoy it; and that was the end of the nine days' wonder of the young Roscius.

Bliss at Bushy

William had followed the course of the war against France with great interest and as great a resentment. Through the years he had kept up a friendship with Nelson and he followed the latter's exploits with admiration and delight.

'I should have been a Nelson,' he told Dorothy, 'if they had not stopped me.'

William, Dorothy admitted to herself, was inclined to see himself rather larger than life. In the Lords he believed himself to be a Chatham when in fact his verbose speeches were yawned over by his fellow peers and ridiculed in the press. But he was never meant to be a politician. It might have well been that he would have been a great Admiral.

When Nelson was wounded and lost an eye and arm William had mourned with him; and he had been the first to congratulate him when he came to England and insisted on his visiting Bushy that William might fight over his battles with him in his imagination while Nelson drew plans and explained how everything had taken place.

William would rage and storm after Nelson went because he was not going to sea with him. He was rather difficult to live with at such times; particularly when he suffered from one of his gouty turns.

When he heard that Nelson had fallen at Trafalgar his joy in the great sea victory was diminished by his grief. He came to Bushy to be comforted by Dorothy. He took Frederick on his knee and George and Henry stood beside him while he talked of the glorious sea battle which crippled the wicked Napoleon's power and how Admiral Lord Nelson had saved England from the tyrant. He told of how he himself had served under the great man and that if he had not been his father's son and been held back from following his career he would have been with Nelson on that great day.

The boys listened bright-eyed. They had all decided they would be sailors or soldiers.

Dorothy, watching and thinking of Lord Nelson dying in Hardy's arms on the flagship *Victory*, rejoiced that they were so young. The war would be over before they were of an age to fight.

William asked that the bullet which had killed Lord Nelson be given to him; it was brought to him by Nelson's surgeon and he declared he would treasure it for ever. He had a bust made of the great sailor and kept it in his study at Bushy House.

He was sad for a long time and talked to Dorothy of Nelson and how he had been present at his marriage to Mrs Nisbet, that marriage which had not made Nelson a happy man for the rest of his life, as he had thought it would. But then he had not known he was to meet Lady Hamilton.

But the battle of Trafalgar which was so important to the country brought relief to William in his pecuniary difficulties.

The King sent for four of his sons and when they arrived at St James's he received them all together.

William thought how feeble the old man was getting, and his speech was becoming even more rapid and incoherent. He glared at his sons with those wild protuberant eyes of his and watching him William could not help wondering whether the madness still lurked in him.

The two elder sons, the Prince of Wales and the Duke of York had not been summoned. The King was going to speak of their debts and those of the two elder brothers were so vast that this matter could bring but little relief to them.

William's three brothers, who had joined the group, were the Dukes of Kent, Cumberland and Sussex.

The King glared at them. 'I've had reports,' he said, 'reports I don't like. Debts! Why are there these debts? Why can't you live within your income, eh, what? Every one of you ... Scribblers ... lampoons. Criticism. It's not good for the family. Don't you understand that, eh, what?'

None of them spoke. They knew that the King's questions were merely rhetorical. He would probably go through a list of their sins. They all led irregular lives, it seemed, except Cumberland. William could not remember any scandal about Cumberland. Perhaps he had not been discovered. But Kent had been living with Madame de St Laurent for years in much the same state of respectability as he himself maintained at Bushy; and Sussex had married without the King's consent when he was about twenty and there had actually been a court case to prove that he was not married at all even though he had gone through the ceremony, because a marriage of a royal person under twenty-five without the King's consent was no marriage in the eyes of the State no matter if it might be in those of the Church.

The King thought of them all and particularly William with that nice actress and all those children. Why did his sons have to be perverse? Why couldn't the Prince of Wales be the father of a brood like that ... a legitimate brood.

'Too much talk about your extravagance,' he said. 'The people don't like it. People can turn ... against royalty. Look at France! What if it happened here, eh, what? It would be the fault of libertines and spendthrifts. You ... all of you. With your debts and your women. What have you got to say to that, eh, what?'

Sussex began to protest that he had wanted to live respectably but the King said: 'Don't interrupt me. I've brought you here to tell you these debts must be settled ... without delay ... and then there must be no more. Now at Trafalgar we captured several ships and these have yielded us a certain sum of money. I have £80,000 which I am going to distribute among you four and it is for one purpose, understand me, eh, what? It is to pay off your debts, you understand? Not to be used for jewels and women ... or banquets and drink and gambling. No, nothing like that. Those debts are to be paid. Understand, eh, what?'

They did understand. They would be delighted. It would not settle everything, of course, thought William, but creditors were satisfied with a little to go on with if it came from a royal duke.

He went down to Bushy in an excellent frame of mind. £20,000 to settle some of his debts. Moreover, recently Parliament had voted him an extra £6,000 on his income. He was better off than he had been for some time.

When he reached Bushy it was to find Dorothy there. He had not expected her so soon and when he discovered the reason he was alarmed.

She had felt too ill to go on playing and had decided she must have a short rest. The pain in her chest which recurred when she was tired had been worse than usual. And when she coughed there was a little blood on her handkerchief.

William was all concern.

'You're going to retire,' he said. 'We're going to settle down, both of us. We'll live quietly at Bushy. I have this extra income and I have to tell you why the King sent for me.'

Listening to the good news Dorothy felt better.

This was her dream come true. She would retire and devote herself entirely to the family.

Retirement was all that she had dreamed it would be.

Each morning she awoke to a sense of freedom; no more rehearsals, no more rivalries; no more long and tiring 'cruises', no more sighing as she forced herself into Miss Hoyden's costume and worried whether she had put on more inches about the waist. Now she could grow fat at her ease. She was pleasantly plump, she decided; plump and motherly; and after all that was what she was now: a mother.

They had started a farm on the estate and William enjoyed it as much as his father would have done. The boys liked to make the hay and ride the horses round the fields, even milk the cows. They played games in which William joined – usually of a nautical character; though George who was all for the Army introduced a military note. Fanny, Dodee and Lucy came often to Bushy and were now beginning to regard it as one of their homes. William tolerated Fanny but was quite fond of Dodee and Lucy; and

Dorothy was delighted to see how the two families mixed and behaved towards each other as brothers and sisters.

Fanny's inability to find a husband still worried her; she had taken a house in Golden Square where the two younger girls lived with Hester still and she often made the journey there and stayed with them so that they should not feel that that was not her home too.

But it was Bushy she loved – Bushy with its gracious rooms and its lovely gardens and its noisy military and nautical Fitz-Clarences. Even little Molpuss had decided on his career and toddled about in the sailor's hat which William had bought for him.

William announced that on his forty-first birthday they would have an elaborate party.

It was a sunny day. William and Dorothy were awakened early by the young children coming into their bedroom, headed by Elizabeth.

'Happy birthday, Papa.'

Molpuss, wearing his sailor's hat, scrambled on to the bed and saluted his father. Dorothy lifted up little Augustus and they were all chattering excitedly about Papa's birthday and the party.

'You cannot have your presents yet, Papa,' said Molpuss sternly. 'George said we were all to wait until breakfast.'

William pretended to look disappointed which made Molpuss shriek with laughter; but Augustus put her arm round his neck and whispered: 'Shall I go and get mine so that you can have it now?'

William whispered back that he thought he would wait for fear of offending George.

Dorothy, lying back with little Augustus in the crook of her arm, thought: This is perfect happiness.

They were up early to make sure that everything was in order by the time the guests arrived. William had spent a great deal on having new bronze pilasters fitted up in the hall and new lamps which hung from an eagle fixed to the ceiling. Several new adornments had been added to the dining room, including some beautiful lamps at the doors, of which he was very proud. 'George will be interested in these,' he said. 'Not that we can compete with

Carlton House or the Pavilion, but I think he'll be impressed. The servants look magnificent in their new liveries.'

His brothers York and Kent had offered their military bands to play in the grounds and this offer had been gratefully accepted.

At five o'clock the party was opened by the arrival of the Prince of Wales, whose glittering presence added grandeur to any celebration. With him came his brothers York, Kent, Sussex and Cambridge and other members of the nobility. They walked about the grounds commenting on the excellence and tasteful displays of the flowers while the bands played Haydn's Oratorio of *The Creation*.

This promenade continued for two hours when the bells rang for dinner.

The Prince of Wales had been at Dorothy's side during most of the promenade and when the bells rang he took her hand and led her to her place at the top table in the dining room. He sat on her right hand and the Duke of York took the place on her left.

There could not have been any more obvious indication that in the Prince's eyes Dorothy was his sister-in-law the Duchess of Clarence. William looked on with misty eyes at those two whom he loved so well engaged in pleasant animated conversation while he himself took his place at the extreme end of the table.

The discourse about the Prince of Wales continued witty and lighthearted while the most sumptuous foods were passed around and the bands continued to play in the garden just outside the open windows.

The Prince of Wales congratulated Dorothy on many of her performances and talked knowledgeably of the theatre so that it was a pleasure to discuss the merits of plays and players with someone of such discernment. She appreciated the more intellectual approach he could bring to the subject than William was able to; but looking at her lover at the end of the table she believed she was indeed fortunate to have won his affection.

The Prince wanted to hear about the children, particularly George.

'I daresay they are stationed somewhere not far off,' said Dorothy, 'listening to everything that is going on down here.'

'Could they not come down ... for a little while ... just to have

299

a look at the company – and to give the company the pleasure of looking at them?'

'If Your Highness would not be bored with them . . .'

'My dearest Dora, bored with my enchanting nephews and nieces! But I adore them . . . every single one.'

So Dorothy called to one of the liveried attendants and told him that it was the Prince's wish that the children come to the dining room.

And very soon there they were – all eight of them, led by the intrepid George with Henry marching like a soldier – Sophia, Mary, Frederick, Elizabeth, Molpuss and Augusta. A round of applause, led by the Prince, greeted them. Dorothy found herself weeping with pride in them. They were a healthy, handsome band indeed. They came and made their bows and curtsies to the Prince of Wales who had a word with each of them, and Molpuss almost succeeded in removing the royal diamond shoe buckles so the Prince took the young miscreant on to his knee and fed him with sweetmeats from the table until he was rewarded with a sticky kiss which seemed to please him. Augusta preferred to view her glittering uncle from her mother's knee, and the children made a delightful domestic contrast to all the grand ceremony of the occasion.

The Prince asked about the youngest of the children, and Dorothy sent a servant to tell the nursemaid to bring down the baby; and young Augustus appeared, somewhat startled, from his bed and everyone exclaimed on his beautiful white hair.

William sat back in his chair, the proud father of such a family.

The public had been allowed to come into the grounds for the occasion and while this pleasant scene was enacted they strolled round and looked in at the windows. They saw the Prince of Wales with a FitzClarence on either knee and the rest of the family amusing the guests. The band went on playing. And the people of Bushy said how pleasant it was to have the Duke of Clarence for a neighbour.

The dinner over, the children retired and the Prince of Wales rose to announce a toast.

'The Duke of Clarence.' And when this was drunk he gave 'The King, the Queen and the Princesses', followed by 'The Duke of York and the Army'. When the toasts were drunk the bands played once more and the guests strolled in to the gardens where they mingled with those members of the public who had come in to see them.

It was a happy day, they decided, a worthy celebration of a forty-first anniversary.

When all the guests had gone William and Dorothy together went into the nurseries to see their children, all fast asleep.

'God bless them and keep them safe,' murmured Dorothy; and she wondered what Grace would have thought had she been present on this occasion.

It was not the marriage for which she had hoped, but surely even Grace would have been satisfied.

It was hardly to be expected that the birthday party would have been allowed to escape without comment. The extravagance of the entertainment for one thing was taken up by the press.

Cobbet, the editor of *The Courier* who was constantly attacking the royal family, wrote:

'The representing of the oratorio of *The Creation* applied to the purpose of ushering in the numerous family of the Duke of Clarence whereby the procreation of a brood of illegitimate children is put in comparison with the great works of the Almighty, is an act of the most indiscreet disloyalty and blasphemy. We all know that the Duke of Clarence is not married and that therefore if he has children those children must be bastards, and that the father must be guilty of a crime in the eyes of the law as well as of religion . . .

'I am confirmed in my opinion when I hear that the Prince of Wales took Mother Jordan by the hand . . . taking his place upon her right hand, his royal brothers arranging themselves according to their rank on both sides of the table, the post of honour being nearest Mother Jordan, who the last time I saw her cost me eighteenpence in her character of Nell Jobson.'

The King read of the party and almost wept rage and frustration.

'I help him to pay his debts and what does he do, eh, what? He immediately sets about incurring some more. What can I do with these sons, eh? All very well to honour Mrs Jordan in private . . . nice little woman . . . good actress, good mother, so I hear, eh, what? But an affair like this. Think of the cost! What was the cost of that, eh? He'll be in trouble before long if he goes on like this. Nine children to keep, eh? That place at Bushy. He'll be in debt, you mark my words, and then who's going to get him out of trouble, eh, what?'

The Queen replied: 'There's one thing he can do.'

'What's that, eh, what?'

'He'll do what George did before him. He'll have to marry. Then the Parliament will settle his debts and his income will be increased and he'll be in time, I hope, to give the family some legitimate children.'

'But it won't do. Debts. Extravagance. The people are not so fond of us. There was that bullet. It wouldn't take much . . . I think of France. Sometimes I don't sleep all night thinking of France . . . and those boys. Could be a difficult situation. Should be careful. Shouldn't have parties. Shouldn't drink and gamble. Shouldn't show off their women. People don't like it.'

'I can see the day coming,' said the Queen, 'when William will be in the same position as George was. Then he will have to marry – and marry the wife who is chosen for him.'

The Queen's warning

The idyllic scene at Bushy was too good to last. The usual troubles arose. William could never understand that what he bought would eventually have to be paid for. The cost of his birthday party had been enormous; he had had no idea it would be so expensive.

Dorothy frowned over the bills. 'You couldn't possibly have spent so much.'

'It's all there, all set out,' he replied irritably. His gout was bad that morning. It always was when he was agitated.

'But we're almost as much in debt as we were before you paid off that £20,000.'

'Am I to be blamed because the price of things is so high?'

The decorations to the house had not been necessary. It had been beautiful as it was. So much of the expensive food had not been eaten.

She pointed this out.

'My dear Dora, I fancy I have more experience of entertaining Princes than you have. Not to have given of the very best would have been an insult to the Prince of Wales.'

Dorothy shrugged her shoulders. It was no use continuing with recriminations. They had to find the money – or some of it – enough to keep their creditors quiet for a time.

There was only one thing to do.

She must return to work. On a cold January day she opened at Drury Lane as Peggy in *The Country Girl*.

She was as popular as ever in the early parts, which was amazing considering she was almost fifty years old. She often felt ill; the pain in her chest had grown worse and she was spitting blood again. But the audience was faithful. She could still charm them; she had that indefinable quality which the years could not destroy. Dorothy Jordan was a draw again.

There was the money – always the money. They would manage somehow as long as she worked.

One evening she found Fanny in the Green Room, an excited Fanny, with a secret she was bubbling over to tell.

'Mamma,' she said. 'I'm going to be married.'

Dorothy embraced her daughter. At last she had found a husband! Poor Fanny was about to enter that state which Dorothy herself for all her genius, for all that she had thirteen children – little Amelia had been born to bring the FitzClarence children to ten in number – had never been able to achieve.

'Who is he?' she asked.

'Well, Mamma, he is not in a very good position. He has a post in the Ordnance Office.'

'A clerk.'

'Oh, I know that is not to be compared with a duke, but at least he can marry me. And a clerk in a government office like the Ordnance is no ordinary clerk.'

'That's true,' said Dorothy. 'And are you happy, my darling?'

Fanny nodded. Of course she was happy. She had found a man willing to marry her. She had thought she never would and she was twenty-six years old.

'Then I am happy, too,' said Dorothy.

She was less contented when she met Thomas Alsop; she could not rid herself of the uneasy feeling that he had heard of the dowry which was to be Fanny's when she married. He would know of course that she was the daughter of Dorothy Jordan and there had too been all that publicity when she had inherited the Bettesworth money.

However, Fanny was happy and determined on marriage so preparations must go on.

When she told William of the forthcoming marriage he was not so pleased. The dowry would have to be provided, £10,000 in all. £2,000 was to be paid to the husband on the marriage and the rest at £200 a year. Dorothy had managed to invest in an annuity which would provide for Fanny, but she had been obliged to lend the money which she had saved for the other girls to William; and the fact that she would have to ask for this in the event of the others marrying worried her – and him.

His gout flared up, he was touchy and irritable. A gloom had settled over Bushy House.

But the marriage of Fanny to Thomas Alsop took place and it was arranged that Hester with Dodee and Lucy should share a house they had acquired in Park Place.

This was settled, but somewhat uneasily; and as she was now working hard in the theatre and not feeling very well, Dorothy was beset by fears of the future.

Soon after Fanny's marriage Dodee was betrothed to another clerk of the Ordnance Office, whom Thomas had brought to the house. He was Frederick Edward March, a natural son of Lord Henry Fitzgerald.

'We plan to get married soon, Mamma,' said Dodee.

Dorothy said she was delighted to see her daughter so happy; and then she began to think about the money.

She had found Fanny's dowry but Dodee's would be another matter. It was going to be necessary to ask William to return the money he had borrowed.

He was not well, and he always hated talking of money. There was something undignified, he always felt, when a member of the royal family was asked to pay. The Prince of Wales felt the same;

but he dismissed these matters with an elegant shrug and allowed the debts to mount until they were of such proportions that only the Government could settle them for him. Then they came up with conditions. It was such a condition which had brought him to marriage with the wife he loathed.

Marriage, thought William. What if they were to demand it of him!

Perhaps Dorothy did not understand this.

'I have promised the girls this money,' cried Dorothy in distraction. 'I must have it. Everything else must be put aside but I must have it.'

'They will have to wait for their money like everyone else.'

'Not the dowry, William. They must have it.'

'What about their father?'

She drew back as if he had struck her. It was not like William to refer to those unfortunate incidents in her life. She had thought he understood them. She had told him of the persecution of Daly, her devotion to Richard Ford and the latter's promise to marry her.

'I could not ask him now.'

'Why not. He's comfortably placed. Sir Richard now – and didn't he marry a rich wife?'

'I would not ask him,' she said. 'I have promised this dowry. You must let me have it. I have your bond.'

There was nothing that could infuriate him more than the reference to a bond. He owed her money, he admitted it. He believed it was somewhere in the neighbourhood of £30,000, but to think that she could refer to the *bond* in that way. As though she were a moneylender.

'So what will you do?' he demanded. 'Send me to a debtors' prison?'

'William, I only meant . . .'

'I know full well what you meant, Madam Shylock. I have had money from you . . . which you were pleased to give me and now I must repay it. It says so in the bond.'

She was distraught. So was he. He hated to see her so worried. But he thought of all the creditors who were crying out to be paid. So how could he let her have the money he owed her?

His frustration whipped up his temper. He was saying things

he did not mean, unkind things which were untrue; and she had turned and hurried away.

They were reconciled afterwards but the question of money was between them. It hung over them and would not be dismissed.

He would find the money, he declared, if he had to go to the moneylender he would find it.

'I must take more engagements,' she said. 'I shall work all through the season if I can get them.'

George was now fourteen and William had said he should join the Army as a Cornet.

'He's far too young,' she argued.

'Nonsense!' retorted William. 'I was sent to sea when I was thirteen. It did me no harm.'

So she lost her darling George, and not only did he become a soldier but one on active service. She was distracted when he was sent out to Spain to join Sir John Moore's army. This made a further rift between herself and William, because she blamed him for sending George away at such an early age.

There was the continual round at the theatre. She had to go on stage and play parts like Miss Hoyden, for which she felt far too old and tired when all the time she was conscious of great anxieties. What was happening in the Alsop household? Would Dodee be happy? Would William be able to find the money? What when Lucy's turn came? What of George – such a boy to be thrust into battle!

In May of that year there were riots among the weavers of Manchester. The military were called in to deal with them and two people were killed while several were wounded.

In September Covent Garden was burned down and the rumour was that the fire had been started on purpose. The roof collapsed and nineteen people were killed; the losses were tremendous and a shudder of horror ran through the theatrical world.

Dorothy was concerned about George, for young as he was he was engaged in the battle of Corunna where Sir John Moore the commander was killed. As news of the battle reached home she was frantic with anxiety and so was William until news came of George's safety. This brought them close together again; and Dorothy was at least grateful for that.

That January there was another spectacular fire. It occurred in

St James's Palace and this was declared to be very strange following on the burning of Covent Garden; and as that part of St James's which suffered was the royal apartments, some significance was attached to this.

The Queen said: 'It was done purposely. I always said people would not endure the Princes' behaviour. Our sons will not do their duty. Just think – there is not one who is respectably married. At least the King and Queen of France were that. At least they had *legitimate* children.'

The Princesses were in a state of nervous anxiety. Amelia was growing steadily more and more feeble and the King asked every few minutes what the doctors had said about her and had to be told, untruthfully, that she was in good health. The tension in the royal household was mounting; it was very bad for the King.

At the beginning of February the New Sessions House at Westminster was burned down. There was clearly a dangerous arsonist at work. But was this the work of one person? Was it intended as a warning? The Queen was sure that it was. The King was becoming so vague that he was not sure of anything.

Then there was real panic in the royal family for the biggest scandal since the Delicate Investigation broke upon them.

The trouble had begun with the startling revelations that a woman named Mary Anne Clarke, who had been a mistress of the Duke of York, had been selling commissions in the Army – which his position as Commander-in-Chief of the Army gave her the opportunity of doing.

What would the royal brothers do next? The subject of the Duke and Mary Anne Clarke was discussed in every club and coffee house. The affair could not be hushed up. The truth must be brought to light. The profits may have gone into Mary Anne's pocket, but how deeply was the Duke of York involved?

The publicity was enormous and when the case was heard in the House of Commons the Duke's love letters – ill-spelt and naïve but intensely revealing – were read during the hearing. People were talking about the 'Duke and Darling' and quoting from letters; and although the Duke was acquitted of having been a party to the sale of commissions and it was judged that he was ignorant of what was going on, he could no longer hold his position of Commander-in-Chief.

George came home for a short leave – full of vitality and eager to talk of his adventures as a soldier. General Stewart, whose aide George had been, called at Bushy and told the proud parents that George was going to be a fine brave soldier and that there was no one he would prefer as his aide de camp. William was delighted, but Dorothy was apprehensive, fearing that George would be leaving them soon; and she was right.

The next fire broke out in Drury Lane itself. It started in the coffee room on the first floor which led directly to the boxes; and as the safety curtain did not work all the highly inflammable material on the back-stage made a mighty conflagration when the walls crashed in and the crowds were in danger of being suffocated by the smoke.

Sheridan was at the House of Commons at the time, where the reflection from the fire could be seen through the windows. On the Surrey side of the river people could see the glow for miles; and from Westminster Bridge the effect was startling.

When it was known that it was the Drury Lane Theatre which was ablaze it was proposed that the House should adjourn since the tragedy so deeply concerned one of the House's most distinguished members.

Sheridan would not allow this, although he himself left the House with a few friends and made his way to the burning building.

His theatre in flames! But what could he do to save it? He saw his financial difficulties increased, for the theatre was insured only to the extent of £35,000 which could not cover the entire loss.

Sheridan turned into the nearest coffee house and ordered a drink.

'Mr Sheridan, how can you sit there so calmly?' asked one of his friends.

To which Sheridan replied: 'May not a man sit and drink at his own fireside?'

The remark was repeated with the pleasure that was taken in all Sheridan's witticisms; but no one else could joke about this great calamity.

And when later there was a fire in Kensington Palace, happily soon put out, and the Prince of Wales received anonymous letters that more fires would follow, it was clear that there was some purpose behind these conflagrations.

Almost immediately afterwards there was a rumour that Hampton Court was ablaze. This proved to be false, but this was not the case in the Quadrangle of Christchurch College, where fire did £12,000 worth of damage.

'There is mischief in the air,' said the Queen, and it was the Queen who was becoming more and more influential at court. 'We shall have to consider carefully what should be done.'

The fires stopped suddenly and soon everyone ceased to expect them. In September there was great excitement in the theatrical world because the new Covent Garden was about to be opened with *Macbeth*, and Kemble was to speak the address.

Carriages blocked the street and people jostled each other to get into the theatre; but when it was discovered that prices had been increased they were indignant; they had paid the prices and gained entry but they had no intention of accepting them for the future.

During the weeks that followed they crowded into the theatre for the purpose of creating what were known as the Old Prices Riots; and the fear that the new theatre would be wrecked if they persisted caused the management to relent and to declare that the boxes should remain at seven shillings and sixpence and the pit three shillings and sixpence and that there should be no more private boxes.

It was an uneasy year for Dorothy. William was ill again, suffering as he did from his periodic gout; he had developed asthma and this grew worse as the Queen harped on the damage he did the royal family by living openly with an actress. She pointed out the comments of that man Cobbett whom William knew wielded great influence.

He should abandon his mistress; or at least he could pension her off; and as for all those children, he would have to make provision for them, but that should not be an insuperable task.

He tried to explain that he regarded Dorothy as his wife.

'An actress,' retorted the Queen. 'A woman who parades stages in men's clothes for anyone to pay to go to see!'

'She is the best and most generous woman in the world. I cannot tell you how often she has given me money.'

'You should have been ashamed to take it. That's another thing

I've heard about you. They say you keep her working to keep you. That's a very unpleasant thing to be said of His Majesty's son, I must say. You should put an end to that connection as soon as possible . . . and in view of all that is happening the sooner the better. Your sister Amelia is very ill. If anything should happen to her it would completely turn the King's mind. And all these fires and that bullet at the theatre. Where do you think all this is leading? And you – making an exhibition of yourself with an actress!'

'The people love her. They crowd to the theatre to see her.'

'Yes, to see the actress who is keeping a royal Duke. You should think about this. You should think about us all.'

William went to Brighton for the birthday celebrations of the Prince of Wales while Dorothy, taking a rest from the theatre, was at Bushy with the family.

She was sitting on the lawns with the young children playing about her when Fanny arrived with Thomas Alsop.

They had driven over to see her, they said, because of the news.

'What news?' she wanted to know.

Hadn't she heard that there had been a battle at Talavera?

'Talavera,' she cried. 'That is where George is.'

'Yes, Mamma,' said Fanny. 'There were five thousand killed.'

'Oh, God!' she whispered.

'George will be all right,' said Fanny. 'George would always be all right.'

'I must know.'

'Where is the Duke?' Fanny asked.

'At Brighton. It's the Prince's birthday. He has gone to help him celebrate.'

'He's with the royal family more than he used to be,' commented Fanny, a little maliciously. She had always felt that she with Dodee and Lucy were slighted compared with the Fitz-Clarence children – herself especially.

'I wonder if he has heard,' said Dorothy. 'If so he will come at once.'

'Perhaps the celebrations will be too exciting to miss.'

Dorothy did not answer.

'Mamma, are you ill?'

'I feel my old pain . . . here.' She touched her chest.

'You should be resting. Let me help you to your room. Then I'll stay awhile and play with the babies.'

Dorothy lay in her room. She had been awake all through the night.

They shouldn't have let him go. He was only a boy. Henry was training to be a sailor. They were too young to be sent from their homes. She should have refused to allow it. After all they were her children.

She rose from her bed and paced up and down and sat at her window looking out across the gardens.

Five thousand dead! So many. And among them one young boy?

It was five o'clock in the morning when she heard the sound of carriage wheels.

Her heart began to beat madly. It was William, she knew. He had driven all the way from Brighton and had come as soon as he had heard the news, for he would know how she was feeling.

She ran down to meet him. He looked tired and haggard, but he was smiling.

Surely he could not look like that if George were dead?

'William!' she cried. 'I heard . . .'

'I knew you would,' he said. 'That's why I came right away. He's safe, Dora. There's no need to fret. He's been slightly wounded – his leg grazed by a shell splinter, but he's safe. He'll be home to see you soon and tell you all about it.'

She was sobbing with relief.

'Oh, William, my good, good William. I knew you would come.'

Another scandal occurred in the royal family – and this was the greatest of all.

The Duke of Cumberland's valet was found murdered in the Duke's apartment at St James's in most mysterious circumstances. The popular theory was that the valet had found the Duke in bed with his wife, had attacked him and then either been murdered by the Duke or committed suicide.

This was the greatest scandal of all. The Prince of Wales might be guilty of profligracy, Frederick of dishonesty – and all of the Princes of immorality; but this was the first one who had been involved in murder. Of course the Duke was exonerated but the general opinion was that there was one law for a duke who committed murder and another for ordinary men.

'Such terrible scandals,' groaned the King. 'I never knew the like. What does it mean, eh, what? What will become of us all?'

The Queen sent for William to discuss the affair.

'I do urge you to show some sense,' she said, and added ominously: 'Before it is too late.'

Dodee had married and an arrangement had been made that William should pay the dowry – borrowed from Dorothy – by instalments. He found the position humiliating but he saw no way out of it. He was deeply in debt – more so than he had ever been. When he confided this to his eldest brother the Prince advised him to forget about it, but it was not easy. William knew the reckoning must come.

Meanwhile Dorothy had undertaken extensive tours to bring in more money. For some time Fanny had been talking wistfully about a chance to go on the stage; she had always wanted to act, and married life, she confided to her mother, was not all she had hoped it would be. She would welcome the opportunity of being separated from Mr Alsop for a while and would Mamma consider taking her with her when she went on tour?

'Think, dearest Mamma, I should be company for you and it would give me the chance I never had.'

Dorothy considered this and finally agreed to take Fanny with her.

It turned out to be not such a bad arrangement for Fanny proved herself to be a tolerable actress. She would never be great and she was not pretty enough nor was her personality charming enough for her to succeed to any great extent with audiences, but she could manage a small part and Dorothy was delighted to see her momentarily satisfied.

The tour took them to Bath, Bristol, Chester, up to Liverpool and over to Ireland. It was exhausting and she was constantly thinking of Bushy and home and longing to be there. She was terrified that something would befall George and she had five sons with whom to concern herself. Henry had started off in the Navy which had disappointed him and had begged to be transferred to the Army; and even little Molpuss was being sent to a nautical school to prepare him for his future.

She wanted them to stay young and be babies for ever.

In any case, she told herself, they are too young.

When she returned home it was to receive the news that Lucy was engaged to be married.

Pretty, charming and modest Lucy had been the most amiable of the three girls and had consequently been more welcome at Bushy House than the two elder ones. She could not remember the time before her mother had been the mistress of the Duke of Clarence and being nearer to the age of the FitzClarence children she had been more at home with them than Fanny and Dodee.

It was at Bushy House that she had met Colonel Hawker of the 14th Dragoons. He was fifty, married, with a daughter of Lucy's age, but he had always been fond of her. As aide de camp to the King he was often in the company of the Prince of Wales and was a frequent visitor at Bushy. When his wife had become ill Lucy had comforted him and on Mrs Hawker's death the Colonel asked Lucy to marry him which she consented to do.

Dorothy was not sure whether to be pleased or not. She liked Colonel Hawker; he was a man of good family, but he was so much older than Lucy. Still, Fanny's marriage was far from successful and she had married a young man. Dodee, however, seemed happy and was expecting a child. As for Lucy and Colonel Hawker they had made up their minds and Lucy seemed contented.

So that April Lucy was married to her Colonel in the parish church at Hampton and Henry and Sophia with their mother were witnesses to the ceremony.

The three girls were now settled, but once more there was the tiresome problem of the dowry with its resultant scenes and humiliations.

Dodee's daughter was born in May and Dorothy was delighted to become a grandmother; Dodee and Lucy were happy; it was only Fanny who was disgruntled. But then had she not always been?

Money was the predominant need, so she must undertake more tours. She was growing more easily exhausted and longed for the peace of Bushy.

I will retire definitely next year, she promised herself.

William was suffering from his periodic attacks of gout and asthma; he was very often at Windsor and St James's because the King's health was giving the family great cause for anxiety. The alarms over the fires had subsided but one of the Queen's favourite themes was the need for reform throughout the family.

She took every opportunity of pointing out to William that he was living a most unsatisfactory life.

'You are no longer a boy,' she would tell him. 'Mounting fifty!'

William protested at that. He was only forty-five.

'There is not much time left for you to get a legitimate heir,' the Queen warned him. 'When I think that the only heir all my children have been able to give to the country is Charlotte I despair.'

'Charlotte is a very lively heir,' William reminded her.

'The child is not as strong as I would wish.' The Queen's lips tightened. Charlotte was a wayward child who more than once had expressed her dislike for Grandmamma. Her famous remark which had been bandied about the court was, 'There are two things in the world I dislike – apple pie and my Grandmother.'

'Only this child . . . and a girl.'

William liked his niece, who had a somewhat difficult time because she was denied the company of her father and mother; her mother was often forbidden to see her and her father could never look at her without remembering that she was her mother's child. He was sorry for her. She was a hoyden but bright, intelligent and an interesting child. She was rather fond of his own young Fred and was always glad when Fred paid visits. They went riding together and she would order Fred about, telling him that she was his future sovereign, which Fred seemed to enjoy.

He wondered what the Queen would say if she knew of Charlotte's friendship with her cousin, the son of an actress.

'I always hope,' said the Queen, 'that you will see reason one day . . . and it will have to be soon. I think you should consider this . . . very seriously.'

Dorothy had no idea of the Queen's determination, for William never mentioned it to her.

She continued with her tours, going from one provincial city to another, earning money, trying to ease the financial situation; but she had no idea how deeply in debt William was.

It was a momentous year.

That November, the King's best-loved daughter, the Princess Amelia, died. The King was overcome with grief, and this loss, with the fears and scandals of the last years, sent him tottering to insanity.

The King was mad, and incapable of ruling. The Prince of Wales became the Prince Regent.

'For the last time'

William was on his way to Carlton House where the Prince Regent was giving a fête. This was his first as Regent and although he could not say it was to celebrate his accession to the Regency, for to do so might seem that he was rejoicing in his father's misfortune, that was in fact what it was.

Everything would be different now, William mused. The tiresome restrictions which the King had imposed on the court would be swept away. The court would be gay and carefree. That ridiculous Marriage Act would be annulled. George had always sworn that one of the first things he would do would be to abolish that. Their sisters would be allowed to marry, if they could find husbands. Poor things, it was a bit late. He was sure that George would see that they had allowances of their own which would give them some measure of independence from the Queen. What lives they had led! The men had been the fortunate ones, although the King would have liked to restrict even them.

And now the poor old man, who for years had been on the edge of madness, was a raving lunatic.

He would be well looked after so there was no need to waste sympathy on him. The fact was that George, his dear friend and brother, was now in all but name ruler of the realm.

The Queen had realized this and had decided to ally herself

with her eldest son this time – not work against him as she had before.

The Queen was wise.

Dorothy could not accompany him to the fête – it was a very different affair from the birthday party when the Prince had led her in to dine and sat at her right hand. This was an official occasion, and the Regent would have to be more careful than the Prince of Wales had been. Perhaps that was why he had broken with Mrs Fitzherbert, and Lady Hertford was the reigning mistress now. It was sad in a way when one considered what Mrs Fitzherbert had meant to George; their relationship had been like that of himself and Dorothy, but his and Dorothy's had been on a firmer basis; all those years, all those children. Twenty years with one woman! It was as good as a marriage. But it was not a marriage. Royal princes could not marry actresses and there was only one legitimate heiress, the Princess Charlotte – the only one they had produced between them.

He was reasoning like the Queen.

Carlton House in all its splendour! No one could design a house like George! The Pavilion was different from any residence anyone had ever seen before and there wasn't a house in Europe which was more magnificent than Carlton House – as there was no prince more courtly, more elegant, than the Regent.

He was proud of his brother.

Poor George, he *was* a little sad about Maria Fitzherbert, but their connection was severed and he was devoted to Lady Hertford.

George had explained to William. 'I love Maria,' he had said. 'I always shall. It's this damned religion of hers. If she hadn't insisted on marriage . . . But the main point of contention is that she's a Catholic. How could the Regent have it said that he was married to a Catholic? It would be enough to shake the throne. We have to consider that, William. All of us.'

Was he reminding William that like the rest of them he had his duty?

George was receiving his guests, magnificent as ever, the diamond star glittering on his coat. Then he led the way into the banqueting hall with its treasures, its works of art. The table was a work of art too, with a stream running down the centre in which gold and silver fishes swam.

It was during the banquet that William became aware of the beautiful young woman. She was exquisitely gowned, animated and in conversation with a young man who appeared to be paying court to her.

'Who is the young lady?' asked William of his neighbour.

'Did not Your Highness know? She has caused quite a stir since she has come to court. She is Miss Catherine Tylney-Long, daughter of the late Sir James Tylney-Long.'

'I'm not surprised that she causes a stir. She is very beautiful.'

'Oh, it is not her beauty which causes a stir, Sir. It is her fortune. She is worth £40,000 a year.'

'£40,000 a year!' cried William. 'She must be one of the richest young ladies in England.'

'That is the general opinion, Your Highness.'

'And who is that who is talking to her so earnestly?'

'Wellesley-Pole, Your Highness. Lord Maryborough's son.'

'Is he related to the Duke of Wellington?'

'Yes, Sir.'

'Interesting,' said William; and he thought: £40,000 a year. And a beauty too. Young, lovely and rich.

When the banquet was over he asked that Miss Catherine Tylney-Long be presented to him. He found her even more charming than he had believed possible. Witty, amusing, not the least impressed by the interest of a Royal Highness, in fact very diverting.

He insisted on keeping her at his side, much to the chagrin of Wellesley-Pole, but the young lady seemed to enjoy this; and it was a gratifying experience.

He was very loath to leave her and when he said good-bye he had discovered what functions she would be attending and decided to making a point of being there.

He did not go to Bushy afterwards, but to his apartments in St James's.

I have been leading a strange life for a royal prince during twenty years, he thought. I have forgotten what it is like to be in fashionable society. People noticed it and did not like it. A prince should live like a prince not like some bourgeois gentleman dominated by domestic concerns.

*

Everywhere he went there too was Catherine Tylney-Long. So beautiful, so enchanting and so . . . rich. He could not think of her without thinking of £40,000 a year, and what it would mean to him.

He realized that he was in love. He was in love with the beautiful face and figure of Miss Tylney-Long and her beautiful income.

When thoughts of Bushy crept into his mind he pushed them away. Twenty years was a long time to be faithful to one woman and princes had more temptations than most men.

He could not expect Miss Tylney-Long to be his mistress; her family would never agree to that, but doubtless if he offered marriage they would be overcome with delight. Their heiress would become a Duchess and no ordinary Duchess because it was just possible that if anything happened to Charlotte, one day Miss Tylney-Long would be Queen of England.

William remonstrated with himself. What am I thinking of? What should I tell Dorothy and the children? How could I possibly go down to Bushy and say: 'I'm going to be married.'

And yet . . . he was a Prince and he had his duty. His mother was constantly instilling that into him. His duty . . . his duty . . . to marry a beautiful young girl and £40,000 a year!

Debts were mounting. He dared not think what he owed. If he married he would get a settlement and his debts would probably be paid by a government grant. They would be delighted, for everyone must be rather uneasy while there was only a young girl to follow her father. If Charlotte died without offspring what would happen to the House of Hanover?

It was his duty to marry . . . and to marry Miss Catherine Tylney-Long.

He went to Carlton House to see his brother.

George had changed since he became Regent. He was very much aware of his greater responsibilities, and less approachable. Matters of State occupied him a good deal. He was keeping the old government in power, much to the disappointment of his friends, and it was clear that he was going to act cautiously at first. He had made an impression among the artistic section of the public by letting it be known that he intended to support them as his father had so lamentably failed to do. He was serious, aware of new responsibilities, but none the less ready to listen to William's troubles, good brother that he was.

'I am in a dilemma, George,' said William. 'It sounds incredible and foolish at my age. But I have fallen in love.'

'It is never incredible or foolish to fall in love,' said George.

'Do you think that? I am relieved. She is young and very beautiful. Miss Catherine Tylney-Long.'

'And rich,' said the Regent.

'I admit that that is no bar to marriage.'

'So you want to marry her?'

'There would be no other way of gaining her favours . . .'

'Or her money,' added the Prince. 'Forgive me. There is so much talk of money about me that it is constantly in my mind. So you have fallen in love with this delightful girl and want to marry her. What of Dora and the children?'

'That is what worries me. But I think Dorothy would see reason. She is very fond of me.'

'Perhaps for that reason she would be reluctant to let you go.'

'I have long been disturbed because I have failed to do my duty by the State. The Queen is constantly making it clear to me that I should marry. It would be my duty to make sure that Dorothy and the children were well taken care of and then . . .'

'So you really want to marry Miss Tylney-Long?'

'I am aware,' said William, 'that I should need your consent. But somehow I don't think you would withhold it. You have always deplored the Marriage Act.'

'If you wished to marry Miss Tylney-Long of course I should not withhold my consent.'

William was suddenly light-hearted. 'George, you have made up my mind for me.'

'I hope not. I hope your feelings for the young lady have done that.'

'Of course. Of course. But you have always been the best of brothers . . . kind and helpful . . . always ready to make my concerns your own.'

The Prince looked sad and William knew he was thinking of Dorothy and the children. He had always been fond of them all.

'I hope,' he said, 'that you will be very gentle with Mrs Jordan.'

'George, you know I will. I have a great affection for her.'

The Prince nodded. He was thinking how sad it was that so many men found it impossible to be faithful to one woman; and he was thinking of himself as much as William.

'There is one thing,' he said at length. 'Before you begin your courtship of Miss Tylney-Long you should make your arrangements with Mrs Jordan.'

'You mean . . . tell Dora now?'

The Prince looked sadly at his brother and nodded.

'It is the only way,' sighed William.

It was inevitable that Dorothy should hear rumours. The name of Catherine Tylney-Long was constantly being mentioned. Who was this lady? she wanted to know. One of the richest heiresses in England, was the answer. There was a great deal of angling going on among the fortune hunters, and no wonder. Such a prize was not to be won every day.

Wellesley-Pole was reckoned to have caught her fancy, but the Duke of Clarence seemed to be at those functions which she attended, which was strange when it was considered how he had been hiding himself from society for years.

One day Dorothy went in a library to read the papers; she did not go out much when she was on tour because she was so well known that it was difficult for her to evade the stares of passersby; on this occasion she had evidently remained incognito, for two women were discussing the Duke of Clarence and Dorothy Jordan.

'It's over,' said one to the other. 'Fancy! After all these years.'

'Has he left her, then?'

'Oh, yes. Left her and the children.'

'Ten of them. Fancy. What a family!'

'And now he's chasing that young girl, that heiress. She's very beautiful, they say, and the Jordan is now fat and fifty.'

Dorothy was unable to resist the temptation of speaking to them. She said: 'I could not help hearing you mention my name.'

They stared at her, overcome with confusion.

'I was very interested to hear your comments,' she said. 'You know so much more of these matters than I do.'

With that she left them.

There had always been these scandals. It was not the first time she had heard that William was considering leaving her; and more frequently the gossip had concerned her. There had been many occasions when she had been accredited with lovers.

William was writing to her regularly, sending her news of the children. Everything must be as usual.

She was not sleeping well. She would wake in the night and think of the acrimonious words they had exchanged over the girls' dowries. William had never forgotten that she had made a legal matter of his debts even though she had explained again and again that it was only the girls' money that had to be treated in this way. Everything else he had had from her he was welcome to.

Money. It had been the constant theme of their life together. Was it to be the reason for their parting? Money! She dreamed of it; and when she awoke the words were ringing in her ears: 'One of the richest heiresses in England.'

She was playing at Cheltenham when she received a letter from William.

He believed that her engagement there had finished but she had arranged to stay one more night to play Nell in *The Devil to Pay* for the benefit of one of the actors, and she was about to go on when the letter arrived.

She read it and could not believe it. It was as though all the rumours she had overheard came echoing back to her. It's not true, she thought. It can't be true.

Feeling sick and faint she gripped a chair for support. There were the words written in William's familiar handwriting. He wanted to see her immediately and he wished her to meet him at Maidenhead *for the last time*.

For the last time. Oh, God, she thought. What does it mean? She thought of the women in the library, all the gossip of the last months, all the sly allusions in the papers.

It couldn't be. There was some other explanation.

She must go to him at once. She could not play tonight. But what of Watson's benefit.

She *must* play tonight, but as soon as the play was over she would go to Maidenhead, for she could not endure the terrible suspense longer than was necessary.

'Mrs Jordan on stage!'

The familiar cry. The call which must always be obeyed.

She stumbled on. Strangely enough she did not forget her words; she played so that no one would guess that her thoughts were far away. At Maidenhead. At Bushy with the children. With William.

She thought: My carriage is at the door. As soon as the curtain falls, I shall not stop to change my clothes. I will go in Nell's costume. I must know ... soon or I shall die.

She felt near to fainting; but she tried to think of poor Watson who was so urgently in need of his benefit.

The audience did not notice her abstraction. So many times had she played Nell that she could play her absentmindedly. But when she came to the scene when the character of Jobson says: 'Why, Nell, the Conjuror has made you laughing drunk!' before which words she fell into fits of laughter, she found it impossible to laugh and to her dismay – and that of Jobson – she burst instead into tears.

Jobson's presence of mind saved the scene.

'Why, Nell,' he said, 'You're *crying* drunk.'

Such quick wits brought her relief, reminded her of the need to go on playing no matter what the trouble.

And so she played through to the end and when the curtain fell hurried out to her carriage and drove through the night to Maidenhead.

He was impatiently awaiting her arrival in the inn at Maidenhead which he had chosen for their rendezvous.

'Why, William,' she cried, when she saw him. 'What has happened? You are ill.'

He looked at her and shook his head. He was almost weeping.

'I did not understand your letter. "*For the last time.*" What does it mean?'

He hesitated, seeking for words and failing wretchedly to find the ones he needed.

'It has to happen, Dora ... dear Dora, it has to be.'

'You mean we are to ... part?'

He nodded.

'But why ... why ... after all these years?'

'It ... it has to be.'

'You have been ordered? The Regent has . . . ?'

He said: 'Dora, we have to bear this . . . together.'

'We have borne so much together, William, these last twenty years. If we are together I can endure anything.'

'But not . . . living together. We have to separate. I have to marry. My mother, Her Majesty the Queen . . . has made my duty clear to me.' He started to speak very quickly. 'There is only Charlotte. The Regent has refused to live with his wife. Fred's wife is barren . . . They tell me that it is my duty . . .'

'To marry . . .'

'Before it is too late.'

'And that means . . .'

'That we must part.'

She thought: I am going to faint. But I must not. I must be strong. I must try to understand. I must be brave.

'The children . . .'

'They will all be taken care of. *You* will be taken care of.' Again that almost pathetic eagerness to assure her that all would be well.

'But now . . . after all these years . . .'

'Dora, believe me, I shall always love you. But I have my duty to the State . . . to my family. This has been gradually borne home to me. I *have* to do my duty.'

She was silently groping her way to a chair that she might sit.

'So you will marry.'

'I must, Dora.'

'And you wish to marry?'

'It is no wish of mine. I am in debt. I cannot go on like this. My creditors will not allow it. And I must do my duty to the State and my family.'

It was like a theme. Duty to State and family; and if that were not enough: Money.

'I see,' she said slowly.

He came swiftly to her and placed his hands on her shoulders. 'I knew you would. You have always been a wonderful woman. Dora will understand, I told myself.'

Understand? she thought wildly. That this is the end of my life? I cannot lose him, for to lose him is to lose everything . . . everything that I care for. She had always known that it was not fame

323

she wanted. It was her home, her husband, her family.

'The children,' she said faintly.

'All taken care of. You must not worry. It will all be drawn up legally. There is nothing to worry about.'

'Nothing to worry about! I am to lose you . . . and there is nothing to worry about?'

'I shall not separate the children from you,' he said. 'You shall see them whenever you wish. You will have an income. I shall see to this. I shall have it all drawn up . . . You are all right? You are feeling ill?'

'I am feeling,' she said, 'as though my life is ended.'

'The lovely little nice angel'

There had, she reflected, never been a time in her life for happiness; now there was no time for grief. How often during those happy hours she had spent at Bushy had she been reminded of the transience of the peace she was enjoying? Always there had been the contracts to fulfil, the money to earn. Now sick and weary, wanting to do nothing but to shut herself away from the world, she dared not give way to the momentary comfort of mourning; she must think of the children's future.

The elder boys were away from home, but the younger ones were there. She had their future to think of. William had said it would be secure, but how far could she trust William? All the time when she had believed him to be the faithful husband – in every way but one – he had been planning to leave her.

Bushy – with its lovely lawns, its gracious rooms, the home that she had loved as she would love no other, was where the happiest days of her life had been spent. It had changed – with her life. The servants were different. They looked at her covertly. They knew. Did they always know . . . before one knew oneself?

The little ones shrieked their joy to see her.

'Mamma is home,' cried nine-year-old Molpuss. He hugged

her. How long, she wondered, shall I be able to keep him? How long before he is taken away to train for the Navy?

Elizabeth, Augustus, Augusta and Amelia. She kissed them all in turn.

'And where is Sophie?' she wanted to know.

'She went away with Papa,' she was told, and her heart sank. Was he planning to take the children away from her, too?

Her lips set firmly. She would never allow that. Oh, yes, there was no time for grief. She had to fight.

That day the girls and their husbands came over. Fanny with Alsop, her eyes alert with speculation. She distrusted him and had always known he had married Fanny for what he could get. Poor Fanny! Then Dodee and Edward March. She liked Edward best of all her sons-in-law although she thought that perhaps Colonel Hawker would be a better friend to her. He was after all most knowledgeable of affairs; he had moved in the circle which she had frequented with William. It would be different now, she supposed.

Lucy kissed her fondly – always the most affectionate of the girls.

'Oh, Mamma, we have heard the news. I couldn't believe it. That's why Samuel said we must come over and see you at once.'

Fanny said spitefully: 'He's like all men. He's not to be trusted. I never liked him. He couldn't forget he was the King's son. He pretended he forgot it but it was all a sham. When you think of the money he's had . . .'

'Hush,' said Dorothy sharply. 'I do not want to hear a word against the Duke. He has always behaved with courtesy and kindness. This has ended . . . for State reasons.'

Fanny looked at her mother in amazement.

'You believe that? Why, he's been chasing this heiress all through the summer.'

'Fanny, I said be silent.'

Colonel Hawker laid his hand over Dorothy's.

'What is done is done,' he said. 'Now we have to make sure that everything is taken care of.'

Yes, thought Dorothy, she had reason to be grateful to Samuel Hawker.

*

William could not wait to continue his courtship. He had made with all speed to Ramsgate, taking his fifteen-year-old daughter Sophie with him to show that there was nothing clandestine in his courtship.

William had always been seen in the lampoons and cartoons as the rough sailor and although it was long since he had been to sea he was known as the 'royal tar', and was reputed to be without finesse and the courtly graces of his brothers.

He now started to prove this picture of him to be true. His courtship of the heiress was clumsy in the extreme; so was his gesture in taking Dorothy Jordan's daughter with him to Ramsgate to witness it.

Sophie was bewildered and therefore sullen. She had been brought up in the homely atmosphere of Bushy where she had believed harmony reigned between her parents. Now she was suddenly exposed to the antics of an ageing father paying court to a young girl.

She was bewildered, bad-tempered and uncertain whose side to be on. She wanted to be with her mother to ask what this was all about; and on the other hand she liked the gaiety of all the festivities at Ramsgate that were to celebrate the naval fête which was in progress and was the reason why fashionable society was there.

Catherine was amused by the Duke's pursuit. She thought him old and scarcely attractive, but he was a royal duke, and her mother had pointed out the glorious possibilities which marriage with him could bring.

Lady Tylney-Long, widow of Sir James, had had two sons and three daughters – the two sons having died and Catherine being the eldest of the girls, as one of the wealthiest heiresses in the country, was certain to have a host of suitors. Lady Tylney-Long hoped her daughter would choose wisely; but Catherine was a girl who would have her own way.

William could not help being a little piqued. He had expected that his title would have bemused Catherine to such an extent that she would have accepted him immediately.

Her mother was aware of what marriage with him could mean; but she was also aware of the difficulties of achieving it. The consent of the Prince Regent was essential; the Queen would have to approve, she supposed, and it was the custom of the family to marry German princesses.

She talked this over with Catherine.

'It would be absolutely necessary to know that a marriage could take place before you accepted him,' she said.

'My dear Mamma. I am by no means certain that I am going to accept him – so we need not concern ourselves at this stage.'

'He is devoted and impatient.'

'And you must admit a little ridiculous. A man with a left-handed wife living – an actress who has borne him ten children! Oh, Mamma, it is an *extraordinary* situation in which to find oneself.'

'You are very frivolous and thoughtless, Catherine.'

'On the contrary, Mamma, I am both serious and thoughtful. That is why I shall keep my Lord Duke dangling for some time yet.'

And she did.

She was fascinated by William Wellesley-Pole, who was young, handsome and much more suitable than that other William of Clarence.

But a duke! her mother continued to remind her. Did she realize that there was a possibility – a remote one admittedly – of her becoming the Queen of England? The Duke of Clarence was fourth in the succession to the throne. She did think Catherine should consider that.

Catherine retorted that there was only one thing she would consider and that was her own inclinations.

Her aunt, Lady de Crespigny, who was on very friendly terms with the Duke and to whom he wrote of his passion for Catherine wrote to Catherine and to her mother to tell them that the Duke's intentions were of a very serious nature; and she thought Catherine would be foolish not to give them the utmost consideration.

But Catherine was perverse.

'Marriage,' she said, 'is a serious undertaking. I should be no more impressed by the possibility of his having a crown than he should be about my fortune. But I admit,' she added judiciously, 'that these considerations will not be ignored on either side.'

Meanwhile she continued to flirt with her admirers at the head of whom were William Wellesley-Pole and the Duke of Clarence.

While Dorothy waited at Bushy House for William to come and discuss the settlements which would have to be made on their separation, William stayed on at Ramsgate, behaving like a young and ardent lover.

He was writing frequently to Lady de Crespigny giving her accounts of the progress of his courtship.

'Dear Lady Crespigny,
'I write at this singular moment because I have just left your lady-ship's lovely and truly amiable niece after having had the happiness of dancing with Miss Long the whole of the evening . . .

'Of course my attentions are clearly pointed to Miss Long, and I really flatter myself the lovely little nice angel does not hate me . . .

'I went to Lady Catherine's in the evening and escorted over to the library Miss Long. She had promised to dance two dances with Pole. I had previously obtained Lady Catherine's consent for the whole night, and made her promise in future whilst we remain here to dance with me, and to cut the matter short I told Pole very civilly I would not give her up to any man . . .

'Her dear consent is all that is wanted. Her relations wish it and so do mine. Mrs Jordan has behaved like an angel and is equally anxious for the marriage. Miss Long therefore cannot be afraid of any éclat from that quarter . . .

'My two elder brothers are married and I am therefore at this moment the first unmarried man in the kingdom . . . The character of the third son of the King cannot be a secret and I know she likes what she has heard of me . . . She must be persuaded I really love her; why come to this place but to see and converse with her? In short, can Catherine Long love the Duke of Clarence?'

But in spite of his devotion and his assurances to her family that his intentions were honourable William was obliged to continue his courtship and Miss Long kept her suitors waiting on her decision.

Ernest, Duke of Cumberland, who liked to meddle, called at Bushy House. He was smarting from the affair of the murdered valet which had happened only a year or so before and it was pleasant to have the limelight turned on one of his brothers. The Dukes of Kent and Cumberland had never been on the same terms of friendship as the rest of the royal brothers. The Duke of Kent, it was said, had been in some way responsible for the exposure of the Duke of York over the Mary Anne case; now Cumberland wanted to play his part in Clarence's affair. It was for this purpose that he went to see Dorothy.

'My dear,' he cried, embracing her, 'this is terrible news. I came to commiserate with you on the misdeeds of my brother. I am ashamed that he could treat you so.'

Dorothy immediately came to her lover's defence.

'I am afraid it has been forced on him.'

That made Cumberland laugh.

'Did you not know that he has been angling for Catherine Tylney-Long all through the summer? He is declaring himself passionately in love with her.'

'All through the summer,' she echoed, thinking of those affectionate letters he had written to her at that time, telling her about the children, never giving a hint that he was courting this girl. She thought of the money she had sent him, money earned by her performances when she was far from Bushy and longed to be there but dared not give up because they needed what she could bring in to the home.

'As for the family's wanting him to marry. They might think it advisable for him to marry a German Princess, but do you think they will give their approval to marriage with Miss Long? They might . . . as she is so rich and he's in debt up to his ears . . . but I thought you should know that he is treating you shamefully. And you should make sure that you get a good allowance from him. He should pay for his sins. I am sure the Regent will be of this opinion.'

Dorothy was overcome with grief. This changed everything. He was deceitful as well as unfaithful. She felt weary of everything.

If it were not for the children she would go right away, go abroad, hide herself, prepare to die for she felt so ill that she could not believe that death was not far off.

Cumberland went on to give her details of the gay doings at Ramsgate. Clarence was not there because it was a naval occasion but because the Tylney-Longs were there. He had deceived her completely. He made a point of dancing throughout the evening with the heiress; he never left her side; he was quarrelling incessantly with Wellesley-Pole because he was one of Miss Long's favoured suitors.

It was too humiliating.

But it was true. Cumberland had brought the papers to show her.

There was one cartoon in which was portrayed a boatman bringing his boat to shore. The boatman was clearly the Duke of Clarence and standing on the shore was a girl, her apron full of gold coins. Beside the girl was another figure – Wellesley-Pole – and in the background Dorothy herself surrounded by ten children. From her mouth came a balloon in which were the words: 'What, leave your faithful Peggy?'

A verse reputed to be Miss Long's response to the importuning of the Duke ran:

'Sir, if your passion is sincere,
I feel for one who is not here;
One who has been for years your pride,
And is, or ought to be, your bride;
Shared with you all your cares and joys
The mother of your girls and boys.

Tis cruelty, the most refined
And shows a mean, ungenerous mind,
To take advantage of your power
And leave her like a blighted flower.
Return to Mistress Jordan's arms,
Soothe her and quiet her alarms;
Your present difficulties o'er,
Be wise and play the fool no more.'

'So you see,' said Cumberland, 'I tell you only the truth. I feel it right that you should know it. Don't trust him, but make sure he does what is right by you and the children. I am sure the Prince Regent will agree that this should be.'

Dorothy thanked him. She wanted to be alone with her misery.

After a while her grief gave way to anger.

To be so deceived! After all these years, how could he do this? She remembered how ardent he had been when he had sought her. Then she had regarded herself as Richard Ford's wife, and who knew he might have married her. How much happier she might have been as Lady Ford, the respected wife – and widow now – of Sir Richard.

But she had loved William; she had borne his children, her own beloved family.

What would become of them all if he married this heiress?

He was making a fool of himself. The writers said so. 'Be wise and play the fool no more.' An ageing man, chasing a young girl ... and for her fortune. It was too humiliating to be endured – for him and for her.

She sat down and wrote two letters, one to William in which she told him that she was aware of his antics at Ramsgate and that she knew that he had lied to her about being forced to make a State marriage. She realized that it was Miss Long's money he needed – for she could supply him more liberally than an actress, however hard the latter worked.

Then she wrote to Cumberland and thanked him for calling on her and telling the truth of what was happening in Ramsgate.

In her agitation she put the letters into the wrong envelopes, so that Cumberland received Clarence's and Clarence Cumberland's.

Everyone was talking about the great quarrel between Clarence and Cumberland. It was whispered that the elder would challenge the younger to a duel.

There were always spies to report royal actions and the great joke was that Cumberland had told tales of his brother to Mrs Jordan who, naturally indignant, had written to her ex-lover telling him what she thought of his conduct ... but the letter had gone to Cumberland and her letter of thanks for his revelations to Clarence.

What a joke! What a genius these brothers had for supplying the gossip writers with exactly the material they needed.

Miss Tylney-Long did not care to be involved in such a controversy. Her name was constantly in the newspapers and she was always depicted with her arms full of rent rolls of gold coins on which the lusting eyes of the Duke rested – not on her pretty face.

She refused to take the advice of her friends and family who saw that her fortune might purchase a crown.

She accepted William Wellesley-Pole. She preferred him in any case.

So William was the rejected suitor.

The refusal of Miss Tylney-Long did not deter William from looking for another heiress; and almost immediately he was seeking to make Miss Mercer Elphinstone his bride.

Miss Elphinstone was less rich than Miss Tylney-Long, but only a little less. She was young and good-looking and had ingratiated herself so completely with the Princess Charlotte that she almost controlled all the Princess's actions.

She pretended for a while to consider the Duke of Clarence, but never seriously. William was hurt and bewildered. He had thought that royalty was a passport to marriage with any woman who could only achieve it through marriage with a member of his family.

He was mistaken. The young ladies saw William as a ridiculous old man; he had not waited long to mourn the loss of Miss Tylney-Long. He was determined on an heiress obviously and had not the wit to pretend that he wasn't.

Miss Elphinstone was not the sort of woman who cared to be ridiculed and she soon made it clear that she had no intention of taking the Duke seriously.

To be rejected so publicly was humiliating to the family and the Prince Regent was displeased.

'Good God,' he cried, 'aren't we unpopular enough? Do you have to make us *ridiculous*! You would have done better to have stayed with Dora.'

William agreed, but he would try again. He would find one heiress who was glad to have him.

Dorothy meanwhile had done her best to put the Duke in a good light, but insisted on his paying her an adequate income with which she could support the younger children.

The Duke knew he must concede to her request and promised to allow her £1,500 every year for the maintenance of his children, and £1,500 for herself; for her house and carriage she should have £600, and £800 to make provision for Fanny, Dodee and Lucy.

There was a condition. Should she return to the stage the £1,500 a year paid for the maintenance of her children should not be paid and the children should return to their father.

The settlement was completed.

Dorothy found a house in Cadogan Place and decided that this should be her new home. To this she took the younger Fitz-Clarences, the Alsops, the Marches and the Hawkers. At least she had all her children under one roof.

And there she proposed to live quietly for the rest of her life.

The choice

Dorothy was trying to settle down in Cadogan Square and make something of her life. She had lost William; she would not wish to have him back now. He had disappointed her; he had not only deserted her but had made a fool of himself publicly. Why had he thrown away everything they had built up over the years for the pursuit of a young girl whom he could not have cared greatly about since as soon as she had refused him he was courting Miss Elphinstone?

Why did people whom one believed one knew thoroughly suddenly become as strangers? For the sake of what looked like a whim he had broken up and brought great unhappiness into the family.

She would do without him. With the help of her children she could reshape her life. She had engaged a governess for the children, a Miss Sketchley, who was a great comfort to her and favourite throughout the household. She heard regularly from George and Henry who were together now in the Army. Only Sophia was remiss, but then Sophia had always been unpredictable. She wondered what her daughter had thought when she had to watch her father dancing attendance on Miss Tylney-Long as she had had to do at Ramsgate.

What had possessed William to behave in such a way? Perhaps it was because he had suddenly realized that he was no longer young. He had, as some people did, tried in vain to rekindle his youth.

Oh, the folly of it!

But as the months passed, although she was not exactly happy, she was at peace. For one thing it was pleasant to be shut away from public life. Her name was appearing less and less in the scandal sheets. She was living within her own family; and she had the three eldest girls all married and settled, beside the little FitzClarences who had always been a joy to her.

She was very fond of her son-in-law Frederick March, and Colonel Hawker was very good to her and looked after her affairs. She could not endure Thomas Alsop, but she was not so foolish as to hope for perfection. Thomas could be endured when she had two such sons-in-law as Frederick and the Colonel.

When the children were in bed and her daughters with their husbands, for she had made it quite clear that she had no wish to intrude into their privacy, she and Miss Sketchley would sit together and she would gossip to the governess of her theatrical adventures and it was the pleasantest way of reliving them because she would laugh over her misfortunes and enjoy her triumphs afresh.

Yes, life had become bearable.

But it seemed that peace must always be denied her. For some time she had noticed that Miss Sketchley was uneasy. She realized how much the governess meant to her when she feared that perhaps she wanted to leave.

She broached the subject one evening as they sat together.

'Miss Sketchley,' she said, 'have you something on your mind?'

The governess started guiltily.

'I hope you are not planning to leave us.'

'No,' said Miss Sketchley. 'Never.'

'That is a weight off my mind,' said Dorothy. 'But something is worrying you.'

Miss Sketchley hesitated. 'I . . . er . . .'

'Come now, please tell me. I'd rather know the worst.'

'I . . . I don't think all is well between Mr and Mrs Alsop.'

Dorothy laughed. 'My dear Miss Sketchley, all has never been well between Mr and Mrs Alsop. I can say this to the dear friend you have become. The marriage was a great mistake.'

'I fear so,' said Miss Sketchley.

'Pray tell me what you have discovered.'

'I think that Mrs Alsop is taking laudanum every night.'

'Laudanum!'

'I have seen quantities of it in her room. I know I should not have opened her drawer. But I was alarmed because I suspected . . . and I found a very large bottle of the stuff there.'

'Oh, my God, what does this mean?'

'I fear that she is taking drugs for some reason.'

'For what reason? Is she unhappy? She is here . . . I care for her. What can be wrong?'

'Perhaps she will confide in you.'

'Oh, Miss Sketchley, that girl has been a great trial to me. I would do anything on Earth for her – but somehow I fear she will never bring happiness to me or to herself. I blame myself. When I think of her coming into the world . . . But you know the story. I loathed her father and when I knew I was to have his child . . . perhaps I loathed her too . . . before she was born. As soon as she arrived I loved her . . . but perhaps it was too late then.'

'No mother could have done more for a child than you have done for Mrs Alsop.'

'Oh, God, how I've tried! All my quarrels with the Duke began through Fanny. They did not like each other. There was always conflict when she was at Bushy. But I must find what is wrong. I will go to her now. Fanny has always terrified me.'

Fanny was in her room, sitting at her mirror, idly twirling a lock of her hair.

'Fanny, my child, is anything wrong?'

Fanny swung round to face her mother. 'What . . . do you mean?'

Dorothy leaned forward and opening a drawer took out a bottle of laudanum. Fanny had turned pale.

'Fanny, what does this mean?'

'I had to have it,' cried Fanny hysterically. 'I couldn't sleep. I felt so miserable. I wanted to take an overdose.'

'For God's sake, don't talk like that. Tell me what's wrong. You know that I will put it right if it is humanly possible for me to do so.'

'It's Tom . . . he's in debt. We can't pay. He's lost his job. They've turned him out. There is nothing we can do. And we owe £2,000.'

'£2,000! How could you owe so much as that?'

'You don't know Tom. He'd double that in a week or two. He only wants time.'

'Where is he going to find this £2,000?'

'I don't know. He'll be in the debtors' prison. He's threatened with it . . . and that'll be the end.' Fanny picked up the bottle.

'I will take this away.'

'No,' cried Fanny. 'I'd die without it!'

'How long have you been taking this?'

335

'For months. I couldn't sleep. I thought I'd kill myself. I had to . . . I had to . . .'

'Now listen,' said Dorothy, 'we're going to be sensible. As soon as Thomas comes in bring him to me. We have to find that £2,000 and he will have to live within his income.'

Fanny burst into wild hysterical laughter. 'But Mamma, he has no income to live within.'

This nightmare, thought Dorothy, this nightmare of money!

She thought she had escaped it, but as she had feared the Duke was finding it difficult to pay the income he had promised. Perhaps she had always guessed he would.

And she desperately needed £2,000.

If she did not find it quickly Thomas Alsop would be in a debtors' prison, and she knew what that meant. Disaster and degradation, and once people were incarcerated in such a place how could they ever earn the money which would buy their release?

And if she did not act, what would happen to Fanny? Hysterical and unbalanced, already familiar with drugs, drinking too freely whenever the opportunity arose!

She must find £2,000 and how could she? There was one way. She could return to the stage. But if she returned to the stage she could not keep the children, for William would not permit the mother of his acknowledged children to act on a stage when she was not living with him. She had always known that he would have preferred her to retire at the beginning of their liaison; but he had wanted the money. Now that the money she earned would be of no concern to him he was determined that she should not earn it and keep their children.

For days this was the great question in her life. She could give up the young children to their father's care and go back to the stage by which means she could soon earn the money she needed to save Thomas Alsop from disaster. Or she could keep the children and let the Alsops take care of themselves.

There was no middle way. It was one or the other.

What could she do? She lay tossing on her bed and thought of the laudanum which she had seen in Fanny's room.

Then she thought of the little children with whom she must part.

She talked over her trouble with Miss Sketchley.

'You see, the children will be well cared for. They will have the best governesses and tutors; they will be received in royal circles as they always have been but more so without me. It is a matter, dear Miss Sketchley, of who needs me most. When I look at it like that I have no doubt. I could never abandon Fanny. I must always do my best for her no matter what it costs me. I feel I owe it to Fanny . . . more than anyone else in the world.'

'If the children go,' said Miss Sketchley, 'I will remain with you.'

So the decision was made. Dorothy parted with the children and went back to the stage.

She was playing again in the new theatre of Covent Garden. The audience went wild with joy. They were determined to show her how glad they were that she was back.

The *Morning Post* wrote:

'She was greeted with reiterated bursts of the most ardent applause. Her performance throughout was such as fully to merit the warm testimonials of approbation by which in every scene in which she appeared she was honoured. She is increased in size but there is no abatement of her natural vivacity or that wonted gaiety of deportment and sweetness of expression which have ever formed so distinguished a characteristic of the performance of this inimitable and most favoured votary of Thalia.'

She was back on the stage. She was back in the news, for naturally there were those to detract as well as those to applaud.

They were delighted with her. They had missed her – theatre and press. And they were glad that Dorothy Jordan was back.

She played her light-hearted comedy roles with zest; but she was sad at heart.

She had lost her lover and her young children. But she had saved Fanny and her husband from disaster. That must be her reward.

Treachery in the family

William was penitent. He knew why Dorothy had returned to the stage. She was not doing it for herself but for that family of hers – that ungrateful Fanny and her worse than ungrateful husband.

He wished that he could go back to her. But how could he now? The parting was too far behind him; too much had happened; and he was determined to marry. He must. It was for this reason that he had given up Dorothy; so he must have a wife to justify his act.

Was it his fault that Catherine Tylney-Long and Mercer Elphinstone had refused him? He had forgotten what they looked like now. Yet he could see Dorothy's face as clearly as though she were beside him.

He must not think of Dorothy. It was a phase of his life which was over. But he would put no obstacle in the way of seeing the children; and although they could not *live* under her roof while she followed her stage profession they could visit her and write to her when they cared to.

George was a constant correspondent. So was Molpuss who was very interested in the theatre and wanted to know all about it.

Her children's letters were her greatest comfort and she wrote to them in the same prolific way in which she had once written to William.

William wrote to her suggesting that he might help over Alsop. Lord Moira, who was an old friend of his and the Prince Regent, had been appointed Governor-General of Bengal and it had occurred to William that there might be a place for Alsop on his staff. It would be an excellent post for Alsop whom he understood had no employment; and would at the same time remove him from Dorothy's roof so that he would cease to be a burden to her. In due course his wife could follow him there. If she thought it was a good idea and let him know he would speak to Moira and do what he could to arrange it.

Dorothy was gratified – not only because it seemed a good prospect for the Alsops but because William and she were friendly again.

When Alsop heard of the offer, he was delighted. Most certainly he would take it, he said; and if Dorothy would take over his creditors, as she was doing, there was absolutely no reason why he should not go to India.

Alsop had left, to Dorothy's great relief. Fanny talked of going out after him but with no real intention of doing so, and Dorothy believed in her heart that if her eldest daughter did go there might be a chance of that peaceful life for which she had craved.

She had settled Alsop's debts and if she went on commanding the high prices which theatre managers were willing to pay her she reckoned that in a year or two she would be able to retire.

She had lost he children, but several of them wrote to her regularly and she carefully followed all their activities. Sophie was the only one who never wrote; she was always in her father's company; but George and Molpuss were good letter writers although George's spelling was a little wild and she often jokingly rebuked him for not using his dictionary. The household in Cadogan Square was a tolerably happy one. Colonel Hawker was the strong man who looked after her affairs and Frederick March was her favourite son-in-law; he was affectionate to her and to Dodee and as far as possible he made up for the loss of the Fitz-Clarence boys. Then there was Lucy and Dodee with dear Miss Sketchley who was so good and useful and who had become as one of the family.

Fanny was a problem. Her addiction to drugs was growing alarmingly and she was behaving oddly. One rainy day she was missing and they were very alarmed and not greatly comforted when she returned home, her clothes soaked, her shoes letting in the water. She would give no reason for her disappearance; and after that she would walk about the streets in the oldest clothes she could find, a torn dress, a bonnet with ribbons that looked like rags and stockings which she had dyed bright pink.

Fanny was decidedly odd and needed especial care. It would be a great relief if she joined her husband. Sometimes she would grow quite excited about this; at others she would shrug the idea listlessly aside.

But it seemed there was no lasting comfort. Dorothy was horrified when she heard that George and Henry were in trouble and were to be court-martialled. This angered her because, as she saw it, it was no fault of the boys. They had done what they thought was their duty and she was amazed at the sternness of the Commander-in-Chief of the Army, the Duke of York, who had been reinstated by the Regent about a year or so after he had been forced to resign as a result of the Mary Anne Clarke scandal.

During the fighting against the French in which both brothers had been engaged – George as Captain and Henry as Lieutenant – in their opinion, and those of some other officers, the Commander, Colonel Quentin, had been negligent. A complaint was lodged by these officers and Colonel Quentin was court-martialled.

But the Duke of York was incensed. He wanted to know what right junior officers had to question the actions of a commanding colonel. He declared that discipline was at stake and action must be taken.

Since two of the officers concerned were his own nephews he believed that they had taken advantage of their relationship with him and he decided on drastic punishment. All the officers concerned were dismissed from their regiment of the 10th Hussars and their swords confiscated and the two FitzClarences were to be sent to India.

When Dorothy heard this she was overcome with grief. George was her eldest son and if he was her favourite it was understandable. He had always been devoted to her and during those heartbreaking months when she had first been separated from the Duke it had been his letters which had helped to sustain her.

When George wrote to her and told her that he was shortly to leave the country she wept with despair. To Miss Sketchley who was accompanying her on her tours as companion, secretary and in fact filling any post that was needed, she said: 'This is the only letter I have ever had from George that did not fill me with happiness.'

That night she was taken ill on the stage and her part had to be taken over by her understudy. It was the first time that had happened.

The trouble which had fallen on George and Henry resulted in William's writing to Dorothy. He too was worried about the fate of the boys and had tried remonstrating with his brother; but the Duke of York, who had previously been an easy-going and goodhearted man, was adamant. However, the Regent was sympathetic and so was the Queen and it was for this reason that they were being transferred to another regiment for the Duke's first intention had been to dismiss them from the Army. His instructions had been that when they arrived in India they were to be treated by the commanding officer there to the utmost discipline; but the Regent had made it known that it was his wish that this should not be so.

It was pleasant to hear from William and to know that her concern for their sons was shared by him. But she did wonder whether there was an inclination in the royal family to disown the Fitz-Clarence children now that their mother and father were separated and to treat them as any other illegitimate offspring – which owing to the long-standing relationship and the respectability of its nature had not been so before.

She must not fret too much and so upset the boys when they came to see her. And perhaps as the Regent was kindly disposed and she had never had any reason to doubt this, they would soon be home from India.

The case of Colonel Quentin and the part the young FitzClarences had played in it naturally called attention to their parents and there was a further spate of comments.

William was extremely unpopular, and Dorothy, although subject to criticism and ridicule, was a public idol. Now she was the deserted woman; and her two sons had been unfairly – most said – sent to India, just when the war was over and she could have hoped to be freed from anxiety concerning them.

Dorothy was away again on tour, working hard, trying to accumulate money for her retirement.

'If only this hadn't happened,' she often said to Miss Sketchley, 'I could have become reconciled. Why is it that as soon as I believe myself to have emerged from my difficulties another one appears?'

'It is often so with families,' said the practical Miss Sketchley. 'And you have a large one. But remember that while there are some to give you anxiety there are others to bring you joy.'

'How right you are!' said Dorothy. 'And I have had a great deal of happiness in my life. I know Alsop was a trial but I have two good sons-in-law. Samuel is so firm and strong . . . such a rock and dear Frederick so reliable. And the dear girls . . . Fanny, of course.'

'Fanny's place is with her husband,' said Miss Sketchley firmly.

'I wonder whether she would be happy there.'

Miss Sketchley did not answer. She knew that Fanny would never be happy anywhere.

It couldn't be true. Was there not enough trouble. How could Fanny do this? Had she not caused enough anxiety already?

The letter reached her while she was playing in Carlisle and it was from Frederick. He did not know how to begin to tell her but there had been trouble in Cadogan Place.

Fanny had been writing threatening letters to the Duke of Clarence – letters which carried a hint of blackmail. She had threatened if he did not give her mother more money that certain facts of their relationship of which she was aware would be given to the newspapers.

As a result the Duke had sent his lawyer to Cadogan Place and there had been an alarming scene.

Frederick was outraged because, as he said, the Duke suspected him of being concerned in these threats. He had not believed that Fanny could have composed the letters herself but that Frederick had helped her.

'I was able to prove my innocence,' wrote Frederick, 'and not only that, but let it be known that I had tried to prevail on Fanny to stop doing this foolish thing.'

'Oh, God, what can I do?' Dorothy demanded of Miss Sketchley. 'I really begin to wonder what will happen next. I must go home.'

'You cannot break your contracts,' Miss Sketchley pointed out, 'or you will be sued. You don't want further financial worries.'

'How can I go on acting? What can I do? Fanny will have to go away. I wonder if she would go to India. Perhaps I could send her to my brother in Wales. Anything . . . anything to get her away.'

'Frederick is capable. He should be able to manage this in your absence.'

'I will write to him. What can we do for poor Fanny? For she is ill, you know. That is the trouble. My poor, poor Fanny! First, she must be stopped writing these letters.'

'I daresay she had been thoroughly frightened out of that by the lawyers.'

'As soon as I get home I shall have to make some arrangement for her. In the meantime I am asking Frederick to increase the premiums on the life insurance I took out for Alsop, so that if he should die out there Fanny will be all right for the future. My head is simply whirling. I don't know what I should do without you. How I long for this tour to be over!'

'Frederick will manage everything,' soothed Miss Sketchley.

'Thank God for Frederick.'

Frederick told Dorothy that he had control of affairs in Cadogan Place and she could trust him to carry out her wishes. So she wished to raise the insurance on Alsop's life; he would deal with the matter. He was not sure of the amount but if she would send him a blank cheque he would fill in the amount required. He was also advising Fanny that she should, after the trouble with the Duke, make plans immediately to leave for India, or if she did not wish to go so far he was sure it could be arranged for her to go to her relations in Wales.

Fanny said she would consider which appealed to her more. And one day she went out and did not return.

When Dorothy – still on tour – heard the news she was heart-broken; but Miss Sketchley said that Fanny would always fall on her feet and she probably had been making plans to leave home for some time. It was clear that she would not go to her husband; and now that she had made everything so uncomfortable at home, preferred to leave.

It was very likely, added Miss Sketchley, that she had gone to Wales.

Dorothy remained in a state of great unhappiness. It was all very well for others to say that all would be happier without Fanny. Dorothy could not forget that she was her daughter and she loved her in spite of all the trouble she had caused.

'What will become of the child?' she asked distractedly of Miss Sketchley.

'Child! She is scarcely a child. If it were not for her and her husband you would not be here now working yourself into a state of exhaustion. You would be living peacefully at Cadogan Place.'

'She did not ask to come into the world. Nor did I ask that she should. It's that man Daly . . . he has been an evil shadow across my life from the day I met him. If I had never known him, everything would have been different.'

'Fanny would never have been born, but would the Duke have remained faithful?'

'It might have been different. Who knows? We had quarrels and I think I irritated him beyond endurance with my preoccupation with money and it was for the girls, I suppose.'

Miss Sketchley did not think highly of the Duke and conveyed it in her silence when he was mentioned. But Dorothy insisted on defending him. 'He was always good and generous. It was money which separated us.'

Miss Sketchley said nothing. She was maliciously amused by his inability to find an heiress. She hoped that one day he would realize what he had lost.

Dorothy was waiting anxiously for news. There was none. Touring was so exhausting particularly when one felt so ill. She was spitting blood more frequently now and the pain in her chest was recurring. She must go on playing the old roles. Peggy in *The Country Girl*, Prue in *Love for Love* and Letitia Hardy in *The Belle's Stratagem*. She could no longer play Priscilla Tomboy or the Little Pickle. Those days were over, but there was some satisfaction in knowing that audiences felt very lukewarm about anyone else's playing of the parts.

So weary she was after a performance that Miss Sketchley had to help her to bed where she fell into an exhausted sleep.

Every day she would wait for news. 'Any news of Fanny?' she would ask, fear showing in her voice and eyes. What next? she was wondering. What else could happen?

The next blow came from an unexpected quarter and was all the more cruel for that.

She was deeply in debt. Someone had been drawing on her account; bills which she had believed to have been paid had been left outstanding. Her creditors were threatening that they could wait no longer.

She read the letter from Frederick several times and Miss Sketchley who was always alarmed when the mail arrived came in to find her sitting staring blankly before her.

'May I?' she asked, picking up the letter.

Dorothy nodded.

'Good God!' cried Miss Sketchley. 'This can only be Frederick March.'

'Impossible.'

'It seems to me,' said Miss Sketchley sadly, 'that it is the unexpected that often happens.'

'I must go home,' said Dorothy.

'You are certainly in no fit state to go on the stage. Leave it to me. I'll make all our arrangements. We must leave at once for London.'

That very day they drove out of Margate; and when Dorothy returned home it was to find Frederick in a state of near dementia.

He threw himself at her feet. He deserved her reproaches. Nothing she could say or do to him would be hard enough punishment.

Yes, he had been wicked. He had been criminal. He had needed the money. He had stolen from her. He had filled in the blank cheques she had given him for double and treble the amounts she had intended.

They were ruined.

That it should be Frederick, her favourite son-in-law!

She did not know what to do. She could only think of her poor mother who had feared insecurity and so longed for the respectability of marriage. Marriage! What had it brought to Fanny? And now Dodee's husband had done this to her!

Colonel Hawker offered to help but how could he? He was not a rich man. He had not the sums at his disposal which they would need.

She read through the demands for payment. The veiled threats if the bills were not met. She understood them well. They pointed to the debtors' prison from which there was no escape, for how could she earn money while in prison to pay her debts, and how could she escape from prison until she did?

What to do? Where to turn?

She thought of the one man who had been good to her. Yes, he had, she insisted, until his family had demanded that he marry for State reasons and pay *his* debts.

William would never desert her.

But she could not plead to him personally. She would write to his agent, John Barton, who had arranged the settlement. He would most certainly inform the Duke and everything that could be done to save her would be done.

It was a relief.
She wrote to Barton and waited.

When John Barton received Dorothy's appeal for help he began to see how he could use the position to the advantage of his master.

Since his desertion of Dorothy the Duke of Clarence had become a figure of fun to the people. They did not approve of the desertion. He had lived with Dorothy for twenty years. They had had ten children and then like a silly lovesick schoolboy he had started to court young women. Heiresses, of course. There was something ridiculous about an ageing man pretending to be a young one; and the fact that the heiresses had the good sense to refuse him made him all the more ridiculous.

The people did not like this treatment of one of their favourite actresses; and while she appeared on the stage and was constantly in the public eye, they could not forget.

After being refused by Miss Tylney-Long and Miss Elphinstone, William had tried for royalty. The Princess Anne of Denmark had declined to marry him, so had the sister of the Tsar, the Duchess of Oldenburg.

William was depicted in all the cartoons as the lovelorn suitor who could succeed nowhere and on these cartoons Dorothy was invariably in the background with her ten children about her.

Barton had a brilliant idea. He might extricate his master from this humiliating position and win his eternal gratitude.

With this plan in mind he went to see Dorothy.

'I know,' he told her, 'that the Duke would wish me to do everything possible to ease your situation. I beg of you show me all the accounts.'

This she did and when Barton had calculated how much money was needed he made a wry face.

'It will take months to raise this money,' he said. 'And in the meantime your creditors will take action.'

'What am I to do?'

'There is only one thing. You must get out of the country.'

'What?'

'It's the only way you will be safe. You must slip quietly away. Leave these bills with me. I will settle your affairs as speedily as I can and when I have done so send word for you that it is safe for you to return.'

'Do you mean . . . ?'

He looked at her intently.

'I mean, Madam,' he said, 'that from the threatening tones of your creditors they will have you in a debtors' prison within the month. I should say you have at most three weeks to get out of the country.'

Dorothy was aghast.

She thought of that day long ago when Daly had threatened her with a debtors' prison. She had given way and as a result there had been Fanny . . . and because of Fanny she was in her present dilemma, for she believed deep down in her heart that it was their differences over Fanny which had begun to make the rift between her and the Duke and that had it not been there he would never have deserted her no matter what family pressure had been exerted. It was as though she had completed a circle.

'I could not face prison,' she said. 'It is so . . . impossible. How should I ever get out . . . and what would become of my family?'

'Take my advice,' said Barton. 'Get away. I will do all I can to help. Sell up everything you have here and go. I shall be in touch. Your allowances will be paid . . . and in a short time you will be able to settle your debts and come back.'

She trusted Barton. There was no one else to trust.

Barton went away satisfied that he had done an excellent thing for the Duke. He would not tell him at present for the Duke was a sentimental man. But he would never regain the dignity of his rank, nor would he find a bride, while Dorothy Jordan remained in the public eye.

Dorothy frantically started to sell her furniture at ridiculous prices; she disposed of the lease of her house, and with the faithful Miss Sketchley as her company set out for France.

The order of release

The little cottage at Marquetra was small but the surrounding country was green and reminded her poignantly of England. There were two cottages side by side and in the second lived her landlady Madame Ducamp, the widow of a gardener. Madame Ducamp's maid Agnes also looked after Dorothy and was soon charmed by her. So beautiful although she was no longer young; so graceful although she was no longer slim; so different from anyone Agnes had ever known.

Agnes would talk of Dorothy continually to Madame Ducamp and to Miss Sketchley.

'I have never known anyone like the dear sad English lady,' she said. 'I am sure Madame James has been a grand lady in England. Of course, I do not believe Madame James is her real name. Ah, I can see it is not, Mademoiselle Sketchley. I believe she is a princess . . . or a duchess. She has the airs of one for all that she is so kind.'

Why did she wait so eagerly for the mail which did not come to her direct but had to be collected?

'When it is time for it to come,' said Agnes, 'she becomes so anxious that I am afraid she will die if she does not get what she wants. I hear her coughing at night and I fear for her. Is she very ill? How I wish that the letter she longs for would come.'

Miss Sketchley gave nothing away. Calm, discreet, she looked after Dorothy who often wondered what would have happened if this dear good woman had not come to her.

One day she was wildly happy. It was due to a letter. Agnes wondered but Miss Sketchley did not tell.

It was not the letter for which she had hoped; the letter from Barton to say that it was safe for her to come home. But it was from sixteen-year-old Frederick FitzClarence who although he did not know her address did know that she was living in France under the name of Mrs James and that he must address letters to her in this name c/o the Post Office at Boulogne.

Frederick was already in the Army and had written: 'If you want money . . . take my allowance because with a little care I could live on my father's.'

She wept over the letter, kissed it and slept with it under her pillow.

The children loved her. Dodee and Lucy were in despair because she had left home; George had always been a good son and so had Henry, but they were in India, and now dear Fred had offered his allowance.

She felt that she was not entirely forgotten.

'I feel,' she told Miss Sketchley, 'that soon release will come.'

After a few months she left Marquetra for Versailles and there found rooms. She spent her time writing letters and reading, and each day she would ask herself: Will the letter come today – the order of release?

She longed to be with her family. Dodee and Lucy wrote regularly. Dodee was sad because of the disaffection of her husband. They missed her and longed for her return.

She wrote to Frederick telling him not to worry, that she understood his difficulties; she was sure he had hoped to repay her before the deficiencies were discovered; and when Mr Barton had so settled her affairs and she could return to England they would all set up house together.

Versailles did not suit her and she went to St Cloud and took rooms in the Maison du Sieur Mongis, a gloomy place with a dark overgrown garden and shabbily furnished rooms. It was ill-heated and as it was winter she felt chilled and thought longingly of the comforts of Bushy House.

She would lie on the shabby old sofa and say to Miss Sketchley: 'Sometimes I feel that this old sofa will be my death bed. One day I shall lie down on it and never get up. Do you know, I don't think I should greatly care.'

'Nonsense,' said Miss Sketchley. 'What of the girls? They are expecting you to go back and make a home for them.'

Yes, the girls. She must always think of the girls.

A new year had started. 1816. One weary day followed another, bringing no letter of release.

'Have they forgotten me?' she asked Miss Sketchley.

Her health did not improve with the coming of the spring. She developed jaundice and her skin turned yellow. Miss Sketchley, alarmed, wrote to Dodee.

She waited for the reply.

Meanwhile Dorothy was growing worse. The coughing fits were frequent and alarming.

'Are there any letters from England?' she asked constantly.

Miss Sketchley could only shake her head miserably.

'My dear, ask them to go to the Post Office . . . let them go now . . . There may be some waiting for me.'

Miss Sketchley knew it was useless, but nevertheless, to satisfy Dorothy, she sent the messenger.

She sat by Dorothy's side at that old sofa. She thought: 'Will her daughter come? Is none of her family – for whom she lived, and for whom she is dying – to be with her at the end?'

Someone was knocking at the door. But it was only the messenger.

'Are there any letters?' asked Dorothy.

'No, Madame, nothing at all.'

In weary resignation she sank back on the sofa and turned her head to the wall.

Miss Sketchley sat still, afraid to look at Dorothy because in her heart she knew.

The July sun filtered through the window showing the dust on the furniture and Miss Sketchley sat listening as Dorothy had listened for the family to come to take her home, for the letters which would never come.

The favourite exponent of the Comic Muse had died from an inflammation of the lungs at St Cloud in France, so said the English papers.

She was buried with only Miss Sketchley and strangers to mourn her; but one of these strangers put up a granite slab to her on which he had the words inscribed:

'Sacred to the memory of Dorothy Jordan, who for a series of years in London as well as other cities of Britain pre-eminently adorned the stage. For Comic Wit, sweetness of voice, and imitating the manners and customs of laughing maidens as well as the opposite sex, she ranked second to none in the display of that art. Neither was anyone more prompt on relieving the necessitous. She departed this life, the 5th July 1816. Remember and weep for her.'

Jean Plaidy
The Regent's Daughter 95p

The ninth book in the Georgian Saga

The marriage of the Prince of Wales to Caroline of Brunswick was strewn with private skirmish and public scandal yet it did bear a daughter – Princess Charlotte, heiress presumptive to the English throne. Ever bewildered by her bizarre collection of royal relatives, Charlotte grew up honest, forthright and always sure of her destiny . . .

The Heart of the Lion 80p

The third book in her magnificent Plantagenet Saga

The death of Henry II brought his son Richard to the English throne – his destiny was to be one of the greatest warrior kings of the medieval world, to ride against the Saracen at the head of his army of Crusaders, sworn to win back the holy city of Jerusalem for Christendom. At court, Berengaria, Richard's queen, struggled to hold the place in his life that was ever beyond her reach, while his treacherous brother John cast greedy eyes towards England's crown . . .

Here Lies our Sovereign Lord 75p

The third book in the Charles II Trilogy

Charles II intrigues with Louis XIV for the money that will keep him independent of Parliament and dispel the shadows cast over the throne by his son Monmouth and his own brother, the Duke of York. When politics tire the Merry Monarch there are always women ready to please him – Nell Gwynn, Hortense Mancini, Louise de Koroualle . . .

'Fascinating' MANCHESTER EVENING NEWS

Daphne du Maurier
Mary Anne £1.25

In the glittering, corrupt world of Regency London, Mary Anne Clarke had beauty, brains and wit – but no money. Spurred on by the demands of a drunken husband, a wastrel brother and four children, she chose an exacting profession aimed for the top – and soon became the mistress of the Duke of York.

For her family she needed a fortune – and she got it the wrong way. The scandal rocked the country from palace to Parliament and Mary Anne Clarke became the most famous woman in England.

Frenchman's Creek 80p

While the gentry of Cornwall strive to capture the daring Frenchman who plunders their shores, the beautiful Lady Dona finds excitement, danger and a passion she never knew before as she dares to love a pirate – a devil-may-care adventurer who risks his life for a kiss . . .

'A heroine who is bound to make thousands of friends, in spite of her somewhat questionable behaviour' SUNDAY TIMES

You can buy these and other Pan books from booksellers and newsagents; or direct from the following address:
Pan Books, Sales Office, Cavaye Place, London SW10 9PG
Send purchase price plus 20p for the first book and 10p for each additional book to allow for postage and packing
Prices quoted are applicable in the UK

While every effort is made to keep prices low, it is sometimes necessary to increase prices at short notice. Pan Books reserve the right to show on covers and charge new retail prices which may differ from those advertised in the text or elsewhere